Praise for *New York Times* best‑selling author Lindsay McKenna

"McKenna provides heartbreakingly tender romantic development that will move readers to tears. Her military background lends authenticity to this outstanding tale, and readers will fall in love with the upstanding hero and his fierce determination to save the woman he loves."
—*Publishers Weekly* on *Never Surrender*

"Talented Lindsay McKenna delivers excitement and romance in equal measure."
—*RT Book Reviews* on *Protecting His Own*

"Lindsay McKenna will have you flying with the daring and deadly women pilots who risk their lives... Buckle in for the ride of your life."
—*Writers Unlimited* on *Heart of Stone*

Praise for Nicole Helm

"An intimate, rewarding romance with a hot hero whose emotional growth is as sexy as his moves in the bedroom."
—*Kirkus Reviews* on *Want You More*

"Nicole Helm has done a great job of writing three-dimensional characters... A super beginning to this series. I look forward to the next book in the series, *Wyoming Cowboy Protection*."
—*Harlequin Junkie* on *Wyoming Cowboy Justice*

LINDSAY McKENNA

STALLION TAMER

ISBN-13: 978-1-335-40995-9

Stallion Tamer
First published in 1998.
This edition published in 2021.
Copyright © 1998 by Lindsay McKenna

Wyoming Cowboy Justice
First published in 2018.
This edition published in 2021.
Copyright © 2018 by Nicole Helm

Recycling programs
for this product may
not exist in your area.

This edition published by arrangement with Harlequin Books S.A.

For questions and comments about the quality of this book,
please contact us at CustomerService@Harlequin.com.

Harlequin Enterprises ULC
22 Adelaide St. West, 40th Floor
Toronto, Ontario M5H 4E3, Canada
www.Harlequin.com

Printed in U.S.A.

CONTENTS

Lindsay McKenna is proud to have served her country in the US Navy as an aerographer's mate third class—also known as a weather forecaster. She was a pioneer in the military romance subgenre and loves to combine heart-pounding action with soulful and poignant romance. True to her military roots, she is the originator of the long-running and reader-favorite Morgan's Mercenaries series. She does extensive hands-on research, including flying in aircraft such as a P3-B Orion sub-hunter and a B-52 bomber. She was the first romance writer to sign her books in the Pentagon bookstore. Visit her online at lindsaymckenna.com.

Books by Lindsay McKenna

Shadow Warriors

Running Fire
Taking Fire
Never Surrender
Breaking Point
Degree of Risk
Risk Taker
Down Range

The Wyoming Series

Out Rider
Night Hawk
Wolf Haven
High Country Rebel
The Loner
The Defender
The Wrangler
The Last Cowboy
Deadly Silence

Visit the Author Profile page
at Harlequin.com for more titles.

STALLION TAMER

Lindsay McKenna

To Dan York,
who's way ahead of his time, and a good friend.

Chapter 1

No! The cry careened through Jessica Donovan's head. She tossed and turned on her old brass bed, one of the few items taken from her life on the Donovan Ranch before she'd fled at age eighteen. Her blond hair swirled across her shoulders as she moved from her back to her side. The dark cloud was pursuing her again. Only this time it was even more malevolent. More threatening. She began to whimper. Her small, thin fingers spasmodically opened and closed in terror.

That black cloud reminded her of one of the torrential thunderstorms that every summer rolled across the Mogollon Rim and then across the expanse of the Donovan Ranch. Those terrifying downpours of her Arizona childhood were every bit as devastating and unrelenting as the monsoons of Southeast Asia and India, or so she'd been told. As lightning and thunder now careened and rolled through the black cloud in her dream, Jessica's breathing became shallow. Faster. Her hands curled into fists as she saw the black cloud begin to take shape.

For whatever reason, the normally lethal, roiling cloud that often chased her was now, for the first time in a year, beginning to take form. Jessica saw herself on the mesa, on the Rim, watching the bubbling cauldron of a storm racing toward her. The wind was tearing at her clothes, punching and pulling at her. Her blond hair streamed out behind her shoulders. As scared as she was, she lifted her chin and directly faced the oncoming, savage storm.

Her mother, Odula, an Eastern Cherokee medicine woman from the Wolf Clan, had not taught her to be meek or mild in the face of fear. No, Odula had always counseled Jessica to face her fears. Not to run away from them, but to work through them and stand her ground no matter what.

Jessica moaned and rolled onto her back. The storm cloud was taking on the appearance of something. An animal? A man? She expected it to be her abusive ex-husband, Carl Roman. Her heartbeat sped up as she saw the lightning stitch and lance through the black-and-green clouds. The winds began to screech like a banshee. An old memory surfaced…old and wonderful. Exhilaration momentarily wiped away the fear she could taste in her mouth. And then it slipped away from her, blotted out by the savagely moving storm.

Jessica felt as if she were going to die. It was a feeling she'd felt often in real life, while married to Carl. Was she remembering the time he'd sent her to the hospital? Tears trickled out of the corners of her eyes as she faced the storm. This time, she knew, it was going to consume her. Kill her. Oh, she'd been near death too many times already! She was tired of being afraid. Her soul was dying. She knew that. Somehow, even while caught in this nightmare, which haunted her several times each week, Jessica knew her soul was withering, dying like a beautiful flower not given enough care, love or nurturance.

The wind picked up, pummeling her bodily. Jessica's turquoise eyes widened as she watched the black clouds take shape.

It was a horse! A black horse. Her breath hitched in her throat as she watched the beautiful, threatening animal form midway up that spiraling, anvil-shaped mass towering forty thousand feet above the Mogollon Rim.

For an instant, her fear turned to awe. She saw the finely dished head of an Arabian stallion—ebony colored, his nostrils red and flaring. His eyes were black and wild. White and red foam trailed from the sides of his mouth. As the front half of his magnificent body formed out of the clouds, Jessica gave a cry of recognition. It was Gan! The Donovan Ranch Arabian stallion! Gan was the horse that her father, Kelly, had repeatedly abused, trying to beat him into submission. During one of his frequent drunken rages, Kelly had even used a whip.

Jessica sobbed. She watched as the figure of Gan developed fully in the writhing, roiling clouds. The stallion was at once beautiful and terrifying as he seemed to gallop, free at last, across the darkening sky. Jessica's hands flew to her mouth as she watched Gan's savage, primal beauty. He was big boned for an Arabian, his raw power evident in the taut muscles that rippled with each long stride he took. His black mane and raised tail flew like banners, proclaiming his freedom from man's hands—or more to the point, from Kelly Donovan's cruel hands.

Jessica felt tears streaming down her face. She began to sob harder as she watched the powerful celestial vision. Gan had wanted nothing more than to roam freely with his herd of purebred Arabian mares. Her father had always kept him in a small, eight-foot-high corral where he couldn't stretch his long limbs or truly exercise. And a stallion servicing a hundred mares a year needed exercise. Kelly had been so cruel to the stud.

During one of his drunken bouts, Kelly had won Gan in a high-stakes poker game in Reno, Nevada. Gan was brought home by Kelly to procreate black Arabian offspring. Black was a rare color and in high demand in the equine world, for there were few true black Arabians. Gan was able to throw that color eighty percent of the time. Often Kelly had lost mammoth sums with his gambling ways, but this time he'd walked away with a prize.

But what he'd won, Jessica thought as the stallion and the thunderstorm began to fade away in her dream, was trouble with a capital *T.* Kelly had expected a submissive stallion, not the fighter that Gan turned out to be. In some ways, Gan was like her—badly beaten. And like the stallion, she was bloody, but unbowed. Thanks to her mother's spirit, her nurturing, Jessica had managed to hold her head up through her disastrous marriage and successfully carry on.

It was Jessica's own sobbing that awakened her. In the early morning grayness, she opened her eyes and slowly pushed herself up into a sitting position. As she leaned forward and brought her knees up beneath the downy quilt, she placed her hands against her face and felt the wetness of spent tears on her cheeks. Her silky hair fell around her face, covering it like a curtain as she took in a deep, unsteady breath.

That dream, that nightmare…why did it haunt her still? It had since she'd gotten the call that her father had died unexpectedly in an auto accident. Lifting her chin, Jessica sniffed and reached for a tissue on the nightstand. Blowing her nose and wiping away the remnants of her tears, she gazed out the window near her bed. Her mother had been a medicine woman, and she was Odula's daughter. She had the mystery, the magic of her mother's blood running through her veins. She knew dreams were not sent without a reason. Jessica knew she had to try and understand the context of the nightmare.

Shafts of grayish dawn penetrated the Victorian lace curtains at her bedroom window. Jessica lived north of Vancouver, British Columbia. How she loved the area, having been here since age eighteen. The pristine big Douglas fir forest that surrounded her home provided a wall of safety for her. She loved the scent of the pines, and unconsciously breathed in deeply now. Even in the coldest of winters, Jessica kept her window slightly cracked to let in just a little fresh, outside air. Odula had had the same habit.

A soft smile played on Jessica's lips. In so many ways, she was the image of Odula—at least inwardly. As far as outward looks went, she wasn't. Kate and Rachel, her older sisters, had gotten her mother's black hair. Where Jessica's blond hair had come from was beyond her! It certainly wasn't in Odula's Eastern Cherokee lineage. At least her large, expressive blue eyes were her mother's gift to her. The Cherokee people were

lighter skinned than other Native American tribes, and
some had blue, green or hazel eyes. The Cherokee people also had brown and reddish brown hair in their ge-
netic background, too. Odula had had ebony hair, shiny
like a raven's wing in early morning light. And while
Kate had Odula's dark hair, Rachel's strands had a decided reddish gold cast to them.

Jessica had to get up. Today was the day. The day
she would leave Vancouver to start her long drive home.
Fear struck her as she eased her slender legs from beneath the covers. The white, knee-length flannel gown
she wore kept her warm against the chill of her room.
Even in early May, Canadian weather was cool. In her
hometown of Sedona, Arizona, it would already be in
the nineties on some days, with lots of brilliant blue
skies and unrelenting sunshine—unlike Vancouver,
which had days of grayness interspersed with shafts
of rare sunlight.

Jessica would miss her little cabin, surrounded by its
massive tree guardians. Her lovely fir trees had acted as
a barrier against the world. Hurriedly, she got dressed in
a pair of well-worn jeans and a pale pink, long-sleeved,
jersey shirt. With a colorful scarf she tied up her hair
in a ponytail before heading for the warmth of her tiny
kitchen to make herself some scrambled eggs and coffee.

On the maple table stood one of her favorite orchids.
Spontaneously, Jessica went over and stroked one long,
oval leaf, which felt like leather.

"You didn't have any nightmares, did you, Stone
Pinto?" She smiled admiringly at the lovely Phalaenop-
sis orchid's first blossom. Phals were known as moth orchids, their blooms looking like the outstretched wings

of a very huge moth—only the orchid's colors were far more spectacular than any moth! Stone Pinto was a white Phal with violet-colored dots all over her large petals. Although it emitted no fragrance, Jessica admired the plant's incredible beauty as it graced her table. How could anyone live without an orchid in each room of the house? It was beyond Jessica, who was sensitive to the energies not only of people, but of animals and plants as well, and knew how much certain plants improved the atmosphere.

Hurrying back to the stove, she added some sprinkles of shredded cheddar cheese to her scrambled eggs and placed the lid over the skillet for a moment. She looked sadly around her small cabin. She'd lived here since her divorce, two years ago, and loved this place. So had her orchids and the other flowers she'd raised for her company, Mother Earth Flower Essences. Yes, the dream her mother had had for her daughters had really taken root in Jessica. Of the three sisters, Jessica walked most directly in her mother's medicine footsteps—but in her own unique way.

At ten o'clock she would be leaving her place of safety and moving home—back to the Donovan Ranch. It would be different this time, Jessica told herself sternly as she dished up the eggs onto a stoneware plate covered with a bright, pretty wildflower design. Very different.

A knock on her door interrupted her thoughts.

"Come in," Jessica called breathlessly. She quickly brought down another plate from the cabinet as the door opened. A young woman about five foot ten, with long black, shining hair and lively forest green eyes, entered.

"You're just in time, Moyra," Jessica said in greeting.

She placed half her eggs on the other plate and beckoned her best friend to come and join her for breakfast.

"Oh," Moyra whispered, waving her long, ballerinalike hand, "you go ahead and eat, Jessica! I'll just grab a cup of coffee." She took the percolator off the stove and reached for two cups decorated in a flower design.

Jessica eyed her. "Have you *had* breakfast?"

"Well…" Moyra said in her low, purring voice, "not really, but—"

"Then sit," Jessica demanded with a flourish. "Here you are, helping me pack my orchid girls for the trip, and what kind of hostess would I be if I didn't feed my help first?"

Moyra grinned broadly and placed the steaming cups of coffee on the table. She sat down and graciously accepted a plate with half the scrambled eggs on it. "I'm going to miss you terribly," she said, picking up the fork and knife.

"I know…." Jessica felt a terrible sadness. Moyra had entered her life unexpectedly two years ago when Jessica had been in the middle of a messy and life-threatening divorce. A young woman in her thirties, Moyra had come from South America. In Jessica's eyes, she was an incredibly gifted person with a wild beauty to match her mysterious lineage. Because Moyra had been raised in the jungle of Peru, she was quite knowledgeable about orchids. She had helped the Mother Earth company grow and become financially solvent, assisting Jessica in expanding the distribution of the healing orchid essences around the world.

"Well," Moyra prompted between bites, "you'll get on well back home. I just feel it, here in my heart."

Jessica tried to smile. "I hope you're right…." She

had tried to talk Moyra into coming south with her to Arizona, but her friend had refused, saying the hot, dry weather wasn't for her. She was used to the warm, humid Amazon jungle and loved the rain, which Vancouver had a lot of. Now Jessica would be without help. She would have to train someone down at the ranch. But who? It was a real problem, because orchids needed unique care and sensitivity on the part of those who worked with them. And most people didn't have the level of sensitivity that Jessica desired.

"Besides," Moyra continued, wrinkling her long, chiseled nose, "leaving Vancouver and getting away from Carl stalking you is the best thing that has happened to you."

Glumly, Jessica nodded as she sipped her coffee. Normally, she loved this time of day, the talking and sharing that went on between her and Moyra. Each morning, Moyra would come and they'd talk over what had to be done during the day: what orders needed to be filled, which essence was to be made or what orchids carefully tended, watered or fertilized. But today Jessica felt her heart breaking.

"I had that nightmare again," she finally confided.

Moyra's eyes narrowed. "Again?"

"Yes." Jessica finished off her eggs and put the plate aside. She wrapped her slender fingers around the warm mug of coffee. "Only this time it was different…." She shared the frightening vision with Moyra.

Tossing her head, her black, long hair thick and curled with the humidity, Moyra nodded thoughtfully. "Where I come from, my people—my grandmother, who was a jaguar priestess—would say that your nightmare is telling you something. The threat of the clouds turned into a stallion. What does that mean to you?"

"Isn't that the sixty-four-thousand-dollar question?" Jessica asked with a chuckle. She sipped her coffee, wanting to prolong her last morning with Moyra as much as she could. She would miss her wisdom. Perhaps they were so close because Moyra's background paralleled her own. Her Peruvian friend came from a mixture of Indian and Castilian Spanish aristocracy. Her mother's side of the family were known to be members of the powerful and mysterious Jaguar Clan. Legend had it that those who carried the blood, the memory of once having been a deadly, powerful jaguar, could, when they wanted, go from a human form into a jaguar form in times of threat or emergency. It was called shape shifting. Jessica had only seen Moyra turn into a jaguar once, but she felt her friend's incredible energy— an energy that was very different from any other person she'd ever met. At times, Moyra's green, almond-shaped eyes, would turn a distinct yellow color when she was angry, and Jessica would almost swear she could see a jaguar overcome Moyra's human shape, could see the face of a jaguar staring back at her.

Nonsense? Maybe. Moyra had been Jessica's right hand since the divorce. And on more than one occasion, Moyra had stood up to Carl, who'd come to stalk Jessica, to harass her and hurt her. In this way, Moyra truly was a jaguar who had guarded and kept her safe. Now, where Jessica was going, there was no safety. Carl had threatened to fird her and kill her—that hadn't changed. But perhaps it was time for this chapter of her life to close. A new one was certainly beginning for her. Would Carl try to follow her to Arizona? A shiver of dread wound through Jessica.

"Are you glad to be leaving? Going home?" Moyra asked as she finished off her eggs with relish.

Shrugging, Jessica sighed. "I don't know. Part of me is. I've missed my family terribly. It's like a hole in my heart that never got fixed."

"Family wounds are the worst," Moyra murmured, buttering her toast and adding orange marmalade. And then, with a husky laugh, she said, "Not that I'm one to talk!"

Jessica nodded. The air of mystery around Moyra was always intact. After two years Jessica still knew very little about why Moyra had moved to Canada. Family meant everything to her. So why didn't she go home?

Home was several places to Moyra, though. She had family in the jungle of Peru as well as in Lima, its capital. Jessica did not pry, however. Like a typical Native American, she figured if Moyra wanted to tell her something, she would share it. Otherwise, it was not on the table as a topic to be discussed.

"The only thing I've got to do this morning is put my orchids in my pickup, and then I'll be ready to go." Once Jessica had made arrangements to bring the plants across the Canadian border, she had rented a large trailer to bring the rest of her supplies—the beautiful one-ounce, cobalt blue bottles, the eyedroppers, labels and other office items that were needed. Her computer, printer and files were already packed. She had fifty orchids of different varieties and types from around the world, and they would need careful temperature and humidity control. To expose them to chilly Canadian temperatures could kill them, as most orchids could not survive below fifty-five degrees Fahrenheit. Only her truck with the cap on it would be able to transport them properly. Moyra had fixed the heater in the truck so that the warm air would flow back into the bed where the orchids would be packed.

The Peruvian woman stood up, tall, lean and graceful. She even moved like a jaguar, Jessica thought, smiling to herself. Moyra was, indeed, more jaguar than human most of the time. Maybe that's why they got along so well, hidden out in the forest, absorbing the peace and quiet of their natural paradise. But then, Jessica knew her own Cherokee blood had given her a need for such surroundings rather than the craziness and the stress of city living. She could never survive in a city! Nor could her orchids, which were quite sensitive to air pollution.

"I'll start up the truck and get the heater going," Moyra said. "We need to warm that bed area for them. I'll make sure there are no leaks so that colder air can't get back there. I've got the temperature gauge set so you can just turn your head, glance at it and know that it's in the right range for your girls." Moyra leaned over and delicately touched the Phal. "How I'm going to miss Stone Pinto. She's so lovely!"

"I know." Jessica rose and put the plates in the sink. "Worse, I'm going to miss you...."

Moyra hugged her. "I'll be around in spirit. You know that. Once a jaguar priestess adopts you into her family, you are one of us, and you come under the protection of the jaguar goddess herself." She frowned, her thin brows knitted. "And I hope Carl has the good sense not to follow you to Arizona."

"He wouldn't dare," Jessica whispered, her throat automatically closing with fear.

Moyra threw back her head and chuckled. "Ha! That poor excuse of a man would do anything! He's capable of anything." The smile disappeared from Moyra's full mouth and she studied Jessica, who was inches shorter than her. "And you, my fine, delicate wisp of a friend, need to embrace the power of your Wolf Clan. You've run from your own power all your life. You're so much your mother, and yet you're afraid of the power of the wolf." She gripped Jessica's shoulders, deadly serious now. "I ran from the Jaguar Clan for years, but don't do as I've done. Our life path is part animal, part human. We are here in this lifetime to learn to integrate both halves into ourselves so that we are whole."

"I know you're speaking the truth. I feel it here, in my heart," Jessica admitted.

"Well," Moyra growled, sounding exactly like a jaguar in that moment, "you are going home to complete the first circle of your life. Claim the Wolf Clan power that is rightfully yours. Don't keep running from it." Allowing her hands to slip from Jessica's shoulders, Moyra added primly, "That dream of Gan, the Arabian stallion, has something to do with this. I know it."

Jessica felt lost suddenly. "What am I going to do without you?"

Moyra smiled enigmatically. "My jaguar sight tells me there is a man in black who will be near you soon. He will be someone you can trust, so run to him."

Jessica eyed her jadedly. "Oh, sure, a man. My track record with men is horrible and you know it. Besides, I don't trust them anymore...."

"Carl was a mistake." Moyra closed her eyes and

took a deep breath. "This man who is coming into your life is dangerous—not to you, but to himself." She continued in a low voice "I see him…swathed in black. Covered in darkness. But it's not a dangerous darkness like Carl has around him." Opening her eyes, she smiled down at Jessica. "And don't ask me any more questions because we both know that discovering the truth on your own is the only way to do it. I've said enough! I'm off to the truck. Meet me when you're ready and I'll help you load your orchid girls."

Jessica felt a heaviness in her chest and knew it was sadness at leaving Vancouver, Moyra and the many other friends she'd made here. Canada had been good for her—a home away from home. How she loved this beautiful country and its wonderfully friendly inhabitants!

Jessica's heart ached. And yet, as she finished washing, drying and packing the last of the kitchen supplies into one final box, another part of her was very excited about seeing Kate again. Their sister Rachel could not come home for a while because she had to fulfill her teaching contract at a college in England. But by December, Rachel would be moving back, too, and then what was left of the Donovan family would truly be home for the first time since their chaotic childhood.

As she carried the box outdoors, Jessica saw that the dawn had brightened, revealing a pale blue sky. She smiled. Even Canadian weather was going to bless her travels—blue sky and sunshine in early May was wonderful!

At least she wouldn't have to struggle through snow, sleet or rain on her southward journey back to the States…back to Sedona, Arizona.

Moyra had the pickup backed up to the small, glass greenhouse that housed most of her orchids. Going to the trailer, which would be hitched on afterward, Jessica packed away the final boxes. One of them contained her goose-down quilt, her most precious possession, made by her mother when Jessica was fifteen. Odula's energy, her love, her heart, was in this quilt and no matter how alone or bereft Jessica felt, even in the darkest days with Carl, she could wrap that quilt around her and feel the love and healing energy of her mother being absorbed into her battered spirit.

Closing up the trailer, her breath white and wispy, Jessica hurried to the greenhouse. Opening the door and quickly shutting it, Jessica saw that Moyra had carefully packed the orchids in plenty of newspaper and then moved them into cardboard boxes so that they wouldn't tip or fall over during the three-day trip down to Arizona. Jessica appreciated Moyra's attention to detail. Many of the orchids were just coming into bloom, their long, thin green spikes about to yield inflorescences or buds.

"Ready?" Moyra asked, looking up from the last box she'd packed with larger orchids already in bloom.

"I think so," Jessica whispered. She looked around the greenhouse. Kate had made her one exactly like this back at the ranch and it stood waiting and ready for her orchids—for her new life.

Moyra smiled gently. "Little Jessica is once again closing one chapter in her life and opening up a new one. You have to be excited."

"And scared," Jessica admitted softly, easing her arms around the first box of orchids.

Laughing, Moyra took another box and followed her

out to the pickup. "Be scared, but stand in the storm of fear and walk through it, my friend."

"Spoken like a true jaguar priestess," Jessica teased, smiling over her shoulder at Moyra. The woman positively glowed with life, her green eyes sparkling mischievously. Jessica knew that Moyra was psychic. In the past, she had used her abilities to warn her when Carl was in the vicinity. Jessica had been able to call the police and avert Carl's stalking each time. She shuddered now. She didn't know what Carl would do if he got his hands on her again. For two years, ever since Moyra had magically walked into her life to become a big, cosmic guard dog of sorts, Carl had not been able to fulfill his threat that he would hunt her down and kill her if she divorced him.

They put the first boxes in the pickup, the warmth satisfactory for Jessica's orchid girls. Hurrying back and forth, both women finally got all the boxes in place and the cap closed to protect the orchids from the chill of the Vancouver morning. Then Moyra maneuvered the pickup to the trailer and they quickly hitched it up.

"There," Moyra said, rubbing her hands and grinning. "Don't look so sad, little sister. I'll be with you in spirit, looking over your shoulder. You know that."

Tears filled Jessica's eyes as she looked up at Moyra. "You've been a true sister to me. I don't know what I'd have done without you, Moyra. Really, I don't feel like it's been a fair exchange. You've given me so much and been such a wonderful role model for me—"

"Hush, sister. You are going home to reclaim your power.

"You know, a shaman is always most powerful where she was born. You are a long way from your

source of empowerment. Go home. Don't be afraid."
Moyra moved closer and placed her hands on Jessica's
small, slumped shoulders. "Listen carefully, Jessica. I
see much." Her fingers dug more deeply into Jessica's
shoulders. "You are in great danger. You will be tested
once you reach home. In order to survive this test, you
must embrace your power. If you don't…" Moyra looked
upward, tears in her eyes. "But I know you will. You
are a frightened little shadow of your true self. There
is a man clothed in black who will help you, guide you,
if you allow him to."

"I don't *trust* men!"

"I know that. Carl has hurt you so deeply, he's
wounded your spirit, Jessica…but this man, whoever
he is, can help you heal at a soul level." She gave Jessica a gentle shake, her voice turning raw with emotion.
"Your test is twofold, my sister. You must face your fear
head-on and you must learn to trust men again. Neither is an easy task, but you are the daughter of a medicine woman. You must learn to embrace your inherited
power from her, and become it. If you do this, your life
will be spared. But you will be in danger. Just embrace
your wolf senses—your exquisite hearing, your sense
of smell—and remain on guard.…"

"Sometimes I wish you wouldn't speak symboli-
cally," Jessica said with a little laugh, taking Moyra's
hands into hers. "Sometimes I wish you'd just spit it
out."

Moyra grinned. Her laugh was a husky purr. "I was
raised by my grandmother, an old jaguar priestess. I was
taught at an early age to discern and not say too much.
Life is a process of discovery, little sister, and it's not
my right to take that way from you." She hugged her

fiercely and then released her. "Go, Jessica. Drive toward your new life. Trust this man in black. Open your heart to him. See what happens."

Jessica nodded and climbed slowly into the pickup. The sun was just edging the tops of the spruce, making the sky look like a crown of pure, white light surrounding the small meadow where they stood. "And you? What of you? Where will you be?"

Moyra smiled sadly. "I must go home to Peru now, little sister. My people have called me home."

"Which ones? The Jaguar Clan or your family?" She started the engine, her heart already crying for the loss of her friend. Jessica knew that she'd probably never see Moyra again—except in her dreams, where the jaguar ruled night journeys of all kinds.

With a laugh, Moyra said, "One and the same."

"Stay in touch?"

"I will see you on the Other Side."

Jessica blinked back her tears. "Okay.... I love you, Moyra. You're like a fourth sister to me. You know that."

"Yes, and you've helped heal my heart, you know." Moyra's voice became choked. "You gave me a place to heal, Jessica, whether you knew it or not. You taught me about the goodness, the positiveness of family once again. I needed that. In your own way, you are a great healer." Moyra motioned to the orchids in back of the vehicle. "And look what you do for thousands of people around the world who buy your orchid essences. Look how many you heal in that way. Go, my little sister. Drive toward your destiny. I must go to mine now. I promise, I'll be in touch...."

The driveway blurred in front of Jessica as she put

the truck in gear and drove away, leaving behind her cloistered, safe existence. The sunlight glared brightly down on the rutted dirt road. She drove slowly and carefully, not wanting to jar her orchid girls. Sniffing, she wiped her eyes on the sleeve of her shirt. Fumbling for her dark glasses, she put them on. In the rearview mirror, she saw Moyra standing so proud and tall. And then she saw her form change—suddenly a jaguar with a gold coat covered with black spots stood in her place. Blinking the tears away, Jessica almost slammed on the brakes. Blinking once more, she saw Moyra again in human form.

Jessica was grateful that her mother had called Moyra from South America to be her guardian for these past two years, since her divorce from Carl. Jessica knew her mother could use her power from the Other Side. Odula had embraced her Wolf Clan power, but she herself was afraid of it.

And what about this man in black? Jessica shook her head and paid attention to the winding road. The greenhouse and the log cabin disappeared one final time as she drove around the curve that would take her to the asphalt highway—that would take her home. Her real home.

Fear warred with expectation and joy. Jessica had felt little joy in her life—except when she worked with her orchid girls and made the essences. There she was free—like Gan, the black Arabian stallion—to run wildly without fear. She examined her dream of the night before. A man in black…who was that?

Suddenly, Jessica felt a trickle of hope—something she'd not felt in a decade. Hope had been torn from her the day she'd fled from the Donovan Ranch. Now, miraculously, she felt it coming back—a small tendril of flame, so tiny and weak—yet it was there. Yes! Taking in a deep, shaky breath, Jessica absorbed that wonderful feeling. Just thinking about this mysterious "man in black" lifted her wounded spirits. Maybe, just maybe, as Moyra had said, she was going home to face her old fears, to try to work through them and walk out the other side, healed—finally. With the help of this man in black....

Chapter 2

The darkness gripped Dan Black's belly, twisting his fear into pain. Sweat trickled down from his furrowed brow, running into his eyes and making them sting. The low, husky voice of Ai Gvhdi Waya, Walks with Wolves, trembled through the darkness of the sweat lodge where Dan sat. Ai Gvhdi Waya was an Eastern Cherokee medicine woman who lived up on the Navajo reservation where he'd been born, thirty years ago. She wasn't Navajo, but she was known to be one of the most powerful healers on the res. He focused on her now as she poured ladle after ladle of cooling water on the red-hot lava rocks making them glow eerily through the steam. Why the hell had he come here? Why had he thought this would help?

The pain knotted in his stomach. The heat was building. Her voice was low, powerful and searching. His fear heightened. Squeezing his eyes shut, he tried to control the fear. Wasn't that why he'd come? To walk through his fear, not control it? He'd been taught that fear was not to be ignored or denied. By walking through it, feeling it, allowing it to consume him, he would be healed.

He felt anything but healed. He was scared to death. Death…yes, how many times had he faced that horrible possibility? It hurt to admit he had a fear of dying. Dan hadn't realized the depth of his fear until he'd gone over with his marine reconnaissance unit during the swift-moving Gulf War. Desert Storm had been a living, fiery hell for him—externally as well as internally. *No!* He shook his head, moving his long, roughened fingers along the hard curves and lines of his sweaty face. He tried to wipe away the bubbling fear that was snaking up his gullet.

The medicine woman stopped singing. Dan opened his eyes. He could not see her in the sweat lodge, the darkness was so complete. So terrifying. All he saw was the vague outline and shape of glowing red rocks. He centered all his attention on them. He had to or he was going to scream. And then what would she think of him?

"You are frightened, Dan Black."

Her voice sounded like a bullhorn over his head. Dan instantly jerked upright. It was as if Ai Gvhdi Waya was leaning over him, talking directly into his right ear. Automatically, he moved his right arm outward, but the space was empty. Though he was sitting opposite the door she sat next to, he could not see her at all.

"Tell me of your fear."

His throat closed. He felt the penetrating heat of the steam burning the back of his shoulders and neck. His flesh prickled and he cried out, feeling another type of pain.

"Fear is walking around you. I see you clothed in black. Are you going to become your namesake?"

"No…" Though Black was an honored name on the Navajo reservation and there were many branches of the family, Dan's mother had done the unthinkable—she'd wed an Anglo schoolteacher. Dan was a half-breed, and he'd been mercilessly teased about it as he'd gone through the school system on the res. He'd regained his honor among his family by becoming a tamer of horses. Horses were still a powerful, moving force on this reservation today.

"Sometimes we take on a name to walk through it. How far into your journey are you?"

Dan closed his eyes. "It's so dark I can't see daylight at either end," he rasped, forcing the words between his thinned lips.

She threw more water onto the rocks. The hissing and spitting threw up more billowing, steamy clouds into the closed, confined space. "There are people who have a black heart. You are not one of those. I see your heart in pieces, but it is not dark. It is bleeding. You do not have a black spirit, but I see your spirit clothed in darkness, instead."

Was there any good news? Dan felt his heart pumping wildly in his chest. The heat scored his flesh. The sweat ran in rivulets from his head down across his naked body to the white towel he wore around his waist. He dug his fingers into the earthen floor he sat upon. There was something soothing about the red sand. He'd been born on this red desert, in a hogan in Monument Valley, a hundred miles from the nearest hospital. It was one of the most sacred places on the res. The medicine woman in attendance at his birth had proclaimed him a light among his people.

Some light. His last name was Black. And he was clothed in darkness. His spirit sagged. He felt so damned alone, so afraid and unable to help himself. Maybe part of it was his own fault. He never reached out and asked for help because of his childhood on the res as a half-breed. The Navajo children had tortured him daily at school because of his lighter skin and gray eyes. He had black hair like they did, but that was where similarities ended. They said his eyes looked colorless, like those of a predatory owl. And owls were not looked upon kindly in Navajo cosmology. No, they were the symbol of death.

"I'm dying...." he managed to say, his voice low and terribly off-key.

"Sometimes, in order to move forward, a part of us must die. Cut out the old. Let it go and die. And then you will have space for something new, something better, to take its place."

He wished she wouldn't speak in such riddles. But then, all medicine people did. His head was swimming with terror, with trying to control the pain in his stomach. He was overcome with the same fear he'd felt over in the Gulf War when— Instantly, Dan slammed his mind shut, obliterating that scene.

"Look into the stones. The stone people talk to us in many ways," she directed in a low voice.

Eagerly, Dan focused his smarting eyes on the red-colored rocks in the fire pit. Any attempt to take the focus off his terror and pain was worth doing. The clouds of steam came and went. For a moment, he thought he saw the shape of a face in the glowing rocks. And then it vanished. Was he seeing things? His Anglo side pooh-poohed this stuff. His Navajo side was starved for it. Which to believe? Was he hallucinating or did he truly see a woman's face in those rocks?

"There is a woman coming."

Dan's breath hitched. He snapped a look across the blackness to where Ai Gvhdi Waya was sitting. She saw it too? Then he wasn't delusional? Holding his breath, he waited and prayed that the medicine woman would say more.

"Look again."

Disappointed, he shifted his gaze back to the rocks. She poured more water on them. It was so hot now, so strangling with humidity that Dan thought he was going to die for lack of cool, clean oxygen. Everything was becoming claustrophobic to him—again. A new fear, the fear of being in too tight a place, raced through him.

Concentrate!

He had to concentrate or he would begin sobbing.

His gaze fell to the red rocks, where clouds of mist swirled and moved. He blinked, trying to get the stinging sweat out of his eyes in order to see the rocks better. Would he see the woman's face more clearly this time? It had been so vague before.

There!

He gasped.

Yes! It was her—again. Only this time, the face was far more distinct. Its outline wavered in the clouds and heat rising off the rocks. An oval face. He saw huge blue eyes staring back at him—blue like the turquoise color of the endless sky that blanketed his beloved Southwest. The expression in them tugged directly at his heart. He felt a strange spasm there and the sensation was so real that he automatically rubbed his chest. The feeling continued. There was more pain as he felt something opening inside him like a rusted door that had never been opened before.

Gasping, Dan felt his breath leaving him. He clung to the vision of her face, wavering inches above the heated stones in thick, misty clouds of steam. Pain surged outward, like ripples from a pebble thrown into a quiet pond, each one a wavelet of more intense agony. The sensation continued inside his heart and tripled as it moved outward, expanding rapidly across his chest.

"Release it!"

Ai Gvhdi Waya's order came as a physical blow, her voice low and snarling. His hand fell from his chest and he straightened up and tipped his head back, gulping for air as the knifelike sting continued to ripple outward across his chest. He was having a heart attack. Dan was sure he was going to die.

"Lie down!"

It didn't take much for him to do that. He practically fell over, feeling the warmth of the sand on the side of his face, arm and lower body. Air! There was cooler air near the bottom of the sweat lodge. He gulped it greedily, his breath ragged.

"Let the pain continue."

He couldn't have stopped it if he'd tried. Rolling helplessly onto his back, he dug his fingers deep into the red sand on either side of him. The pain deepened and felt like a red-hot brand now, centered in his heart region. Oh, no, he *was* going to die! The air in his lungs was shallow and he was unable to get enough oxygen because it hurt so much to breathe.

Suddenly, Dan felt a swirling sensation around his head, and then it moved down, inch by inch, across his body. The more he became enveloped in this cloud, the less of a coherent hold he had on reality. Somewhere in the distance, he heard Ai Gvhdi Waya beginning another song. He tried to hold on to her voice, to where he was, but found it was impossible.

There was a deep, snapping, cracking feeling emanating from within him. He not only felt it, but distinctly heard it. It sounded like good crystal being smashed with a hammer. Almost instantly, he closed his eyes and he felt himself become featherlight. He was drifting in the darkness, but he had no idea where. The need for breath no longer mattered. He wasn't breathing, he realized, but he was still alive. Or was he? Dan was no longer sure. Miraculously, he no longer felt the fear from the Gulf War. No, he felt an incredible sense of peace—and love.

Shaken by the experience, he allowed himself to move. At times, he felt like a leaf that had fallen off a tree and was gently wafting on an invisible breeze. There was a rocking motion to his weightlessness, reminiscent of a cradle. It was nurturing. Supportive. How wonderful it felt not to be pursued by the demons from hell that had lived within him twenty-four hours a day since the war. He breathed in a sigh of absolute relief.

And then he realized that this was what death must feel like—a warm, embracing cocoon that made him feel like an infant swaddled in a blanket, lovingly held. Held by what, he wasn't sure, and his mind wasn't functioning all that well to ask or to care. Little by little, he thought he saw a grayness somewhere above him. It seemed as if he were moving upward, slowly but surely, toward that emanation of light.

Dan watched in awe as the blackness changed to gray, and then transformed into an incredible gold-and-white light that surrounded him. He should have been blinded by it, but wasn't. Instead, it embraced him, cradled him and held him in a loving security he'd never known before. How he liked being in this place! There was no fear, only an incredible sense of being loved for who he was—faults and all. There were no judgments in this place, only an incredible sense of nurturance. Perhaps this was what white man's heaven was all about.

Out of the light, colors began to congeal. Sometimes they would disappear, but they'd always return, more vibrant than before, eventually taking the shape of a blossom. He had no idea what kind of flower he was looking at. It was white with purple spots all over it.

The apparition danced and moved slowly in front of him, and then it faded. In its place he saw the most beautiful turquoise blue he'd ever seen. In this reality, wherever it was, colors were more vibrant, more dramatic and pure than what he saw with his physical eyes.

The blue color began to take the shape of a set of large, wide eyes. Beautiful eyes, Dan thought as he clung to the gentle love that seemed to emanate from them. And then he began to see the rest of a face fill in around those eyes—the same face he'd seen in the fire. Only this time the vision—of a lovely woman about his own age—was very clear and unmistakable. She had long, straight blond hair that shone like precious gold in sunlight. Her face was oval, her lips full and delicate. Dan didn't know which of her features he liked better. She was smiling, and the fact sent his heart skittering with unaccustomed joy.

He watched as she raised her small, stubborn chin and laughed, her pink lips curving deliciously. The sound of her laughter reminded him of angels singing. It was soft, low, and held such love and nurturing that it brought tears to his eyes. He felt the heat of his tears mingling with the sweat that ran across his face and body in rivulets.

And then her face began to fade. *No!* He tried to call out to her, but he had no voice. His chest region was throbbing with warmth now, not pain. The light began to fade and he felt himself being pulled rapidly back into the cloistered blackness once again. This time he didn't fight it. He surrendered totally to it because he knew he was safe and loved.

The spinning began again, sharp and violent. Within seconds, he felt heaviness. He was in his body once more. He could feel the sand he still gripped beneath his fingers, could hear the ending of the song Ai Gvhdi Waya sang, could feel the prickling heat against his taut flesh and the endless streams of sweat washing off of him.

"You have returned."

He lay there in awe. Dan had no idea how long his journey into the other world had taken. He'd never had such an experience before—ever. But then, he had never sought out the help of a medicine person, either. He'd always gone the anglo route when it came to medicine, rather than rely on his Navajo heritage. Maybe he should have come long ago, he thought wearily. He moved his hand across his chest where an intense, branding warmth still throbbed. There was no pain, just a wonderful feeling of joy. What had happened? What had the medicine woman done? And who was the woman he'd seen in his vision?

"Come out when you want," Ai Gvhdi Waya instructed as she threw open the blanketed door. "Go to the hot springs down the path, wash off and dress. Then come see me at my hogan."

Dan felt incredibly tired, as if his body weighed twice what it should, and he was thirsty, too. It was probably dehydration, the loss of water during the hour-long sweat lodge ceremony. As his mind slowly began to function again, he felt the grit of the sand on his naked back. It felt familiar, comforting. He watched as the medicine woman, who was dressed in a faded cotton shift, crawled out of the sweat lodge and then got to her feet. Outside the door, the sun was shining brightly, the shafts of light piercing the darkness of the lodge.

Closing his eyes, Dan gasped for the cooling air moving into the heated, humid confines. Air! Fresh air. All he could do was lie there and allow his weakened body to recuperate. His mind spun with questions and no answers. Emotionally he felt lighter. The fear was less. Why? What had the medicine woman done to make it so? The questions drove him to sit up and then weakly crawl out on his hands and knees.

The midafternoon May heat moved across the red desert as he stood up on unsteady legs. Rewrapping the white towel low on his hips, Dan picked up his clothing and cowboy boots and headed down a well-worn path toward the hot springs behind Ai Gvhdi Waya's hogan. In the distance, he heard the familiar and soothing sounds of bleating sheep. Right now, he just concentrated on putting one step in front of the other.

At the springs, a natural well of hot water surrounded by smooth red sandstone guardians, Dan lay with his head on a stone that served as a pillow and felt the healing effects of the water on his body. His mother would be proud of him—going to see a medicine person. His father would have told him to see a psychotherapist— which Dan had many times.

Oddly, his fear remained at a distant from him. Before, he'd anesthetized the fear with alcohol. That had gotten him into a lot of trouble, too. When he was drunk, he was violent. He'd spent some time in the Coconino jail in Flagstaff. He'd recently gotten fired from his job on a ranch, where he'd been the head horse wrangler. Alcohol had made his fear lessen, so that he could continue to function in the world. And yet, because of his Navajo blood, he had no enzymes to break down alcohol once it entered his bloodstream, so he went "crazy." His father used the word *berserk*. His mother cried and begged him to seek help of her medicine people.

A tired half smile tugged at Dan's mouth. He lifted his head and knew it was time to climb out, dry off and get dressed. Well, he hadn't been much of a prize to his family, had he? He'd shamed them repeatedly. Now his name was mud. Any honor he'd gained for being one of the best horse wranglers they'd ever seen was now destroyed. It had hurt to see his mother cry when she visited him in that damned jail. It made him angry when his father did nothing but castigate him and tell him to go to a shrink to get cured.

Dan had disappointed them. Shamed them in front of the rest of his large, extended family. Gossip was one of the worst habits Navajos had, and there was plenty about Dan Black, the "black sheep" of the family, and his crazy ways. He was shunned by his own people. Well, why not? Since returning from the Gulf War six years ago, he'd pretty much made a disaster of his life.

Before going into the marines, he'd had a good job on a ranch near Flag. He'd joined the marines because his father had been one. Dan had wanted his dad to be proud of him. And he was, until Dan was sent to the Gulf, where all hell broke loose. He'd come back broken not only in body, but in spirit. His mother had pleaded with him to walk the Navajo way and get his spirit healed. His father had said that in time his fear would go away and that he didn't need help from some medicine person.

Why the hell didn't he listen more to his mother? Dan thought as he got out of the spring and quickly dried off in the ninety-degree, midday heat. He donned his light blue, short-sleeved shirt, his faded jeans, and settled a dusty, black felt Stetson on his head. Sitting down, he pulled on his socks and badly scuffed cowboy boots. The boots looked like how he'd felt before coming to this incredibly powerful medicine woman.

Standing, he stretched his arms toward Father Sky. The blueness of the sky reminded him of this unknown woman's turquoise eyes filled with such loving warmth. Just remembering the vision of those eyes caused his heart to expand with joy. It took him off guard. What was going on? What was happening to him? Maybe the medicine woman could tell him. Dan hurried up the slope, looking for answers that would explain his vision.

As he rounded her hogan, Dan saw Ai Gvhdi Waya with a white man. Word had gotten around that she was living with an Anglo named Dain Phillips. Gossip had it that he was very, very rich. If he was, Dan didn't see it. The tall, intense-looking man stood near a beat-up old blue pickup that looked a lot like his own—in dire need of a paint job and some bodywork. He saw Ai Gvhdi Waya reach up and kiss him quickly on the mouth. She was once again dressed in familiar Navajo clothes: a long-sleeved red velvet blouse and a dark blue cotton skirt that hung to her ankles. Her hair was in two thick braids, tied at the ends with feathers and red yarn.

Dan stood near the door to the hogan, his eyes averted. But he hadn't missed the love for Ai Gvhdi Waya shining in the Anglo's eyes. Dan wondered if he'd ever find a woman who made him feel that way. So far, his luck with life in general, not to mention women, was pretty bad. He supposed it had something to do with that curse of darkness that surrounded him. When he was growing up on the res, the children had always teased him that his skin was lighter because the copper color had faded away due to the blanket of darkness wrapped around him since birth. And because of this owl darkness, his skin seemed lighter to those who looked at him. Dan hated that explanation. He'd fought repeatedly to defend his honor throughout the twelve years of schooling here. Fighting didn't come naturally to him. No, he'd rather work with horses, to feel in tune with their wild, free spirits, than take on the school bully.

"You feel lighter."

Dan lifted his head, suddenly realizing he was staring down at his dusty, booted feet. Ai Gvhdi Waya stood directly in front of him, no more than six feet away. He looked past her and saw that the Anglo had driven away in the pickup, down the rutted dirt road. Shaking his head, Dan rasped, "I don't know what's happening."

"Come in. You need to drink water."

Her hand felt comforting on his arm. He liked this woman, her quiet power, her ability to soothe him and make him feel decent and not ashamed. "Thanks," he mumbled, and followed her into the cooling comfort of her hogan.

He always felt at home in the hogan, an eight-sided structure made of mud and logs. The door faced east, to welcome Father Sun as he rose each morning. The odor of sage filled his nostrils and he saw that some was burning slowly in an abalone shell on top of the old pine table. She gestured for him to sit down at the table while she went to the kitchen counter and poured two large glasses of water.

"Thanks," he said sincerely as she handed him the glass. Dan drank the contents quickly, his body eager to replace what he'd lost in the sweat. She placed a pitcher of water between them and he poured himself a second and third glass before he was satiated. When he was finished, he sat opposite her at the table, the tendrils of sage smoke drifting upward and spreading out across the hogan. Sage, for the Navajo, was purifying and healing. Whenever he got a cold or flu, Dan would make sage tea and drink quarts of it to flush and cleanse his body. It always worked.

"Tell me what you saw in your journey," Ai Gvhdi Waya urged softly.

He took off his hat and set it on the table. "You'll probably think I'm crazy." He tried to smile, but failed miserably. "Everyone else thinks I am, anyway...."

She smiled gently. "One person's craziness is another's sanity. So who is sane and who is really crazy?"

He laughed a little and tried not to feel so uncomfortable. "Listen, this is my first time with a medicine person. I didn't know what to expect."

"Expect nothing. Receive everything."

He stared at her, more of the tension draining from him.

"You've been called crazy by many, but you are not. Your spirit is sensitive. Things that wouldn't wound others wound you. The road you walk, Dan Black, is a hard one." She closed her eyes and gestured with her hands. "I see a man walking with one foot on one road, an asphalt one. And then I see him walking with the other foot on the good red road of our people." She opened her eyes and smiled a little. "You carry the blood of two worlds in your body. You are *heyoka,* a contrary. You must learn to blend these two paths you walk into one road and then make it your road."

"Easier said than done," he muttered.

"One path is that of a warrior, the other of a healer. A warrior healer. You have tasted and done both. But neither is comfortable with the other. Your spirit hungers for the touch of our mother, the earth. And for her living things. Today I saw horses surrounding you. I knew of your reputation before you came here—of being one of our best horse wranglers. Horses are important to you. They are part of your healing. Stay with them."

He nodded. "Yeah, I just got a job down at the Donovan Ranch. The ranch foreman gave me a chance. He knew I was a—that I drank too much…."

"Yes." She nodded. "I know him. Sam McGuire is a good man. He will give you the chance you deserve."

Earnestly, Dan met and held her sympathetic gaze. "Look, I came to you to try and stop this fear. That's why I drank. I had to make it go away somehow…it was the only way."

"Not the right way and you know that, Dan."

Grudgingly, he nodded. "My father calls me an alcoholic. My mother cries for me all the time. I had to do something."

Reaching out, the medicine woman closed her workworn hand over his. "Listen carefully, stallion tamer. You drink to run from the pain you received while being a warrior. There is only one way out of this and that is to walk through it. Alcohol will not cure you. Only

your heart's desire to do this for yourself will cure you."
She lifted her hand, all the while her gaze holding his.

"I know… I agree," Dan rasped.

"The path you walk is a hard one. There is no disagreement on that. The Great Spirit gives you the
strength you need to walk it. All you have to do is surrender to a power higher than yourself and trust what
you know instinctively. You use it to tame the mustangs.
Why not use it on yourself?"

Dan watched her smile. It reminded him of the coy-
ote, the trickster. He smiled a little, too. "I'm going
to try. I've got to save my family's reputation. This is
tearing my mother apart. I don't mean to hurt her—I
really don't.…"

"I understand," Ai Gvhdi Waya soothed. Tilting her
head slightly, she asked, "What else did you see in your
vision?"

Shaken, he stared at her. "You saw it, too?"

"Yes, but I want to hear in your words what you saw
and experienced."

Dan took a deep breath, and, risking everything, told
her the details of the vision. She nodded wisely now and
then, as if to corroborate his story. Little by little, he
didn't feel so foolish. By the time he finished, Dan felt
oddly comfortable. He wondered if everyone had such
visions in a sweat lodge, but didn't ask.

"What do you make of it?" he asked instead.

She shrugged. "It's more important what you make
of it."

Quirking his mouth, he leaned back and tilted the
chair onto its rear legs. "I knew you were going to say
that."

Ai Gvhdi Waya laughed deeply. "It is your life, your

interpretation of events, that counts. What I think about it is unimportant compared to how you feel, how you respond to what you saw."

Nodding, Dan looked up at the earthen ceiling. His voice dropped. "I feel lighter, almost happy…expectant that something good is coming my way—finally. I don't know this woman I saw. I've never seen eyes like hers. She's so beautiful…like a dream I might have. And the flower…it was white and purple. I've never seen anything like it, either." He shifted his gaze to her. "Do you know this flower?"

"No. I've never seen one like that."

Shrugging, Dan eased the chair downward. He placed his hands on the table and folded them. "A woman and a flower. Got me."

"And what did you feel when you saw this woman's face?"

He gave a shy grin. "A lot of things."

The medicine woman smiled back. "Your heart opened. By just seeing her face, some of your injured heart was healed. It is no longer as fragmented. Do you have the feeling that she could heal your heart?"

Dan felt telltale heat creep into his face. That was one of his flaws—blushing. "Yeah… I think she could—"

"No," Ai Gvhdi Waya admonished, "stop saying 'I think' and switch to saying 'I feel'. You must disconnect from that Anglo head of yours and move down to the true center of your being, which is your Navajo heart. There you feel and you *know*. You can know without knowing why you know." She smiled enigmatically. "Your father is Anglo. Anglos think too much. They think only their brain has answers. That is not true. Our heart is our only true voice. You use your heart when you break and train horses. Why not use it *all the time* with regard to yourself? Switch off your thinking. Not all of life is logical. And reality?" She laughed deeply once again. "The Anglo mind sees only what it can weigh, measure or perceive with these two things we call eyes." She pointed to her own eyes. "There are many other realities. When you're with a wild horse, you move into his or her reality, don't you? You are no longer a human, a two-legged. You become like a four-legged, a shape-shifter. You become the horse to feel him, his fears or whatever, don't you?"

Dan had never thought of what he did in those terms, but looking at it her way, he had to nod his head. "Yes," he said slowly, "something does happen, but I couldn't tell you what, or how it happens."

"That," Ai Gvhdi Waya said firmly, "is your skill, your power. That is what you need to embrace twenty-four hours a day. I call it your flow. It is a flow of life. If you can get into it and stay in it, life becomes one unfolding miracle after another. If you will try to stay in your flow, this woman with the flower will come into your life."

He chuckled. "I wish. I'd be happy just to see her now and then in my dreams." Instead of his terrifying nightmares, he thought, but didn't say it.

The medicine woman rose. "Become more aware of what feelings and sensations you have when you work with the wild horses. And then start to feel them in other situations. Watch what happens."

Dan stood and placed the black cowboy hat on his head. He'd brought fifty dollars' worth of groceries to the medicine woman in exchange for her help. He wished he had more, but he was broke—as usual. "I don't know how to thank you...."

"You can thank me by getting into your flow." She led him out of the hogan and walked him to his rusty white pickup. In the back was all his horse-training equipment and other meager belongings. He would head down to the Donovan Ranch and be there by sunset.

Entering the pickup, Dan tipped his hat in her direction. She stood six feet away, with a white wolf now at her side. There was an ethereal presence to this medicine woman; an inner beauty and power resonated from her person. Dan was in awe of her, and he was grateful. As he drove away from the hogan, the woman's face, the one with the incredible turquoise eyes, seemed to hover like a mist in front of him. He shook his head. He had to concentrate on his driving or he'd end up stuck in one of these sandy washes.

Today, he thought, *is the first day of my life. My new life.* In a sense, he felt reborn by the experience in the sweat lodge. He also knew Ai Gvhdi Waya saw a lot more than she was telling him, but then, she was right: his personal discovery of his own process was far more empowering to him than her just telling him. He understood her reasoning.

Dan knew this was his last chance at a good job—a way to salvage his family's name. The foreman at the Donovan Ranch was giving him a break when he deserved none. His first order of business was to tame a black Arabian stallion known as Gan. *Gan* was an Apache word for devil. From what the foreman had said, Gan hated humans, and had been badly abused by his alcoholic owner. Dan's fingers tightened momentarily on the steering wheel. In front of him rose the red sandstone buttes that were scattered over the red desert of the Navajo res. It was a beautiful sight, one that Dan never got tired of looking at.

Hadn't he been abused daily by his schoolmates when he was growing up? Been called names? Been shunned? He'd always had to defend himself. And how many fights had he lost? How many times had he come home with a black eye or a bloody face? Or worse, a broken hand or nose? Navajo children were not kind to one who did not fit their concepts. Dan wasn't a fighter. All he wanted was peace. So why the hell had he joined the marines and gone into the warrior branch, the Recon Marines? He knew now that he'd been trying to make his father accept him. It hadn't been the right choice.

No, Ai Gvhdi Waya was right—he had to stand in his power as a horse trainer and not always be apologizing for not being a teacher, as his father wanted to be, or the marine Dan had once tried to be for his father's sake. He had to find himself and like himself for what he was. Or else the man clothed in darkness would become a homeless person on some cold street of Flagstaff, looking for handouts, for money to go buy his next bottle of whiskey.

The alternative was no alternative at all to Dan. Somehow, he *had* to save his own life. This was his last chance and he knew it. And the woman with the flower was part of his healing. Did she exist? Would he be blessed by getting to meet her in physical reality? He fervently prayed that it would be so.

Chapter 3

"Welcome home!" Kate cried as Jessica parked her truck in front of the main ranch house and got out. The midday sun beat down as her older sister took the steps two at a time to get to her. Though she was tired and stressed out, Jessica rallied and gave Kate a big smile in return.

"Oh!" she cried, throwing her arms around her tall, lean sister. "It's so good to see you, Katie!" She basked in the love that emanated from Kate, before she finally stepped away.

"I don't mean to be in a hurry here, Katie, but my girls, my orchids…" She pointed to the rear of her pickup. "They've got to have a cooler temperature or they're going to die!"

Sam McGuire, the foreman, came out of the house. He grinned and tipped his hat respectfully to Jessica. "Did I hear a call for help? Welcome home, Jessica.

Kate couldn't sleep at all last night because she was so excited about your coming home today."

"Hi, Sam," Jessica whispered, and hugged the tall, strapping Arizona cowboy. "It's great to be home. Where did you put the greenhouse you and Kate built for my girls? I have to get them into it pronto or they're going to die of heat prostration." Jessica quickly pushed a wisp of blond hair away from her brow. She saw the love in Sam's eyes when he and Kate shared a warm look. If only she could someday find a man like Sam— who loved her, warts and all.

Sam put his arm around Kate's shoulder and pointed to the house that stood to the left of the main ranch house. "That's your new home, Jessica, over there. I'll drive your truck around and back it up to the greenhouse door. Kate put on the humidifier, and the temperature was reading eighty-five just about half an hour ago."

Relieved, Jessica nodded. "That's wonderful. Thanks so much, Sam."

He brushed past her and drove the pickup around to the other side of the cottonwood-enclosed main house.

Jessica gazed up at her sister. "You look so happy, Katie. Love really does work, doesn't it?"

Kate nodded and said softly, "Sam is wonderful. I'm afraid that it's all a dream and that I'll wake up some- day and be without him," she confided as she put her arm around Jessica's shoulders and guided her toward her new home.

"Pshaw. Sam isn't some dream. Judging by the way he was looking at you, he's never going to leave under any circumstances," Jessica responded. It felt so good to have Kate's tall, lean body against hers. "Boy, to tell you the truth, Katie, I'd sure like to find a guy like Sam, but my record isn't so good in that department."

Kate touched Jessica's flyaway blond hair. The ninety-degree weather in early May was sending waves of heat across the canyon floor, where the ranch head-quarters sat. "Give yourself time. Carl was a real bas-tard. Not all men are that way."

"I'm worried, Kate. Carl might try to follow me here. He threatened to hunt me down and kill me. I seem to have a curse. All I pick are abusive types."

"Is it any wonder? Kelly was abusive to us. That's all we know." Kate sighed. "And as for Carl following you here, if he has any brains at all, he won't."

Jessica looked up into Kate's face, which was darkly tanned despite the fact that she wore a straw cowboy hat today to protect her skin and shade her eyes. "Then tell me how you ended up with Sam. He's certainly not an 'abuser' type."

Mystified, Kate shrugged her shoulders. "I don't know, Jessica. I really don't." And then she grinned down at her. "You tell me. You're our little spiritual sister out here in the desert wilderness."

Jessica chuckled as they rounded the corner of the ranch house. About three hundred feet away was a beau-tiful cream-colored, Santa Fe adobe home. It was one of three houses that Odula had insisted be built for her daughters. Kelly had built them, but he'd been angry about doing so. In Odula's world, children not only were raised together, they lived in close proximity to one an-other even after they were grown. Jessica remembered how Kelly had railed at spending what little money they had on building these homes. Sadly she recalled how their mother had wanted her daughters to stay on after high school, but it had been impossible with Kelly's continual drinking and abusive behavior toward them.

"The house…" Jessica said with a sigh. "You've given it a new coat of paint!" A thrill went through her. Home! She was really home—and it felt so good! A bubbling joy kept moving up through her and expanding her heart until she was breathless from it. Not until this moment had Jessica realized just how much she'd missed her family.

"Actually," Kate murmured, releasing Jessica and opening the gate in the white picket fence, "our new wrangler, Dan Black, just finished painting it."

"Oh, you've got help finally."

Kate grimaced. "We're not in any financial shape to be paying anyone yet, Jessica. Sam knows Dan Black. He's part Navajo and part Anglo. Got a real chip on his shoulder, but Sam said he was good at breaking and training horses. And he's going to be working at taming Gan." Kate moved to the front door and opened it for Jessica with a flourish. "Welcome home, little sis."

Jessica stepped into the much cooler environment of the house. It was empty, but the colorful flower-print curtains on the windows made tears come to her eyes. "Oh, Katie, it's beautiful. I'd forgotten how much I'd come to love this house after Kelly built it." She wiped tears from her eyes as she looked around. Happiness deluged her.

"Grudgingly built," Kate reminded her grimly. "Why don't you go unload your Mother Earth Flower Essence stuff from the back of your pickup into your new greenhouse? I'll get Dan to help unpack your trailer, and he and Sam can move the contents into here."

Jessica sighed, relishing the cool interior of her

home. "Which of the two guys would be more sensitive to my orchids?"

Chuckling, Kate moved to the door. "Sam is all thumbs. If you need help unloading the orchids, I'll call Dan over from Gan's corral to help. Okay?"

"But you said he's got a chip on his shoulder."

"Ah, he's shy and doesn't say much. Like most Navajos, he won't look you in the eye. He looks up, down or to the side, but not straight into your eyes. They think it's rude to stare at a person. Sam says the only time he ever got ugly was when he hit the bottle after coming back from Desert Storm. Dan hasn't touched alcohol since that time, so I think it's in the past. He's been here for a week, and so far, so good. Dan's really wonderful with animals, Jessica. Far more sensitive than Sam. He'll be okay. He takes orders well. I'll go get him and he can help you unload your orchids. Sam and I will move your furniture into the house in the meantime."

Nonplussed, Jessica nodded and hurried out the back door. It was so hard to concentrate on the care the orchids demanded at a time like this. All Jessica really wanted to do was settle into her new home, spend time with Kate and simply reacquaint herself with the place where she'd grown up. With a sigh, she opened the side door to the hothouse. Checking the thermometer and humidity gauge, she noticed the rows and rows of lattice type, wrought-iron shelves that had been set up for the bulk of her orchids to sit on. The environment within the greenhouse felt wonderful compared to the much drier, hotter air outside. The swamp cooler kept the greenhouse at a reasonable seventy-five degrees.

"I hear Dan's going to help unload your orchids with you?" Sam called from the front door.

"Yes," Jessica said, hurrying to where Sam had

parked her pickup near the door. "Thanks for helping, Sam."

He nodded. "Dan will be better at this than I am. I'm all thumbs."

She smiled up into Sam's rugged face. "Okay, thanks. I think Katie wants you to help her move my furniture into my house." Sensitive to the need of others, Jessica could feel that he was trying his best to be warm and welcoming to her. She knew Sam was a strong, silent type, and for him to be putting out this much for her meant a lot. She appreciated his trying to make her feel comfortable about coming home.

"Yep, that's where we'll be. When you're done here, come back to your house. Kate's got some nonalcoholic grape bubbly to toast your coming home."

Touched, Jessica nodded. "I will! Thanks for everything, Sam. It means so much...."

Nodding in turn, Sam left.

A few minutes later, Jessica heard a slight, hesitant knock at the side entrance to the greenhouse. It must be the wrangler, the one with a chip on his shoulder, she thought. Jessica chided herself for thinking of the man in that way. It wasn't right. She hurried to the door and swung it open.

For a split second, Jessica froze before the open door. A man, tall and lean, his skin a dark golden brown, and his eyes gray and intelligent, stared back at her. Her heart pounded in her breast. She felt her breath torn from her. It was as if time had halted and frozen around them. She studied the man before her more closely. He wore a dusty, black felt Stetson hat low across his broad forehead. His prominent nose was crooked, as if it had been broken a number of times. A scar along his left cheek scored his hard flesh. His face was narrow, and the lines at the corners of his pale, almost colorless eyes showed he squinted or laughed a lot. On closer inspection, Jessica surmised that he probably squinted more than laughed. This was a man who wore sadness like a huge blanket around himself.

Because of her sensitivity to people, to the feelings surrounding them, she felt an incredible weight settle within her, the weight of his absolute sadness. And yet he stood lean and tall, his shoulders strong and thrown back with an unconscious pride. She saw the Navajo in him, from his shining, short black hair to the leanness of his body to the golden color of his skin. She liked the warmth she saw banked in his gray eyes, eyes that seemed to change color slightly as he stared down at her. He seemed surprised—shocked—at seeing her. Why on earth would he be shocked?

Almost unconsciously, Jessica touched her hair. She was sure it was in disarray and needed a good combing. Why was he looking at her like that? Had she spilled something on her skirt or blouse when she ate that veggie burger on the road? Nervously, Jessica touched her lacy cotton blouse. No, no ketchup there. How about her skirt? She quickly flattened her hands and brushed them over the dark green print decorated with various shades of pink and lavender morning glories. She found no damage to her skirt, either.

Lifting her chin, she frowned as she felt his shock deepen. He was staring at her as if he'd seen a ghost! His gray eyes had widened considerably. Those black pupils had enlarged and she saw an almost predatory intent in his gaze, as if he were an eagle checking out a possible prey. Laughing at herself, Jessica quirked her lips.

"Hi, I'm Jessica Donovan. You must be Dan Black. Come on in." She stepped aside and he slowly entered, still continuing to appraise her sharply. Closing the door, Jessica offered him her small, slender hand. "You can call me Jessica…."

Dan stared at that very white, delicate-looking hand with such slender, artistic fingers. This was the woman he'd seen in his sweat lodge vision! His heart was pounding like a sledgehammer in his chest. An internal trembling began deep within him and he felt outwardly shaky. Unable to tear his gaze from her beautiful turquoise eyes, Dan stood there, looking like a gaping fool, he was sure. How could he tell this beautiful woman of the sky that she'd been in his vision? Automatically, he felt a strange, warm tendril curling around his heart.

"Do you shake hands?" Jessica demanded a little more briskly. "Because if you don't, we have to get to work. My orchids must be cooled down quickly or they'll die."

Rousing himself, Dan jerked his hat off his head and quickly raised his hand, swallowing hers up in his. Her fingers were so soft and firm compared to his dirty, range-worn and callused ones. "Sorry," he mumbled. "I'm Dan Black. Most folks call me Dan unless they don't like me."

Jessica felt the warm strength in Dan's hand. It was a hand that had known hard, even brutal physical labor. Suddenly she felt a new sensation and she didn't want to release his hand. Though she could feel energy and emotions around people, if she touched them she got a far more intimate portrait of them. Dan's strength was there, quiet and deep, like the cold Canadian lake near Vancouver that she loved to sit beside, watching the wildlife. The sadness she'd felt melted away, and instead she discovered the man who was hidden within it. Yes, he was terribly shy, and unlike the typical Navajo, he *was* staring at her. As if she were a specimen or something.

Laughing softly, she reluctantly released his hand. "Am I a ghost to you, Dan Black?"

Shaken, Dan placed the hat back on his head. How pretty Jessica Donovan was in person. The blouse she wore had Victorian lace around the throat. The skirt was full, brightly colored with flowers, and fell to her thin ankles. She wore some kind of sandals on her small, perfectly formed feet. As his gaze moved up again, he noticed how her mussed golden hair fell in a tumble around her shoulders. She reminded him of the clouds that moved along the Mogollon Rim above the ranch, fleeting, ethereal and transparent with beauty. But in the sunlight, those clouds disappeared. Dan wondered if she was an apparition. He hoped not.

"No, ma'am…you're not a ghost. You, uh, remind me of someone I saw one time, that's all. I'm sorry for staring. It's not polite."

Jessica felt heat rise in her cheeks as he averted his gaze. "Oh, that's okay. I hope I reminded you of someone who was good and not bad." She chuckled, gesturing for him to follow her. A new thrill moved through her. How handsome he was! Twice in the span of a short while, Jessica found herself detoured from the care of her orchids. On a feminine level, she found herself helplessly drawn to Dan Black. There was an air of mystery around him and it drew her effortlessly.

Even the way she moved reminded Dan of a wispy cloud. It was as if Jessica's feet weren't really touching the gravel of the greenhouse floor at all. He shook his head. What was going on? Was he hallucinating? How could this woman be real? Yet his fingers tingled wildly where he'd touched her hand. If she was a ghost, a vision, she certainly felt real. His entire body was resonating with her presence, her impish smile and the kind warmth that danced in her eloquent eyes—eyes that were a window into her sweet, vulnerable soul.

As he followed her to the door where the truck was parked, Dan realized that as closed up and guarded as he was, Jessica was just the opposite: she was open, available, trusting and sweet. So very, very sweet. How did she survive in this harsh world? Early in his life, he'd been a lot like her, but the meanness of the schoolchildren had forced him to close up and protect himself against such attacks.

Looking at Jessica's flyaway, spun-sunshine hair, the almost ethereal way she walked, he realized life hadn't treated her in the same way. Halting, he watched her pull a box out of the pickup, and he opened his arms to receive it. All he saw were a lot of lumps of newspaper in it.

"These are orchids, Dan," she said a little breathlessly. As she slid the cardboard box into his waiting arms, she found herself *wanting* to make physical contact with him again. Jessica felt such hesitancy around him, such excruciating shyness and…what else? As her arms brushed his darkly haired forearms, bared because he'd rolled up the sleeves of his dark red cowboy shirt, she felt something else. It was so hidden and elusive… and yet, as she slid the box into his arms, it was there. What was it?

"Treat them gently. Just start putting the boxes over there, on the metal table." Jessica found herself wanting to touch him again. How strange! After her experience with Carl, she had learned to distrust men, yet here she was, wanting more contact with Dan. Her emotions were like a roller coaster and she simply couldn't stop the blazing joy that curled through her heart every time she looked at Dan Black.

For the next twenty minutes, Dan helped her bring in box after box. He'd heard of orchids, but he'd never seen one, so he was curious. When Jessica finally shut the door to the greenhouse, her cheeks were flushed a bright red and her gold hair was growing slightly curly in the humidity, framing her oval face beautifully. Dan tried not to gawk at her. He tried not to rudely stare into those beautiful, bottomless eyes that shone with such life.

"Now, watch what I do," she directed softly as she brought the first box over to where he stood.

Dan moved closer. He liked how he felt around her. Remembering Ai Gvhdi Waya's instructions about opening himself up to that mystical flow he always had with horses, he allowed that to consciously happen now. Jessica felt safe to him. In fact, he'd never felt more safe with a person than her. There was nothing dark, manipulative or abusive about her. She was like an incredible rainbow of color to him, and just as otherworldly. He still wasn't sure he wasn't hallucinating. But each time he got to brush her hand or her fingertips, he knew she was very human.

In his world, the Navajo world, he had heard tales of gods and goddesses who turned from animal form into human form. Sometimes, they became human in order to instruct the Navajo people. That was how he saw Jessica—as a goddess from the Other Side, come to instruct him. She couldn't really be human. She was too beautiful. Too loving and open to be like him or the people he knew.

Jessica gently began to unfold the newspaper from one of the orchids she had taken from the cardboard box and set on the metal table in front of her. "Have you ever seen an orchid, Dan?" She thrilled to his nearness. There was such raw, barely controlled power around him. He was a stallion tamer, a man who could handle a thousand-pound horse and not be afraid. Admiration for him spiralled through her and a hundred questions about him sat on the tip of her tongue.

He shook his head. "No, ma'am, I haven't."

She glanced at him out of the corner of her eye. "Please call me Jessica. Ma'am sounds *so* formal. I'm afraid I'm not a very formal person." The warmth in his eyes melted her and she saw one corner of his mouth gently curl. It was a slight response, but she felt the feathery, invisible touch of it upon her.

Out of habit, he tipped the brim of his cowboy hat in her direction. "Yes, ma'am! I mean... Jessica." Her name rolled off his tongue like honey. He liked the sound of it. In his world, names had meanings. Someday he'd like to ask her what her name meant.

Smiling warmly, Jessica met his shy gaze. She saw color rising in his cheeks. Dan was blushing! What a delightful discovery. This hard-bitten man, whose face was carved with sadness, could blush. Jessica felt her pulse speed up as his gray gaze met hers for a fleeting moment. She saw again the hint of thawing in his eyes and felt a shy smile emanating from him. But it never appeared on his hard, thinned mouth. She wondered if Dan's lips would seem fuller if he didn't keep them so tightly compressed, as if to protect himself from what

she might say. She sensed that he was like a beaten animal—a beaten, wary animal that didn't quite trust her.

As much as she wanted to be nosy and ask him more,
Jessica had grown up with Navajo people and knew they
did not like to be asked direct questions about themselves. Perhaps with time and careful watching, Dan
Black would be like one of her mysterious orchids. As
he blossomed and began to trust her more, she would
understand more of these feelings she picked up around
him.

"Watch me carefully," she said, and unfolded the
newspapers one by one and set them aside. "Orchids are
very sensitive plants. They must have a certain range
of temperature in order to survive. For instance, many
of my orchid girls like the temperature no lower than
fifty-five degrees at night and no higher than eighty-five
during the day. And—" she pointed to the two temperature gauges hung on a redwood spar "—humidity is
an absolute must or they won't bloom or flourish. The
humidity has to be set around eighty to ninety percent
to create the best environmental conditions for them."

He watched, mesmerized as her hands flew know-
ingly around the packed orchid. Although Dan wanted
to see what one of these plants looked like, her long,
beautiful fingers were worth watching. There was nothing but grace to Jessica Donovan. No move she made
was jerky or hurried. Everything she did flowed from
one gesture directly into another, making it seem as if
she were always in motion. He smiled to himself, absorbing the warm, sunny energy that emanated from
her. Getting to stand only inches from her, looking over
her shoulder as she worked quickly, was pure, unadulterated pleasure for Dan.

"See?" Jessica said excitedly as she pulled the last

remaining newspaper away. "This is Stone Pinto!" Her voice softened with excitement as she turned the orchid in the red clay pot around so that Dan could see the spike with twelve blossoms on it. "Isn't she lovely? Oh, I love this orchid so much. She's one of my personal favorites. Here, look at her. Carefully touch her leaves and her flower."

Jessica was delighted to see real interest in Dan's eyes as he moved closer, much closer to her. She unconsciously absorbed Dan's nearness; it was a powerful sensation, but one that did not put her on edge. Ordinarily, if any man got this close to her, she would shy away. But she wasn't afraid of him. Although she was puzzled as to why, Jessica had enough intuitive sense to allow the exchange of energy to take place. In some ways, she was like a starving animal and Dan was giving her what she needed. But when she remembered he was a man, wariness invaded her. Yet her heart whispered that he could be trusted. Could he?

Dan stared at the orchid. "The flower..." he began, choking up. Without thinking, he reached forward and delicately touched the white blossom with the field of purple dots across it. "I've seen this flower before—" He felt his throat close up completely. When he touched the orchid blossom, he felt the strength of it, as well as the velvety softness of the petals.

Jessica saw so many different emotions cross his once hard, unreadable face. She was amazed at his response to Stone Pinto. She'd seen similar responses to other orchids when she'd allowed friends and customers to come in and see the plants from which she'd created the flower essences that cured them.

"You like her?" she whispered, touched by his emotional reaction to the orchid. As he leaned over and carefully examined the orchid, he grazed her arm with his. Being with him, Jessica realized, was wonderful! She'd never felt this way around any man. Ever. Absorbing his profile, she felt confused and exhilarated all at once. "When I did tests with Stone Pinto, I found out her essence was for people who carried too much responsibility on their shoulders or worked too hard. People who saw life as just one big responsibility and had lost their ability to play, to laugh or even smile...."

She reached out and stroked the long, leathery leaf of the orchid. "Stone Pinto is for people who usually have had a very hard, rigid life, Dan. If you took her essence, it would help you unbend, allow you to feel more vulnerable and to be able to laugh or smile again." She shared a soft smile with him as he turned and looked down at her. The predatory look was gone from his eyes now; instead, they appeared to be a soft dove gray, showing his emotions.

"Already," Jessica whispered, "she heals you as you touch her...."

Dan stood there, mystified. He withdrew his hand and stood looking at the orchid on the workbench. "But how... I saw this flower in my vision...." And then he stopped. Most people would never understand. He didn't trust that Jessica would. And when he saw her eyes change, and tears swim in them, he felt his heart opening like that orchid bloom. He was helpless to stop the reaction as their gazes met and locked. There was such an incredible sense of love moving from her to him in that moment that it made his breath hitch in response.

Stepping back, he looked away, unable to understand or digest all that was happening. Embarrassed, Dan moved the hat around on his head. It was a ner-

vous gesture, something he did when he was afraid he'd
humiliated himself once more in front of a stranger.

Jessica reached out, wrapping her fingers around his
arm and drawing him back to the bench. "Let me show
you something. You're part Navajo. You're close to the
land, the plants and animals, like we are. My mother
was a medicine woman and she passed on much of her
skills to all of us." Jessica didn't want to release his
hard, muscled arm, but she forced herself to do it. How
strong and capable Dan was. Her hands tingled wildly
from contact with him. Sliding her fingers around the
six-inch clay pot, she drew the Stone Pinto forward.

"You understand that all living things have a spirit,
don't you?" Her gaze dug into his widening eyes.

"Yes." He took the clay pot she placed in his hands.
The spike on the Stone Pinto arched close to his face,
like a bower full of beautiful blossoms.

"All right, then take what you know about plant
spirits. They are just like people, aren't they? There're
grumpy ones, happy ones, shy ones and everything
else in between." Jessica moved her fingers along the
leaves in a loving, caressing motion. "They have an aura
around them, just as we do. Like people, not all plants
are created equal. We know from our belief systems
that there are young souls and old souls down here on
Mother Earth."

Jessica became very serious as she placed her hands
around his. "Dan, when I share this with you, I know
you'll understand what I'm saying. I don't normally tell
people this because they'd think I was crazy, but orchids
are the most evolved plants on the face of Mother Earth.
They are the pinnacle, the most spiritual of all the spe-
cies of flowers that grow down here. Why? Because—"
she slid her hands off his and tapped the bottom of the

pot "—orchids do not live in soil like every other plant we know. No, they are air plants. They require absolutely no soil to grow. All they need to not only survive, but flourish, is humid air and the right temperatures. They absorb all the water they need right out of the air."

Jessica sighed and held his awed gaze. "Isn't that something? I'm so amazed by these plants. I feel like a child among very old, learned teachers when I work with my orchids."

He nodded, slowly turning the clay pot in his hand. "So, they are like the stone nation. Stones are millions of years old and hold much knowledge, too."

Jessica clapped her hands delightedly. "Exactly! Yes, you've got it!" She saw the redness in his cheeks and realized she'd embarrassed him. "I'm sorry, I didn't mean to seem to make fun of you, Dan. Just the opposite. Do you know how few people I can talk to about orchids and their spiritual qualities and evolution?" She held up one hand and spread her fingers wide. "Not even five people for the five fingers on my hand!" She laughed.

A hint of a smile tugged at the corners of his mouth as he gently placed the orchid back on the workbench. Jessica's childlike joy was infectious. She made him want to return her sunny smile, her uninhibited joy. "I see. They are flower teachers to us because they are so advanced on their own path of learning?"

With a sigh, Jessica whispered, "Yes. Oh, yes. You've got it, Dan. I'm *so* glad you're working here at the ranch. You really understand. And I need someone to help me. Would you like to do that? I can teach you so much about them, but in the long run, they will teach you ten times more. Just to get to work with orchids is like being in the most wonderful school of life you've ever experienced. I love it! I love working out here most of the day with them. They are so loving, so warm and giving to us." As she gazed at him, she realized the woman part of her wanted him around for other reasons. She savored his maleness because it did not threaten her, rather, it made her wildly aware of herself and her femininity. Each time he looked at her, she felt as if her heart would explode with raw joy.

Stunned, he muttered, "I don't know anything about them, though. I'm afraid I'd hurt them."

"Pshaw!" Jessica handed him another orchid clothed in protective newspaper. "Unwrap this one. Let's see which one she is! I don't believe for a second that you'd hurt a fly, Dan Black." And then she became serious. "Maybe you've been hurt, like Gan out there, but you're not mean and neither is that stallion."

Shaken, Dan stared at her, the silence building. "How—no, never mind...."

"I'm pretty psychic," Jessica said, quickly going about the business of freeing up the orchid in front of her. "It was a gift from my mother, Odula. She had the Sight, as we call it. Kate has good gut feelings and intuition. Rachel has the same thing, but I got gifted with more than them in some ways. I can feel people, and sometimes I'll know something about them without ever having been told beforehand. Don't let it shake you up. If you want to work in here with me and my orchid girls, you'll just have to get used to it."

As he unwrapped the orchid, a beautiful yellow one with a spicy scent, Dan nodded. "I know a medicine woman who sees like you."

"Will it bother you?" Jessica demanded primly. But from his expression, she knew it wouldn't. As she watched Dan carefully unwrap the orchid, she almost smiled. Despite his long, large-knuckled hands toughened with calluses, he had been ultracautious unwrapping that orchid. Yes, he was the perfect helper for her. Even if he was a man, he had that wonderful gentleness that many Navajo men possessed. She sent a prayer of thanks upward to the Great Spirit for sending such a person to her. Jessica had been very worried about not having help, since Moyra was no longer at her side. And she certainly couldn't ask Kate or Sam to help. They were already working sixteen hours a day to keep the Donovan Ranch afloat. She could not expect help from them.

"You know," Jessica whispered as she set the orchid on an upper shelf, "you are an answer to my prayers, Dan."

His head snapped up and he momentarily froze, the orchid in his hand. "What?"

"I said you're an answer to my prayers. Is that so awful? Judging from the look on your face, it is. Do you not want to help out in the greenhouse? Maybe Sam's given you other duties that I don't know about?"

"Oh…no," he muttered, placing his orchid next to hers on the wrought-iron shelf. "It's not that—"

"What then?" Jessica removed two more pots from the cardboard box. Her heart broke a little at the thought that Dan didn't want to work out here with her and her orchid girls. He seemed so perfect for it. Besides, if she was really honest, she had to admit she liked having him around, shyness and all. He was terribly handsome in a rugged, western kind of way. Maybe he was married, she thought as her gaze went to his left hand. There was no wedding ring on it, but a lot of Navajos never wore much jewelry on their fingers—just on their wrists and around their necks.

"No… I'd like to work out here," he admitted in

a low voice. "I'll have to have Sam okay it. He's my boss. My other duty is to try and tame Gan and get him under saddle."

"Big order," Jessica said, relieved that Dan wanted to work in the greenhouse.

For the first time, Dan chuckled. He began unpacking another orchid. The pleasure of having Jessica less than a foot away from him was all he needed. "Gan is wary and he hates men. I've got to get him to trust me even if I am one. That's the first order of business."

"When my father drank," Jessica said in a low voice filled with pain, "he used to beat Gan with a rubber hose." She slid Dan a pained look.

Dan's hands stilled around the orchid. "What did he do to you when you tried to stop him?" He saw her face go pale and those glorious turquoise eyes of hers veil with deep grief and sadness. In that moment, he wanted to reach out and cup her small face protectively.

"I don't want to talk about it," she managed to answer, hurriedly unpacking the next orchid.

Dan felt her anguish and heard it in her strained voice. He'd heard a lot about Kelly Donovan; he knew he had been a mean bastard when he hit the bottle. Frowning, Dan returned his attention to the orchid he was unwrapping. It wasn't the Navajo way to ask personal questions or intrude into someone's life. He'd already overstepped the bounds with Jessica. It was so easy to do, he was discovering, because she was accessible and vulnerable.

Sighing, he realized his vision had been real. And the woman he'd seen in it was Jessica Donovan—a woman completely out of his reach. She was the owner of this ranch. She was rich and had land. He was nothing but a horse wrangler with no money, no savings. Pain racked his chest. Life was cruel, he decided. Cruel and hard and merciless. Here was the woman in his vision—unreachable. Untouchable. In a different class from him. In a different world from him.

His hands trembled slightly as he picked up another orchid. Great Spirit help him, but he wanted Jessica. He wanted her breathless laughter against his mouth, the warm touch of her hands exploring his hard body. He longed to discover every inch of her and love her until he died, knowing he'd given her every ounce of his passion.

Dan was even more unsure about life now than ever before. It had thrown him a curve he could never have imagined. Not ever. What was he going to do? How was he going to handle this hotbed of bubbling emotions in his chest that refused to be stilled or denied? Could Jessica feel it? Feel how he *really* felt toward her? He lived in fear of her finding out because he was afraid she'd misinterpret his feelings. Yet just watching her hurry back and forth, like a fluttering, beautiful butterfly, Dan felt his fortitude dissolve like honey in hot sunlight. He ached to remain in Jessica's presence. And somehow he was going to have to control himself, his emotions and his desires in order to keep his job on this ranch. How was he going to do it?

Chapter 4

Jessica awoke suddenly. She sat up in her old brass bed, the quilt falling away from her. Sleepily, she pushed her blond hair away from her face and looked toward the open window. Outside, she heard wonderful, familiar sounds from her childhood. The soft lowing of the cattle, the call of the rooster and the snort of horses were a welcoming balm to her. Inhaling, she could smell the scent of juniper in the cool, damp dawn air that flowed through the window into the small room.

Looking at her watch, she discovered it was only five a.m. She never got up this early in Vancouver. As Jessica sat there, Dan Black's face seemed to waver in front of her. Her heart tugged, gently stirring her sleep-filled thoughts. A soft smile pulled at her mouth as she eased from bed. Her feet touched the shining cedar floor, which had been waxed to perfection days earlier. Bless Kate and Sam for their help. Jessica knew that

Dan had helped prepare her home, too. That made her feel inexorably good.

Quickly taking a hot shower, she pulled on a short-sleeved white blouse, a pair of jeans and very old but comfortable cowboy boots. She smiled as she stood up. She hadn't worn these since she'd left the ranch. Noticing that the leather was cracked and worn, she ran her fingers across the roughened texture of one of the toes. Despite their condition, the boots were steel toed and would protect her if a horse or steer accidentally sidestepped and came down on her foot. Cowboy boots were an important part of the uniform of the day here at the Donovan Ranch.

Humming softly, Jessica moved to the small kitchen and made some hot, fresh coffee. The odor filled her nostrils as she stood leaning against the beige tile counter decorated with the Cherokee colors of the four directions—red, yellow, black and blue.

As her gaze moved around the silent room, she saw many places for some of her hardier orchids, which would love to live here part-time and bring more color and life into the adobe house. Again Dan crossed her mind. How much fun she'd had yesterday unpacking the orchids with him! He was so gentle. So sensitive. Many times during the day she'd watched him carefully unpack one of her girls, enjoying the sight of a man with work-worn hands using a delicacy she'd rarely seen. She hoped Sam would allow Dan to continue to help her set up her business. She needed to get back on line with her company as soon as possible to take care of her back orders.

Pouring coffee into a dark red mug, Jessica moved out to the roughened log porch that enclosed her home.

As she gently sat down in the swing, her ears picked up music—a Native American flute being played, she realized. The rasping, husky notes seemed to waft on the coming dawn. The sky in front of her was turning from gray to a pale pink color. High above the ranch a few wisps of cirrus, which reminded Jessica of a galloping horse's mane flying outward, turned a darker pink. Sighing because she'd missed the intrinsic beauty of the Southwest, Jessica stood and followed the sound of the flute.

As she rounded the large, freshly painted red barn, which housed thousands of bales of hay for the horses and cattle during leaner times, Jessica saw that both ends of the structure were open to allow maximum flow of fresh air to the broodmare stalls that lined the aisle. A few of the mares near foaling nickered as she walked by, probably thinking she was bringing them their oats for the day. But their meal would come later, when Dan made his rounds.

Behind the barn were several huge, rectangular corrals. All of the barbed wire had been replaced either with heavy wooden poles or, in the case of the Arabian horse corral, with solid and safe pipe fencing. Jessica was glad to see the wicked, scarring barbed wire finally replaced. Kelly had never wanted to spend any money on suitable fencing.

The Arabians in the corral all pricked up their ears as she approached, and a few of them nickered in welcome. Jessica smiled and continued to follow the flute music, which was coming from farther north. Who was playing it? She hadn't had time yesterday to explore the ranch and get a feel for it.

In front of her was a huge, enclosed wooden arena.

As she headed toward it, she realized it was the place where horses were broken and training was begun. The walls were ten feet high so that the horse could not look anywhere but at the trainer and the animal's attention would be focused one hundred percent.

Moving around the training area, Jessica halted. Her breath hitched momentarily. There was Gan, the black Arabian stallion. And Dan Black. Neither saw her, and she remained perfectly still, gazing at the unbelievable sight. Though Gan was now twenty years old and middle-aged, the proud stallion looked larger than life. Gan's size had come from Raffles, a stallion of English lineage and one of the most profoundly influential bloodlines in North America. Gan wasn't more than fourteen hands three, but what he didn't have in height he made up for in muscle and power.

The stud had been a year old when he'd come to Donovan Ranch. Because of Kelly's abuse, the stallion hated all people, and men especially. The only person who'd ever gotten close to Gan was Odula.

Now Jessica's gaze moved from the stallion, which stood frozen, his wide nostrils flaring, his full attention on the opposite side of the corral, to Dan. He was sitting outside the pipe fence, his back to a post, playing his flute. The soft, plaintive notes filled the air, bringing tears to Jessica's eyes.

The music was subduing Gan, she realized. She watched with fascination as the stallion snorted and pawed the ground angrily, the dirt and red sand flying from beneath his sharpened hoof. And then he'd stop, fling his magnificent head upward and listen. At no time did Dan pause to see what the stallion was doing.

Luckily, he was in a protected place, where Gan was unable to charge and bite him.

The sky turned a darker pink. Jessica heard the familiar call of quail families, which lived around the ranch. She saw a flock of mallards skimming northward, heading toward the Rim and Oak Creek. Slowly, she lifted the cup of steaming coffee to her lips and took a sip. Enthralled by Gan's attention to the stallion tamer, she smiled. Sam had said Dan was the best horse wrangler in the state of Arizona. Well, his methods were certainly surprising. As the last notes of the mournful flute song ended, she watched Gan.

The stallion shook his head from side to side. He pawed the ground again, a wary look in his eyes as Dan slowly eased away from the post and stood up. It was at that moment that Jessica saw Dan raise his head, take his attention off the stallion and look directly at her. Her pulse skittered. Her heart opened like an unfolding orchid bloom. His gray eyes were dark, the pupils huge and black. For the first time, she saw relaxation in his features—not that hard, guarded look that had been on his face yesterday. Jessica realized Dan was happy. Even more, his mouth, which was usually tightly compressed into a thin line, was now full, the corners tilted upward. She realized she was seeing the real Dan Black now—the man without the mask in place.

Suddenly she felt like an interloper; heat swiftly moved up from her neck, warming her cheeks. She gripped the coffee mug a little more tightly and an apology came to her lips.

As if sensing her embarrassment, Dan pushed his black Stetson off his forehead with his thumb and gave her an uneven smile of welcome.

"May I come closer?" Jessica asked in a low voice. She knew that horse trainers liked to work alone, without interference from other people. They needed one hundred percent of the animal's attention at all times or training didn't occur.

Dan nodded. "Walk very slowly," he told her in a low voice. "No fast movements."

"Right…." Jessica said. She paid attention to the uneven red clay and sand beneath her feet as she walked carefully toward the corral. Gan started, snorted and leaped from the center of the corral to the opposite side, away from her. Her heart sank. She hadn't meant to scare the stallion.

Her pulse skipped erratically as she approached Dan. He stood completely at ease, one foot hitched up on the bottom rail, the flute in his left hand resting across his thigh. How terribly handsome he looked today, Jessica thought, despite the fact that the long-sleeved, white shirt he wore had seen better days. She saw a number of places where the material had been torn and sewn carefully together again. Still, she couldn't help but admire the broad shoulders and powerfully sprung chest beneath that shirt. His blue jeans outlined his lean, hard lower body to perfection and a red bandanna was wrapped loosely around his neck. His cowboy boots were in just as bad a condition as hers, worn and cracked by years of use.

Dan's eyes narrowed as he watched Jessica approach. Had the Great Spirit ever made a woman more beautiful, more untouchable than her? As she closed the distance to him, he thought not. Her gold hair was drawn back into a ponytail that moved with her graceful movements. Her white blouse was feminine and enhanced the blush staining her cheeks. Yesterday she had worn a skirt, but today, he noticed with more than a little interest, she wore snug-fitting jeans and cowboy boots. She was small and delicate. Dan wondered if she had been sick as a child, because she seemed so fragile compared to Kate, who was more solidly built and much taller.

When Jessica lifted those lashes and revealed her turquoise eyes, Dan felt heat gather in his lower body. And when her pink lips drew into a hesitant, almost apologetic smile, his heart opened wide. Again that same warmth he'd experienced during his vision in the sweat lodge avalanched through him. How beautiful she was! How untouchable! Pain moved through him and doused the joy he'd felt. His fingers closed more firmly on the flute as she halted about four feet away from him.

"Your music was beautiful," she whispered with a sigh. "I woke up early for some reason and made coffee. When I came out on the front porch, I heard your song. It was so incredibly beautiful, Dan." Jessica closed her eyes and sighed again. "You should record what you play. It's as good as any other recording I've heard of Native American flute music."

He felt heat tunneling up his neck. With a shy laugh, he pulled his hat back down on his brow, unable to accept the look of admiration in Jessica's eyes. "I'm afraid, ma'am—I mean, Jessica—that my playing is pretty basic. I learned from my uncle, who died when I was a kid and passed on his flute to me."

"So what if you're mostly self-taught?" Jessica said, some indignation in her voice. "You have a natural, raw talent for it. Don't apologize."

With a shrug, he lifted up the flute for her to take a look. "My uncle made it out of cedar. He carved it himself. I remember he used to play it for us kids when we'd get in bed at night. I always liked his music." Sadness moved through him at the memory. "He died of liver cancer. I was real sorry to see him go. He's the one who brought laughter to us."

Jessica set her coffee cup down on the ground and gently took the nearly three-foot-long flute in her hands. The wood was a warm color, a mixture of red and yellow. There was a beaded band of red, blue, green and black around one end of it, and several red-tailed hawk feathers hung beneath the rust color of the feathers matching the reddish hue of the wood.

"This flute feels so warm. So alive…."

Dan studied her widening eyes. "You feel it, too? Why should I be surprised? You're sensitive like your mother."

Shrugging, Jessica moved her fingertips lightly over the wood. "Wood has spirit. So do these hawk feathers. You have a tree and a hawk spirit who work with you when you play this flute."

"Yes." He smiled inwardly, liking her understanding that all things were connected and that all things had spirit. Even though Jessica looked more Anglo than Cherokee, she still had the powerful blood of her mother moving through her, as Kate did. "I guess I have to get used to the fact you've got blond hair, but you're still Indian."

Jessica chuckled as she continued to examine the flute. "I'm the renegade in the family. Mom said she had no idea where my blond hair came from. It sure wasn't from her side of the family."

He enjoyed watching her, studying how she stroked the wooden flute. How would it feel if she touched him the same wonderful way? Dan surprised himself with the thought. Generally, he didn't pay much attention to women, because he'd never had any luck with them. Who wanted a drunken Navajo cowboy for company? Not many, that was for sure. But he couldn't help wondering what Jessica's light touch would do to him. His skin tightened in response. Deep down he knew, but he didn't dare follow that line of thinking. She was part owner of a large ranch. And him—he was just a tumbleweed cowboy without money or property. She would never be interested in him.

"On your father's side, I thought they were all redhaired like he was."

"No, looking back in family photos, I can see that many of our descendants from the Bay of Donovan had black hair or reddish blond hair." She reluctantly handed the flute back to him. Their fingers met briefly and Jessica absorbed Dan's warmth. She withdrew her hand quickly because her heart sped up again, as if to underscore how much she enjoyed his touch.

Dan felt his hand tingle wildly as a result of their contact, and the heat in the lower part of his body flared for an instant. Would she sense how much he liked touching her? He hoped not, or his shame would be complete. Shaken, he unhitched his boot from the rail, leaning down to pick up the carefully folded leather flute case.

"How long have you been working to tame Gan?" Jessica asked.

"Sam and Kate hired me less than two weeks ago. I've been working with Gan about a half hour a day. That's all he'll put up with for now." Dan lovingly slid the cedar flute back into the case and then hitched his boot up on the rail again. Balancing the flute across his thigh, he tied the leather strings at the top so that the instrument would not slide out.

Jessica studied the stallion, which was watching them from across the corral with large, intelligent brown eyes. He was switching his black tail from side to side, as if peeved with their continued presence. His fine, small ears kept moving back and forth.

"I never thought anyone could tame him," she admitted.

"I may not be able to. I'll try. But I'm not going to get killed in the process of trying." Dan placed the flute against the pipe fence and rested both his arms on the rail in front of him.

Jessica moved closer to Dan. She liked his lean, masculine grace. There was never a wasted motion with Dan. She sensed an underlying steadiness in him and knew that he would be someone to rely on in a time of emergency. He was someone she could trust. Moving to the fence, she placed her hands on the rail and watched Gan. The stallion's coat gleamed in the dawn light.

"He's so terrifyingly beautiful," she whispered.

"Well, he wouldn't be so terrifying if people hadn't made him that way," Dan said, absorbing her closeness hungrily. "I sometimes wonder what he would be like if your father had not beaten him into hating two-leggeds. In my mind, when I play my flute for him, I see him coming over to me." He pulled a carrot from his back pocket. "Coming to take this from me."

Jessica shared a brief smile of understanding with him. "Gan, if I remember correctly, loves apples and carrots. That is how my mother got him to trust her.

She always brought him an apple or carrot a day. He always waited for her right over there, next to the gate."

"Did Gan ever try to charge her or bite her?"

"No, he was a gentleman with her, like he was to the mares he was bred with." Jessica shook her head. "Gan is a paradox in some ways. He'll bluster and charge you, and I've seen him take a pound of flesh out of Kelly two different times. And he charges with the intent to hurt you bad. But if you turn a mare ready to be bred into his corral, he's such a gentleman. He's never hurt a mare."

"There are some stallions that hurt their mares. But Sam said this stud's gentle with them. He never bites or scares them."

"Then there's hope," Jessica said, "that you can tame him and get his trust. Gan is not completely bad. No animal or human ever is."

Dan grimaced. "I don't know," he muttered, "some of us two-leggeds have pretty bad reputations that we aren't ever going to live down. People's memories are too long."

She looked at him and felt his inner pain and deep sadness. Jessica almost asked him if he was referring to himself, but something cautioned her not to be too nosy about Dan Black. He was a lot like that stallion in the corral—wary of people and not all that trusting. She felt him wanting to reach out, to trust her, and she hoped she could be there for him when he did. She liked his easygoing nature when his mask wasn't in place. Out here on the desert with his untamed stallion, she was privileged to see the real Dan Black.

"I know what you mean," Jessica said. She shrugged painfully. "My track record isn't one I'm proud of, either. Thank goodness it's in Canada, not here. But I know what you mean about gossip and people never forgetting. If you're bad, you're always bad in their eyes. There's no way to reclaim yourself or try to better yourself. People hold on to what's bad about us, not what's good or decent."

He held her sad, blue-eyed gaze. "Somehow I don't believe that you are bad."

Sighing, Jessica said, "I married a guy, Carl, up in Canada. I'd just arrived there after leaving this ranch. I didn't want to leave, but Kelly was driving us all out. He didn't want women running his ranch. Me and my sisters each left at age eighteen, as soon as we graduated from high school." Her fingers tightened around the coolness of the pipe railing.

"I didn't want to leave Mama. I was the baby of the family, the last to go. She wanted me to stay, but I just couldn't stand what Kelly was doing to her, to the ranch and to himself."

"Or," Dan said gently, "to you?" He knew he shouldn't ask, but something drove him to. He wanted to know more about Jessica, about how life had treated her. In his heart he knew without a doubt that Jessica had the goodness he'd searched for and never found in himself, much less anyone else. It anguished him to think that Kelly might have struck her, for the rancher had been known to be violent and abusive to friends, neighbors, strangers and family alike. Dan could hardly stand to think Jessica might have been hurt by him.

She closed her eyes. "Let's just say that my growing-up years followed me to Canada, Dan." Opening her eyes, she stared sightlessly into the corral, no longer seeing Gan, but her past. "My marriage to Carl Roman was like my life with my father. I spent eight years in a hell with him. *Hell.*" The word came out bitter and hard.

Dan watched her closely. He fought the desire to ask more personal questions. His Navajo heritage told him not to—that if she wanted to, she would divulge what she felt he should know. He tightened his mouth and stared down at the ground in front of him.

"Hell comes in many forms," he said. "It sounds as if you were not at fault, but you walked into a bad situation with a person with a dark heart."

Jessica took in a deep, shaky breath. "What was it my mother called a person who was a liar? Who chose to use only their bad traits instead of their good ones? A two-heart? Yes, that's what Carl was. He had two hearts, not one good heart. I was too young, too naive and blind to see the real him."

"That is the past now. You're home and you are loved here. Kate has done nothing but talk of you, of your arrival. Sam cares for you as a brother." Dan gestured toward the rising sun in front of them. "Here you are wanted and cared for."

"But I'm not safe here," Jessica muttered, unable to meet his eyes. She felt wave after wave of concern coming from Dan. How protective he was of her! His care was like a warm blanket that could assuage her pain, fear and worry all at the same time.

His black brows knitted and he blurted, "Safe? What do you mean?" Damn! He hadn't meant to probe! Inwardly, Dan chaffed over his rudeness.

Jessica looked up at him, searching his intense features. She was discovering that when Dan was upset, that mask came down across his face. No longer was he relaxed or at ease. Every line in his body had gone rigid with tension. His face was hard now and his eyes nearly colorless. It reminded her of a hawk ready to strike its unsuspecting prey. A shiver ran through her and for a moment Jessica had to remind herself that Dan's demeanor was not aimed *at* her, but rather was a protective response to what she'd just said. Shaken, she managed to whisper, "Carl had always told me that if I divorced him, he'd hunt me down and kill me. He said he couldn't live without me. That if he couldn't have me, no one would."

Dan's nostrils flared and he released a held breath. "The man's crazy, then."

"No kidding. I divorced him two years ago and the most wonderful and strange thing happened. I know if I tell you, you won't think it's bizarre. I was in the middle of divorcing Carl, and I was hiding out in an apartment in Vancouver under an assumed name so he couldn't stalk me. At the time, I ran my flower essence company from my apartment. I was trying to keep my business afloat and stay hidden. I desperately needed help, someone who could assist me with my orchids, fill orders and answer mail.

"One day, I went out in disguise to the grocery store. I was so scared that I dropped a bottle of orange juice in one of the aisles. It broke all over the floor. I was so ashamed, I just stood there looking down at the mess at my feet and burst into tears. I was sobbing almost hysterically when this tall, dark-haired woman came out of—I swear—nowhere. She took me by the shoulders and moved me away from the mess in the aisle, talking soothingly. She just kept patting my shoulder and telling me that it was all right, that I was safe.

"When I looked up through my tears, I saw not this

woman's face, but the face of a jaguar! And then the jaguar disappeared and I saw her human face. I was so stunned by it, I stopped crying. I saw her smile and she offered me a handkerchief for my tears. She said her name was Moyra and she was from South America. She told me in a low voice, as an employee from the grocery store cleaned up the mess I'd made, that she had been sent not only to protect me, but to help me for the next two years."

With a nod, Dan said, "She was a shape-shifter."

"Yes," Jessica admitted. "She's a jaguar priestess from South America. She came from an unbroken lineage of the Jaguar Clan."

"The Great Spirit sent her to protect you, then."

"And she did, too. I could never have survived and flourished in these last two years without her help, Dan. Moyra had a jaguar's senses, and she was completely clairvoyant. She knew exactly where Carl was at all times. She helped me find a beautiful cabin out in a meadow north of Vancouver. We moved everything out there and she helped me build a greenhouse for my orchid girls. And if Carl got too close, she always knew it and would tell me."

"You avoided your ex-husband for two years, then?"

"Yes, thank goodness." Jessica shuddered. "I don't know what I'd have done if Carl had found me. I—I'm still afraid. I talked it over with Kate and Sam, and they said for me to come home, that I'd be safe here." She looked beseechingly up at Dan. "I don't know that for sure. I have bad feelings about it. I feel pretty naked and alone without Moyra around. She said she had to go home, that her family was calling her back to Peru, that she was needed there."

"You're feeling vulnerable," Dan said.

"Yes, unprotected. Moyra was a real friend."

Dan saw Jessica's eyes swim with tears and he laid his hand gently on her shoulder. How badly he wanted to say "come here," to open his arms to her and embrace her until she no longer felt so alone and unprotected against her predatory ex-husband.

Dan's hand felt firm and stabilizing to Jessica. She closed her eyes and absorbed his care and concern. "I shouldn't be telling you all of this. You barely know me...."

"What are friends for if you can't unload what worries you?" he asked huskily, and removed his hand reluctantly. "I'm not Moyra. I'm not a medicine man, but if you want, I can be like a big guard dog for you. I'll protect you, Jessica. If you want...." Never had he wanted to do anything more. Dan suddenly realized that he *could* help protect Jessica. He hadn't been trained as a Recon Marine for nothing. No, he was very good at such things. Far better than most men ever would be. Besides, his Navajo side, the man in him, would automatically protect the woman he felt so strongly about. Maybe it was a knee-jerk reaction, but it felt right to offer her his protection.

Reaching out, Jessica briefly touched his arm, feeling the hard, lean muscle beneath her fingertips. There was a dangerous quality to Dan that she'd never encountered until now. She saw it in the wild look in his almost colorless eyes, and she heard it in the grate of his voice. This side of Dan surprised her for a moment, because he'd shown her only his softer, more sensitive side. Now she saw the warrior unveiled. She allowed her hand to drop back to her side.

"No… I couldn't put you or my family at risk if Carl decided to get even with me, Dan. I don't want to put anyone else in danger. He's—he's horrible and he's insane at times…just like Kelly was when he got drunk. Only," she said, her voice dropping with terror, "Carl was never drunk. He was that way all the time. And I never realized it until it was too late, until after we were married. He hid the real person inside of him until it was too late for me to back out and run from him."

"Listen," Dan said, cupping her shoulders and turning her toward him, "you don't have any say in this matter. There are things you don't know about me, either—good and bad. One thing I can do is help you, protect you, should he ever come here to the ranch." He saw her open her lips to protest. "No," he ordered tightly, "this is not up for more discussion, Jessica. I now know why the Great Spirit sent me here—to help protect you. Because this man is coming here. I don't possess the Sight like you or Moyra do, but I feel it here, in my gut. And I've been in enough situations to trust my gut completely. It's never been wrong."

Trembling, Jessica tried to breathe, but she felt suffocated by the possibility of Carl stalking her once again. Her intuition told her it was only a matter of time. Only Dan's reassuring, strong hands on her shoulders gave her any sense of hope or stability. "Oh, no… I hope you're wrong. Leaving Vancouver, I tried to cover my tracks completely, so he'd never find out…."

Her terror avalanched over him, catching Dan completely off guard. As he felt the depth of her fright, he realized just how much danger she was really in. He wasn't expecting to be that open, that vulnerable to another human's pain or emotions, but it was happening. He felt this exchange of feelings when he worked with horses, but never with humans. Not until now. He remembered Ai Gvhdi Waya's words about allowing himself to shift into that flow, and he did everything in his power to keep his heart and mind open to Jessica.

"You're going to be all right," he said, giving her a small shake. "Look at me, Jessica. Please...." Her eyes opened and he drowned in the blueness of them. "The Great Spirit didn't leave you defenseless by coming here. You traded Moyra for me. I'm just a poor tumbleweed of a horse wrangler, but I have abilities and skills that can protect you. Do you believe me?"

The confidence in his speech cut through her terror. She stared up into his rugged features and absorbed the toughness of his rasping voice. His hands were firm and protective at the same time. "Dan, I can't ask you to do this. Carl is insane and he's manipulative. He was in prison for second-degree murder, but just escaped. The police are after him, but he's smart. They still haven't caught him. He's already killed one human being. I—I couldn't ask you to do this for me, don't you see?"

"Shi shaa, I am not much of a warrior, but I will be like a shield in front of you when Carl comes here, and he will. I know that now. That is my promise to you. Your jaguar priestess may have left, but in her place you find the spirit of the cougar, instead. My spirit guide is just as powerful in some ways as that of my jaguar sister. Trust me. I will be your eyes and ears from now on. You will be able to live here safely...."

Chapter 5

"Hey, how are you doing?" Kate called from the door to the greenhouse.

Jessica jumped at the noise. She whirled around, a plastic sack filled with redwood chips in her hands. "Oh! You scared me, Kate."

Kate grinned and closed the door behind her. Wiping her brow, she took a deep breath. "Whew, it's a lot cooler and nicer in here. Must be close to a hundred degrees outside." Moving over to the workbench, she perused the four orchids in clay pots sitting there. "I dropped by to see how things were going. Sam and I just came off the north range, moving some pregnant cows to a greener pasture." She wrinkled her nose. Untying her dark blue bandanna from around her slender throat, she wiped her perspiring face with the cloth. "Not that there's much green. This drought is a killer. I've never seen anything like it in all the time I've lived here."

Jessica nodded and placed the wood chips back on the bench. "I know. It's awful. So much is dying. And the money you're having to use up to buy bales of hay…yuk."

Kate grinned a little and retied her bandanna. "Little sis, you do not want to look at the accounting books, believe me. Or you'll spend your nights like I do—tossing and turning and wondering when the bank is going to foreclose on us."

Jessica looked up at her oldest sister. Kate had her dark hair in a ponytail, a straw cowboy hat, stained with dust and perspiration from many hours of work, on her head. Tall and angular, she was a living testament to the rugged Southwest and what hard work did to a body. She looked good in her bright red T-shirt, faded blue jeans and dusty cowboy boots. Jessica had always admired Kate in so many ways, even though her sister had spent time in prison for a crime she'd been unjustly accused of. Now Kate's eyes sparkled with happiness, and Jessica knew it was because she was so in love with Sam. Jessica was so happy for Kate. It was about time her sister had something good happen to her.

"Well, if Sam and you will okay it, I could use Dan's help in here to begin processing orders for Mother Earth Flower Essences and start collecting money for that hay you need."

Kate shook her head and put her arm around Jessica's slim shoulders for a moment. "You're so generous, Jessica. I don't know what possessed you to help out so much, but we're all grateful for it."

Jessica put her own arm around Kate's waist and hugged her in return. "I wouldn't have it any other way. Besides, we're going to get out of this financial nightmare with the ranch someday."

"I hope sooner rather than later," Kate said, her voice strained. She sat on a tall wooden crate next to the workbench and watched Jessica begin to repot the orchids. "Hey, on a happier subject, if you want Dan Black to be your assistant, go for it. Sam would like him to divide his day into working at taming Gan, helping you in the mornings and then helping Sam run the fence and handle the other ranch duties in the afternoon."

Jessica turned the first pot upside down. Old redwood chips fell onto the bench, and she gently drew the orchid's long, white root system to one side. "That's fine." Taking fresh redwood chips, she leaned down, retrieved a new clay pot and put some into it.

"What do you think of him?" Kate asked, watching her sister work quickly and efficiently.

"Who?"

"You know who. Dan Black."

"Oh…" Jessica risked a look at her sister's frowning features. "He's, uh…"

"Aren't you getting along? Did he say something?"

"Now, Katie, don't go jumping off a cliff, okay? No, Dan didn't say anything wrong to me."

"You look…" She searched for the right word. "Uneasy?"

With exasperation, Jessica picked up the orchid, carefully arranged the root system in the larger pot and began to drop small pieces of bark around it. "It's just me and my big mouth, Katie. I barely know the guy, right? What do I do the second day I see him? I blurt out my whole life story."

Grinning, Kate took off her hat and set it on her thighs as she propped her heels up on the box. "What else is new? You always trusted everyone without wondering what their ulterior motives might be. Me? I'm just the opposite of you. I walk in wondering what the son of a bitch wants from me—a pound of flesh?" She chuckled indulgently.

"A little paranoia is good," Jessica admitted, frowning.

"Especially in *your* case," Kate warned heavily. "This thing with Carl isn't over. We both know that."

Jessica shot her a look of anxiety. "I'm worried, Katie."

"The guy is nuts. He's a sick stalker. He killed a guy. He could kill you. He might try it."

"Now you're talking just like Dan."

"Oh," Kate murmured, raising her brows, "you told Dan about Carl, too?"

With a sigh, Jessica placed the newly repotted orchid into a small dish of water so that the clay would absorb some of the moisture for the plant's root system. "That's what I mean—I blurted out everything about my life to Dan this morning."

"And?" Kate asked carefully. "How did Dan react to Carl's potentially showing up here to finish what he started in Vancouver?"

Agitated, Jessica felt fear and consternation roiling within her. She raised her eyes to the ceiling and then back down to Kate. "I was surprised at his reaction, to tell you the truth."

"Tell me about it."

Shrugging, Jessica took another orchid and turned it upside down to loosen the old wood chips around the roots. "He said that he knew now why he was sent here to the ranch." She glanced at Kate. "To protect me...."

"Hmm..."

"That's all you have to say? I mean, I was a little taken back by his passion for wanting to protect me. He doesn't know me! I mean, for all he knows, I could be a murdering thief in disguise."

Kate laughed and shook her head. "No, Jessica, you just don't fit the profile, and Dan knows that." She tapped her fingertip on the workbench. "Dan's a lot like Sam. He's a realist. He's pragmatic, too. He may not value himself as much as he should, but he's good with animals and some people. He's been kicked around enough to know the world isn't a goody-goody place. Unlike you, Miss Idealist."

Jessica grinned a little and set the unrooted orchid aside. "Okay, okay. So I think ill of no one. I don't question people's motives or their reasoning like you do. In most cases, my view of life works."

"That's what got you into trouble with Carl," Kate growled. "You believed the facade he put up for you. You didn't bother to ask what might be behind it."

"Carl's manipulative. It took me a year to know the real man behind the mask. I don't think anyone could have known." Her hands trembled slightly as she put redwood chips into a new pot.

"Listen," Kate whispered gently, "Carl's insane, as far as I'm concerned. And he's dangerous. Sam and I think he'll try and get to you here, at the ranch."

Her heart plunging in terror, Jessica set the pot down and fully faced her sister. "If you honestly believe that, why on earth did you let me come here? Carl could kill *all* of us if he goes off into one of his ballistic rages. He has an arsenal of guns he keeps hidden from the Canadian authorities. He could bring them down here and begin shooting up the ranch."

"Hold on," Kate said, putting up her hands. "Don't get upset, Jessica. First of all, you've got three big, bad guard dogs here at the ranch—Sam, me and Dan. We are being watchful."

Grinning a little, Kate continued, "Besides, Dan Black is a hell of a lot more dangerous than his mannerisms might show. He was a Recon Marine for four years, and according to Sam, he was damned good at what he did. Those men are taught to be invisible until the right moment. Dan got a lot of experience during the Gulf War. He was in the thick of things. And if a worst-case scenario happens and Carl is stupid enough to come down here thinking he can hurt you, well, he'll be in for a few surprises. Dan may not be able to be everywhere with you all the time, but when he is, Sam told him to watch out for you. And if Dan isn't there, Sam will be. Twenty-four-hour protection, Jessica."

"So Dan knew about me already? About Carl?"

"No, Sam told him that you needed to be watched, that was all."

Miffed, Jessica put the repotted orchid aside. Her fingers trembled badly now. "That's why Dan was so intense with me, then. He was all worked up about protecting me."

"He's not getting paid any extra to do this, you know. I don't know where his passion is coming from." And then Kate tilted her head and smiled a little. "Maybe he likes you?"

"Oh, please, Katie! I'm not exactly a great gift, am I? I've got an ex-husband who wants to kill me. Who might be really stupid and drive all the way from Canada to do it. If I were Dan Black, I'd sure stay away from me, with good reason!"

"But you have a lot going for you that any man worth his salt would be interested in. You're pretty, smart and ultrafeminine, just the way a man likes a woman."

"Please...." Jessica begged, truly upset now. She took the third clay pot, forcing her hands to stop shaking so much. "I just wish I had your nerves of steel, Katie. Look at my hands. I'm such a wimp. I think of Carl coming to stalk me, to hurt me, and I feel like I'm falling to pieces all over again. I think about the time he put me in the hospital. The pain. The horrible thought that I had to go back and live with him again. It's as if this nightmare is never going to end." She stopped and forced back the tears that stung her eyes.

"It's not easy," Kate whispered gently, her face soft with sympathy as she got up and walked over to Jessica and hugged her. "It's my fault. I shouldn't have brought this up. You're still tired from your trip. You've got a lot of pressure on you to get your orchid girls taken care of, not to mention a lot of orders that haven't been filled."

Shrugging painfully, Jessica looked up at Kate. "Compared to you, Katie, I've got the spine of a jellyfish. I wish I didn't let day-to-day pressures and stresses get to me like this...."

"It's not every day you realize your life is in danger," Kate answered wryly, releasing her. She settled her cowboy hat more firmly on her head. "Look, you need help here. Let's rearrange the schedule for the next week. I'll talk to Dan. He can still work with Gan in the early morning, but I think I'm going to ask him to work with you the rest of this week full-time, to help you get on your feet with your business. That way, that's one more stress off your shoulders. Okay?"

Jessica's heart pounded briefly and this time it wasn't

out of fear, but rather something else she couldn't identify. Whatever it was, it felt good and steadying. When she realized Kate was watching her like a hawk, she said, "Ask Dan. He may not want to do this. I don't even know if he likes working in a greenhouse with orchids. I mean, he's a wrangler, for heaven's sake. He's used to doing a man's work outdoors, not spending time in some hothouse...."

Chuckling, Kate headed for the front door of the greenhouse. "Oh, Jessica, you are so funny! I swear, sometimes you wouldn't see a Mack truck barreling down on you."

"What's that supposed to mean?"

Kate turned, her grin widening considerably. "You really are naive, little sis. When a man brings 'passion' into conversation with a woman, there's something there, you know? Yep, I'd say that horse wrangler likes you just a little bit."

Heat washed across Jessica's face as she stared at Kate. "You mean, personally likes me?"

"Arrgh, I give up!" Kate lifted her hand in farewell and left.

Muttering to herself, Jessica returned to her work. Her fear over Carl's possible appearance and her apprehension over Dan's feelings for her warred within her. Yes, she'd felt something when Dan had gripped her by her shoulders early this morning. She'd felt his care, his powerful protection blanketing her, like something warm and good. Oh, why wasn't she wiser about people? Or, better, wiser about men? She supposed the fact that she'd married Carl at age eighteen, shortly after leaving home and moving to Vancouver, was to blame. She really didn't have any experience with men except for Carl.

No, Kate was right—her naiveté was getting her into a lot of hot water. But how did one become wise in that way? Too bad there wasn't a flower essence she could take to give her that wisdom. She laughed out loud at the thought as she repotted the next orchid. She could make millions if that were possible.

Suddenly Jessica heard the door open and close. She looked over her shoulder and her pulse leaped. It was Dan Black. His mask was in place, that unreadable, hard expression, and his eyes were nearly colorless, measuring her.

"Hi, Dan. Did Kate send you?" The corners of her mouth moved upward in greeting. How handsome he looked!

She absorbed his tall, lean frame and the easy way he walked. She saw his expression soften just as soon as she smiled at him. His eyes changed from colorless to a soft dove gray. The tightness around his mouth eased, revealing the fullness of his lower lip.

"Yes, she did." He gazed hungrily at Jessica's petite form as she stood at the workbench. She had on a dark green canvas apron that fitted her body to midthigh. In her hands was a large orchid in a clay pot. "She said you needed help this next week," he continued, taking off his cowboy hat and wiping the sweat from his brow with the back of his arm. "This place is a lot cooler and nicer than out there, anyway."

She brightened. It was so hard not to stare into his large, intelligent eyes, which seemed banked with so many emotions he fought to hide from her. There was a sparkle in them today, and she felt their penetrating power. Shaken by the sensation, she stammered, "W-well, if it's okay with you, I can use some help getting set up the rest of this week. I know you're probably used to being outside and doing ranch work, and this sure isn't anything like that, but—"

"I want to help."

The words, husky and filled with emotion, silenced Jessica. She saw the honest sincerity burning in his eyes, and the roughened quality of his voice was like a cat's tongue licking her flesh, making it tingle deliciously.

"Oh...." she replied, at a loss for words.

"My people honor the plant nation," he said simply, looking around at the hundred or so orchids sitting at various heights on the wrought-iron steps. "My uncle, the one who died of cancer and gave me his flute, knew a lot about plants. He wasn't a medicine man, but he passed on his love of them to me. I know a lot about the plants that live on the res." He shrugged slightly. "Not in a scientific sense, but I know which ones the Navajo people use for medicine purposes."

"That's wonderful! I've been thinking of expanding my business line to include plants from the Southwest now that I've moved my company down here! Maybe you could help me identify some of them and tell me what you know of them?"

Dan felt her unbridled enthusiasm, her childlike awe and joy. There wasn't anything not to like about Jessica Donovan, he decided. All morning he'd tried to find things to stop himself from liking her so much—from wanting her, man to woman—but he'd found nothing. Now, for better or worse, he was being put to work with her for seven whole days, except for the early morning training sessions with Gan. He frowned. Either this was heaven or his personal hell, he couldn't decide which. It was heaven just to be privileged to be in Jessica's exuberant presence, but it was hell trying to keep his hands off her, to maintain a respectable distance from her and treat her like the owner of the ranch. He had to remember he was only a ranch hand.

"I'd like to learn about your orchids. I know nothing of them."

"And you were so gentle with them," Jessica said. "I would never have thought a man could be like that, but you are."

He held her wide, innocent gaze. "Not all men are like your ex-husband, Jessica. There is a man in Sedona who owns a nursery, Charlie McCoy. He loves his plants like you do. They grow well for him because he cares for them with his heart—like you."

Chastised, Jessica nodded and returned to the workbench. "You're right, of course. I shouldn't be projecting that every man is Carl." And then she laughed sharply. "It's a good thing they aren't!"

Dan followed her over to the workbench. "Show me what you'd like me to do."

For the next hour, Jessica went through everything that Dan would need to know about the care, watering and repotting of orchids. He proved an apt student. Time flew by as she became immersed in her love of the brightly colored orchids that lived in the greenhouse. She enjoyed his nearness, though he seemed somewhat distant compared to earlier this morning, when he'd become impassioned about protecting her.

Finally, she said, "Enough for now. I'm sure your head is spinning with too much information on my girls."

Dan nodded and rested his hands on his narrow hips

as he surveyed the many orchids. "There's a lot to them. More than I realized." He noticed a light veil of perspiration across Jessica's furrowed brow. Her blond hair was slightly curly from the high humidity in the greenhouse, and he had an urge to move several strands away from her eyes, but he resisted.

"When you talk about them," he told her, "do you know your eyes light up, your voice becomes excited?"

Laughing, Jessica nodded. "Yes, I've been told that many times before."

"It's your love of them that does it." Dan followed her back to the workbench.

"Don't you think that whenever a person loves, he or she should show it?"

"Maybe," he hedged. "But not many people I know are willing to reveal themselves, their real feelings, like you do all the time."

"Kate's warned me about that. She says I'm too transparent. That I need to put up some barriers until I get to know people better."

"I don't agree," Dan said.

"No?" She looked up and smiled as she washed her hands in bleach and water to keep from spreading potential viruses among the orchids.

"No."

"You hide behind a mask like Kate and Sam do."

"Guilty."

Jessica laughed a little as she dried her hands. She stood aside for him to rinse his hands and dry them off. "But I shouldn't be like the three of you?"

"No." Dan replaced the towel on a hook on the side of the workbench. "I don't pretend to know orchids very well yet, but I think you're a lot like them. You're differ-

ent. As you said, they don't need soil to survive in, just
air and moisture. In my mind, they are plants of Father
Sky, not Mother Earth." He turned and held her warm,
soft gaze. How badly he wanted to reach out and caress
her reddened cheek, touch his mouth to those parted lips
that were begging to be kissed. Battling his needs, Dan
said, "You are like the sky people. Like the clouds that
form and disappear. You respond to sunlight, moonlight
and the temperature of things around you, as these orchid
people do. You *are* different, Jessica, but that doesn't
make you wrong or us right. In some ways you are able
to see things better. You don't think badly of anyone."

Maybe he'd said too much. Dan supposed he had. But
Jessica's expression changed to one of such sweetness
that his hand itched to reach out and stroke her cheek.
"Father Sky sees all that goes on down here on his lover,
Mother Earth. His eyes are set differently. So are yours.
You belong to the cloud people, who see above and be-
yond what we mere two-leggeds, who are root bound on
Mother Earth, can see. So no, do not change. Do not try
to become like us." He touched his face momentarily.
"Masks are shields. We put them on to protect our soft,
inner side. Cloud people do not need masks. They have
the safety of Father Sky's embrace to protect them."

Jessica stood there for a long, silent moment, digest-
ing Dan's heartfelt words. His sincerity touched her
heart as nothing else ever could. "How you see things
is so beautiful," she began in a strained, low tone. "I
wish—I wish…well, never mind."

Dan saw her eyes darken. "What is your wish?"

"Oh, it's a stupid one. An idealistic one, as Kate would
say." Jessica could not bear to look at the compassion she
saw burning in his eyes. For a moment, she wanted to

take those two steps forward and simply embrace Dan, lean against him and feel the solid, hard beat of his heart against hers. This man was surprising her on so many levels all at once that she felt flustered emotionally.

"Would you share it with me?" he asked, moving next to her at the workbench.

His closeness was wonderful. Jessica was only beginning to realize how *hungry* she'd been for a positive male presence in her life. Moyra had often teased her that she didn't know how Jessica had survived two years without male companionship. Moyra had a boyfriend who she saw on weekends in Vancouver, and Jessica had wished for something similar for herself, but it had never materialized. Maybe because she lived in abject fear that Carl would unexpectedly show up to hurt her, she supposed.

Jessica also realized she hadn't been ready to reach out and trust a man, either. Until now. Dan was different, very different from any man she'd ever encountered. He was so in tune with nature, with her flowers and most importantly with her. It was amazing—and scary. Carl had come on to her like that, too, pretending an interest in her flowers, and in the philosophy of life that she lived every day. Her memories of Carl warred with what she saw in Dan. Was he really like Carl? Her heart said no, but her head was screaming at her to be wary, to watch out and to give things time, instead of rushing willy-nilly into some kind of relationship that might turn out similar to her marriage.

Heaving a sigh, Jessica wrestled with her confusion. Who to trust? Who not to trust? Frustrated, she finally said, "It's a stupid wish built on fantasy."

Dan heard the finality in her voice, the strength that

came up unexpectedly from deep within her. Her tone implied that he was to drop the subject—completely. He would respect that for now. There were many feelings he was picking up around Jessica, he realized, noticing how her fingers trembled slightly as she removed an orchid from an old clay pot. From the stubborn set of her lower lip and the darkness haunting her glorious turquoise eyes, he knew the beautiful cloud person was gone, at least for now. Somehow their conversation had brought up ghosts from her past that now stood between them. He felt badly about that. All he wanted was to see Jessica remain in the clouds, to be that magical, wondrous, happy creature he'd first met.

For the next fifteen minutes, Jessica concentrated on showing Dan how to repot an orchid. He no longer questioned her, but stood respectfully nearby, just far enough away to keep her from feeling threatened.

When Jessica handed him another orchid to repot, he went through each step perfectly. Just the way he touched the plant made her ache for him to touch her in the same way. It was a ludicrous idea, but her body was responding to him even if her mind whispered warnings to her. Unhappy with how she was feeling, she sat on the wooden crate beside the workbench to watch Dan complete the repotting process.

The silence remained between them for a long time, except for the occasional instructions he needed from her. By noon, Jessica felt her stomach growl. Glancing to the left, she watched Dan's angular profile as he worked. His mouth was relaxed now, not thinned. His black brows were drawn down in concentration as he worked with the fragile orchid, his touch light and careful. A light perspiration made his dark, golden skin gleam beneath the diffused light in the greenhouse. Sweat dampened his white shirt beneath each arm and around his upper chest. She saw the creases and lines at the corners of his mouth and eyes and she wondered how he'd gotten that scar on his left cheek. But, she remembered, there were a lot of things she wanted to know about Dan Black.

"This morning," Jessica began awkwardly, trying to find a diplomatic way of asking what she wanted to know, "you said something to me I didn't understand."

Dan glanced over at her. "Which part of it?"

Knitting her hands nervously, Jessica looked away. In that moment, the brief smile that pulled at the corners of his mouth made him look years younger. Dan had a beguiling face; she knew his rugged features had yet to reveal his every emotion to her. She wondered what it would be like if he really smiled, or laughed fully.

"You said something in Navajo—*sh* something. I didn't know what it meant."

Dan's hands stilled over the orchid. His heart plummeted. "That…" he muttered self-consciously.

"Yes?"

He didn't *dare* let Jessica know what it meant. "It was…nothing. When I get excited, I drop into my own language, that's all."

She watched him closely. His expression had closed up faster than a snapping turtle. It was surprising to her. Her head whispered, *See, he's not to be trusted. He's lying to you. He knows what it means, but he won't tell you.* Jessica tried to ignore her mistrustful thoughts.

"Oh…"

He felt her sadness and looked at her sharply. "It wasn't anything bad, Jessica. I promise you that." And it wasn't. It was a beautiful expression that a man used for the woman he loved. He knew Jessica had grown up with Navajo people, but he was grateful she didn't recognize the wonderful endearment that was only shared between two people who were deeply in love with one another. He had no wish to embarrass her with his slip of the tongue, or the wild way his heart and his passion had galloped away from him in those moments out of time with her. At all costs, he must hold how he felt toward her to himself. She must never know his real feelings, because if she did, he was sure he'd be fired from the job and asked to leave the ranch. And right now, Dan was helpless, unable to walk away. Jessica was like an answer to his lifelong prayers—a woman who could fulfill him on every level. And she could. He knew that as surely as he took each breath of air into his lungs.

Jessica sighed and stood up. "You did a great job of repotting that orchid. Let's go get some lunch. I'm starving to death."

Relieved that she wasn't going to pursue the topic, Dan nodded. He put the orchid on the bench and, grabbing his hat, followed her out of the humid, moist depths of the greenhouse. He wondered how he was going to handle his unraveling feelings for her in the days to come. Yes, he felt like a man with one foot in heaven and the other in hell. Or maybe he was like that man in the Greek myth, who ached to capture the golden fleece that was guarded by a killer giant, but knew he never could. Not ever…

Chapter 6

Where had the first three weeks of her time at the ranch gone? Jessica stood out on the porch of her house, the hot breeze ruffling her hair. In frustration, she caught the tousled strands and put them up in a ponytail. The sunlight was blindingly bright, the sky an incredibly deep, cobalt blue. It was a beautiful day, she thought as she watched Kate and Sam riding off to the north pasture. A lot of new calves had been born, and she knew they wanted to check on them and the mothers today.

In her hand was a list of things to pick up at the Sedona Hay and Feed Store. Sam had asked her to get veterinary items they were running low on, such as antibiotics, hypodermic needles and thrush ointment. At the clip-clop of horse hooves coming around her house, she turned expectedly. Instantly, her heart rate increased. Dan Black sat tall and proud on a dark bay gelding with four white socks. His face was a sheen of perspiration, and she admired once again his powerful chest outlined by the sweat-damp, dark blue shirt he wore. Oh, how she'd missed his company!

Jessica had become spoiled by Dan's presence that first week at the ranch. He'd worked sixteen hours a day helping her get her business set up and running smoothly once again. The only time she saw him now was for an hour—if that—in the morning. Their time with one another was extremely limited. How often she had gone over to the bunkhouse to invite him to her house to eat, only to learn that he was still out on horseback, doing ranch chores somewhere.

She saw Dan's gray eyes narrow heatedly upon her. That mask he always wore softened considerably as he pulled his dusty, sweaty horse to a halt. Putting his fingers to the brim of his hat, he tipped it in her direction.

"Going somewhere?" he asked. Dan knew he should continue to avoid Jessica all he could, but when he'd seen her step out onto the porch, he couldn't help himself—he'd had to ride over to visit with her. It was a selfish decision on his part. He'd just finished herding some broodmares from the south pasture to the west one and was coming back in to grab a late lunch. Now he was hungry on a much different, more galvanizing level.

"Hi, Dan." Jessica held up the paper in her hand. "Sam wants me to go to the feed store and get some antibiotics for him."

He nodded. "Yes, we're going through them lately. A lot of sepsis with the cows and their babies." He squinted at the dry, yellowed pastures. "Might be the drought doing it. Everything's dying."

She sobered and stepped off the front porch. "I can hardly wait until Rachel gets here. She's got homeopathic remedies that can cure sepsis better than an antibiotic, and it will cost us a lot less, too. She left a few kits here on her last visit, but we've already used them." She paused, then said, "Hey, why don't you come into town with me?"

The idea was tempting. "I can't, I got—"

Jessica pouted prettily. "Dan, I'm going to need some help. Sam wanted me to take the pickup truck and get about eight hundred pounds in feed. I'm going to need a strong body to help lift that stuff into the truck. Sam said Old Man Thomas at the store is in his eighties and he's too stingy to hire help. The poor old gent can't handle hundred-pound sacks of grain, and I can't, either." Flexing her arm, she pointed to the almost nonexistent bulge of her biceps. "I'm a wimp."

He chuckled. The sparkle in her eyes was one of warmth and welcome. Instantly, Dan felt embraced by her bubbly enthusiasm and humor. "Okay, Miss Jessica, let me get my horse unsaddled and cared for. It'll take about ten minutes."

"Great! I'll drive over to the barn in about ten and meet you."

Her heart exploded with happiness as she saw him grin. How little Dan laughed. The more she pried, the less he allowed her entrance into his unknown life. She longed for his companionship again. Kate and Sam had been so busy that Jessica largely left them alone. They worked from dawn to almost midnight every day and then fell exhausted into one another's arms, and slept deeply. The drought was putting a terrible edge on the struggle for life at the ranch, and they were doing everything in their power to save the lives of their stock.

She knew Dan was working every bit as hard, but she wished she could spend more time with him.

Jessica couldn't still her excitement as Dan drove the beat-up pickup into town. There was no air-conditioning in the truck, so both windows were down as they pulled slowly into uptown Sedona, the area known to the locals as the "tourist trap."

"Can you imagine, six million people a year visit us?" Jessica asked, looking at the line of tourist shops crowded together along the highway.

Dan grimaced. "I stay away from this place as much as possible."

"Why?" She looked at his chiseled profile, her gaze settling on his mouth. His lips were thinned, which meant he was tense. She wondered if this trip was the reason. Rarely did Jessica see Dan leave the ranch premises. It was as if he were hiding out there.

With a shrug, Dan turned the truck into the hay-and-feed-store parking lot. "Crowds bother me, that's all."

"Oh…" She looked at the storefront. It was badly weathered and in dire need of a coat of paint. The wood was graying and splintering from the heat. A rusted old sign hung at an angle and moved slowly back and forth in the inconstant afternoon breeze, creaking in protest. Dan backed the pickup against the wooden loading dock at the barn portion of the building, where the grain and hay were kept.

Jessica caught sight of an old Indian man sitting beneath the cottonwood tree near the entrance. He was probably in his seventies, his white hair down to his shoulders, a bright red wrap around his head as he sat with his back against the tree and weaved from side to side. He was drunk, Jessica realized as she stepped from the truck. The clothes he wore were rags, and very dirty looking. She frowned. Instead of going up the stairs into the store, she moved to the man's side.

Jessica had forgotten most of the Navajo she'd learned as a child. She'd been multilingual, knowing English, Eastern Cherokee, some Navajo and Apache. Now she worked to remember Navajo phrases.

The old man opened his bloodshot eyes and looked at her as Jessica knelt down in front of him. *"Ya at eeh,"* she began tenuously. That was Navajo for "hello." She wasn't sure he *was* Navajo, even though the reservation ended where the city of Flagstaff, an hour north of Sedona, began.

The old man's tobacco brown skin crinkled. He gave her a toothless smile, his gums gleaming. *"Ya at eeh..."* he slurred.

Jessica knew there was a mission in West Sedona that helped the homeless. She was distraught by the man's condition. The odor of alcohol assailed her, and she spotted an empty one-gallon wine bottle lying next to him.

"Jessica, leave him alone."

She looked up to see Dan scowling darkly over her.

"No. He needs help."

"You can't help him. That's Tommy Wolf. He's the local drunk here in Sedona."

She heard the embarrassment in Dan's voice. He was edgy and nervous, looking around as if he were ashamed to be seen with her and Tommy. "I'm not leaving him, Dan. Look at him. He's filthy! He needs a bath and some help. Can you speak Navajo to him and tell him we'll take him to the mission? It's only a few blocks from here."

Pulling his black Stetson lower on his sweaty brow, Dan frowned in irritation. "Jessica, you're throwing your care away. Tommy knows where the mission's at. He'll eventually get over there when he wants a decent meal and a bath. Right now, he's drunker than hell. Just leave him alone."

Her jaw became set. "Dan, just go get the feed and antibiotics, okay? I'll take Tommy over while you do it." She moved forward to lift the old man's arm, placing it around her shoulders. Instead, she felt Dan's strong hands on her arms. He lifted her up and away from Tommy.

"Dan!" She stood there, staring up into his angry features.

"I'll do it," he rasped. "Just get the door of the truck open for me."

Jessica's eyes widened as she heard the grating in his deep voice. She watched as Dan easily hefted the old Navajo to his feet and aimed him in the direction of the pickup. Tommy began a slurred conversation in Navajo with Dan as they walked toward the truck. Jessica hurried ahead of them.

The honk of a horn startled her. She halted as a brand-new pickup truck roared into the hay and feed store next to where they were parked. If she hadn't stopped when she did, she would have been sideswiped by the swift-moving vehicle. Her mouth dropped open in shock as she stood there, the truck passing only a foot away from her. Blinking, she realized she knew the two cowboys in the cab—Chet and Bo Cunningham from the neighboring ranch. Old memories flooded her.

Angrily, Jessica moved around the red pickup and quickly opened the passenger door for Dan, who was slowly easing Tommy along on not too steady feet. The old Navajo had no shoes or socks on, and her heart bled for his condition.

"Well, well, another one of the prodigal daughters has returned to the Donovan Ranch. Whad'ya know...."

Snapping her head to the left, Jessica met the dark eyes of Chet Cunningham. A two-day growth of scraggly beard shadowed his narrow, pale features, and his straw cowboy hat was low over his eyes as he swaggered around the front of his red truck toward her.

"Little Jessica Donovan," he crowed, and then laughed. "Out saving the world again?" He slapped his hand on his jean-covered thigh.

To her consternation, she saw the taller, darker brother, Bo, appear around the front of the truck in turn. "Mind your own business, Chet," she said.

Chet snickered and put his hand over hers where she held the door to the pickup open. "Naw, that's too easy. The Cunninghams run Sedona. You're trespassing, missy."

"Get your hand off her."

Jessica jerked her head toward the dark, lethal-sounding voice. She realized belatedly that it was Dan speaking. He stood there, still holding Tommy in his grip, and glared past her to Chet. She'd never heard Dan speak in such a tone, nor had she ever seen the expression his face held now. There was a dangerous quality radiating around him that made the hair on the back of her neck stand up in reaction. His eyes were colorless, his mouth a hard line, his face emotionless.

Chet snickered again and glanced over at Bo, who came and stood at his shoulder. "Go to hell, you drunken half-breed. You got guts coming into Sedona in the first place," he roared, raising his gloved hand and jabbing it at Dan. "You takin' Tommy over to the

mission to dry out again? Together?" And both brothers laughed loudly.

Jessica jerked her hand away from Chet's and held it
out to Tommy, who weakly grasped her fingers. "Pay
no attention to them," she ordered the older man as Dan
helped her maneuver the Navajo into her truck. Before
she knew it, she felt Dan's hand on her arm. It was a
strong, guiding grip, not hurtful, but meant to remove
her from between him and the Cunningham men. She
opened her mouth to protest, but it was too late.

"You two sidewinders go about your business," Dan
snarled. "And leave off your jawing, too."

"Whooee!" Chet crowed, slapping his brother's
shoulder. "Listen to this drunken Indian give orders,
Bo. Whad'ya think about that?" Chet's eyes narrowed
in fury. "Take your bottle and the old Navajo rug your
granny made for you and crawl back into your hole,
Black. Better yet, crawl off to Flag, where you were
the butt of everyone's jokes."

Dan felt the heat creep into his face. He saw the leer-
ing anger in both men's expressions. Worse, Jessica was
hearing what they said about him. His heart pounded in
fury and dread. Now she would know the truth about
him. A serrating pain scored his heart. "Get the hell
out of here, Chet. Just leave us in peace and we'll do
the same for you."

Chet took in a couple of deep breaths and stuck his
chest out. He glanced again at Bo, who barely nodded.
Pulling his stained leather gloves a little tighter, Chet
grinned. "Gonna be the cock of the walk here, Black?
Showing off for Miss Goody Two-shoes, who rescues
drunks like you?"

Dan heard Jessica's protest. Before he could answer,
he saw Chet draw back his arm, his fist cocked. To hell

with it. If he was going to go to jail on assault charges, he might as well make Chet Cunningham pay in full for his actions.

Jessica gasped as she watched Chet's fist barrel forward to strike Dan. Suddenly she saw Dan move with the speed of a striking rattlesnake. Only he didn't use his fists, he used his entire body in a karatelike motion. Blinking, Jessica cried out as Chet went flying backward with a grunt, slamming into the dock and letting out a loud *ooooff* sound.

Bo cursed and leaped toward Dan. Jessica put her hands to her lips and cried out a warning. Dan moved with the grace of a ballet artist and swung around, his booted foot arcing out and catching Bo in the stomach. The older brother was slammed into the side of the red truck. Chet, his nose bloody and crooked, scrambled off the ground and leaped at Dan.

Jessica stood there, stunned by Dan's prowess in fighting. All of a sudden the easygoing, mild-mannered cowboy had turned into a lethal warrior she'd never known existed. She watched as Dan's open hand caught Chet just beneath the nose. Cunningham went down like a felled ox, unconscious this time.

"Stop it!"

A shotgun went off.

Jessica leaped and screamed. She saw Old Man Thomas hobbling out onto the dock, the shotgun aimed at the three cowboys below.

"Now, galdarnit, you three young roosters take yore fights elsewhere. You got that? Or you want yore pants full of buckshot?"

Dan eased out of his karate position. Breathing hard, his hands aching, he looked up at Old Man Thomas, who was red-faced and angry as hell. Holding up his hands, Dan said, "We'll leave, Mr. Thomas."

"Damn right you will! Get outta here! All of ya! Chet, Bo, get a move on. I'm a callin' yore daddy and tellin' him yore up to yore same ol' tricks again. Dagnabit, yore nothing but trouble! Now git! The lot of ya!"

Dan moved swiftly over to Jessica, who stood white-faced and frozen, her hands pressed against her stomach and her eyes large and glazed. Damn! "Come on," he rasped, grabbing her by the arm and leading her around the front of the truck. "Let's get Tommy over to the mission. We can pick up the supplies down at Cottonwood Hay and Feed, instead."

He looked over his shoulder just to make sure the Cunningham men weren't foolish enough to try and attack again. He saw Bo holding a hand up to his bloody nose and mouth.

"You drunken bastard," Bo snarled as he got to his feet, "I'm callin' the sheriff. You're going up on assault charges—"

"No, he ain't!" Old Man Thomas roared, glaring down at them from the dock. He aimed the shotgun directly at Bo. "You two started it. I saw it with my own eyes. You two ain't got the sense of a rock. Get the hell outta here! Any sheriff to be called, I'll be doing that, ya hear? And if you put charges against Black, I'll be slappin' them against you. Understand?"

Bo glared over at Dan, wiping his nose with his gloved hand. "Yeah, I hear you, Mr. Thomas."

Chet stood on wobbly feet, his face a mass of blood coming from his nose and the corner of his badly cut mouth. Bo strode over, jerked his younger brother forward and pushed him back into the pickup. He looked up at them.

"Black, you're on my list now. You'd better watch your back, you drunken son of a bitch." His mouth curved into a hard grin. "Yeah, you'll hit the bottle again and I'll come looking for you. Next time, things will be different," he finished, punching his gloved index finger toward Dan.

"Come on," Dan urged tightly, getting Tommy out of the truck in front of the mission. He didn't dare look at Jessica. Now she knew about his sordid past. Damn! Gently moving the old Navajo up the sidewalk to the two-story wooden house that served as a center for the homeless in Sedona, he avoided Jessica's gaze. But he could feel her eyes on him, his skin scorching hotly at her appraisal. She hadn't said a word as he drove the three blocks to the mission.

The ache in his heart widened. Well, he was stupid to hope that Jessica wouldn't find out about his past—his bout with the bottle after the war. He brought Tommy into the cooler depths of the front lobby, sitting him into a chair near the reception desk.

Jessica moved to the desk and talked to the young woman with glasses behind it, while Dan stood back, his hands shoved into the pockets of his jeans. His knuckles hurt, but it was nothing like the pain he felt in his heart or the shame that burned through him. When Jessica turned, he saw her avoid his gaze and stare down at the floor instead. Humiliation avalanched through him. Grimly, Dan opened the door for her. Tommy was in good hands now and the folks who ran this mission would get him a bath, clean clothes, shoes, some hot, nutritious food and a place for him to sober up.

The heat of the sunlight laced across them as they

walked to the pickup parked beneath two huge cottonwoods. He opened the door for Jessica.

"Thank you," she whispered. She got in, pressed her
hands into her lap and hung her head. She felt Dan get
back in and heard the door slam. Closing her eyes, she
took a long, shaky breath.

"Jessica," he began awkwardly, "I'm sorry..."

She slowly opened her eyes and lifted her chin. Dan
sat tensely beside her, both his bloodied hands gripping the steering wheel. As she met and held his sad,
dark gray eyes, tears stung hers. The incredible sadness around him enveloped her and she just stared at
him, at a loss for words. Finally, she saw him scowl and
push the cowboy hat off his wrinkled, glistening brow.

"Something came over me," he muttered. "I saw Chet
trap your hand against that door and something just
snapped inside me. That little rattler is no good. He
knew what he was doing."

"Y-yes, I think he did," she managed to answer halt-
ingly. Her gaze shifted to his white-knuckled hands. "At
least let me clean up your hands, Dan. They're bleeding pretty badly."

He hadn't even noticed, Dan realized as he watched
Jessica lean down and pick up the plastic quart bottle of
water she'd brought along for them to drink. From the
glove box, she took a clean cloth. Turning in the seat,
she eased his right hand off the steering wheel after
dampening the cloth. Her touch was incredibly gentle
and warm. He felt his heart breaking. It would be the
last time she ever touched him this way. The last.

"You don't have to touch me," he muttered, and tried
to draw his hand out of hers.

"Stop!" Jessica cried, her voice rising. "I'm upset,

Dan. The least you can do is sit still and let me clean you up. Now just relax, will you?"

He heard the strain in her soft voice. Her full mouth was compressed and he knew she was angry—at him. Still, he relished each touch of the cooling cloth against his aching knuckles. He never wanted her to stop. "You make the pain go away," he murmured unsteadily, catching and holding her fleeting blue gaze. "Just your touch...."

Heat swept through Jessica. She closed her other hand over his. Taking a ragged breath, she said brokenly, "Dan, you could've been killed by those two! I've rarely seen evil in this world, but I think Chet and Bo were *born* that way! It's just so upsetting."

Without thinking, Dan tugged his hand from between hers. "Listen to me," he rasped, pulling her into his arms. He felt her trembling like a frightened fawn. Closing his eyes, he buried his face against her soft blond hair. Slowly her trembling ceased and he felt her relax against him. He expected Jessica to fight him, to push away from him in disgust. Instead, he felt her moan softly, her face pressed against his, her arms sliding around his torso.

"It's all right...." he whispered against her ear. She smelled like a meadow full of wildflowers. Her hair was thin and fine, like soft, spun gold against his cheek and nose. All of his barriers dissolved as she sought his protection. "Stop shaking. It's all over, *shi shaa.* You're safe...safe...."

His voice was low and singsong. Jessica felt the strength of Dan's arms around her, holding her protectively. She smelled the odor of hay and horses on his roughened cheek. She felt the powerful thud of his heart against her breasts as he pressed her hard against him. Everywhere she contacted his lean, whipcord strong body, her skin burned with desire.

She heard him speaking low, in the beautiful, rhythmic Navajo language, and she sighed softly and sank more deeply into his arms. She felt his mouth against her hair as he pressed a kiss to her head. How she'd longed for his kiss all these lonely weeks! Summoning all of her courage, all of her driving needs, Jessica turned her face slightly, and this time, as his mouth came down to press another kiss to her hair, his lips met hers instead.

A jolt of heat tore through her as his pliant mouth closed over hers. At first she felt surprise vibrate through Dan, and then, as she moved her lips softly, searchingly against his, she felt the surprise dissolve into a swift, returning pressure against her lips. Suddenly, the world ceased to exist. She was enclosed within his strength, the searching boldness of his mouth. The molten heat of his tongue moved slowly across her lower lip, making her moan with a pleasure she had never before experienced. His roughened hand moved slowly up her bare arm, his touch eliciting fire, yet gentling her at the same time.

This was the Dan Black she had wanted all along, Jessica hazily realized as she sank more deeply into his searching, molding kiss, which stole her breath and bound their aching souls into one. As she ran her hand up across Dan's shoulder, she felt every muscle leap and harden beneath her foray. He felt so good to her! So solid, warm and giving. For an instant, she had thought he would be not only hurt, but killed by the Cunninghams. They were dangerous men. But she'd never realized how dangerous Dan was. To know that the hands that now roved roughly across her arms and shoulders were hands that could hurt as well as protect was shocking to her. He was a man of many surprises. A man wrapped in the darkness of his past.

That realization caused Jessica to pull away unexpectedly. She gazed up into Dan's eyes, which appeared almost silver and black as he studied her. Their breathing was ragged. Their hearts were pounding in unison. Blinking, Jessica realized that Dan was the man Moyra had told her about—the man wrapped in darkness! Her lips tingled wildly from his onslaught. She stared at that mouth, that full lower lip, and then back up into his narrowed eyes. He seemed like a predator right now, and she his willing quarry. Her fingers opened and closed against his broad, powerful shoulders. Her legs felt weak and she didn't want to move. All that existed, all that she'd ever dreamed of having, was here, in Dan Black.

"No...." Jessica whispered faintly.

Chastened, Dan released her. His body was on fire. He ached for her, the pain making him want to bend double. What the hell was he doing? Why had he kissed Jessica? What demon from his darkness had driven him right over the edge to take her? Helping Jessica sit up on her side of the seat, he leaned back, taking off his hat and allowing his head to rest against the rear window. What the hell had he just done? His heart was pounding like a wild horse in his chest. His mouth was warm from her soft, breathless kiss. She tasted like sweet honey and warm sunlight. His skin throbbed wherever she'd touched him with her delicate, hesitant fingertips. Dan cursed himself richly. He could feel shame flooding through him as if a dam had burst. What kind of fool was he? He'd not only overstepped his bounds, he'd probably be getting his walking papers from Sam McGuire tonight when his boss got off the range. Dan had no business kissing the owner of such a huge ranch.

Taking in a deep, ragged breath, he tried to tame his fear and shame. But his desire to make Jessica his, to couple with her not only on the physical level, but to entwine their souls in beautiful lovemaking, overwhelmed him. He ached to take her all the way with him. He wanted to feel her small, firm body against his, to feel their flesh sliding hotly together.

It was all just another broken dream, Dan realized as he opened his eyes and sat up. He risked a look at Jessica. She sat there, hands clasped tightly in her lap, her head tipped back and her eyes closed. Those delicious, pale pink lips were softly parted, and he wondered if he'd hurt her with the power of his kiss. His brows drew downward as he replaced the hat on his head and started the pickup. By tonight, Sam would be asking him to pack his bedroll and leave. By tomorrow morning, the sheriff would probably be out looking for him, to slam him into the county jail on assault charges. Dan couldn't fool himself. Old Man Cunningham ran Coconino and Yavapai Counties, including Sedona.

Dan's hands shook momentarily as he backed the pickup away from the mission. Heaven and hell. He'd just held heaven in his arms and stolen a wild, hot kiss from Jessica. The hell was that he was going to pay for all his indiscretions. Every single last one of them. Worse, he'd never see Jessica again, and he felt his heart crack and begin to break into anguished fragments deep in his chest.

Chapter 7

Dan leaned moodily against the last hundred-pound sack of grain that he'd stored in the barn. The hundred-degree heat was making him sweat profusely. His knuckles ached and he automatically flexed them. Taking his red bandanna from around his neck, he removed his cowboy hat and wiped his perspiring face. Through the large open doors of the red barn, he could see Jessica's house.

Hell and damnation! He might as well pack what few belongings he had into the old carpetbag that he'd inherited from his great-grandmother. It was only a matter of time, Dan concluded, until Sam came to the bunkhouse to give him his walking papers. Especially now that he'd got entangled in a fight—and he'd kissed Jessica.

His lips tingled hotly in memory of her soft, sweet mouth against his hungry, searching one. Frowning, he settled the black Stetson on his head and walked out to the pickup. Climbing in, he drove it around to the front of the main ranch house where it belonged. His gaze caught a rising cloud of dust from the dirt road that led into the ranch from 89A.

Trouble. He could feel it. Getting out of the truck, he looked toward the greenhouse. It was probably the Coconino County sheriff come to slap him in cuffs and take him to jail on assault and battery charges. Rubbing the back of his neck, Dan felt a storm of emotions roll through him. He needed more time. He *had* to talk to Jessica about their unexpected, shocking kiss. He wanted to apologize. Afterward, she'd retreated into a silent shell, and they'd passed the entire trip to the hay and feed store and back to the ranch in stilted, embarrassed silence.

Dan knew she was sorry. The look on her face—the chagrin written across it and the high, red color in her flushed cheeks—told him everything. She didn't like him. He hadn't asked her permission to touch her, much less kiss her. What the hell was the matter with him? He was acting crazy, like that black Arabian stallion when he got around a mare in heat. No brains, just hormones.

Dan decided to wait for the approaching vehicle. As it crested the top of the hill that led down the winding, narrow dirt road to the canyon below, where he stood, he scowled. It wasn't a white car with lights and sirens. No, it was a red car with antennae sticking out of the trunk area. Someone from the fire department. But why? Stymied, Dan folded his arms against his chest and waited, leaning tensely against the back of the pickup. The shade of an overhead cottonwood cooled him slightly and the off-and-on breeze felt good to him.

He was sweating plenty, probably out of fear of being jailed again. He never wanted to return to that hateful place.

As the red car drove up and parked near him, Dan saw a man with black hair and blue eyes at the wheel. When the stranger opened the door and unbuckled the seat belt, Dan got a better look at him. Wearing dark blue, serge pants, highly polished black boots and a light blue, short-sleeved shirt, he had a tall, lanky build, reminding Dan of a cougar's lethal grace. He looked vaguely familiar, but Dan couldn't place him. On his shirt he wore a silver badge and his left sleeve bore a red-and-white insignia that said Emergency Medical Technician. Dan tensed as he caught the nameplate affixed to his left pocket: J. Cunningham.

Slowly uncrossing his arms and spreading his feet slightly for balance, Dan studied the man before him. He was the youngest of the three Cunningham brothers, and from town gossip Dan knew that Jim had recently quit his forestry job as a hotshot firefighter and come home to try and mend fences with his cantankerous father and brothers. Rumor had it that Jim had left years ago during a hellacious family fight, swearing never to return. For ten years, he had remained up in Flagstaff. The only time Dan had heard of him coming home was at Christmas. But he always left shortly after to resume his fire fighting duties around the U.S. Now that he was working for Sedona's fire department, everyone wondered if he'd stay for good.

As he quietly closed the car door, Cunningham's blue eyes were dark and disturbed looking, though he held Dan's gauging look. His full mouth was pursed as he moved in Dan's direction.

Dan didn't know what to expect. Had Jim Cunningham come to finish off the fight? His heart began a slow, hard pounding as adrenaline began to pour into his bloodstream.

"You Dan Black?" Cunningham demanded, halting about six feet away, his hands resting tensely on his narrow hips.

"I am."

"You know who I am?"

"Got an idea."

"My brothers just came over to the fire department to get patched up from the fight they just had." Giving Dan a frosty smile, he continued, "I'm an EMT, on the medical staff of the Sedona Fire Department. I came to apologize to you in person for my brothers' actions and to see if you were okay."

Stunned, Dan stared at him in disbelief. Cunninghams weren't known for apologizing for anything they did—they played by their own twisted rules and their reputation in Sedona was nasty. They never had any compassion for folks they chose to take on and destroy. Dan knew many people Old Man Cunningham had torn apart over the years. The father was a merciless bastard just like his two sons. But as Dan heard it, Jim Cunningham had always been different, set apart from the rest of the family, like a black sheep of sorts. Or rather like a *white* sheep.

When Jim thrust out his hand, Dan swallowed hard. "My knuckles are bruised up a little," he muttered, taking the man's offered hand. Cunningham's grip was firm, and Dan found himself respecting the guy for what he was doing. It was absolutely unheard of that a Cunningham apologized for anything.

Jim nodded and released his grip. "And Miss Jessica Donovan? Is she okay? Chet said she slapped him, but I don't believe my brother. Maybe you can tell me what really happened?"

Dan nodded and told him the entire story. The EMT's oval face and strong chin became tight with anger by the time he'd finished.

"I see," Jim rasped. "Well, both of them have broken noses out of the deal. Just deserts, I'd say." He cocked his head and perused Dan speculatively. "I heard you were in the Corps for four years, or is that just gossip?"

Dan relaxed. He liked Jim Cunningham, even though something about his stance reminded him of a dangerous cougar ready to strike. "Yes, I was."

"What part?"

"Recons."

Cunningham grinned a little. "Thought so."

"Oh?"

"My brothers said they couldn't lay a hand on you. That you'd done all the damage to them. I figured you had some special training to do that."

"I don't like to fight, Mr. Cunningham. It's not in my nature. I'd rather have peace."

He nodded. "I'm with you. Coming back to this family of mine this last month has been hell. I'm going to try and stick it out, but I don't know...." He looked up at the clear blue, cloudless sky for a moment.

"Family troubles are the worst kind," Dan agreed quietly.

Jim looked over at him. "Look, if it's okay with you, I'd like to meet Jessica Donovan and make my apologies directly to her."

"You shouldn't be cleaning up the messes your brothers make."

"No, but if I'm going to break the patterns of abuse that run through my family, somebody is going to have to take responsibility and start changing things, aren't they? My two brothers don't have a clue yet." His eyes flashing, Cunningham muttered grimly, "They sure as hell will when I get off duty tomorrow morning and we have a friendly little chat over breakfast with Dad about it. That's a promise."

Dan didn't envy Jim's position, but he respected the man. He wanted to say that the Cunninghams were a barrel of rotten apples and that if a good apple like Jim were put in among them, they'd infect him, too. Instead, he said, "I admire your mission."

Jim grinned tightly. "Not a job for the faint of heart, is it?"

"No," he murmured, "it isn't." In that moment, Dan realized Jim knew all the sordid tales of his brothers' and father's escapades in Coconino and Yavapai Counties, and that he was well aware of the hatred many people had toward the Cunninghams. Their greed, stinginess and manipulative, underhanded business dealings were famous in these parts. "Come on, I know where Jessica's at. I think she'll feel better hearing that there's one Cunningham who cares about other people's feelings."

Dan was going to leave once he showed Cunningham to the door of the greenhouse, but the EMT persuaded him to come in and make introductions. It was the last thing Dan wanted to do, but he had no choice. Opening the door, he felt an immediate drop in temperature inside the structure and the high humidity enveloped him. He saw Jessica perched up on a stool tending to one of her orchids at the workbench. When she turned to see who was coming in, her eyes widened, first with shock and then surprise mixed with some hidden emotion. Probably disgust for him, for his earlier actions, Dan thought.

Getting a grip on his own feelings, Dan led the EMT over to the workbench and made introductions. Then he stepped back, tipped his hat in Jessica's direction and left. He could see that look in her flawless turquoise eyes. She was so heartbreakingly innocent and beautiful—and he'd abused the privilege of being with her. As he shut the door behind him and crossed the yard, he felt suffocated by his own feelings toward Jessica. How could he have fallen so in love with a woman he'd known only three weeks? How? It had never happened to him before. Not ever.

"I wanted to apologize directly to you for my brothers' actions, Miss Donovan," Jim said to her in an apologetic tone. "I drove over here after they came into the firehouse to get some medical treatment from me and my partner. That's when I found out about it. They told me their side of the story, and I just got the truth as to what really happened from Dan Black. I'm sorry. I want to know if there's anything I can do to patch things up between us."

Stunned, Jessica stared up at the tall, well-muscled EMT. "Y-you're *Jim* Cunningham?"

"Yes, ma'am, I am."

"But," Jessica said, putting the orchid aside, "I thought—"

"I just came home a month ago. Permanently, I hope. My father's ill and—"

"Oh, I'm sorry to hear that." Jessica saw the sadness in his narrowed gaze. She immediately liked Jim Cunningham. "This is such a change from normal Cunningham actions."

"I realize that. I'm trying to break the old habit patterns. They die hard, but someone has got to make Chet and Bo straighten out and become better citizens of Sedona and the county, don't you think?"

His easy smile made him look more handsome, and Jessica warmed to him even more. She wondered if he was married. There was no wedding ring on his left finger. "So, you're home for good now?"

"Yes, I am. For better or worse, I'm afraid."

"Gosh, I admire your tenacity, Jim. You don't mind if I call you by your first name, do you?"

He relaxed slightly, his hand on the edge of her workbench. "No, ma'am, I don't. To tell you the truth, my own lack of formality has gotten me into a lot of trouble with superiors all my life." He looked down at his fire-department uniform. "I'm kinda the wild card around here."

She smiled, enjoying his openness toward her. Jessica was the youngest Donovan girl, and she vaguely remembered Jim in school, but they'd been many grades apart. She knew he'd been a very shy young man, a mere shadow, compared to his two brothers, who were always in fights of one kind or another. Shortly after graduation, he'd been hired by the forest service and had taken a job as a hotshot firefighter. It was the last Jessica had seen of him.

"Sometimes it takes a wild card—or a black sheep—

to make the changes, you know?" She saw him relax completely, his broad shoulders drawn back proudly.

"Your reputation around here seems to be true," he murmured.

Jessica raised her eyes and laughed. "Oh, dear, Sedona gossip, I suppose?"

"Well," Jim hedged, "you know there's some truth to gossip. Not much, usually, but there's a seed in it somewhere."

"And what's the gossip going around about me? I imagine because you're in the fire department you hear a lot of it."

Jim pushed his long, strong fingers through his short black hair. "Just that you were insightful, that you always thought the best of a person and his behavior, that's all. After what my brothers pulled, you didn't have to see me or be this kind to me. I think that speaks volumes about you, personally. At least, it does to me." He scowled. "I want peace between our families. I know the Donovans and Cunninghams have fought for decades, mostly because of our stubborn, wrongheaded fathers." Spreading his hands open in a gesture of peace, he continued, "I want to bury the hatchet, Jessica. I want to come over here some time and tell Kate and Sam the same thing. I've only been back for a month, however, and my hands are full with my new job, plus trying to help run the ranch on my days off."

She felt his commitment, as well as his incredible anguish. Noticing the tiny scars on his brow and right cheek and all over his hands and darkly haired arms, she knew without a doubt that Jim Cunningham carried the scars not only of his own life, but those of his family, too. Her heart went out to him.

"I'll tell Katie and Sam that you dropped by to apologize, Jim. I'm sure they'll be relieved to hear this. We don't want to fight, either. We just want to be able to work with your ranch in the event of some crisis or emergency. We're just as tired of the bad blood between us as you are. Kelly's dead now, so most of the problem is gone. Right now Kate's trying to pick up the pieces, and Sam's trying to help her save our home." Jessica sighed and looked at his serious, dark features. She saw the Apache blood of his mother in him, in the set of his high cheekbones, his glossy black hair and the reddish tone to his dark golden skin. "I know Katie will be glad to hear you're back and trying to change things."

"I don't know if I can," Jim admitted heavily, frowning down at his hand resting on the workbench. "But I'm going to give it one heck of a try."

"You're a catalyst," Jessica said. "The lightning bolt your family needs. By you coming home, things must change or else."

He grinned a little recklessly and held out his hand to her. "Thanks for the vote of confidence. It's the only one I've gotten around here so far. Maybe I should come over once a week and get a pep talk from you so I can carry on."

Giggling, Jessica shook his proffered hand. "I'll tell you who's a real cheerleader. My sister Rachel. She's coming home in December from London, England. Talk about someone cheering people on to strive to be all they can be—that's Rachel!"

"I remember her. She was two grades behind me in high school," Jim said.

Jessica heard a sudden wistful quality in his voice and saw longing in his blue eyes. It occurred to her that maybe Jim had had a crush on Rachel in school. But Rachel hadn't said anything about it back then, so Jessica shrugged off the intuitive hint. "Hang tight until December. I'm sure Rachel is going to be thrilled to death to hear you're home to change the ways of the Cunningham family. Besides, she's going to be setting up a clinic in Sedona to practice homeopathy. You're an EMT, I see. You two will have a lot in common—medicine."

"Sounds good to me, ma'am."

"Call me Jessica. Please."

He smiled a little. "Okay… Jessica."

"You already talk to Dan?" she asked, sliding off the stool and walking out of the greenhouse with him.

"Yes, I did. And I apologized to him, too."

Jessica felt the dry heat strike her as they walked around the main ranch house to his dark red car. "I think he was worried the sheriff was going to come out and arrest him or something. I think he worries too much, sometimes."

"Chet and Bo started it. He was only defending himself, you and Tommy." Jim halted at the car and opened the door. "If you wanted, you two could press charges against them and land them in the county jail."

Jessica shook her head. "Why perpetuate bad feelings, Jim? I'm willing to let bygones be bygones."

He climbed into the car and shut the door, rolling down the window. "I hope someday my brothers and father have your kind of understanding heart, Jessica. Thanks." He lifted his hand after starting the vehicle. "If you get a chance, drop over to the main fire department and take a look at our emergency medicine facilities. I hope you don't ever need us out here, but if you do, dial 911 and we'll be here."

Jessica lifted her hand. "I'll do that, Jim. I'm sure Rachel would love to see your medical station, too."

"You've got a deal. Next time I see you, I hope it's for happier reasons."

Jessica watched him drive slowly up the winding road that led out of the canyon. With a sigh, she turned to find Dan. It was time to talk. More than time.

Jessica found Dan in the barn, moving hay that had been brought in by truck earlier that morning. Her heart beating rapidly, she stood at the doorway, absorbing his lean, hard body and graceful movements as he lifted the hundred-pound bales as if they weighed next to nothing. He had put his cowboy hat aside, and she saw damp black tendrils clinging to his sweaty brow and neck. It was stifling in the barn, and except for the breeze that blew through the open doors, there was little fresh air.

"Dan?" she called, her voice swallowed up by the barn. At first she didn't think he'd heard her, and she was about to call his name again when she saw his head snap in her direction. Instantly, she watched his stormy gray eyes go colorless. She knew that meant he felt he was in danger. Or at least he didn't feel safe—with her. That hurt more than anything, and fear threaded through Jessica as she stepped forward, her fingers twisted together.

"I know you're busy, but could you take a break so we can talk?" Her throat felt dry, and her heart was pounding relentlessly in her breast. Whether Jessica wanted to or not, her gaze settled on Dan's mouth. Oh, that kiss he'd given her had been so incredibly galvanizing! She felt as if he'd breathed life back into her wounded soul, such was the power he'd shared with her in that exquisite moment.

"Yeah, hold on...." he rasped between breaths.

She stood to one side as he grabbed his hat, wiped his face with his bandanna and moved out into the aisle, where there was at least a breeze now and again. She saw his eyes narrow, making his wariness more than evident. She went over and unscrewed the cap from the jug of water he always kept with him, and taking his beat-up, blue plastic cup she poured him a drink.

"Here," she whispered, "you need this."

In that moment, Dan wished for something a lot stronger to anesthetize the pain he felt in his heart. Alcohol always stopped him from feeling and took the painful knots out of his gut, too. He saw her unsureness; her eyes were shadowed and that soft, delicious mouth was compressed. He knew what was coming. Inside, he cried. Outwardly, he took the glass with his damp, gloved hand.

"Thanks," he said.

Jessica watched as he tipped his head upward, his Adam's apple bobbing with each swallow. Some trickles of water ran down his chin to the strong, gleaming column of his throat. Trying to gird herself emotionally, Jessica sat down beneath his towering form on a bale of hay.

Wiping his mouth with the back of his hand, he placed the blue cup next to the water jug. He saw Jessica hang her head, unable to meet his gaze. She was twisting her fingers nervously in her lap. Crouching down, his hand on the bale behind where she sat, he took a deep breath. "Okay," he rasped in a strained tone, "what do you want to talk about?" He pushed the brim of his hat upward with his thumb.

Jessica tried to smile but couldn't. She risked a very brief glance in his direction. Dan seemed to realize she didn't want him towering over her. Instead, he'd crouched down to be at eye level with her. Her heart mushroomed with strong, powerful feelings toward him. Touching her breast, she managed to say in a strangled voice, "This is so hard for me, Dan. I hope you can forgive me if I bumble through this. I—I just feel so scared and unsure right now. And I feel a lot of other things that I've never felt before."

She gave a helpless little laugh and met and held his gaze. His eyes had gone from colorless to a dove gray and she knew he'd let down some of his guard. Opening her hands artlessly, she said, "Here I am, a woman who was married for eight years. You'd think I'd be a lot less naive than I am. Or I'd know a lot more than most people think I should when it comes to relationships. Or—" her voice shook "—about men and what they want from me…"

Dan shut his eyes tightly for a moment. "Jessica, I never meant to—"

"No," she whispered, twisting toward him. "Please, Dan, let me finish. This is so hard for me to come to terms with, and you more than anyone should know the truth." She watched his eyes open slightly to study her. "Right now, my heart's pounding in my chest. I can taste my fear."

Concerned, Dan reached out and gently grazed her flushed cheek. "Jessica, I swear to God, I *never* meant to make you feel fear…."

Jessica drowned in his darkening, stormy gray eyes,

but his gentle touch gave her courage. "Oh, Dan, I was hoping you'd understand, and I believe you do without even realizing it. My heart said you would." She looked away, tears choking her voice. "When you kissed me earlier today, my world just fell apart around my feet. It wasn't your fault. It was my past coming to meet me. I didn't expect it. How could I know?" Jessica opened her hands and gave him a pleading look.

"Your kiss made me feel so clean and good inside, Dan. I would never have thought it was possible to have a man's kiss do that to me instead of...well, making me feel...awful." She avoided his sharpening gaze, hanging her head and staring down at the fingers she'd nervously clasped together. "When I married Carl, I fell in love with the mask he wore, not the man beneath it. I guess if I'd been older, more experienced, or maybe not such an airhead, I'd have realized he was a two-heart underneath that facade. He presented such a wonderful mask to me, Dan. I thought he was the kindest, gentlest, funniest man in the world. I fell for him so hard that I married him three months after meeting him.

"Within a year of being married to him, I realized I'd married an insanely jealous, controlling monster, not a man. He didn't care about me. Over the years, I realized that he just needed someone else to control, to be a slave to his whims and needs, to cook for him and keep house for him. My love, or whatever it was, died over those years. I felt so trapped, like I was in a prison, or a bad nightmare that just got worse and worse with time. It got so I hated his touch. My skin would crawl when he'd touch me...when he'd kiss me. Toward the end, I'd get physically sick to my stomach if he tried to make love to me."

There, the words were out. Jessica took a deep, ragged breath and risked a look at Dan. To her surprise, his face was open and so readable. Gone was his mask; here was the real man beneath. More than anything, she saw anguish in his dark gray eyes, and his lips were parted, as if he wanted to say something to her.

"There's more," Jessica continued in an unsteady whisper. "Only my sisters know about it, and now Sam, because…well, you'll see. I need to tell you all of this, Dan, because it's not fair to you to walk into something without knowing the whole truth. That's why I have to tell you…." She closed her eyes, unable to stand the judgment she knew would be on his face when she was finished.

"Carl would question my every move. If I went to the grocery store, he would accuse me when I returned of seeing another man. He'd accuse me of sleeping with someone else. But he made up everything in his own sick head. I *never* had an affair, Dan. I never could. I'm just not made that way. It got so I had to not only tell Carl where I was going, but what time I expected to be home. If I wasn't home at that time, all hell would break loose. He'd fly into a fury and he'd accuse me again of having an affair. I tried to tell him I would never be with another man…but," Jessica whispered, "he never believed me."

Rubbing her face, she dropped her hands in her lap and stared across the aisle of the barn, her voice losing all trace of emotion. "The last three years of our marriage were pure hell for me. Carl would hit me and knock me down when I denied I was having an affair. At first he'd just shove me around. Then, later, he'd use his fists and hit me in the stomach. He never hit me anywhere a bruise would show. Over time, his attacks escalated. At the end of the third year, he beat me up so badly that I ended up in the emergency room."

Dan whispered, "Jessica—"

"No...please...let me finish this, Dan. You must." Jessica was too ashamed to look at him. She heard the heartbreaking tone of his voice and it drove tears into her eyes. She fought them back and went on, her words coming out stiltedly, in fits and snatches. Caught up in those terrifying times, she could feel the terror eating her up once again.

"That final time, when I was in the emergency room because of what Carl did to me, I lost consciousness. I remember waking up two weeks later in a Vancouver hospital. The nurse told me I'd been in a coma. I was amazed, because when I lost consciousness, I went into the light. I saw my mother, Dan. She held me while I cried. I had needed her so much over those years, but I was afraid to call home, to tell her what I'd done, what I'd gotten myself into. Carl was just like Kelly, only worse. I'd left home and then married someone just like my father. I felt so humiliated, so stupid, that I didn't want my mother to know...but then she died, too, so I was alone. I didn't call Rachel or Kate because of the same reason. I just felt stupid and shamed.

"When I was with my mother in that beautiful white light, I told her everything. I knew she had gone over the rainbow bridge, and I knew I was talking to her spirit. I thought I'd died, too, and now I could be with her forever, which made me very happy. We had so many wonderful talks and I was able to tell her everything.

"Her love was so great that she told me it was all right, that what I had to do when I got 'back' was to leave Carl. This was a test, she said, to break the bondage of the past with my father, and to move forward, free to soar like the eagle I really could become. My mother said someone would be sent to help me leave Carl and my worthless marriage. She said I would always have protection, from the day I decided to divorce Carl.

"When I regained consciousness, I remembered everything my mother had told me. From my bed, I called an attorney, and then I called the police and got protection. I started divorce proceedings that day. I was so scared, but I was more scared of the hospital releasing me, of going back to that house and Carl. I knew he'd kill me eventually." Her voice broke. "I didn't want to die that way.... I knew life had more to offer than this kind of horrible abuse. I didn't feel I deserved it, but Carl kept telling me how worthless I was, that I was no good, that I was a bad seed. After a while, I bought it. I was brainwashed."

Gently, Dan sat down and put his arms around Jessica. Hot tears stung his eyes as he enclosed her in a light embrace. He felt her tremble, and then she leaned back against him, her head against his shoulder as she surrendered to him completely. The precious gift of her trust sent an incredible joy tunneling through him. Closing his eyes, Dan pressed his face against her hair.

"Listen to me," he whispered unsteadily, "you aren't bad, Jessica. You never were. I—I don't know how you stood eight years of something like that. I couldn't have...." He felt her hands fall over his where he'd clasped them against her torso. "You're a survivor. You know that? Just like that black stallion out there who was beaten within an inch of his life by Kelly."

Jessica relaxed in his arms. She could feel the powerful beat of his heart against her back where she lay against him. His arms were strong and caring. His voice was riddled with emotion—for her. "I don't know how you can hold me, Dan. I really don't...."

He smiled softly and squeezed her momentarily. "I know one thing brings an animal that's been abused out of his pain, and that's love and care."

Jessica wanted to tell him she needed his love, but she didn't dare. It was too soon. Her past had taught her that hurrying into a relationship was not smart or healthy. The other thing she'd discovered was that the fact that she had been raised by an abusive father had led her to marry an abusive man. The clarity of that realization was sinking into her now. But Dan was nothing like her father or Carl.

Then she remembered the fight he'd had that day. "When you protected me against Chet, I was so shocked. I don't know why. When he put his hand over mine to trap me at the door of the truck, I panicked inside. It brought back horrible memories of my abusive marriage."

Jessica stirred in his arms, slowly sitting up and turning to him. Dan's face was filled with sadness, and she saw anger burning in his dark gray eyes now, but she knew it wasn't aimed at her. Placing her hands over his, she whispered, "When you fought them, it just shocked me. I never thought of you as a warrior. And the way you fought..."

"I picked up karate when I was a Recon Marine," he told her. "It comes in handy sometimes."

"Yes...it did. You protected Tommy and me." Looking up at the thick rafters of the barn, Jessica said, "I was so shaken up by it all. I'd escaped Vancouver, the violence, to come here and live in peace."

"And your peace was shattered this morning."

Jessica nodded and knew Dan understood better than anyone else what she'd felt. "Yes," she said simply. "I guess it was stupid and idealistic of me to hope that violence wouldn't follow me. But it has...and will...."

Dan gave her a strange look. "The Cunningham boys and I have tangled before, Jessica. They were after me because of my own past, not because of you."

She held Dan's earnest gaze and felt the powerful blanket of his care enveloping her. "There's something else you need to know, Dan, before this goes any further. You need to know the whole truth."

Dan gave her a puzzled look.

"I already told you about my friend Moyra, how she watched out for me while I was living in Vancouver. When I moved down here because Katie needed me to help try and save our home, Moyra warned me that Carl would come after me. Somehow, he'd find out I'd left Canada and would come and hunt me down. She warned me that he would kill me this time if he got a hold of me." Looking at Dan, she said, "But Moyra also said a man 'clothed in darkness' would be sent to me, to protect me and help me. I believe that's you. The day I first met you, I felt something here, in my heart." She touched her breast with her fingertips. "I don't know what it is, but being around you, Dan, makes me feel clean and pure again, like I felt before I met Carl and married him."

Heat thrummed through Dan—a delicious, warming heat that made his heart open wide like a flower in his chest. Jessica was pale as she spoke now, her face etched with strain and so many emotions. He reached out and captured her hand. Normally, her fingers were warm and dry. Now they were cool and clammy.

"And when you kissed me…" She sighed and closed her eyes, relishing the feel of his roughened fingers wrapping around her cooler hand. "I felt things I'd never felt before in my life." She opened her eyes and held his gaze. Tears slipped down her face. "I felt a joy like I'd never knew existed, Dan. All I had known was one man's kisses… Carl's. Your kiss was like life. His were like death. You were so gentle and coaxing when you kissed me. You didn't take, you shared. I was so stunned by your kiss. Nothing had ever felt so right, so good, to me." Quickly, Jessica looked away, unable to stand the pity she saw in Dan's eyes. "That's why I had to tell you everything," she said hurriedly. "I don't know how you really feel toward me, but I know my feelings for you are growing. I don't want to put you in harm's way. Carl could find me. He's so insanely jealous that—that—if he knew you liked me, just a little, he might kill you, too." Pressing her hands against her face, Jessica cried out brokenly, "And I couldn't stand for that to happen, Dan! I just couldn't!"

Chapter 8

Dan slowly released Jessica and turned her around on the bale of hay they sat on, so that she could look directly at him. It was time to be as completely honest with her as she had been with him. Taking off his sweat-stained leather work gloves, he dropped them to the floor of the barn. Her cheeks glistened with spent tears, and her eyes were red rimmed, filled with sadness, betrayal and fear. And yet as she lifted those thick blond lashes, met and held his intense, burning gaze, he felt his heart lift euphorically in his chest, as if for the first time in his life he was flying.

The sensation was new and startling. Beautiful and filled with hope. Hope wasn't something Dan had ever felt much of. Lifting his hands, he brushed away her tears with trembling fingers. Her skin was soft and warm beneath his touch. He ached to lean forward and kiss her mouth, kiss that trembling lower lip as she clung to him.

"Your life path has been hard," he murmured huskily, allowing his fingers to drop from her cheeks and fold around her hands. "I barely knew any of this. Sam only told me that you would need watching out for when you came here. He didn't say more than that."

"It's pretty sordid, don't you think?" Jessica said. How gentle Dan's face had become. She would never have believed he could be so tender if she hadn't seen it for herself. The harshness of the land he'd been raised on made men hard. All she saw now was his dark, stormy eyes burning with a powerful, intense emotion that caught and held her gently in its embrace. His touch was firm and yet gentling. Perhaps it was the same touch he applied to a scared mustang he was breaking for saddle.

He shook his head. "It's a crime what Carl did to you. You're stronger than I believed." One corner of his mouth hitched upward for just a moment. "If you weren't telling me all of this, I'd never believe it secondhand." Gazing at her face, he touched some tendrils of blond hair and smoothed them across the top of her head. "You don't look scarred, Jessica. You're untouched by the darkness life can wrap us in. Like it did me." He saw the puzzled expression in her eyes. "It's funny how we see other people without really knowing them, or what path they had to endure. I see nothing but the beauty in you—in the way you walk, the way you treat others, the way you lead with your heart, not your head."

Dan's mouth curled into a sarcastic line. "I know you heard what Chet and Bo said about me today at the hay and feed store."

Sniffing, Jessica pulled a tissue from the pocket of her Levi's. "Yes, I did." She blew her nose, apologizing as she tucked the tissue back into her pocket. "Chet and Bo are well known for lying, so I didn't take it seriously."

Dan held her hands firmly. It took every ounce of his escaping courage to hold her gaze and say, "It wasn't lies this time. They were telling the truth about me."

Jessica stared at him, the silence stretching stiltedly between them.

Dan felt his heart begin to beat hard with fear of her rejection. He saw the question, the shock registering in Jessica's easily read expression. Whatever he'd thought he might have with her was rapidly dissolving. Risking it all, he rasped in a low, pain-filled tone, "I never touched alcohol until I entered the Marine Corps. My father was a Recon Marine. He wanted me to be one. That was always his dream for me—to be like him. He was an officer. I went in enlisted because I didn't have the college education that was needed in order to become an officer.

"I wanted him to be proud of me. When I went into the marines, I didn't like it. But I stuck it out and worked hard, and eventually, I was able to go into Recon training. I became a communications specialist for my team of five Recons. Each of us had a skill. Mine was radios, computers and stuff like that.

"I liked the Marine Corps in one way because it was about teamwork. My team was good. One of the best, at Camp Reed out in California. We worked hard together, we played together and—we drank together. It was real easy, after a hard day humping the hills of Reed, to go over to the enlisted men's club and grab a few beers. It never got out of hand.

"When Desert Storm wound up, they sent ten Recon teams over to Iraq. We worked with army special forces and black berets, as well. We were part of a contingent no one has ever known about to this day. We were dropped way behind the lines, to cause havoc among the elite guard units."

"Oh, dear," Jessica whispered. "It must have been dangerous...."

Dan tightened his hands around hers, staring down at their soft, white expanse. "Jessica, what I'm going to share with you, I've never said to another soul. I—I'm ashamed of it. I see it almost every night in my dreams. I wake up drenched in sweat, feeling my heart trying to beat out of my chest, and I want to die."

Murmuring his name softly, Jessica eased her hand from his and rested it against the side of his face. She saw the harshness and judgment in his eyes. "Dan, whatever it is, you can share it with me."

Taking a deep, ragged breath, he rasped, "I ended up killing five men that night. My team and I parachuted into an Iraqi stronghold. We'd gotten bad information. We were surrounded. Once the captain realized what had happened, we went about our business of causing havoc. The ammo dump was blown up, and that was the start of the whole thing. Then we ran out of ammo ourselves. We had no way to get help or support from either the sky or the land units. It ended up," Dan continued, scowling heavily, his voice dropping to a bare whisper, "that the only way we could get out of there alive was to use our Ka-bar knives as weapons...."

Jessica shut her eyes tightly. "Oh, no...."

Something old and hurting shattered inside of Dan. He felt it, felt the pain drifting from his chest down to his knotted gut. "That night I thought I was going to die. In a way, I wanted to. I had to take five men's lives. Their blood is on my hands to this day. I remember every sound, their cries…. I wonder about their families, their loved ones, and the fact their children no longer have fathers to raise them." He swallowed hard, the lump in his throat making his voice tight. He saw Jessica's eyes widen with such pity that he couldn't handle it.

"Two members of my team were badly wounded. Marines never leave their wounded or dead behind. The other three of us got them out of there, past their lines. Then a rescue team began firing artillery blindly into the night, trying to find us. Well…they did. We were heading down off a sand dune when a shell exploded just behind us. I remember the concussion wave slamming me and the marine I had over my shoulders in a fireman's carry, and that was the last thing I recalled."

Jessica held her breath. "You were hurt, too?"

He shrugged. "The pain I carry inside me every day is much worse than the physical wounds I received."

"How badly were you hurt?"

"I was the only one to survive that blast."

Jessica stared at him, watching his thinned mouth work. He would not look at her, only down at her hand, held so tightly in his own. "Thank the Great Spirit you lived," she breathed softly, leaning over and sliding her fingertips along the hard, unforgiving line of his jaw. She felt the prickles of his beard beneath her flesh.

"I was lucky in one sense. Another returning Recon unit found what was left of us right after dawn. They called in a chopper, which took all of us back to a hospital unit in Kuwait. I didn't wake up until a week later, in some hospital in Germany. I had shrapnel all down my back and both legs. I'd taken a piece of metal into my helmet, which tore it off my head." He grimaced. "I guess the docs thought I was going to die because the shrapnel fractured my skull and caused bleeding underneath. The nurses looked pretty surprised when I woke up. The docs were even more surprised when I didn't seem to suffer any aftereffects of the skull injury. My speech was okay, and so was my memory, unfortunately.

"I got a medical discharge from the Marine Corps after that, and I got transferred to Prescott, Arizona, where they have a Veterans Administration hospital. My wounds were healing up fine on the outside, but inside I was falling apart. I couldn't erase any of what I'd done or seen. As soon as I could, I started drinking hard liquor. It was the only thing that stopped the memories, stopped the sounds careening through my head day and night. By the time I left the VA hospital and headed home to Flagstaff where my parents lived, I was drinking a quart of vodka a day."

Jessica sighed. "Oh, Dan, that's terrible. I can't imagine how much pain you were in, how much you were suffering...."

He held her tear-filled gaze. "I'm not proud of what I had become, Jessica. You realize that?" It hurt him worse to say those words than any others he'd ever said to anyone in his life. "Chet was right. I was a drunk for a while. My parents tried to help me, and asked me to move in with them."

With a little cry, Jessica whispered, "Your pain was

so great. You drank because of the pain, not because you craved alcohol."

"That's right," Dan said with a sigh. "But it doesn't matter. I can't handle alcohol. At all." He couldn't believe she was still sitting there with him. People had disdained him for years because of that painful period of his life. "I dishonored myself, and worse, my parents and their good name. I had hit bottom. I decided that the only way to get out of this cycle was to want to do it. My father looked around for a job for me. He knew if he could get me to stop thinking so much about what I'd done, that I could survive it. There was an opening at a Flag ranch for a horse wrangler. I went over there and got the job. I kept it for five years until they let me go. Then Sam asked me to come down here and be the head horse wrangler for your ranch. He couldn't promise much pay up front, but I needed a change. The people up in Flag remember me as a drunk. The stares, the gossip, the looks they always gave me reminded me of my past, my shame...."

Risking everything, Dan looked up. Jessica's face was filled with suffering. When he realized it was for him, that she was not going to judge him harshly as the people of Flagstaff, and those who had heard gossip about him here in Sedona had, his heart took wing like an eagle that had wanted to fly for a long, long time.

"I know Kelly Donovan was a roaring alcoholic," he admitted hoarsely. "But I'm not like your father, Jessica. I would never hurt you or any other woman. Though I did get into a few brawls, all I wanted to do was go and hide away and—cry. I needed to be alone. The Great Spirit knows, I've hurt and killed enough people already—"

"No!" Jessica said fiercely, grabbing his hands. "You killed to survive, Dan. That's different!"

He shook his head. "It's wrong to take another person's life. I'll never do it again. Not *ever*. I—couldn't. The hell I went through just to get this far away from my past has been the hardest thing I've done in my life. When I finally realized what the alcohol was doing— when I finally got tired of watching my mother grow old because of my choices—I quit." He shook his head. "If I had to kill again, I'd probably go put a bullet in my head afterward because I couldn't handle the pain, the guilt and all the crap that went with it. I'm not that strong. I try and ignore those voices in my head, the faces I see in my nightly dreams."

"Dan, you're an amazing person," Jessica said gently. "You've gone through hell and come out the other side of it. Yes, your spirit was wounded, but you had what it took to pull yourself up by your own bootstraps."

He crooked his mouth a little and looked up at her. "So did you."

"Maybe we don't give ourselves enough credit for our strength and courage," Jessica admitted sadly. "I know I'm horribly ashamed of my past, of my inability to leave Carl before he put me in the hospital."

"Jessica," Dan whispered in a raw tone, "you were like a beaten animal. You came from a family where your father did not respect women. What you have to understand, *shi shaa,* is that when you met Carl, that was the only kind of man you knew. Like draws like. Because you are so intuitive, you, more than most, must realize that. The Navajo have a saying—we attract what we are or we attract what we need. You were young, running away from home, probably homesick, scared and alone in Vancouver. You had no friends, so when Carl saw your beauty, your cleanness, he was like a wolf leaping on an unprotected lamb."

She nodded, amazed by Dan's insight, his understanding of what had really happened up in Vancouver. "You're right—I was scared and alone. I didn't know what I was going to do. I cried all the time because I missed Mama, I missed this ranch…but I didn't miss Kelly. I was so scared of him, Dan. I used to hide under the bed when he was drunk. I remember crawling under it and then rolling into the fetal position, my head buried against my knees. Mama did what she could to protect us, but she couldn't be in three places at once. Kelly usually picked on Kate, not me or Rachel half as much." She shook her head, tears spilling from her eyes. "It's all so sad, Dan. So sad…. Kelly destroyed our family with his drinking binges. And for what?"

"I heard from Sam that Kelly was in the war," Dan murmured. "That he had post-traumatic stress disorder. I'm not making excuses for him, but my gut hunch was that he drank for the same reasons I did—the horror of what we had to do in a wartime situation, or what he saw…."

"Probably," she sniffed. "But it didn't give him the right to abuse us, either."

"No, it didn't," Dan admitted quietly, studying her flushed, glistening face.

She drowned in his dark gray gaze. "You said something in Navajo just a minute ago. I know you've said it to me a couple of times. What does it mean?" She took a clean tissue from her pocket and wiped her face free of tears.

Avoiding her searching look, Dan tightened his mouth. "I have no right to call you what I did. I'm sorry...."

"No!" Jessica slid her hand into his. There were so many white scars across the darkness of his hand. His fingers were calloused and rough, and she ached to feel them once again, moving against her body. What would it be like to love Dan? The thought was exhilarating, scary and appealing to Jessica. She was surprised, because she'd thought she was emotionally dead. She thought Carl had destroyed whatever her heart could feel of desire, need and love. "Please," she begged, "share with me what you said."

Heat crept up into his face and he compressed his lips.

The silence hung between them. Did he dare? Dan knew that once she understood what it was, the utter intimacy of it, that it would reveal far too much of how he really felt about her. Jessica knew Navajo ways. She understood that certain sayings, certain words, such as his endearment for her, were never said unless meant from one's heart.

Yes, she had accepted his sordid, drunken history, but so what? She might see him as the spitting image of her father. Maybe Jessica would never get beyond seeing the overlay of Kelly on him, would never accept him for who he was—a man who was falling helplessly in love with her. Dan wanted to say all of this, but he was afraid to. Right now, he felt raw inside from revealing his dark past. He could see the fragility written across Jessica's sweet face, too.

"I had no right to call you what I did," he repeated. "I'm afraid of what you'll do if I share it with you right now, Jessica. We're both hurting...."

She took a deep breath and straightened her shoulders slightly. "I know we're raw, Dan. Maybe we needed to share our pasts with one another for whatever reason. I'm not sorry we did. Are you?"

He shook his head. "No...."

"And your kiss...?"

He snapped a look at her. "That was a mistake...a stupid reaction on my part, Jessica. I had no right, no—"

"Hush," she whispered, placing her fingertips across his strong mouth. "Don't apologize for that, too," she said, a partial smile on her lips. "I liked it, Dan. And since we're telling the truth here, I think I should share with you how much I liked it...."

He took her fingers in his hand, kissed the center of her soft palm and felt a fine tremble go through her. He couldn't believe what he was hearing. Yet as he ruthlessly searched the depths of her glorious eyes, he saw no lies in them. Only a shining warmth that enveloped him like sunshine on a bitterly cold winter day.

"I never thought," Jessica said in a choking voice, "that I would *ever* want a man to kiss me again. Carl, well, he didn't care what I wanted. Ever. He made me hate his kiss. And soon, I hated him. I guess, in the end, I hated all men because of him. Moyra told me that with time, I'd be able to separate Carl from the rest of the men in my life, but I didn't believe her." Jessica slid her hand against Dan's cheek and held his widening gaze.

"When I came here and I met you, something happened, Dan. I still don't know what it is, or pretend to understand it all—yet. I just know that with you, I feel safe—and good. I can feel again. You know, real feelings. Before now, I thought Carl had killed my heart, beaten my spirit. The only time I felt good, felt alive and happy, was when I was working with my orchid girls. My heart would open and I would feel such joy, such pure love from them surrounding me. I would love them back in my own, wounded way, I suppose.

"With you," Jessica continued, giving him a shy look, "I began to experience feelings I'd never felt before in my life. I'd never felt them toward Carl. And all you had to do was be with me. It's kind of wonderful—but kind of scary, too."

Capturing her hand, Dan kissed the back of it gently and said, "You're like that stallion out there in many ways. He's coming around because I'm gentle with him. I use a gentle touch and voice. I would never do anything to hurt him or make him want to distrust me." He smiled a little. "Although he watches me like a hawk, I give him no reason to think I'm like the other men who he's grown to hate and be wary of."

"We're a lot alike, Gan and I," Jessica agreed painfully. "Now you're able to put a saddle on him and ride him. I find that amazing, but in another way, I don't."

"Why?" Dan absorbed the softness of her skin as he moved his thumb across her palm. Touching Jessica was like feeling the sun shining down into his dark, scarred heart. She gave him hope, and so much more....

"It tells me about your quality as a person, what you bring to the situation, Dan. That stallion out there is smarter than most human beings. He's got a wild, innate intelligence, a survival drive. He knows who he can really trust and who he can't." She reached over and pressed her hand, palm down, against the center of Dan's chest and felt the pounding beat of his heart. "No matter how much darkness you've been wrapped in, trapped within, Gan saw your purity, your heart's intentions. He *knows* you won't ever hurt him. You would never lay a finger on someone to hurt them. Even I know that."

"Then why doesn't that stud pick up the fact that I killed five men?"

"He knows the same thing I do," Jessica whispered unsteadily. "That you didn't do it out of enjoyment or pleasure. Gan instinctively knows that you, like him, have the ability to survive some awful storms in life. You're a survivor, as he is. As I am. He trusts you. So do I…."

Closing his eyes, Dan felt her move her hand from the center of his chest upward. His skin tightened deliciously beneath her light, hesitant exploration of his chest and shoulder. As her fingers curved around the back of his neck, an ache built in his lower body. He wanted her. Great Spirit help him, but he wanted all of her, from her bright, shining soul, to her wounded heart and beautiful physical body. And yet, his heart cautioned, Jessica was no different from Gan—badly brutalized and beaten by a man. Dan realized fully that he couldn't just sweep her off her feet, carry her to his bed and love her wildly, fully and with all the hunger he felt. She was still too emotionally wounded from her bad marriage to an abusive man. Dan knew that he had to move slowly, gain her trust and let her tell him when and if she was ready for him to love her.

His heart broke over that realization. Nothing bad should ever have happened to Jessica. She was an innocent victim in all of this. Completely innocent. She'd been a child scared into hiding deep within herself, and then to have a monster like Carl come and complete the damage to her spirit by destroying her femininity was almost too much for him to bear. But as Jessica explored him now with her sweet, almost shy, exquisite touch, he understood what she was doing. For some reason unknown to him, she was giving her trust to him, as that stallion had done. For him to reach out and respond in like manner would scare her away, too.

Opening his eyes, Dan held her luminous blue gaze. "Whatever we have," he rasped, "is good and clean and pure, Jessica. You never have to be scared of me. You can keep on trusting me. I won't take your trust and twist it like Carl did. You're too beautiful…too pure of heart, to do that to. No human should be disrespected. No one." He slowly reached up for the hand she had wrapped around his neck and eased it away. "Right now, all I want to do is kiss you and return to you in some way the feelings you're sharing with me, but I won't unless you tell me you want me to."

A sweet hotness moved through Jessica as he took her hand between his own. Dan was more than a stallion tamer; he was taming a wounded, hurting woman—herself. His gentleness was real. Still, it seemed incredible to her that any man could possess such sensitivity. And yet, as she clung to Dan's dark gray eyes, she not only heard his words, she felt them in every dark corner of her scarred spirit. Her lips parted and she shyly leaned toward him.

"Yes," she whispered unsteadily, "kiss me. Again." Closing her eyes, she felt his hands fall away from hers. The seconds seemed so long as she waited to once again feel his strong mouth upon hers. She no longer knew what was happening between them or why. She no longer tried to sort it out, nor did she care to.

As Dan's lips covered hers, the warmth of his breath

cascaded down across her cheek. Sighing, she felt his roughened hands move slowly upward, across her exposed flesh, and a delicious prickle began within her. The very motion of his hands massaging the tension away lulled her into a euphoria she'd never felt before. His mouth moved tenderly across hers, giving, not taking. She felt his power, but she also felt him monitoring how much strength he put against her lips, too. His beard was rough and sandpapery against her cheek as she turned her head to more fully press her lips to his. His fingers drifted to her shoulders, then traced the outline of her neck until finally, he gently captured her face between his hands. She felt no fear, only a deep ache throbbing between her legs, longing to have him completely, and in all ways.

With each gliding movement, he rocked her lips open a little more, tasted a little more deeply of her. Jessica sighed, realizing with amazement that she wanted to feel and taste him more deeply, too. For the first time, she felt bold, as if she could risk it all and explore this powerful man wrapped in darkness. Carl had always taken from her, hurt her. Now Dan was asking her to take however much of him she wanted. Pressing herself more surely against him until her breasts barely grazed his chest wall, she embraced his strong, corded neck and felt him tremble. But the sensation didn't frighten her, it excited her.

As she moved her lips in a soft, searching motion across his mouth, she felt desire pouring through her. Each time she kissed him, he returned the kiss with equal strength, but he never did anything more than that. Her hands drifted to his head and she removed his hat. She heard it drop to the floor as she lost herself in the sensation of running her fingers through his thick, short black hair. It was so soft and yet strong, like Dan. Moving her fingers downward, she felt his sculpted brow and then the wrinkles at the corners of his eyes. He trembled again and his hands moved to her face. As she slowly absorbed each line in his skin, each part of his face, he felt hers, too.

It was a delicious, pleasurable exploration, Jessica realized. There was safety here in Dan's arms. *And love,* her heart whispered. At first, she didn't catalog her feelings because she was too caught up in the sensation of Dan's breath against her cheek, the movement of his strong mouth against hers and the thudding beat of his heart against her breasts. Finally, she eased her mouth from his. As she did, she barely opened her eyes before she drowned once again in the burning grayness of his. They slowly drew apart, his hands steadying on her shoulders as she created more space between them. Her world spun out of control and she felt heady, almost dizzy, until Dan's hands tightened around her arms to support her.

Her lips felt lush and full and well kissed. She stared up at him and marveled at what she was feeling. "I..." she whispered. "I've never been kissed like that before in my life, Dan. It was so wonderful. You are wonderful...."

Chapter 9

The hot August sunlight was scorching the ranch and sucking out the very lifeblood from the drought-ridden land, Jessica noted with growing dismay. She had just finished filling orders for her flower essences when Kate stepped into the doorway of the greenhouse.

"Anything's better than that heat out there," Kate groused, taking off her cowboy hat and wiping the perspiration from her darkly tanned brow. "How are things going? We haven't seen each other in the past couple of days."

Kate joined Jessica as she sat on her workbench, the cobalt blue bottles labeled and set in groups on the table before her. Jessica looked up and smiled at her older sister as Kate placed a hand on her shoulder and said, "You've been looking awfully happy lately. What's going on?"

"Questions, questions, Katie," she said with a laugh.

"You won't even let me answer the first one before you fire off one or two more." Placing the order sheets aside, she brushed back a few crinkly tendrils that had escaped from her ponytail as Kate sat down on the wooden crate next to her workbench.

"First, I'm fine. Secondly, there's lots of orders coming in and yes, I'm happy." She grinned. "Now are *you* happy?"

Kate reached for the plastic bottle of water Jessica always had on her bench and took a swig from it. She recapped it and set it between them. "You look happier than usual. And Dan has sure been changing, too," she hinted.

"How has he changed?"

Kate grinned belatedly. "Like he's walking on cloud nine. You know…. Sam and I have been wondering when things were going to gel between you two."

The serious expression on Kate's face was belied by the dancing sparkle in her eyes. Jessica relaxed. "Pretty obvious, huh?"

"A little…but then, when two people are in love, well, it sort of becomes obvious."

"It's not love," Jessica said quickly. "I like him an awful lot, Katie, but—love? No, I don't think so."

Her sister scrutinized her for a long moment without speaking. "It's Carl, isn't it? You're still scared of him finding you. And that's why you can't openly admit you love Dan?"

"No," Jessica said softly as she folded her hands in the lap of her dark pink skirt decorated with bright yellow marigolds, purple irises and pale pink tulips. "It's— I, well, I'm just wary, I guess, Kate. You know how Carl treated me. My stupid head gets in the way when Dan touches me. It triggers a lot of bad memories."

"Yeah." Kate sighed, reaching out and putting her work-worn hand across Jessica's. "I know that one." She squeezed her sister's clasped fingers. "It takes time, Jessica. You have to give yourself that leeway and don't expect miracles."

"Dan has been so patient with me." Jessica pulled her hands from Kate's and gestured with them. "His kisses are wonderful. I've never been kissed like he kisses me." Sighing, she whispered, "And when he touches me, I feel like I'm on fire and I'm so hungry for him…." She laughed, embarrassed by her admission.

With a crooked smile, Kate nodded. "Sam makes me feel the same way."

"I'm just, well, afraid, Katie, that's all. Dan knows it. He's patient with me. And…" She frowned. "And he's afraid you and Sam won't approve of his feelings toward me."

With a laugh, Kate stood up and stuffed her leather gloves into the belt at her waist. "Why not?"

"He's got this thing in his head that he's not good enough for me, Kate. That because he doesn't own land and have money in the bank, he's in a lower class than me. Isn't that stupid?"

With a shake of her head, Kate muttered, "Well, Dan sure as heck isn't getting rich working here. He's got this class thing hammered into his head from the res. There's a lot of Anglos who think they're better than the Navajo people, but that's pure bull. No, Sam and I consider Dan an equal, like you do. So don't worry about it." Her brow wrinkled as she looked around the lush greenhouse where so many of the orchids were in colorful bloom. "If only this damn drought would just end. We've lost so many cattle by having to sell them off because we can't feed them. We've lost money." With a sigh, Kate placed her hand on Jessica's sagging shoulder. "Without your financial input, we'd be waiting for the banker to come down the road to foreclose on the ranch. Damn, I just wish this poverty cycle with the ranch would end."

"I pray for rain every day," Jessica said passionately. "I worry about these hot winds we're having. Lightning could strike one of the tinder-dry pastures and we'd have a ranch fire on our hands. So much could be destroyed."

"This is monsoon season," Kate griped, patting her sister's shoulder one more time, "but whoever heard of *dry* monsoons? Usually, we get four inches of rain in three months. Enough to sustain life around here for the following six months." Her mouth moved into a grim line. "All we have now are incredibly beautiful thunderheads that build around ten in the morning. And when the thunder and lightning start around three p.m., that's when Sam and I begin to worry about forest and range fires."

"Speaking of Sam," Jessica said, trying to dissolve the worried look from Kate's eyes, "have you two decided on *when* you're going to get married?"

She shook her head and settled the hat back on her dark hair. "We're working sixteen hours a day. Who has time to discuss the future? Every day we get up, Jessica, there's a hundred things that need to be done and we divide the list between us. By the time we fall into bed at night, we're so exhausted we can't talk." She pulled the gloves from her belt and jerked them back on her hands. "No, until we become more financially stable, I just don't feel we can take the time and energy to finalize wedding plans."

Sadly, Jessica nodded. "I understand. At least you have one another. Sam loves you so much."

"I know," Kate whispered, tears glimmering in her eyes. "I don't know what I did to deserve him, but Lord help me, I love him with every breath I take into this bruised, beaten body of mine."

"If things start turning for the better, maybe a marriage, say, in December? Rachel's coming home at that time," Jessica hinted.

Kate nodded. "Sam mentioned that time frame, too. We can sell some of the Herefords to meet our expenses. I'm all for it." She grinned and ruffled Jessica's bangs. "And you…when are you going to fess up to doing something more than 'liking' Dan? The guy has cow eyes for you every time he sees you."

"Cow eyes," Jessica protested with a giggle. "He does not!"

"That's what we called boys in junior high, remember? If they got a crush on some girl but never had the guts to go over and tell her because they were too scared?" Kate's smile broadened as she considered Jessica's blazing cheeks. "Sam says that since coming here, Dan has really straightened out. I told him it was your influence. He said it probably was, that Dan wanted to put the past behind him and make a more positive statement with his life. He's done that. He works just as hard as we do and he's getting a pittance of what he should be getting. But—" she winked at Jessica "—he's got something else here at the ranch that's giving him reason to work hard—you."

Touching her hot cheeks, Jessica avoided Kate's laughter-filled eyes. "Oh, Katie, you're reading too much into it. Dan's never said he loved me."

"You said it to him?"

"Well, no… I don't know if I really am in love or not…."

"Silly girl," Kate chided as she walked toward the door, "what's the poor guy to do? If you don't say it, how can he? What's it going to take to get you to see the guy loves you more than life—an act of Congress? I hope your fear goes away soon, or Dan's gonna die of loneliness out there in the bunkhouse."

Squirming inwardly, Jessica watched her big sister open the door to the greenhouse. "Hey, I'm going to leave tomorrow morning and go up near the Rim in the north pasture to try and find some wildflowers to make some new flower essences with."

Kate turned, her gloved hand on the door. "You taking Pete, the packhorse, again? Last time you went out, you made something like ten new essences."

Jessica nodded and slid off the stool. "Yes, Dan's going to get my gelding and the packhorse ready for me tomorrow morning. I hope to scour the Rim itself and see if anything else is up there. I'm taking my wildflower identification books with me and my log and my camera. I'll be up there until about two p.m. I want to be down off the Rim before those lightning bolts start flying."

"Hmm, good idea." Kate patted the redwood frame of the door with her hand. "Okay. But I don't think you're going to find anything alive up on the Rim, especially wildflowers. It's been over a hundred degrees every day and the humidity is so low that the forest service says the pine trees up there are going to start dying off soon because of no rain. I don't know how a wildflower could be alive, much less blooming in those kinds of conditions."

Shrugging, Jessica couldn't disagree. "It's a scouting expedition, is all. I've been wanting to explore that area of the ranch, anyway."

"Probably to get into some cooler air," Kate teased, lifting her hand in a wave. "I'll see you then, tomorrow afternoon sometime? Is Dan going with you? He did last time."

"No, he's at a crucial point in Gan's training."

"Okay, but be careful. There's a lot of rattlers out this time of year."

"I hear you," Jessica said, and watched her sister disappear through the door.

"I wish I were going with you," Dan said as Jessica mounted her small gray Arabian gelding, Jake. Though Jessica wasn't the best of riders, Jake, who was over twenty, was steady and reliable. Dan gazed up into Jessica's face and saw the excitement in her eyes over the daylong adventure ahead of her. She had been working so hard at her business that Dan knew she needed this kind of minivacation from the greenhouse activities.

Jessica reached out and touched his gloved hand, which rested on her thigh. "I wish you were coming, too. Are you sure Gan isn't tractable enough to ride so you could?"

He shook his head. "No, Gan's been backing up on me, testing me. I can ride him in pastures and open areas, but when I try to get him into woods, he starts getting real skittish and hard to handle. He's not given his trust to me fully yet. Until he does, he's a danger to ride anywhere but on the flatlands of the ranch."

Jessica leaned down and quickly brushed his mouth with a kiss, relishing the hot, returning passion of his lips against hers. He gripped her arm, holding her in place to give her a long, thorough goodbye kiss. Her heart pounding, Jessica found herself aching for him again, just as she did every time he kissed her or touched her. "I'll miss you," she said breathlessly, sitting up in the saddle.

"Three p.m. can't come too soon," he rasped, reluctantly releasing her. As he stood there looking up at her, sitting so proudly in the saddle, he wanted to love her so badly he could taste it. He wanted to do more than love Jessica physically. He wanted to speak the words. She wasn't ready for that, he knew, but it didn't help him. Swallowing, he stepped back and smiled up at her. Jessica didn't look like a cowboy, wearing a straw hat with silk flowers affixed to the wide brim. Her white, simple tank top, dark blue jeans and comfortable leather loafers completed the picture. Cowgirl she was not. And he loved her with a fierceness that defied description.

"Hey," Jessica called as she picked up the packhorse's soft cotton lead rope, "do you want to see a movie tonight in Sedona?"

"Sure."

She laughed softly. "Okay, let's make it a date!" Then she clapped her heels and Jake moved off at a steady, slow jog.

Dan watched her form grow small against the towering Rim country that was topped with pine trees thousands of feet above them. The sun was coming up over the canyon wall and he knew it was going to be another blisteringly hot day. He had to get the work done now, while it was still somewhat cool. From one p.m. to seven p.m., he worked indoors because the unrelenting, hundred-degree heat made it nearly impossible to stay outside.

Something bothered him, but he couldn't put a finger on it. Taking off his hat, he rubbed the back of his sunburned neck ruefully before settling the hat back into place. He had an uneasy, gnawing feeling in his gut. The last time he'd had this feeling was when he was dropped behind the lines in Iraq. Why now?

Unable to make heads or tails out of it, Dan moved in long, easy strides back to Gan's pasture to work with the stallion. Right now, he had to concentrate entirely on the stud or he could end up on the ground. That Arabian was smart. Too smart for his own good, Dan thought with a careless grin. But with patience and time, the stallion would reward him with his trust.

Looking over his shoulder one last time, he saw that Jessica had already disappeared behind the ranch buildings. Something niggled at him again. Frowning, he shrugged it off and went to work.

"Dan! Dan!"

Dan was pounding a shoe into place on one of Gan's hooves when he heard Kate's terrified voice. He saw her run into the barn.

"Whoa," he murmured in a low voice to the stallion. "Stand…"

The black Arabian's small ears twitched nervously as Kate came running down the aisle. Dan quickly finished putting the last nails in the shoe and allowed the stallion to stand on all four legs. Automatically, he put a soothing hand on the stud's arched neck. He could feel the sudden tension in him.

"What's wrong, Kate?" he asked as he removed the thick leather blacksmith's apron from around his waist. He saw that Kate's eyes were wide with terror and his gut shrank as he walked down the aisle to meet her. Gan wasn't too trustful of other human beings yet, and he didn't want the horse starting to rear upward in the cross ties.

"Dan!" she cried, breathless. "Jake's back!"

He frowned as he watched her halt, her breathing harsh. "Jessica's back?" It was three p.m.—time she returned.

"No," Kate rasped, holding up her hand, trying to catch her breath. "Jake just came galloping into the yard. He's covered with sweat! Jessica wasn't on him!"

His eyes narrowed. "Jessica…"

"Yes." Kate leaned over, her hands on her thighs as she took in huge gulps of air. "I'm afraid, Dan. I've had a bad feeling since I woke up this morning. Something's happened to Jessica. Sam's in Flagstaff and I can't reach him. We've got to get out to find Jessica. She said she was going to the north pasture. I'm going to drive out there right now. Maybe Jake just spooked and took off. I don't know, but I'm worried."

So was Dan. Frowning, he hung the leather apron on a nail. "Jake isn't the type of gelding to spook or run off, Kate. He's ground trained." That meant that if anyone dropped the animal's reins, he would halt and not move a muscle until those reins were picked up by the rider once again. Terror began to flood Dan as he stood there, his brain racing with questions and possible answers. "What about Pete, the packhorse?"

"No sign of him."

"Well, even if Jake did startle and take off for some unknown reason, Jessica could ride Pete back to the ranch."

Kate wiped her brow with trembling hands. "I've already thought of that, Dan. Oh, God, I'm afraid it's Carl."

Dan froze. *Carl.* How could he forget about the insanely jealous ex-husband of Jessica's? A steel hand suddenly gripped his heart, the pain excruciating. "No!" he rasped, his eyes narrowing to slits.

"I don't know for sure," Kate whispered brokenly. "Jessica's enough of a rider. She's not the type to get thrown off. I'm going to drive out there and see if I can locate her or Pete." She gulped, her eyes filled with fear. "Dan, if I can't find them, I *know* Carl has kidnapped her. Just like he threatened he would."

"That means we need to call the police. A search will have to be mounted," he rasped.

"Yes. Look, I'll drive out right now. It shouldn't take more than half an hour by truck at high speed. You stay here. I'll call you on the cell phone and let you know if I find her. In the meantime, if I don't find her, you're going to have to try and track her. You're the best tracker in the county. If Carl has kidnapped her, he's got some heavy forest to get through before he can get to 89A and then drive off with her."

"*If* he drives off with her."

Anguished, Kate looked away. "He said he'd kill her. Oh, Lord…"

Gripping Kate's arm, Dan propelled her down the aisle and out of the barn. "Get out to the north pasture as fast as you can. I'm going to saddle Gan and take a rifle, ammunition, food and a cell phone with me. If Jessica isn't out there, I'll call 911 and get the sheriff out here, then hightail it toward you. I'll tell the police your location and then meet you out there."

Kate nodded. "Gan's the only horse that has the stamina this is going to take. That Rim country is rough and dangerous, Dan. He's got nine lives."

"Yeah," he whispered, opening the door to the white pickup truck for Kate, "and he's going to need every single one of them." He saw the paleness on her face, the fear in her eyes. He felt the same. Giving her a pat on the arm, he said, "Remember, I'll have the other cell phone with me. Call me as soon as you know…."

Kate choked back a sob. "Y-yes. I'm so scared, Dan. I thought this was all over. I hope I'm wrong. Maybe I'm jumping to conclusions."

He was helpless to assuage her pain and worry. "Drive carefully out there," he cautioned. "Keep your eyes open, Kate. If Carl's half as dangerous as Jessica says he is, the man could have a rifle and could train his sights on you, too."

Grimly, Kate nodded. "I'll be in touch very soon…."

Dan had just finished saddling Gan, packing the leather sheath with the 30.06 rifle and his knife scabbard and strapping a heavy set of saddlebags in place with more ammunition, when Kate's call came. Grabbing the cell phone, Dan pressed the On button.

"Kate?" His heart was pounding in his chest. He could barely breathe as he waited to hear Kate's report.

"It's horrible, Dan!"

He gripped the phone hard. "What do you mean?"

"Pete's dead! The gelding's been shot through the

head," Kate sobbed, trying to speak coherently. "Jessica's nowhere. All her stuff—her bowls, the water and logbook—are scattered around the area. I see some signs of scuffling, but I'm not enough of a tracker to know what the hell it means. Oh, Dan, Carl's got her! Call the sheriff!"

Closing his eyes, his mind whirling, Dan whispered, "Get a hold of yourself, Kate. Tell me exactly where you're located."

"I'm at the most northern part of our pasture, at the gate that leads up the path to the Rim."

"Good. I'll call the sheriff. When's Sam due back?"

"Tonight," Kate cried, sniffling. "Everything is such a mess out here. There's paper that's been torn out of Jessica's sketchbook crumpled up all over the place. She'd never do that. She loved her drawings of plants. He'll kill her, Dan! I know he will! He's an insane bastard. Oh, Lord…"

"Kate, come back. Now. You have to be here when the sheriff arrives. I'm going to mount Gan. I'll take a shortcut to the north gate. Just tell the sheriff I'm tracking them from this end. I'll keep the cell phone in my saddlebags. I'll call you if I see anything, all right?"

"O-okay…" She replied with another sob.

Shutting off the cell phone, Dan carefully placed it in the left saddlebag. Gan, sensing his trepidation, pawed the aisle, snorting and moving his head up and down.

Stay calm, stay calm, Dan harshly ordered himself as he mounted the black stallion. But he couldn't. As he turned Gan out of the barn into the intense afternoon sunlight, he felt like crying. Jessica…sweet, innocent Jessica, had been kidnapped by a man who'd sworn to take her life. No! No! He clapped his heels to the flanks of the stallion and instantly Gan responded. The horse was not large, but he was built like a proverbial bull, heavily muscled in the hind quarters with a wide chest and a long slope to his shoulders, indicating larger than normal lung capacity.

As Dan rode the stallion away from the ranch buildings, he felt the powerful surge of the animal beneath him. What would Gan do in the Rim country? The stallion shied at everything. Gan could throw him, or worse, slam him into a tree to get rid of him. Dan's gloved hands tightened on the leather reins as he leaned low, the horse's black mane whipping into his sweaty face as they sped along the hard, dry road toward the north pasture. He was going to need every ounce of Gan's power, his heart and his spirit. He was going to ask everything of this horse, and he prayed that the stallion trusted him enough to give everything in return. Jessica's life was in the balance. He could feel it. He could taste it.

"You little bitch!"

Jessica shrieked as Carl reached out to grab her by the hair, all because she'd tripped and fallen over some black lava rock hidden by dried pine needles on the forest floor. She felt his hand thrust into her hair, his fingers curl and tighten. Her scalp radiated with pain as he hauled her upward. Hands bound behind her, she had no choice as Carl brought her up hard against him. Staggering to catch her balance, Jessica shut her eyes. She expected him to slap her. Instead, Carl shoved her ahead of him again.

"Get moving faster!" he snarled, poking the rifle barrel into her back. "We've got to be at 89A before sundown. And if we aren't—" he grinned "—I'll shoot you anyway."

She gasped for breath. She had been pushed into a jog repeatedly for the last two hours. With her hands bound, she often lost her balance on the slippery, dry pine needles. Her knees were skinned and her joints ached. But that was nothing compared to the unadulterated terror she felt in her heart. Carl had found her. He intended to kill her. It was that simple. That terrifyingly simple.

Chapter 10

By six p.m. Dan was still moving the stallion along at a brisk walk, following the trail barely visible in the pine needles up on the Rim. Three hours had seemed like a lifetime. He'd called in his findings to the sheriff. Overhead, he could hear a helicopter hovering around the general area where he was tracking.

The prints he saw were of two people. A number of times, pine needles were scattered helter-skelter. He was sure Jessica had either fallen or been pushed down on the ground. His mind refused to contemplate why she would be shoved down on the dry, hard forest floor.

Gan was snorting and wringing with sweat, his ebony skin reflecting every muscle movement. Luckily, the stallion had expended a great amount of energy on his heroic climb up the Rim so that by the time they got on top of the three-thousand-foot crest, he didn't have much energy left to be shying at every pine tree they passed.

All of Dan's old military training had come back in startling fashion. He felt as if the forest had eyes—that every dark apparition and shadow was potentially Carl Roman. He didn't know what Jessica's ex-husband looked like. She never spoke of him except when necessary. She was trying to put him and their terrible relationship behind her. Dan couldn't blame her, but right now, he wished he knew what the man looked like. He could tell a lot by looking at a person's face. There was no doubt Carl could kill Jessica—and probably would try. But was the man good at hiding in a forest? Was he a true hunter in that sense? Or only a crazed, insanely jealous man who would make mistakes out here—enough for Dan to continue to track him?

Or maybe Carl knew how to throw a tracker off a trail. Was he that good? Dan was unsure. All he could do was lean over the stallion and follow the wisps of evidence in the disturbed pine needles. The sun's rays were long now. Sunset wasn't until around eight p.m., and then Dan would have just enough light until nine p.m., when it grew totally dark. He had a flashlight and he would use it to follow the trail if necessary. But he also knew he would be a target with that light on. It was a risk he was willing to take.

His mind went back to the dead packhorse. Because of his Recon background, Dan could see that Carl had used a high-powered rifle to shoot the innocent horse in one clean shot. Carl knew how to use the rifle, there was no question. Mouth compressed, Dan halted the stallion, took the canteen from the side of the saddle and drank a little water. Luckily, he knew this country well. He'd chased his fair share of cattle that had broken through the barbed wire fence—sometimes chased them for days at a time. Carl was heading due west, probably trying to intercept 89A. What Carl didn't know was that the sheriff was patrolling that area, too.

The cell phone rang. Dan retrieved it from the saddlebag.

"Dan? It's Sam."

"Yeah, I hear you, but you're breaking up a lot." Dan knew the cell phone wouldn't work well as he rode more deeply into the forest. "What's up?"

"The sheriff found a Ford camper with Canadian license plates parked on the berm along 89A. They broke into it and found the registration for the truck—in Carl Roman's name. It's him. And he's got Jessica."

Mouth flattening, Dan glared ahead at the murky depths of the dry pine forest. "Yes…"

"The helicopter is up and searching. They haven't seen anything yet, but that forest is thick."

"They'll be lucky to spot anything," he growled as he continued to look around. Sweat trickled down his temples.

"Have you found anything?"

"Just two sets of tracks. They're heading due west."

"Toward the highway?"

"Yes."

"Well, that bastard will have a real surprise waiting for him. They've called in the Yavapai SWAT team. They'll be in position in an hour near the camper if Carl manages to evade you and make it that far with Jessica. The sheriff said that if they get a clear shot of Roman, they're taking him down. No questions asked.

No negotiations. They got the prison info on this guy
and it's not pretty. He murdered a man in cold blood."

A chill ran through Dan. "I understand."

"No, you don't," Sam said harshly. "That means if
you find them, Dan, you're to take Carl out if you can.
You were a sharpshooter in the Recons. If you find him,
take your time, target him and blow him away. He won't
let Jessica live. The sheriff thinks, based upon Roman's
profile, that he'll more than likely try to rape her first
and then kill her. They've got the hospital and police
reports from Vancouver. I've seen them. Believe me,
this bastard is crazy and he'll kill Jessica."

"Rape?" The word almost strangled him.

"Spousal rape. It's on Roman's rap sheet from the
police. Jessica charged him with it after he put her into
the hospital and into a coma."

Dan shut his eyes tightly, tasting even more terror.
"I—understand."

"I'm going to be riding with the sheriff along 89A.
They'll be patrolling it from Flag down to our ranch.
I'll be in touch. Just be careful."

"Yeah…"

Taking a ragged breath, Dan put the cell phone back
in the saddlebags. Rape. Jessica had been raped repeatedly by the son of a bitch. No wonder she was afraid of
him. Dan tasted bile in his mouth and he wanted to vomit.
Closing his fist over the saddle horn, he tried to get a
hold on his unraveling emotions. Jessica had never talked
about rape. Oh, she'd skirt around it when pressed, but
he'd had no idea. None… Wiping his face with the back
of his hand, he grimly swung Gan into a fast walk. Now
more than ever he had to find her, before it was too late.

His heart wouldn't stop pounding. His emotions

whipsawed. He'd have to kill a man—again. In cold blood. So much of him rebelled at the idea, and yet another part of him *wanted* to kill Carl Roman for what he'd done to Jessica. Guilt rubbed Dan raw, but his cold rage toward the man pushed him onward. Carl Roman was less than animal. Animals never killed except to eat, to survive. Roman killed because he enjoyed it. He didn't have to kill the packhorse, but he had.

The fact that Carl savored killing scared Dan more than anything. Roman had no feelings. He was a dead man walking. And he had Jessica. How much Dan loved her! Wiping his mouth, he stared hard at the tracks in front of them. Why hadn't he *told* her that? Why? Maybe it would have given her hope, a fighting spirit to try and escape Carl. A serrating loneliness cut through Dan—along with terror for Jessica. He couldn't begin to imagine how she was feeling. Pushing Gan faster, he urged the stallion into a slow jog. The prints on the forest floor were fairly obvious now and he had to try and catch up with their makers.

Up ahead, he knew the Rim began to drop down to the canyon floor three thousand feet below, where Oak Creek wound through the sharp, pinnacled red sandstone, the black lava spires. After passing through there, Carl would have to climb up the other side, another two-thousand-foot incline, to finally reach the highway where his truck was parked. Now was the time to push the stallion. Once they got off the Rim and down among the dangerous, sharp rocks, Dan would have to be very careful or risk his and his horse's life.

"Sit down!" Carl snarled at Jessica.

She collapsed onto the pine needles. Gasping for

breath, her mouth dry, she sobbed as Carl strode around her. She winced when his leg brushed against her arm as he passed. She had to *think!* She had to stop panicking. Carl shrugged out of his large backpack and dropped it to the ground, digging in it for a bottle of water.

Jessica lifted her head. Her ex-husband was a large man, densely boned and heavily muscled. He was nearly six foot three and weighed over two hundred pounds. There wasn't an inch of fat on him. He was athletic and powerful. And dangerous. The rifle he'd used to kill Pete stood leaning against the pine tree next to where he was crouched, drinking water to slake his thirst. His red hair was short and plastered wetly against his large skull. Jessica shuddered. If anything, Carl was stronger and more intimidating and dangerous than she'd ever seen him.

How could she escape? He'd tied her wrists tightly with cord behind her back. Looking around, she knew they were heading off the Rim, down to the canyon floor and Oak Creek, though she couldn't see it below. The dusky shadows were deep. Threatening.

And Dan? *Oh, Dan!* Shutting her eyes, Jessica drew up her knees and rested her brow against them. Why hadn't she admitted her love to him? If he knew she was gone, he'd know Carl had her. What was Dan doing? Anguished, Jessica wondered if he was searching for her, though she knew rescue was out of the question. Carl had hunted all his life in the mountains near Calgary where he'd grown up, and was quite resourceful in the woods. Several times he'd gone out of his way to create sets of tracks to throw off anyone who dared to follow them. He kept his rifle—one with a high-powered scope on it for long-range shots—locked and loaded. His green eyes were slits as he glanced up from drinking the water.

Jessica quickly looked away. The icy glitter in his eyes made her nauseous. She saw what lay in their depths. She knew Carl too well, as if she were still attached psychically with an umbilical cord to his sick, twisted mind. The helicopter overhead told her that someone was looking for them, so that gave her hope. Every time the chopper flew over at treetop level, Carl would haul her against him under a tree until it left. She knew a helicopter had little chance of locating them. Still, it gave her hope, and she desperately needed some to cling to now.

Something told her Dan was following them. Was it her active imagination? Or some gut instinct? Jessica couldn't be sure because she was so scared.

"Get up!" Roman snarled as he jammed the water bottle back into the pack.

Jessica scrambled awkwardly to her feet. "Can't you untie my hands? We're going down into a canyon, Carl. The rocks are sharp. If I slip, I could hurt myself."

He grinned savagely and hoisted the heavy pack back on his thick shoulders. "Pity. No, your hands are staying tied, little girl." He gestured sharply. "Move ahead. Down that way. We'll follow this deer trail into the canyon. They know the easiest ways to get to the water."

Jessica was sorry she was wearing flat loafers with no tread on the bottom. The brown pine needles were like a slippery carpet beneath her feet, which was why she'd fallen so many times earlier. Carl, on the other hand, had leather hiking boots with heavy treads. He wore army camouflage gear and seemed almost to blend into the dusky shadows of the forest.

Trying to concentrate on the thin trail left by deer

that traversed this area every day at dawn and dusk to go get water, Jessica tried to steady herself as they began to go down the incline. What was Carl going to do? He hadn't said much. All along, he'd pushed her into a trot or a fast walk, obviously trying to get off the Rim as quickly as possible. He had to have a vehicle stashed along 89A. And then what? Jessica knew he wouldn't try and take her back across the Canadian border. No, he wouldn't even attempt it.

She knew what he'd do: he'd get her to the vehicle, rape her and then shoot her afterward, dumping her body somewhere inaccessible. She remembered what he'd done to the man he'd killed in cold blood—he'd stalked him for weeks, plotted and planned and then, at the right moment, kidnapped him. The police had found forensic evidence in the back of a Ford van where the victim had been tortured and then shot.

They'd found the poor man's body fifty miles away, thrown into a ditch and covered with leaves and branches. Only by luck had another hunter, out during deer season, seen Carl dump the body and cover it up. Otherwise Carl would never have been discovered for the cold-blooded murderer he was.

Dan! As her heart cried out for him, Jessica slipped and skidded, then caught herself. The lava rocks poking up through the brown needles were long, razor sharp and could kill her if she struck her head against one. Breathing hard, her mouth parched, she carefully placed each foot as she descended the long, steep slope. Dusk was coming, the shadows growing deeper and darker. Somewhere in her head, she knew this was her dark night of the soul. Would she live to see the sun rise again? Suddenly, life became even more precious than before.

Jessica desperately wanted to live. She wanted to tell Dan she loved him! She wanted a life where she could marry him, carry the children made out of love they shared, have that family she'd always dreamed of. *Oh, Dan, where are you? Where are you?* she silently cried. Part of her knew it was foolish, but still Jessica prayed that Dan would be on their trail, would find them, would save her. *If only...if only....*

Dan knelt down on a promontory of black lava at dusk, the rifle stock tight against his cheek to steady it. Suddenly, through the rifle's scope, he spotted a big, red-haired man with a huge, awkward backpack working his way down into the canyon. Ahead of him—Dan's heart thudded hard—was Jessica! Yes, he saw her! She was alive! Alive! Worriedly, he gripped the rifle tighter. He could barely see her; he only caught glimpses of her now and then, as she slipped and slid down the steep canyon wall. Her hands were tied behind her, and he could make out a rust-colored patch at each elbow. It had to be blood. She must have fallen a number of times.

Rage tunneled through him as he swung the rifle site back to Carl Roman. It was almost dark. The grayness of the dusk mingled with the dark blue of Roman's pack, and the camouflage clothes he wore made him almost invisible now. It was impossible to get a good, clean shot. Dan couldn't risk it. He knew if he only wounded him, Roman would turn on Jessica and murder her on the spot. Lowering the rifle, the pain in his heart tripling, Dan pulled out the cell phone. Punching in the numbers, he heard nothing but static. Damn! Standing up, he slung the rifle across his shoulder and tried facing several different directions while he dialed again. Nothing. He was too deep in the forest and too low into the canyon for the signal to get out and connect with another phone.

He was alone. Grimly, he put the cell phone away and mounted Gan. The stallion was restive. He hadn't had water to drink all afternoon and had to be thirsty. Dan's mind spun with plans and possibilities. Turning the stallion away from an outcrop of lava, Dan moved him down a well-used elk path, a shortcut to the creek below. Could he get down before Carl did? Would he have time enough to set up a shot that would kill the murdering bastard and save Jessica's life?

Dan wasn't sure. The stallion grunted, throwing out both front feet and sinking down on his haunches as they started the dangerous descent toward the creek. Halfway down the slope, the grayness began to turn to blackness. Dan held his breath, his legs clamped like steel around the stud's barrel as they slipped and slid, trying desperately to avoid the larger boulders and outcroppings that could rip into flesh and shatter bone.

Finally, they reached the creek. Dan dismounted and allowed the stallion to thrust his muzzle deeply into the icy cold water. The snowmelt off Humphreys Peak, which rose above the city of Flagstaff, helped to fill this creek. In some places it was over a man's head, while in others it was shallow enough to cross. Dan knew they were about half a mile downstream from where Roman would come off the canyon wall with Jessica.

It was completely dark now and he realized only belatedly that his rifle didn't have infrared. There was no way he could pick Carl out in the darkness. No, he'd have to stalk him, jump him and pray to the Great Spirit that he could subdue him before Roman killed him first. Moving to the sated stallion, which stood eagerly eating at the lush grass along the bank, Dan took out a pair of sheepskin-lined hobbles and put them on the horse's front legs. The gurgle of the stream sounded so happy and soothing compared to the violence he would be heading toward in a few minutes.

He tried the cell phone again, but to no avail. In a two-thousand-foot-deep canyon, no signal was going to get in or out. The helicopter that had been flying overhead from time to time was gone now, too, probably heading to Flag. Unless the aircraft had nighttime capability, such as infrared, more than likely it wouldn't return to the area to search until dawn.

Dan took off the stallion's bridle and hung it from the saddle horn. Patting the Arabian affectionately, he knew the horse would remain at the creek eating and drinking. Hopefully, if everything went right, Gan would be their transportation up and out of here later, carrying them to 89A and safety.

The ifs were huge, Dan realized as he got rid of his cowboy boots, trading them for a pair of soft deerskin moccasins instead. There was no doubt Carl Roman was an expert hunter. Dan had been led off the main trail four different times by him. The fact that Roman wore camos and carried a high-powered rifle told Dan he'd hunted and knew what he was doing. Had Roman been in the Canadian military? As Dan stood up and picked up the rifle, he wished he'd asked Sam about that earlier.

Near the banks of Oak Creek, the grass was tender and the earth soft under his silent moccasins. Dan hurried upstream toward where Roman would emerge off the cliff wall. Maybe they had already made the descent. He wasn't sure. What he hoped to do was find a good place to hide, and then jump Roman, surprise him.

How was Jessica? Sweat trickled down Dan's face as he loped along. Did she know they were hunting for her? Trying to save her? She must. She had to. His love for her vied with his building terror. All the old memories of the war—the stealth, the stalking, the terror, the odor of blood and the grunt of men dying—enveloped Dan. He shook his head savagely. Somehow he had to get clear of all of that and concentrate on the here and now.

For a moment, he crouched near the creek, just listening. Picking up the normal night sounds of crickets chirping and frogs croaking, he waited. Suddenly he thought he heard a woman's cry. Jessica? He almost stood, but harshly ordered himself to remain still.

There! He heard it again. It *was* Jessica! She was screaming. He couldn't hear the words. He only knew it was her voice careening off the walls of the canyon in an eerie echo. It was filled with anger—an emotion he'd not heard from Jessica before.

Rising, he hurried along the creek, being careful where he planted his feet. His night vision was good, and with the slice of moon in the sky, he could make out branches and rocks along the bank just well enough to avoid them. Leaping over a fallen log, he gripped the rifle hard. He heard Carl's voice then and froze. It had a deep, threatening tone.

He had to hurry! Dan's heart began to pound, rattling in his chest. He controlled his breathing—it was important not to be heard. Crouching down, he dropped his cowboy hat aside. He knew the color of his skin would help him hide in the shadows, and he wore a dark blue shirt and dark blue jeans. He looked like darkness itself. Roman wouldn't see him coming—until it was too late.

* * *

Jessica screamed again. Carl laughed as he lunged for her. She rolled along the bank of the creek, over and over, trying to avoid him. He had shoved her on her back as she'd knelt at the stream, thirstily sucking up badly needed water.

The moonlight was just bright enough for her to see that crazed, wild look in his eyes that meant he intended to rape her—once again. That look filled her with such terror that as he shoved her down on the ground again, Jessica lashed out in self-defense with both her feet. Her shoe caught him along the jaw and, thrown off balance, he roared like a wounded bull.

Gasping for breath, Jessica scrambled to her feet as she watched Carl fall backward. She had to run! Where? No matter where she went, she knew Carl would get her. And he'd tear the clothes off her body, like he had before, and he'd hurt her and make her scream all over again. No! No, she wasn't going to be a victim this time! She'd fight to her death!

Turning, she leaped into the stream. Oak Creek was barely knee-deep at this point, but the rocks were algae covered and slippery. She lunged forward, all the time tugging at her numbed wrists. She had to get free! Her sweat and blood had been loosening the rawhide cords all along. Water splashed around her now as she waded forward. The creek was about a hundred feet wide and the bank was covered with thick brush on the other side. If only…

"You bitch!" Carl roared, scrambling to his feet. "You're dead!"

Crying out, Jessica jerked her head around. She saw Carl leap into the water after her, his face icy with fury.

There! She jerked one hand from its bonds. Free! She was free! Leaping from the water, her feet slipping, Jessica crashed up the far bank. Her hands closed over a pine branch the size of her arm. It would do.

She heard Carl's heavy breathing coming up behind her. Thrusting herself onto her feet, Jessica clenched her teeth. She grabbed the limb with both hands and as she whirled to meet her attacker, swung it as hard as she could.

Roman obviously wasn't prepared for her to fight back, and belatedly threw up his arm to protect himself. *Too late!* The wood smashed into the side of his face, catching his hard, square jaw. Her arms vibrated with the impact and her fingers were ripped opened by splinters as the solid connection was made.

With a groan, Carl staggered backward, his hands flying to his bloody, torn face. Jessica blinked uncertainly. Was she seeing things? There was movement, like a dark shadow, back along the creek. Who? What? She froze, unsure, her legs turning to jelly. Carl was roaring and cursing and flailing around in the middle of the creek.

Dan! A cry almost ripped from Jessica's lips as she saw him materialize out of the darkness. Unable to move, she watched in horrified silence as he dropped the rifle he was carrying and pulled out a knife from the scabbard at his side. His face was carved from darkness and light, his eyes narrowed slits of glittering fury as he lunged into the stream after Carl.

Her heart contracted in terror as Dan made two huge leaps. In seconds, he was behind the unsuspecting Carl. She watched in utter fascination and horror as Dan lunged out with one leg and knocked him completely off his feet. Roman grunted hard, falling with a loud splash. Water flew up in sheets all around them.

Dan made one, two, three hard jabs with his fist against Carl's face. In moments, her captor was unconscious, his head sinking below the water.

Jessica trembled, watching as Dan hauled Roman to the other side of the creek, quickly tying his hands and then his feet. Was she dreaming this? Was it all her imagination? No!

"Dan!" Her cry echoed through the canyon as she waded jerkily across the creek toward him.

Throwing the knife aside, Dan whirled at the sound of Jessica's cry. He saw her white face, her eyes huge with horror, her arms outstretched as she slogged against the current toward him. Wordlessly, he jumped into the water. In four strides he was at her side, his arms wrapping tightly around her.

"Jessica…." he rasped brokenly, pulling her hard against him, holding her tightly.

Uttering his name, Jessica felt her knees giving way. Her arms numb, she fell against him, feeling the dampness of his shirt against her cheek.

"It's all right, all right," Dan breathed savagely, whispering the words against her tangled, dirty hair. "You're safe, Jessica, safe. I love you… I need you… you almost died…." He squeezed his eyes shut and held her fiercely. He could feel the rapid thud of her heart against his pounding one. Her body felt limp against his and he realized that she'd fainted. Was she wounded? Alarmed, Dan picked her up in his arms. Jessica was like a rag doll, her head lolling against his shoulder, her face pressed to his chest as he hurriedly got her out of the stream and onto dry land.

Raising his head, he whistled sharply, twice. He knew Gan would hear the whistle. He had trained the stallion to come to him. Even though the horse had hobbles on, Dan knew Gan would easily make the trip upstream in about fifteen minutes.

"Jessica? Jessica?" he rasped as he gently laid her down on the green slope of the bank. "*Shi shaa,* can you hear me?" He rapidly scanned her arms, legs and head with his hands. Her flesh felt cold. Shakily, he held his fingers against the carotid artery at the base of her neck. She had a strong, rapid pulse. Besides the blood on both her elbows, he detected a scratch along her brow, but that was all.

Gently, he began to move his hands slowly up and down her arms as he straddled her, calling her name. Shortly, he saw her thick lashes begin to flutter and he breathed a sigh of relief. Taking her into his arms, Dan sat down and cuddled Jessica against him to keep her warm. She was in shock, her flesh cool and damp from being in the water.

Jessica felt the thud of Dan's heart against hers, felt the warm moistness of his breath against her face, the soft kisses he was pressing against her brow and cheek. This was real. She wasn't dead or imagining this. Just the way Dan held her in that gentle, cradling embrace made her sob.

"You're safe, safe," he crooned, running his fingers through her mussed blond hair. "It's okay, Jessica. It's all over. Just lie against me. I'll hold you for as long as you want. We're going home, *shi shaa.* Home. I love you…. I'll always love you…."

Chapter 11

"Don't leave me, Dan…." Jessica whispered. Sam and Kate had just brought her home from the Flagstaff hospital where she'd been taken. Luckily, the Yavapai SWAT team had contacted the Sedona Fire Department, and the medical team had met Dan and Jessica along the highway, when they crested the canyon rim on Gan. Jim Cunningham was the EMT who'd cared for her. With a gentle, quiet voice, he had talked to her soothingly as he treated her many scratches and cuts. He'd allowed Dan to ride in the back of the ambulance with her as she sat on the gurney, still in mild shock. Once at the hospital, a doctor had examined her thoroughly and said she could go home and rest.

She saw Dan hesitate at the door. It was dawn now; a bleak grayness was visible on the western horizon outside her window. Sam and Kate had left her once she was settled in, and had gone back to their ranching duties, despite how tired they were. Absolute exhaustion played on Dan's features as well. "Don't go," she said pleadingly. "I—I don't want to be alone right now. Will you hold me? I think I can sleep if you hold me for just a little while...."

Dan's heart was torn at her tearful plea. "Sure," he said, slowly turning around and coming back into the gloom of her bedroom. The nightmare they'd lived through had chiseled away his normal sense of decorum, of what was right and wrong. Now, all he wanted, needed, was Jessica—to remain in physical contact with her. Though her hair had been washed at the hospital, he saw that the strands needed to be brushed away from her pale features. Picking up the brush lying on the dresser, he came over and sat down, facing her.

"First things first. They should have at least combed your hair up there."

The fleeting touch of his hand against her jaw made Jessica close her eyes. A ragged sigh tore from her lips as Dan gently moved the brush through her tangled, damp hair. Just his touch stopped the pain and fear she was still feeling. With each gentle stroke of the brush, her raw state began to dissolve. Dan was close, and he was caring for her. He loved her. Hadn't she heard him say that? Jessica lifted her lashes and drank in the strong, tired planes of his face.

"You saved my life."

The corner of his mouth twisted. "I think you saved your own. When I saw you pick up that branch and use it like a club against Roman, I was surprised."

An unexpected giggle came from her lips, sounding slightly hysterical. "You were surprised? I was surprised! I'd never done anything to defend myself against him. Ever."

Grimly, Dan brushed her hair until it shone like fine, molten gold. "Then it was about time, Jessica. You empowered yourself in that moment. For a little thing, you can sure heft one hell of a wallop when you want to." A slight, tired smile pulled at his mouth as he dropped his gaze and held her tired, luminous one. Putting the brush on the bed stand, Dan framed her face with his hands. His smile fled as he searched her features. Jessica had many scratches here and there, all from falling so many times.

"Did you hear me out there as I carried you out of the stream?" he said finally.

His hands were so warm, so steadying. Jessica felt like the desert after a turbulent thunderstorm had ravaged it for hours. "I hope I did," she whispered fervently, clinging to his dark gray gaze. "Oh, I hope I did, Dan. I wasn't making it up, was I?"

Leaning over, he met her soft, parting lips with his own. Her breath was moist and warm against his cheek and her hands fell automatically against his upper arms, her fingers digging into his muscles as he caressed her mouth. "I said I loved you," he whispered hoarsely. "I'll always love you even if you never love me, *shi shaa*...." As he pressed his mouth more surely against hers, he tasted the warmth of her salty tears trickling down her cheeks. It was a taste of life, of her, of her strong, courageous heart inside that small body she lived within. A body he wanted to love and hold sacred forever.

Easing away, Dan felt hot tears gathering in his own eyes as he gazed down at her glistening ones. There was such adoring, fierce light in Jessica's eyes, but he didn't trust what he saw there.

"The one thing," she began, sliding her fingers up across his shoulders, "The one thing I regretted after Carl kidnapped me was that I'd never told you how I really felt about you, Dan." Sniffing, she continued, "I was afraid. So afraid. I was like Gan. Me and that stallion are a lot alike, I think…."

Dan smiled tenderly. "You two are like twins in some ways," he agreed. He released her and reached for the box of tissues on the bed stand, pulling a few free and handing them to her. She blew her nose several times and then blotted her eyes. As she sat there in the gloom, his heart opened wide. Here was how he wanted to be with Jessica, sharing the richness of all their feelings with one another. It didn't matter if they were sad, happy, bad or good feelings, it was the simple, beautiful act of sharing them that was important to Dan.

"I recognize myself in Gan. The more you worked with the stallion—the *way* you worked with him, Dan—I found myself wishing you would be like that with me."

He cocked his head and trailed his hand across her smooth, shining hair. "Why didn't you share that with me? I would have." He shook his head and looked at the light spilling through the fragile lace curtains at the window. "I *wanted* to, Jessica. You don't know how many times I wanted to reach out and touch you, kiss you, tell you how beautiful you are to me, how you made a difference in my life, how you made me feel good inside once again…."

"I was scared," she said.

"I realized that after a while." Frowning, he picked

up her hand and cradled it between his own. "And after seeing Roman, seeing what he'd done to the horse and what he might do to you, I understood very clearly why you were afraid. That man is a two-heart, like you told me earlier. I've rarely seen a human being like that, but as I looked through the scope of my rifle and I saw his face, I knew why you were afraid of all men." He pressed a soft kiss to the back of her hand. "Even of me."

Sniffing, Jessica took another tissue from the box. She wrapped her fingers more strongly around Dan's hand. "Even knowing the Yavapai SWAT team went down there and got him doesn't make me feel any safer. I know he's up in Flag, in jail under heavy guard, but I'm still scared to death, Dan."

"I know, I know...but listen to me." He gripped her hands and made her focus all her attention on him. "They'll deport him, take him back to Canada. He'll go on trial and this time, he'll be put away for life with no possibility of parole. That's what the captain of the SWAT team told me."

"I'll have to go back to Vancouver to testify," Jessica said with a shudder.

"This time," Dan said grimly, "you won't have to go alone. I'll be there, Jessica. At your side. I'll protect you because I love you."

The words fell softly, soothing her emotional turmoil. "I never told you, did I?" she whispered, reaching up, her fingertips softly brushing his cheek. She felt the prickle of beard beneath her hand. The darkness of his beard made Dan look even more dangerous. "I guess I didn't realize just how much of a warrior you really were until today. I know better than anyone what it took to ride Gan into the Rim country. He could have refused. He could have bucked you off and tried to kill you. To know that you tracked me all that way…to have seen you come out of the darkness like that and jump Carl…" Jessica inhaled raggedly and shifted her gaze to the ceiling for a moment. "You're a man of surprising facets, Dan Black. I think I'm one of the few people who have ever witnessed you in action like that."

Jessica saw him avoid her eyes. He pressed her hands between his and she felt his warmth and care radiating out to her. "The reluctant warrior," she whispered. "I know how you said you'd never kill again—ever. Yet when I saw that knife in your hands and Carl starting to get up out of that stream, I knew that you'd do what you had to do."

Lifting his head, his eyes narrowing, Dan rasped, "Yes, I'd have killed him to save you. There wasn't any question in my heart in that moment. I didn't want to hurt anyone, but I wasn't going to let him hurt you, Jessica. Not *ever* again."

Whispering his name, Jessica leaned forward and wrapped her arms around Dan's shoulders, embracing him. She rested her head against his neck and jaw. "I—I know. As I crouched there, I watched you stalk him. I saw the look in your eyes, the way you moved toward him. There wasn't a doubt in my mind that only one of you would come out of that creek functional. I was so scared for you, Dan." Her voice wobbled dangerously and she tightened her arms around his neck. She felt Dan's hands move gently around her torso and draw her fully against his lean, hard frame.

"I knew all the pain, the horror you'd carried for years from the war, Dan. And to be there and see you set aside your own suffering, and possibly add to your nightmares and more pain to yourself to save me…well, it just blew me away. I couldn't believe you'd do that for me. It was then, as I struggled to get out of the water, that I realized you'd come after me because you loved me. It was the only thing that would make you set aside your own values."

Dan turned his head slightly and pressed a kiss against the warmth of Jessica's cheek. Easing away just enough to meet and hold her tear-filled gaze, he felt a self-deprecating smile tug at his mouth. Moving his hand across the crown of her head, he rasped, "Sometimes when you love someone, you do whatever has to be done, Jessica. This was one of those times. And believe me, I'm not sorry about any decisions I made, or what I did or would have done to keep you safe. In my heart, you are my woman. Even if I never told you so, you are. A man keeps his woman safe. He doesn't step back from that line in the sand when her life is in the balance."

It wasn't until today that Dan had come to realize the violence within him wasn't wrong; in every case, he'd acted out of a protective instinct—to defend himself and his team in the Gulf War. And to protect Jessica now. It would be one thing to enjoy killing, but he didn't. In a way, yesterday's event had helped him realize that not only was he a healer instead of a murderer, he was also a good person who was worthy and deserving of Jessica's love.

Looking deeply into his soft, dove gray eyes, Jessica felt the power of his words, the depth of his love for her in those priceless moments. "I don't know when I fell in love with you, darling, and it doesn't matter. What does matter is that I share how I feel with you now. I prayed out there that the Great Spirit would let me live, let me survive Carl, to tell you that."

"Well," Dan whispered, trailing a finger across the high slope of her flushed cheek, "you survived."

Closing her eyes, Jessica rested her head against his strong, broad shoulder. "And now I'm going to live, Dan. With you at my side."

The words sounded good to him and he embraced her tightly for a moment. "Maybe two wounded human beings with dark pasts can walk into the light together, hand in hand?" he teased her huskily.

Jessica moved her head slightly. "Love creates the light for us," she said, feeling safe, warm and so well loved by Dan. She saw the new sense of confidence in him, saw it in the glimmer of his eyes. Somehow this whole nightmarish event had made him realize what she already saw and knew of him—that he was a wonderful man who had many skills and talents to be proud of. No longer would he walk apologetically. Whatever he'd feared before was gone now. She knew love had a lot to do with it. He'd saved her life and that was the gift he'd given her. Life.

"You're tired, *shi shaa,*" he whispered, gently untangling her from himself. "You need to sleep." And he eased her back on the bed and drew up the blankets to her breasts, covering the pink cotton, lace-trimmed nightgown that she wore. He saw a soft smile play across Jessica's lips as her lashes drooped downward.

"Yes, I'm tired now, Dan. I can sleep because I've told you how I really feel...."

Getting up off the bed, he watched as Jessica quickly sank into the depths of sleep. Exhaustion shadowed her face, but as he stood there, he was aware of that inner strength that had kept her going, that had given her the courage to protect herself in those last few deadly moments.

Jessica's inner bravery had come out and she had, in reality, saved her own life. Dan was proud of her. He loved her fiercely. Lifting his head, he looked toward the dawn, the pinkness of the horizon heralding a new day. A better day. Because of his Navajo upbringing, he said a silent prayer to Father Sun. The east was the direction of new beginnings, of a new day. A new way of life.

As he quietly moved from the room, he left the door ajar. Right now, all he wanted was a hot shower to rid himself of the stink of fear, of sweat and terror. And then he'd come back to Jessica's house and sleep at her side, where she wanted him. Where he wanted to be....

"Isn't this a beautiful place?" Jessica asked as she leaned against Dan. Her arms moved gracefully around his shoulders and she gazed up at him, up at his strong mouth and those burning gray eyes. She felt his arms move firmly around her, capturing her and pressing her fully against him. It was late fall and the autumn leaves on the Rim had turned a multitude of colors. Jessica loved autumn, and here on the Donovan Ranch it was a spectacular time of year. Where they stood near Oak Creek, picnic basket and blanket at their feet, the reds, yellows and oranges of the cottonwoods and sycamores surrounded them like a beautiful chorus of joy.

He grinned and playfully pressed a quick kiss to her full, smiling mouth. "What I'm looking at pleases me the most." In the months since the kidnapping, Dan had reveled in the love that had poured forth from Jessica toward him. They had not made love to one another—yet. In many ways, he was glad to wait because he understood Jessica had to not only heal from her past abuse, but to work at trusting him completely, too. He wasn't Carl, but he was a man. And trust in men hadn't been high on Jessica's list—just as it hadn't been with Gan. In the ensuing months since the kidnapping incident, though, Jessica had worked to change her perceptions. More than anything, Dan knew she needed time. Just as that black stallion had needed time to learn to trust him, too.

The warm, woody smell of decaying leaves surrounded them as Jessica leaned fully against him. He loved her fiercely, ached to have her, but he was content in allowing her to explore him in ways that felt safe to her. Today her hair was shining, molten gold in the sunlight that danced down between the falling leaves.

"Shi shaa," he whispered as he stroked her hair. "My sunshine…."

"You," Jessica whispered, as she stood up on tiptoe and found his mouth, "are my life…." And he was, in every way.

Today was special, Jessica admitted to herself as she pressed her lips more fully against Dan's. Today, she knew, was the first day of her life with him. She'd awakened this morning knowing it, as surely as she breathed air in and out of her lungs.

Since the kidnapping, Dan had been incredibly gentle and understanding with her. Sam and Kate understood clearly that they'd fallen in love, and offered no comment when she asked Dan, a month after the kidnapping, to come and live in her house instead of staying out at the bunkhouse. Little by little, day by day, Jessica had discovered that living with Dan was like living life in the happiest of ways. Sure, they had their differences, but what two people in love didn't? Dan never allowed bad feelings to stay between them for long. He'd sit her down and they'd talk until they'd talked it out. So many times, Jessica discovered, it was misunderstandings, not anything else, upsetting her. How different it was living with Dan than with Carl!

As Jessica relished the rich splendor of Dan's lips against her own now, she surrendered completely to his hands, his mouth and his hard, strong body pressed fully against her. Over the months, he had shown her the positive way to live in a relationship. Because she had had such a bad relationship with Carl, she hadn't known what a good relationship consisted of. That was why, by living with Dan for so many months, Jessica knew she was ready to share the final gift with him. And she knew it would occur naturally, wonderfully, between them.

Dan never pressed her or made her feel she had to make love with him. No, not ever. He made it clear that she had to initiate, that she had to tell him how far he could go with her, and when to stop. Never once did Dan cross that line of discretion with her. She saw him struggle sometimes, and she felt guilty, but when he saw her reaction, he'd sit and talk it out with her to make her understand a hurt animal or human being couldn't be rushed or forced into giving something he or she didn't want to give.

But now his mouth was hot and wet and inviting. Jessica smiled to herself as she ran her fingers through his thick, black hair. Yes, today was the day. A day of loving Dan fully, completely. A day of freedom for them. And where else should they spend it but here beside Oak Creek, where her life had almost ended and then been reborn on that tragic night? It made symbolic sense to Jessica. And fall was a time for allowing old things to die, to float away, only to be reborn the next spring. Yes, this was the moment....

Dan felt her tugging insistently at the closures on his dark red, long-sleeved shirt. He smiled beneath her lips.

"You in a hurry?"

Giggling, Jessica eased away from his mouth and looked up into his dancing gray eyes. "I guess I am." She proceeded to open his shirt fully, revealing his firm flesh beneath it, and spread her hands against the dark hair of his well-sprung chest. "Mmm, you feel so *good* to me, Dan Black. Today is special, you know."

He drowned in her turquoise gaze, absorbing her searching, exquisite touch. His flesh burned beneath the exploration of her cool, slender fingers and his heart began to pound with need of her. "Oh?"

She stilled her hands against his chest, absorbing the thudding sensation of his heart beneath her palms. "Yes," Jessica whispered more seriously. "I brought you out here for a reason...."

Dan eased his arms around her and held her, rocking her slightly from side to side. The gurgling creek, the soft, intermittent breeze that danced around them, all seemed playful and joyous to him. "Women *always* have reasons," he teased, laughing huskily as he watched her grin. His lower body began to ache, as it always did when Jessica touched him, kissed him and explored him. As badly as he wanted to consummate his relationship with her, he knew it had to be her call, her choice. He wanted her to come willingly, joyfully, to him. He wanted his woman looking forward to his embrace, to his kisses, his adoration of her in all ways. It was the only way.

"What web do you weave today, my spider woman?" he teased, grazing her flushed cheek with a fingertip. Her eyes were so beautiful to him, a haunting mirror of the depths of her priceless soul—a soul he was privileged to see, to share and love fiercely.

Easing the shirt off his shoulders, Jessica stepped back and began to undo the thick leather belt on his jeans. "It's time, darling." Fingers stilling, she lifted her chin and met his flaring gray eyes. "Love me, Dan," she quavered. "Love me fully. In all ways. I'm ready...."

Frowning, he gripped her hands as she tried to push his jeans off his narrow hips. "Are you sure?" Never had he wanted her more than in that moment. The wind played with her hair, which shone like gold and framed her flushed face and sparkling blue eyes. She was a woman of nature, a child to the tree nation and to the flower people. No one was closer to Mother Earth's heartbeat than Jessica, and he loved her for that connection because life flowed so powerfully through her all the time.

Jessica sobered and held his concerned gaze. "I've never been more sure, darling. I love you. I want to share my love with you." She removed his hands and began to slide his jeans downward.

Dan believed her. He saw the change in her eyes, saw a fierce light there, a hunger aimed only at him. Pushing off his boots, then his jeans, he nodded and moved her over to the blanket. Once he'd set the picnic basket aside, he eased her down on the soft, dark blue surface. "Remember," he rasped as she lay down next to him and he began to unbutton her pale green blouse, "you

can stop me anytime, Jessica. Just say it or show me…."
The blouse opened to reveal her silky camisole. His fingers ached to brush those small breasts beneath it. How would she react to his touch? Suddenly, he was afraid as never before. But he had to push beyond his own fears.

Sighing, Jessica closed her eyes. She took his hand and guided it to the side of her breast. "Touch me, just touch me, Dan. I ache for you. I ache so much…."

Her words fell heatedly over him. Her fingers were so white against his darker hand. He felt the soft, firm roundness of her breast. "You feel so good," he whispered as he leaned down and captured her mouth. "So good…."

The provocative movement of his hand against the swell of her breast, against her camisole and her silken bra, left Jessica wanting more. The sounds of the creek, happy and bubbling, the clatter of the drying leaves moved by the breeze, the far-off call of a blue jay, all blended together in a beautiful song for her. When he tore his mouth from hers, gently removing the soft fabric and settling his lips on the peak of her taut breast, she uttered a cry of absolute pleasure. Her fingers bunched and released on his strong, firm shoulders. A hot, jagged bolt of lightning coursed down through her as he caressed her nipple, suckling it gently. Her body became molten beneath his gentle, exploring touch. A haze of heat throbbed through her, robbing her of any thought processes.

As his lips moved to the other nipple, Jessica arched upward. He slowly removed the rest of her clothing, and when her hip touched his, she realized only belatedly that he was also naked. The movement of his hard, muscular body against her softer one was a mesmerizing experience for her. As his hand grazed her arched spine and he trailed a fiery path of kisses from her throbbing breasts downward, all she could do was gasp raggedly, longing for more of him. The fire between her thighs was hot and burning. She cried out for more of his touch, more of his delicious, dizzying exploration of her. Never had she been touched, kissed, caressed like this.

As she arched more deeply against him, her thighs automatically opened to allow him entrance into her sacred self. Each scorching touch of his lips against her rounded abdomen, moving slowly downward, was a new kind of torture for her. A wild, throbbing ache built and she rolled her head from side to side, frustrated and needing him so badly. As his lips trailed a path of fire to each of her taut thighs and he moved his tongue against her, a moan shattered through her. With each silken movement against her womanhood, she felt the pressure within her build. She reached out, begging him silently to enter her, to consummate their union so that the burning ache within her would be satiated.

Gasping, she felt him move his hand in a languid, caressing motion against that sacred, moist area between her thighs. Consumed in the flames of her need, Jessica lay helplessly in his arms, a prisoner of pleasure to his touches, to kisses that built the fire within her higher and higher, brighter and brighter. Her breath was ragged. Her heart was pounding. How badly she wanted him! She tried to speak, but it was impossible. Just as she sobbed out his name, she felt him move. Within moments, he had opened her thighs even more and she felt the power of his maleness against her, his hard masculine form blanketing her. Jessica barely opened her eyes, her hands coming to rest on his arms. She saw the tender, burning love in his eyes, the way his mouth was twisted in pain as well as pleasure. In that second, she realized he was aching just as much as she was. In the next second, she understood the fierceness of love between a man and a woman.

Without thinking, only responding to the innate knowledge of her body, Jessica lifted her hips upward to allow him entrance into her hot, moist depths. As he surged forward, he bracketed her head with his hands and captured her mouth in a swift, hungry kiss that tore the breath from her. The power of him within her, the rocking motion he established, the cradling of the fire, his hard body pressed surely, provocatively against her—all conspired to dissolve her last coherent senses. In that moment, with that delicious movement tunneling up through her, she understood the mating of moonlight with fierce, hot sunlight that occurs between a woman and a man.

There was such joy, such dizzying elation as he moved within her, taught her the ancient rhythm, that she was amazed by the utter, wild freedom it invoked in her. The pressure, the heat built until she felt as if she would explode internally. And then, as he tore his mouth from hers and suckled her nipple once more, an explosion of such magnitude and power occurred that Jessica arched, cried out and froze in his embrace. It felt as if lightning were dancing across her lower body, sending out forks of light and pleasure through every nerve ending within her.

She felt Dan move his hand beneath her hips and lift her slightly. The sensation, the volcanic molten feeling of pleasure, heightened and continued. He moved within her, danced with her rhythmically, sang in unison with her body, with her heart and soul as he thrust again and again to prolong the incredible feeling for her. Moments later, as the golden light burning within her began to ebb, she felt him stiffen and groan. He buried his head against her breast and held her hard against him and she knew it was her turn to love him, to cherish him as much as he'd cherished her. With a knowledge as old as woman, she moved her hips in a rolling, rhythmic motion and captured him tightly against her with her legs to prolong his release deep within her.

She saw his face tighten almost as if in pain, but with exquisite pleasure, too. With a groan, he suddenly collapsed against her, his hands tangled in her hair, his breathing harsh and shallow against her breasts. An incredible feeling of satiation, of completion, moved through her like soft moonlight caressing the earth. With a sigh of surrender, Jessica understood as never before about real love. What it was really all about. Her abdomen tingled beneath his weight as she slowly opened her eyes, moving her hands weakly through his dark, shining hair, and absorbed his gleaming profile as he lay against her. How fiercely she loved Dan!

In that moment, Jessica felt a breathtaking sensation move through her. Her heart was wide-open, receiving and giving. As she moved her hand languidly across his back and felt the strength of his spine, she smiled softly. To bear his children would be the ultimate gift. Yes, a child created out of love, born not of darkness, but of light, would be welcomed fully. Completely.

As she lay there, the sounds of the forest registering around her once again, Jessica realized that she and Dan would create a child from this first coming together. She

didn't know how she knew it, but she did. Lying there
in the cooling breeze, she gazed overhead as colorful
leaves twirled and spiraled down around them, as if
Mother Earth were celebrating their consummation of
love with them. Smiling tenderly, Jessica slid her hands
around Dan's face. She saw the dove gray of his eyes,
the love shining in them for her alone. He eased up off
her and leaned forward just enough to capture her smiling mouth. The kiss was tender. Filled with love. Her
heart swelled even more and Jessica wondered if it was
possible to die from happiness.

"You are my *shi shaa,*" he rasped, sliding his hand
against her full lower lip, "the sunshine in my life. You're
all I'll ever need or want, my woman of the earth."

His words were filled with passion and love for her.
Dan eased out of her, pulling her into his arms so that
she could rest her head against his shoulder. Savoring
the way he brought her against him, she closed her eyes,
content as never before.

"You are the lightning of Father Sky," she whispered.
"You love me so fully, so beautifully. I thought I was
going to die if you didn't complete me, darling."

He rose up on one elbow and kept her near as he
looked down at her flushed face, her glistening blue
eyes and well-kissed mouth. Smiling tenderly, Dan
traced her cheek with his fingertip. "And you are the
daughter of Mother Earth." His dark hand fell against
her rounded abdomen and he caressed her gently. "Our
children will be welcome here, between us."

"Oh, yes." Jessica sighed as she moved her hand over
his own. She could feel the strength, the roughness of
it against her feminine softness. "Children created out
of our love for one another, Dan...."

"Marry me, Jessica?"

She opened her eyes and met his very serious ones.

"I'm poor," Dan rasped. "And I don't have a college education. I'll probably work myself into a grave someday, but it's good, honest work. I want you by my side every night, every day. We've come so far together. Let's go the rest of the way." He saw Jessica's expression change to one of tear-filled happiness. The luminous look in her eyes, Dan knew, was her way of saying yes. His heart soared in response like an unfettered eagle. Stilling his hand against her abdomen, he murmured, "I want you to be the mother of my children. They'll be so lucky to have you. I want to grow old seeing our children and grandchildren around us. I think they'll have a good life. Good growing-up years, not like what you had, but what we can give them with our love."

Tears choked her and she nodded once. "Y-yes, darling. Yes to all our dreams. And I don't care if you're a horse wrangler and you won't make that much money."

"I don't own any land. I'm poor," he said.

"In one way, maybe," Jessica whispered, "but in so many other ways, you're a treasure to me, Dan. You bring me love, respect and care. What's that worth compared to money?" She touched his cheek and watched his gray eyes narrow with hunger for her. It was a delicious feeling.

"When you put it that way, you're right," he admitted. A slight smile played at the corners of his mouth. "I'm going to love you forever and a day, Jessica. *Shi shaa,* my sunshine. My life and heart…."

Epilogue

"I can hardly wait until Rachel gets home," Jessica eagerly confided to Kate as they sat out on the porch swing in the warmth of late November. Everywhere else in the nation people were experiencing harsh temperatures and even snow, but not here in Arizona. No, on Thanksgiving Day, it was in the sixties and they were enjoying the pale blue sky and sunshine.

Jessica wore a pink angora sweater with a cowl neck, and a soft cream skirt that fell to her ankles. Her hair was caught back behind her head, a beautiful pink-and-white orchid in it. The fuchsia color of the orchid brought out the flushed quality of her cheeks. Dan had given her a gold heart locket shortly after he'd helped rescue her and it hung just above her collarbone as it always did. Inside the locket was a photo of him and her. Together. Like it should always be. He'd also given her a small pair of gold, heart-shaped earrings, which she adored.

Smoothing her fingers over the red velvet skirt she wore with a crisp white blouse, Kate said, "I can't wait to see Rachel, either. I just wish she could have made it home for Thanksgiving, that's all."

"She has to finish up her commitments," Jessica murmured. "Her teaching contract ends in early December. Just think, she'll be home soon." She smiled over at her older sister. Inside, Dan and Sam were finishing up the last of the dishes and cleaning up after the wonderful midday meal. Jessica was so happy to have been able to restart the tradition her mother had begun so many years before—of feeding the homeless of Sedona. A bus from the Sedona mission had just taken twenty homeless people back to town. Yes, Thanksgiving had been very special this year. In so many wonderful, joyous ways.

"December fifteenth, if everything goes according to plan." Kate sighed. "Rachel said she'd rent a car down in Phoenix and drive north to the ranch. I just hope we don't get any of those sudden, unexpected snowstorms."

Jessica nodded. Weather in November, particularly in Oak Creek Canyon, could be unpredictable. "She's probably used to driving in rain at least, having lived so long over in England."

"Probably," Kate agreed. She smiled a little. "I guess I'm just being big sister worrywart, is all."

Warmth touched Jessica's heart as she met and held Kate's gaze. "You love us, that's why." She watched as Kate wrestled with her obvious affection. Little by little, her sister had let down her guard, and over the months, Jessica had watched her begin to bloom in a way she'd never seen before. Kate was more vulnerable, more open emotionally, and Jessica relished those wonderful, unexpected gifts from her older sister.

Kate pointed to Jessica's left finger. "I think it was romantic of Dan to give you his grandmother's engagement ring this holiday morning. He's such a great guy."

Sighing, Jessica rocked in the swing with her sister.

"Isn't he though? Sometimes," she murmured, closing her eyes and fingering the gold-and-diamond ring, "I think I'm in this neverending dream. Sometimes I worry I'll wake up and Dan will be gone." Jessica opened her eyes and stole a look at Kate. "Do you know what I mean?"

Kate laughed. "I sure do." She looked back across her shoulder toward the screen door, through which she could hear the two men working noisily in the kitchen. "I feel the same about Sam. He loves me so much. I sometimes wake up at night in his arms and wonder what he saw in me in the first place. And then I go back to sleep and worry that I'm dreaming it all, and that I'm back in prison again." She frowned. "Boy, are we a jumpy lot or what?"

Giggling, Jessica shook her head, reaching out and gripping Kate's hand. "We have a right to be scared. Dan told me one time that we had such a rough childhood he's surprised any of us turned out so well. He's seen members of his own family who were abused. Some of those kids have scattered to the four winds, and most of them are in trouble in one way or another, lost forever."

Kate became serious. "We were all lost in our own way, Jessica. We all ran the minute we turned eighteen. You went to Canada. Rachel found sanctuary in England. My life went awry and I got involved with fanatical activists and ended up in prison."

"At least," Jessica replied softly, "with the love of two good men who helped us find our way home, we have a chance to change things for the better. Not only for ourselves, but for our children."

"*If* we can keep this ranch afloat for any children that might happen after marriage," Kate warned her grimly. She gestured toward the dried, yellow grass in the front yard. "No rain. Not an inch of it all autumn. I'm really worried about fire, Jessica. And if we don't get rain this winter, I don't know how we can survive. We're going to have to sell off the rest of the herd, the pregnant cows... If that happens, we're done for. Sam and I are counting on that spring crop of calves for—"

"Katie, let it go. Sometimes we just have to have blind faith about these things. Dan says it's the darkness before the dawn for all of us as a family. He sees it in symbolic terms. It's a test. He said all three sisters must come home and pour our lifeblood back into this ranch to get its heart beating again. And once we do that with our care, our love and commitment, he said the rain would come to nourish that seed we've all nurtured here by coming home again."

"Beautiful symbol. But everything still sucks."

Jessica laughed. She shook her head. "Oh, Katie, you're such a pessimist!"

"I have a right to be," Kate growled, though a grin crawled across her mouth. "I'm the one riding the range every day and checking on our cattle and horses, on the drought conditions, the loss of our alfalfa crop."

"Okay," Jessica said, matching her grin, "I'll hold the faith. Rachel was always big on hope. We'll let you be the grouch of the three. I guess every family has to have a pessimist, right?"

Tousling Jessica's hair, Kate laughed. "Right, I've *always* been the grouch in this family. Not much has changed, has it?"

"A lot has changed," Jessica said, more serious now. "On Christmas Eve, we're having a double marriage. You're going to marry Sam and I'm going to marry Dan. Rachel will be our joint maid of honor. *That,* my older, grouchy sister, is *change.*"

Kate enjoyed her younger sister's prim look. "Confident little thing, aren't you?" And she laughed.

"Life is *good,* Katie. Okay, so the ranch is still hanging by a thread, and the bank is salivating over our shoulders, eager to snatch it away the moment we fail to make a monthly payment. On the other side of the ledger, the personal and emotional side, you and I have struck it rich. We've got gold in our hands."

Chuckling, Kate said, "How I wish some of that gold could be alchemically changed into money!"

"Quit!" Jessica playfully hit her sister on the shoulder. "You don't mean that and I know it."

"I guess I don't," Kate said, a little wearily. She lowered her voice so only Jessica could hear her. "What if we can't save the ranch? What will Sam and Dan do? None of us can afford to buy another spread. All we're good for is the open range, being part of this land as cowboys. They might as well shoot us in the head and put us out of our misery if this ranch goes under. I don't want to do anything else in my life except what I'm doing now. I'd like to die in the saddle."

"Ugh. How about in Sam's arms? That's a lot more preferable. I know you love horses, Katie, but geez...."

"You know what I'm trying to say," Kate muttered fiercely.

"I hear you, Katie. Maybe, with Rachel coming home to establish a wellness clinic in Sedona, it will help us with the bills and stave off the inevitable from this terrible drought."

"Rachel isn't exactly rich, you know. She gave us her whole life savings to pay off the bulk of what was owed to the bank so they wouldn't foreclose before. Sure, she's got talent, ideas and plenty of hope, but that's not going to convert into money right away." Kate shook her head worriedly. "No, we've got some long, hard months ahead of us. I just pray for a miracle. Any miracle to help us through, that's all."

"See," Jessica chided, "you're not so pessimistic after all. You believe in miracles."

Chuckling, Kate rose from the porch swing and smoothed out her skirt. "It's all we've got left between us with the bank ready to foreclose on us, you twit."

Giggling, Jessica followed her sister back into the house. The living room had been set up to feed the homeless earlier and the scent of roasting turkey still permeated the air. As Jessica sauntered into the small kitchen, she watched in amusement as Dan and Sam kept bumping unceremoniously into one another as one washed and the other dried dishes. Dan wore a deep cranberry red cowboy shirt, a bolo tie made from silver and a turquoise nugget, dark blue jeans and newly polished black cowboy boots. His sleeves were rolled up to his elbows.

"I should have a picture of this," Kate teased, laughing. She went to the pecan-colored cupboards, opened them and started to put away the plates that Sam had dried.

"I think," Sam grumbled, "we should get silver stars for action above and beyond the duty of males."

Dan grinned and winked at Jessica, who rested her elbows on the white tile counter near the stove. She colored fiercely and smiled that soft smile that was so much a part of her.

"Where I come from on the res," Dan said, up to his elbows in soapsuds, "men did their fair share of housework. About the only thing we didn't do was learn how to weave."

"I'll take dishwashing over that," Sam said, drying the plates furiously with a white towel.

"Thought you might," Dan murmured, grabbing a handful of silverware to wash.

While Kate and the men chatted amiably, Jessica busied herself cutting the last pumpkin pie into four large slabs. Placing the slices on the small oak table covered with a lacy, white linen tablecloth, she added big dollops of whipped cream. Dan had found some pyracantha bushes with bright orange berries against dark green leaves, and had put some cuttings in a small, cut glass vase in the center of the table. It looked Christmassy to Jessica.

Her heart expanded with joy as she saw Dan steal a look across his shoulder to check where she was. Her hands stilled on the last plate as she caught and held his smoldering gray gaze. Automatically, her body responded fully to his unspoken invitation. Surely today was a day of thanksgiving as no other she'd ever had. Her finger burned warmly where his grandmother's engagement ring rested on her hand. Dan had bestowed the gift on her in front of everyone. Jessica had been so humbled and surprised that she'd cried shamelessly. She'd seen tears in Dan's eyes, too. And everyone else's.

There was nothing she wanted more than to have Dan as her husband, her partner for life. Each morning she woke up with him at her side, and it was a miracle to her. A wonderful, unfolding miracle. Jessica realized she had never known love until Dan, the man wrapped in darkness, had walked quietly into her life.

"Is that for us?" Dan queried, raising his brows and eyeing the pumpkin pie.

Grinning, Jessica traded a look with Kate. "Well, we took pity on you cowboys and thought you deserved some kind of treat for doing all this kitchen duty. Right, Katie?"

"Oh, sure, right." Kate looked at them with mock sternness. "We cooked all day, so you boys can clean up the mess."

Dan crowed and shared a laugh with Sam. "Do we get whipped cream on our reward?"

Jessica colored fiercely at the innuendo. "On the pie, yes."

The foursome broke into ribald laughter. The kitchen rang with the sounds of love and joy. How much had changed since she was a child! Jessica realized. With Kelly around, they had always walked as if stepping on eggs, afraid they would break at any moment. Now there was teasing, good-natured competition between Dan and Sam, and obvious love for her and Katie. Enough to go around and then some.

There was a knock at the front door.

"I'll get it!" Jessica said, quickly putting the tub of whipped cream aside and fleeing through the kitchen.

"Who's comin'?" Sam asked, trading looks with Dan and Kate.

"I don't know," Kate said. "We're not expecting anyone else."

Dan chuckled. "By now I think you would have caught on. With Jessica around, surprises are the order of the day."

Jessica appeared at the doorway to the kitchen, breathless and flushed. "Look who's coming for a late dinner!"

All three of them turned in unison.

Jessica smiled and stepped aside. "I found out last week that Jim Cunningham and his crew had Thanksgiving duty at the fire department. None of them could go home and have turkey with their families, so…" She skipped to the refrigerator as Jim entered the kitchen, "I packed up ten meals, for all of his crew at the fire station."

Jim nodded shyly to everyone. "Hi," he said, a bit awkwardly.

Dan shook his head and laughed. "Come on in, Jim."

Sam stepped forward and extended his hand. "Glad you could drop by."

Kate nodded. "Yes," she said, her voice a bit strained.

Jessica knew that the old war between the Cunninghams and Donovans had gone on for a long, bitter time. But Jim Cunningham had reached out to her, Sam and Kate to try and make up for the many wrongs done to them by his cantankerous father. Dressed in his dark blue, serge trousers and light blue, long-sleeved shirt, the silver badge on his chest glinting in the lamplight, Jim gave her a look of thanks for the dinners.

"Can you at least have a cup of coffee with us?" Jessica pleaded as she brought out the foil-wrapped meals and set them on the table. Kate went to find paper bags to place them in.

"Uh, no.... With the permission of my captain, I faked a call to come up here to get the meals, so I'm living on borrowed time as it is," Jim said with a slight, hesitant smile. His dark blue gaze pinned Kate as she returned with the paper bags, her expression grim. "The crew down at the fire station is beholden. Donovan generosity is well known in these parts. I hear you served thirty needy families as well as the homeless at the mission earlier today."

Kate compressed her lips and put the meals into the paper bags. "I'm sorry you have to work today."

Jim shrugged. "Well, with the way things were going at home this last week, I'm kinda glad I have the duty, to tell you the truth."

Jessica gave him a compassionate look. She *liked* Jim Cunningham. He was quiet, clean-cut, terribly handsome in a rough kind of way and respectful toward everyone. "Maybe a meal made with lots and lots of love will help then," she whispered, bringing over both bags for him to carry. "There's pumpkin pie and whipped cream in there for dessert."

Jim brightened as he put the two bags beneath his arms and Sam moved by him to open the front door. "Thanks—all of you." He caught and held Kate's dark stare. "I mean it...."

Kate barely nodded and wrapped her arms defensively against her breasts.

Jessica placed her hand on Jim's upper arm and led him out of the kitchen, with Dan following. She could feel Jim's firm muscles beneath his shirt and noted how fit he was. "I just hope you don't have any calls. I hope you have a nice, quiet night."

"Thanks, Jessica," Jim murmured, smiling down at her.

Out on the front porch, they saw that the sun had set behind the thousand-foot lava wall that protected the ranch property. The sky was a light blue and gold as Jessica, Dan and Sam walked with Jim to the red-and-white ambulance with the Sedona crest on the front door. Dan opened the rear doors of the ambulance and helped Jim place the food where it wouldn't fall over during transit.

Jim hesitated as he opened the driver's door, then turned and extended his hand to Dan. "Congratulations. I hear you're going to marry this flower child at Christmas."

Jessica laughed and felt heat flow into her cheeks as Jim's eyes danced with gentle teasing. "Flower child! Oh, come on, Jim. Is that what the gossip going around in Sedona is calling me?"

Dan released Jim's hand and put his arm around Jessica. "Be happy they're calling you something nice, *shi shaa,*" he said with a grin. "Instead of a blooming idiot or something like that."

Jim laughed, got into the ambulance and shut the door. "No kidding. You don't want to know what they call me. I can guarantee you it ain't nice." He raised his hand in a mock salute to the three of them. "Thanks. All of you. I know everyone at the station will want you to know how much your care means to them."

Her hands clasped to her breast, Jessica leaned warmly against Dan. "Just take care, Jim. I'll see you in town next week. I'll drop by and pick up the dishes and silverware, okay?"

"Okay, Jessica." He started the ambulance and slowly turned around on the gravel driveway.

Back on the porch, Sam rested his hands on his hips as the ambulance disappeared up the winding road out of the canyon. He turned his gaze on Jessica. "That was a good move, politically," he said in congratulations.

She looked at him in surprise. "What do you mean?"

"Hadn't you heard?" he rumbled. "Old Man Cunningham is fixin' to slap our ranch with a lawsuit later this month. Over water rights."

Groaning, Jessica raised her hands to her open mouth. "No! How can he? We've always shared that well between our properties—for nearly a hundred years."

Sam ran his fingers through his hair and looked grimly over at Dan. "Explain it to her, Dan?"

Dan rubbed his hand against Jessica's tense arm. "Yes… I will…."

Sam grunted before slowly walking back inside the house.

Jessica turned in Dan's arms, feeling secure as his hands moved gently down her back to capture her against him. "Dan, what's going on? Is there something you three know that I don't? Is Katie hiding things from me again?"

"Come on," he urged, leaning down and kissing her lips tenderly, "let's go for a walk and let this dinner settle."

Petulantly, Jessica surrendered and fell into step with him as they walked toward the horse corrals near the red barn. "What's Sam talking about, Dan? What lawsuit?"

Dan settled his black Stetson on his head and drew her more surely against him. He wished he could protect Jessica from some of the harshness of life. He saw the consternation in her expression and the worry in her eyes. Everyone hid the truth from Jessica because they knew how easily she could become upset, and how much it distressed her. He tightened his fingers on her shoulder as they walked.

"About two weeks ago, Jim's father called Sam over there," Dan confided in a low tone. "The day before that, Jim had come to the ranch here and talked with Sam, to warn him that the call was coming in. Jim tried to talk his father out of it, but the old man refused to listen to him. The drought has dried up all the wells on Cunningham property and he told Sam he was going to court to get full rights to the well that both ranches have shared for the last hundred years."

"That's why Kate looked so unsettled, then," Jessica said. "She wasn't very happy to see Jim here. Now I know why."

"Kate doesn't trust Jim or his motivations. She thinks that he's in cahoots with his father and he's just bluffing us."

Jessica rolled her eyes. "That's silly! Jim Cunningham is the only good apple from that rotten barrel, and she knows it!"

"That's probably true," Dan conceded, "but Cunningham could destroy us if he goes to court. We don't have the money to fight that kind of a lawsuit. He's got money. And money talks."

"But we need that well, too!" Jessica protested, her voice high with indignation. "All our pasture wells have dried with the exception of that one! What are we to do? Let our stock die of thirst?"

"Take it easy," Dan soothed, placing both hands on her tense shoulders as she faced him. He saw the anguish in her eyes. "It could be a bluff. Old Man Cunningham, from what Sam has said, often uses threat of a lawsuit to scare off someone who gets in his way."

Bitterly, Jessica gripped his upper arms. "But if he takes that well, our livestock will die, Dan."

"I know that...." Helplessly, he caressed her strained mouth with his fingertips. "We can always pump water from Oak Creek if it comes down to that, so stop worrying. At least the creek runs through our property and not Cunningham's. If their well goes dry, we have a second water source. They don't. I was hoping that today would be happy for you in all ways, Jessica."

She gazed down at the ring on her finger. The small diamond twinkled in the early evening light. "I'm sorry. I was happy, Dan. So very, very happy." She struggled to smile for his sake as she placed her arms around his neck.

"I wish," Dan said in a frustrated tone, "that I could make these problems at the ranch go away. This family doesn't deserve any more hard luck than it already has."

Anger, worry and concern warred within Jessica. "Jim isn't a two-heart like Kate thinks," she said fiercely. "I have a feeling he'll fight for us. He won't let his father get away with this. Jim is fair-minded."

Dan nodded. He didn't tell Jessica that Old Man Cunningham owned the ranch until he died, and that the property rights were not to be divided among the three sons. The ranch was going to Bo and Chet. Jim had absolutely no leverage at all, even if he wanted to try and help the Donovans in the lawsuit over water rights.

Gently, Dan stroked her warm, flushed cheek. Instantly, Jessica responded to his touch and he smiled inwardly. Little by little, as he caressed her cheek, her brow and soft, silky hair, she quieted. Much of the worry was replaced with that serene look in her eyes again. The effect she had on him was similar.

"I'm putting Gan out with his band of mares today," he told her as he led her toward the stallion's pen. "Sam agreed. The stallion is tame now and he isn't going to be attacking a man on foot or horseback, so it's safe to let him be with his ladies."

Jessica sighed and wrapped her arm around Dan's waist as they walked. Her heart was heavy with worry, but she knew he had worked hard to get the stallion trained to the point where such a gift could be bestowed upon the animal. It would be one more job they wouldn't have to do. Natural breeding could take place instead. "Yes, let's watch him race out of his pen for the pasture."

Gan was waiting at the corral gate, his head extended, his fine ears pricked forward. He nickered as Dan drew near. Jessica stood back and smiled softly. The stallion, over time, had grown to love Dan. It was obvious in the way the animal nudged his shoulder as he opened the gate. As Gan moved, the shining ripple of his muscles was something to behold. She watched the stallion lift his tail like a flag once Dan had opened the gate, and give a deep, bugling cry that echoed throughout the canyon.

Looking over at the south pasture, where all the broodmares were kept, Jessica saw a number of them lift their heads from grazing on the dry, withered grass, and whinny in return.

Gan dug his rear hooves into the dirt, the dust flying as he lunged out of his corral. His long black mane and tail flowed as he galloped full speed toward his mares, a little over a mile away. Jessica heard Dan chuckle as he closed the gate. She liked the smile on his handsome face, the warm look in his gray eyes as he watched the stallion fly across the hard clay floor of the pasture. Gan's joyous bugling sounded again and again.

Jessica felt her spirits lift unaccountably. With the coming lawsuit she should feel sad and afraid. Miraculously, she didn't, and she knew why. It was because of the man wrapped in darkness who was walking toward her. His eyes were banked with coals of hunger—for her. Reaching out, she touched his fingers.

"He's free," she whispered. "You helped free Gan—and me...."

Sliding his arms around Jessica, Dan nuzzled her cheek. The past few weeks had convinced him that he was worthy of Jessica in every way. Dan was going to let his past go—completely. His bout with alcohol wouldn't be forgotten, but now, thanks to Jessica, he had put it into perspective. She had helped him retrieve his dignity and reembrace who and what he was. He was a man with an incredible gift with horses, a gift that he would use here at the ranch. Over time, the money he'd save from his work would build toward their bright future—together. He no longer worried about his place in Jessica's life. Everything he was had helped to save Jessica. The power of that knowledge had given him back his shredded self-esteem.

Pressing his mouth against her soft cheek, he whispered, "We're free to love one another, like that stallion will love his mares." Gently framing Jessica's face, Dan whispered, "And I'm going to love you forever...."

* * * * *

Nicole Helm grew up with her nose in a book and the dream of one day becoming a writer. Luckily, after a few failed career choices, she gets to follow that dream—writing down-to-earth contemporary romance and romantic suspense. From farmers to cowboys, Midwest to *the* West, Nicole writes stories about people finding themselves and finding love in the process. She lives in Missouri with her husband and two sons and dreams of someday owning a barn.

Visit the Author Profile page
at Harlequin.com for more titles.

WYOMING COWBOY JUSTICE

Nicole Helm

For all the Intrigue readers who took a chance on a new Intrigue author last year. Thank you.

Chapter 1

Laurel Delaney surveyed the dead body in front of her with as much detachment as she could manage.

"Know him?" the deputy who'd first answered the call asked apologetically.

"We're distantly related. But who am I not related to in these parts?" Laurel managed a grim smile. Jason Delaney. Her third cousin or something. Dead in a cattle field from a gunshot wound to the chest, presumably.

"Rancher called it in."

Laurel nodded as she studied the body. It was only her second murder since she'd been hired by the county sheriff's department six years ago, and only her first murder in the detective bureau.

And yes, she was related to the victim. Unfortunately, she wasn't exaggerating about the number of Bent County residents she was related to. She'd known Jason in passing at best. A family reunion or funeral here or there, but that was all. He didn't live in Bent, his parents—second cousins, she thought, to her parents—weren't part of the main offshoot of Delaneys who ran Bent.

"We do have a lead," Deputy Hart offered.

"What's that?" Laurel asked, surveying the cattle field around them. This ranch, like pretty much everything in Bent County, Wyoming, was in the middle of nowhere. No highway traffic ran nearby, no businesses in the surrounding areas. Just fields and mountains in the distance. Pretty and isolated, and not the spot one would expect to find a murder victim.

"The rancher says Clint Danvers broke down in front of his place last night. Asked to use his phone. He's the only one who was around. Aside from the cows, of course."

Laurel frowned at Hart. "Clint Danvers is a teenager."

"One we've arrested more times than I can count."

"Had to be a Carson," she muttered, because no matter that Clint wasn't technically a Carson, his mother was the mother of a Carson as well. Which meant the Carson clan would count him as theirs, which would mean trouble with a Delaney investigating.

Laurel herself didn't care about the Delaney-Carson feud that so many people in town loved to bring up time and again, Carsons most especially. Her father could intone about the generations of "bad element" that had been bred into the Carsons, her brother who still lived in Bent could sneer his nose at every Carson who walked into his bank, her sister could snidely comment every time one of them bought something from the Delaney

General Store. The street could divide itself—Delaney establishments on one side, Carson on the other.

Laurel didn't care—it was all silliness and history as far as she was concerned. She was after the truth, not a way to make some century-old feud worse.

A vehicle approached and Laurel shaded her eyes against the early-morning sun.

"Coroner," Hart said.

Laurel waved at the coroner, Gracie Delaney, her first cousin, because yes, relations all over the dang place.

Gracie stepped through the tape and barbed wire fence easily, and then surveyed the body. "Name?"

"Jason Delaney."

Gracie's eyebrows furrowed. "Is it bad I have no idea how we're related to him?"

Laurel sighed. "If it is, we're in the same boat." It was a very strange thing to work the death of someone you were related to, but didn't know. Laurel figured she was supposed to feel some kind of sympathy, and she did, but not in any different way than she did on any other death she worked.

"All right. I'll take my pictures, then I'll get in touch with next of kin," Gracie said.

Hart and Gracie discussed details while Laurel studied the area around the body. There wasn't much to go on, and until cows learned how to talk, she had zero possible witnesses.

Except Clint Danvers.

She didn't mind arresting a Carson every now and again no matter what hubbub it raised about the feud nonsense, but murder was going to cause a lot more than a hubbub. Especially the murder of a Delaney.

She processed the crime scene with Hart and Gracie.

Even though Hart had taken pictures when he'd first arrived, Laurel took a few more. They canvased the scene again, finding not one shred of evidence to go on.

Which meant Clint was her only hope, and what a complicated hope that was.

Gracie loaded up the body with Hart's help, and Laurel tossed her gear back into her car. "I'm going to go question Clint. You on until three?"

Hart nodded. "Let me know what I can do."

Laurel waved a goodbye and got into her car. She didn't have to look up Clint's residence as Bent was small and intimate, and secrets weren't much of ones for long. He lived with his mother in a falling-down house on the outskirts of Bent.

When Chasity Haskins-Carson-Danvers and so on answered the door, freshly lit cigarette hanging out of her mouth, Laurel knew this wasn't going to go well.

"Mrs. Danvers."

Chasity blew the smoke right in Laurel's face. "Ms. Pig," she returned conversationally.

"I'm looking for Clint."

"You people always are."

"It's incredibly important I'm able to talk to Clint, and soon. This is far more serious than drugs or speeding, and I'm only looking to help."

"Delaneys are never looking to help," the older woman replied. She shrugged negligently. "He's not here. Haven't seen him for two or three days."

Laurel managed a thin-lipped smile. It could be a lie, but it could also be the truth. That was the problem with most of the Carsons. You just never knew when they were being honest and helpful, or a pack of liars trying to make a Delaney's life difficult. Because to them the feud wasn't history, it was a living, breathing entity to wrap their lives around.

Laurel thanked Mrs. Danvers anyway and then sighed as she got back in her unmarked car. Most unfortunately, she knew exactly who would know where Clint was. And he was the absolute last man she wanted to speak to.

Grady Carson. Clint's older half brother and something like the de facto leader of the Carson clan. Much like the men in her family, Grady Carson put far too much stock in a *feud* for this being the twenty-first century.

A feud over land and cattle and things that had happened over a hundred years ago. Laurel didn't understand why people clung to it, but that didn't mean she actively *liked* any of the Carsons. Not when they routinely tried to make it hard for her to do her job.

Which was the second problem with Grady. He ran Rightful Claim, which she pulled up across the street from.

She glared at the offensive sign outside the bar—a neon centaur-like creature, half horse, half very busty woman, a blinking sack of gold hanging off her saddle. Aside from the neon signs, it looked like every saloon in every Western movie or TV show she'd ever seen. Wood siding and a walk in front of it, a ramshackle overhang, hand-painted signs with the mileage, and arrows to the nearest cities, all hundreds of miles away.

Laurel refused to call it a saloon. It was a bar. Seedy. It would be mostly empty on a Tuesday afternoon, but come evening it would be full of people she'd probably arrested. And Carsons everywhere.

Grady wasn't going to hand over Clint's whereabouts, Laurel knew that, but she had to try to convince him she only wanted to help. Grady was a lot of things—a tattooed, snarling, no-respect-for-authority hooligan—but much like the Delaneys, the Carsons were all about family.

Mentally steeling herself for what would likely amount to a verbal sparring match, Laurel took her first step toward the stupid swinging doors Grady claimed were original to the saloon. Laurel maintained that he bought it off the internet from some lame Hollywood set. Mainly because he got furious when she did.

She blew out a breath and tried to blow out her frustration with it. Yes, Grady had always rubbed her completely the wrong way, and yes, that meant sometimes she couldn't keep her cool and sniped right back at him. But she could handle this. She had a case to investigate.

Laurel nudged the swinging saloon doors and slid through the opening, making as little disturbance as possible. The less time Grady had to prepare for her arrival, the more chance she had of getting some sensible words in before he started doing that…thing.

"I see you finally found the balls to step inside, princess."

Laurel gritted her teeth and turned to the sound of Grady's low, easy voice. Doing that…thing already. The thing where he said obnoxious stuff, called her princess, or worse—deputy princess—and some tiny foreign part of her did that other thing she refused to name or acknowledge.

Her eyes had to adjust from sunlight to the dim bar interior, but when they did, she almost wished they hadn't.

He was standing on a chair, hammering a nail into

the rough-hewn wood planks that made up the walls of the main area. Lining the doorway were pictures of the place over the years—a dingy black-and-white photograph of the bar in the 1800s, a bright pop of boisterous color from the time a famous singer had visited in the sixties, and photos documenting all Grady had done inside to somehow make it look less like a dive bar in a small town and more like a mix between old and new.

Much like the man himself. Laurel always had the sneaking suspicion Grady and the Carson cousins he routinely hung around with could straddle the lines of centuries quite easily. Sure, he was dressed in modern-day jeans and a simple black T-shirt that she had no doubt was sized with the express purpose of showing off the muscles of his arms and shoulders along with the lick of tattoos that spiraled out from the cuff and toward his elbow.

But he, and all the Carsons she had pulled over or served a warrant on more times than she could count on two hands and two feet, wore old battered cowboy hats like they were just dreaming of a day they could rob a stagecoach and escape to a brothel.

She wouldn't put it past Grady to *have* a brothel, but for the time being the worst thing he did in Rightful Claim was sell moonshine without a license.

Something she'd reported him on. Twice.

"Gonna stand there and watch me work all day? Want to slap my wrist over some made-up infraction?"

"It's funny you call this work, Carson. You don't have a single patron in here." She glared at the picture he rested on the nail he'd just pounded into the wall. It was a cross-stitched, nearly naked woman. Cross-stitched. Oh, she *hated* this place.

"There are no patrons because I don't officially open until three. But there's nothing like a Delaney coming into *my* place of business and criticizing *my* work ethic when your family has—"

"Please spare me the trip down family feud lane. I have business to discuss with you. It's important."

"*You* have business to discuss with *me*?" He got off the chair, just an easy step down with those long, powerful legs of his. Not that she noticed long or powerful, even when he was roaring his way down Main Street on that stupid, *stupid* motorcycle of his.

"I'm going to need a drink to go with this interesting turn of events," he drawled.

"You're going to drink before three in the afternoon on a day you're working?"

He walked past her, way closer than he needed to, and that wolfish smile was way too bright, way too feral. How could anyone call him attractive? He was downright…downright…*wild, uncivilized, lawless.*

All terrible things. Or so she told herself as often as she could manage to make her brain function when he was smirking at her.

"That's exactly what I'm going to do, princess."

"Deputy. This is official." She followed him toward the long, worn bar. Again, Grady claimed it was original, and it looked it. Scarred and nicked, though waxed enough that it shone. She couldn't imagine how anyone balanced a glass of anything on the uneven wood, or why they'd want to.

"All right, deputy princess—"

She was trying very hard not to let her irritation show, but the little growl that escaped her mouth whether she wanted it to or not gave her away.

The bastard laughed.

Low, rumbly. She could feel that rumble vibrate through her limbs even though there was this ancient big slab of a bar between them. *Hate, hate, hate.*

"Gonna report me again?"

She schooled her features in what she hoped was a semblance of professionalism. "Not this afternoon, though if I see you serve the moonshine when I know you don't have a license for it, I will contact the proper authorities."

"If that's your idea of pillow talk—"

"I know, all those multisyllable words, too hard for you to comprehend," she snapped, irritated with herself, as always, for letting him get to her. "But this is about your brother. And murder." His eyes went as hard as his expression, which gave her a little burst of satisfaction. *Not so tough now, are you?* "Care to shut up and listen?"

Grady had always had a little too much fun riling up the Delaneys, Laurel in particular. She got so pinched-looking, and when he really got her going, the hints of gold in her dark eyes switched to flame. And unlike the rest of the Delaneys, Laurel gave as good as she got.

But her words erased any good humor riling her up had created. Murder and Clint. Damn. Clint might be his half brother without an ounce of Carson blood in him, but he was still family. Which meant he was under Grady's protection.

Grady jerked his chin toward the back of the bar. Though the regulars knew not to swing through the old saloon doors until three on the dot or later, he didn't want anyone accidentally overhearing this conversation.

"I'm sorry, I don't speak caveman. Is that little chin jerk supposed to mean something?"

He flicked a glance down her tall, slender frame. He could see her weapon outlined under the shapeless polo shirt she wore. The mannish khakis were slightly better than the polo because they at least gave the impression of her having an ass. A shame of an outfit, all in all.

"Let me ask you this," he said, leaning his elbows on the freshly waxed surface of the bar. He'd spent most of a lifetime learning how to appear completely unaffected when affected was exactly what he was, and this was no different. "Is this visit personal or professional?" he asked, making sure to drawl the word *personal* and infuse it with plenty of added meaning.

"Professional," she all but spat. "Like I said earlier. Trust me when I say I will never set foot through those pointless swinging doors for anything other than strictly professional business."

"Aw, sweetheart, don't lay down a challenge you won't be able to win."

"I see that even when it comes to your brother, you can't take anything important seriously. How about this? The murder victim is Jason Delaney. The only person around at the time of the murder was Clint Danvers."

Grady swore.

"I need to question your brother before news of this murder and that *he was a witness* spreads through town like wildfire. All we need is for one person to see a Delaney's been murdered, and know Clint is technically a Carson and a witness, and we have a whole feud situation on our hands. Are you going to help me or not?" she said evenly, the only show of temper at this point in her eyes, where he could all but picture the flecks of gold bursting into flame one by one.

He didn't trust a Delaney in the least, but Laurel Delaney wasn't quite like the rest. She hated the feud, and he almost believed she might be more interested in the truth than crucifying Clint without evidence. The rest of the town would be a different matter. This would result in the kind of uproar that could only cause problems for *everyone*.

Clint was in trouble, and Bent was in trouble, and the thing that kept the Carsons and Delaneys in this town, most of them hating and blaming each other for good or for bad, was that something about Bent had been poured into their blood at birth.

Something about the buildings that had stood the test of time in the shadow of distant, rolling mountains, far away from any kind of typical civilization. Something about the way history was imprinted into their fingerprints and their names, even if some people chose to ignore it.

Bent was like an organ in the body of those who stayed, and no matter what side of the feud you were on, Bent was the common good. Usually no one could agree on what that meant.

This wouldn't be any different. Laurel would want to solve the problem with warrants and investigations and all sorts of time-consuming bull. He and his cousins could have it sorted out with a few well-timed threats, maybe some fists, probably within the week.

So, he smiled at Laurel, as genially as he could manage for a man who wasn't used to being genial at all. "Have to pass, princess. Guess you and your gun will have to do all the heavy lifting."

Her eyes narrowed. "Sometimes I can't decide if you think I'm stupid or if that's just you. This is real life, Grady, not the Wild West—especially your lame version of it. If you want to arrest a murderer, you have to conduct an investigation. If you want to save your brother from the possibility of not just being a suspect, but being convicted, you need to work with the police. This isn't about Delaney versus Carson. It's about right and wrong. Truth and justice."

"Guess we'll find out."

She shook her head. "Don't come crying to me when Clint is locked up."

"Don't let the doors slap that pretty little ass of yours on the way out. You might end up enjoying it."

"You know, I don't get to say this enough in a day. Screw you, Grady." She flipped him off as she sauntered out of the saloon. The doors didn't hit her on the way out, but that didn't stop him from watching her disappear.

He waited until she was completely gone, then watched the clock tick by another few minutes. Casually, he pulled out his phone, then gave one last glance at the doors that had gone completely still. As if he didn't have a care in the world, he sent off a text to his cousins.

We need a meeting.

Ty was the first to respond. Mine, cow, or woman?

Grady's mouth quirked at the code they'd developed as teens. *Mine* was property, because the Carsons had managed to eke out some of their own, even with the Delaney name stamped all over this town since the first Delaney bastards had screwed the first Carsons out of their rightful claim to land and gold. Because of that nasty start of things in Bent, the Carsons didn't let anybody mess with what was rightfully theirs.

Cow meant family, because the Carsons and the Delaneys of old had gone to great and sometimes disastrous lengths to protect their livestock around the turn of the twentieth century, and these days, going to great lengths to protect family was still a number one priority for the Carsons.

And *woman*...

Grady stared at where Laurel had gone. Well, she was a woman, and she was a pain. A cop. A Delaney.

Yeah, he had a woman problem, but it was one that he was going to ignore, and it would go away. So, he typed Cow into his phone before grabbing his keys and heading out the back.

Chapter 2

Laurel wasn't big on breaking rules or protocol, but considering she was currently investigating a murder, and Grady likely knew where the only potential witness/ suspect was, following him was necessary.

It was, however, difficult to follow someone surreptitiously in Bent. There weren't any cars to hide behind, and the roads that crisscrossed in and out of town were surrounded by long, wide stretches of plains, the mountains a hazy promise in the distance.

Still, when Grady's motorcycle roared out of town toward the west, quickly followed by another motorcycle, Laurel was pretty sure she knew where the motorcycle parade of doom was headed. Which made her job a hell of a lot easier.

She gave them a few minutes, then drove out of Bent in the direction of the Carson Ranch. Though Grady didn't live there full-time, everyone knew he routinely bunked out at the ranch Noah Carson ran.

Much like the Delaneys tended to congregate around their own ranch on the exact opposite side of town. As if the two ranches were facing off, Bent their no-man's-land in between.

Laurel sighed. This whole thing was going to make that no-man's-land erupt into a chaos they hadn't seen for decades, if she didn't get some information out of Clint, and soon. She'd been stupid to think Grady had half a brain and would grant her access.

But she wasn't stupid enough to give up, and she was too darn stubborn to let Bent get dragged into another foolish war. It might not be the Wild West anymore, but people—many of whom were far too armed for their own good—getting riled up and fighting was never a good thing.

Especially when she had a murder to solve.

Laurel parked her car at the curve in the road, the last place she couldn't be seen. She'd have to hike up the rest of the way and do her best to stay behind underbrush and land swells and whatever she could find. Hopefully the Carson clan would be too busy planning how to hide away Clint to look out the windows and see her.

She pocketed her keys, checked her weapon and set out into the brisk fall afternoon. She remembered to turn the sound on her cell and radio off as she walked, keeping her eyes on where the Carson spread would eventually come into view.

When it did, she paused. She might be the practical, methodical sort, but she never failed to take a moment or two to appreciate where she lived. The sky was a breathtaking blue, puffy white clouds drifting by on the early fall breeze. The grass and brush were a mix of browns and gold. Surrounded by the all-inspiring glory of the majestic peaks of the Wind River mountains and the rolling red hills was a cluster of buildings sitting in the middle of a broad golden field.

The Carson Ranch wasn't much like its Delaney counterpart. It was populated with sturdy, mostly Carson-built buildings. They'd preserved most of the original ranch house, making improvements and expanding only when necessary. Like the saloon, it was a bit like stepping back in time with a modern layer over top.

The Delaney Ranch, on the other hand, was sleek, modern and gleaming, thanks to Laurel's father. The only building on the entire spread that predated her father was the one Laurel used as home right now. A tiny cabin that had supposedly been her ancestor's original homestead, though modernized with plumbing and electricity and whatnot.

It would fit in well enough on the Carsons' land. Laurel frowned at that uncomfortable thought. Nothing about her or her life would fit in with this group of ne'er-do-wells.

She edged along the fence line, trying to stay out of sight from any windows. Two motorcycles were parked in front of the main house, and Laurel had to wonder if they'd come here because Clint was here, or if they'd chosen the place to have some kind of pseudo-planning meeting.

Laurel knew one thing: Grady wasn't as nonchalant as he'd pretended. She'd never known him to bow out of the bar this close to opening before.

Maybe Clint *was* here. She could go to the house, demand to see him and show the three Carson cousins she wasn't scared of them—not Grady and his swagger, not Noah and his quiet stoicism, and not Ty, who'd recently returned after having served years as an army ranger. They might be big, strong men, but she was a law enforcement agent, and she'd faced bigger, badder men than them.

It would set a good precedent to stare them down, to demand access or answers. The Carsons seemed to think they were above the law, especially if it was a Delaney trying to enforce it, and she didn't have to let that stand.

But she didn't see another intact vehicle anywhere, just a handful of rusting, tire-less old cars and trucks. If Clint was here, he'd either gotten here on foot or hidden his vehicle.

There were a ton of outbuildings. While the Carson boys sat inside and planned whatever they were planning, maybe she could find a clue in one of those.

She quickened her pace, making it into the stables first. There were four horses in stalls, huffing happily, and a surprising amount of tidiness inside for the lack of it out. She made her way to the empty stall toward the back. It could fit a motorcycle or—

"Hands up," a husky feminine voice commanded.

Laurel whirled at the sound, hand on the butt of her weapon, and then scowled. "Vanessa, do not point a gun at me."

"Got a warrant?" Vanessa Carson asked, holding an old-looking rifle pointed directly in Laurel's direction.

"Is that a musket?" Laurel asked incredulously, then shook her head. "Regardless, stop pointing it at me. That's an official order."

With a hefty sigh, Grady's sister lowered her rifle.

Laurel felt the same thing she always felt when she looked at her former best friend. Regret, and a pang for a childhood before things had been poisoned by some stupid feud.

"Why are you sneaking around our stables?" Vanessa demanded.

"Official reasons."

Vanessa smirked and pulled her phone out of her pocket. She held it up to her ear. "Hey, Grady. I'm out in the stables. We've got an uninvited visitor."

Laurel threw her hands in the air, frustrated beyond belief. "When will you all realize I am *trying* to help you. Help Bent." It was all she'd ever wanted to do. Help Bent. Even people who hated her because of her last name knew *that* was true.

"Helping Bent usually translates to helping the Delaneys when it comes to your people, Laurel. Why should this be any different?"

Laurel had a million arguments for that. Even though she'd beat her head against that concrete wall time and time again, she had no compunction about doing it again now. But she saw something out of the corner of her eye.

Something that looked suspiciously like a skinny teenager running for the mountains.

Laurel didn't hesitate, didn't concern herself with Vanessa's *musket*, of all things, and most definitely didn't worry about the impending arrival of Grady.

She pushed past Vanessa and ran after the quickly disappearing figure. She ignored Vanessa's shouts and put all her concentration into running as fast as she could.

"Clint Danvers, stop right there," she yelled, gaining absolutely no ground on the kid, but not losing any, either. "Bent County Sheriff's Department, I am ordering you to stop!" She could threaten to shoot, of course, but that would cause more problems than it'd ever solve.

Clint darted behind a barn at the west edge of the property, and Laurel swore, because he could go a couple different directions hidden behind that barn and she wouldn't be able to see which one he chose.

Her lungs were burning, but she pushed her body as fast as it would go, cutting the corner around the barn close. Close enough she ran right into a hard wall of something that knocked her back and onto her butt.

She would have popped right back up, ignoring her throbbing nose and butt, but the hard object she'd run into was Grady himself. And now he was standing there, giving no indication he'd let her pass.

She glared up at him and his imposing arms folded over his chest. "I detest you," she said furiously, even knowing she should tamp down her temper and be a professional.

His all-too-full lips curved into one of those wolfish smiles. "My life is a success, then."

"He's getting away, and if you think that's going to go over well for him, you're sorely mistaken."

Grady jerked his chin toward the house. "Ty's after him on his bike. We'll have him rounded up in a few."

"Oh," Laurel managed to say, blinking. That was not what she'd expected out of Grady. At all. She figured he'd purposefully stepped in her way so Clint could escape.

"But I'm not going to let you talk to him, princess." He held out his hand as if he was going to help her up.

She pushed herself to her feet. "*Let* me?" she muttered. As if he could *let* her do anything in her official capacity.

"But I am going to clean you up. I think you might have broken your nose."

She touched her fingers to her nose, surprised to find a sticky substance there. She'd been so angry, she hadn't even realized her nose was bleeding. "I could arrest you for assaulting an officer."

"Babe, you ran right into me. That's not assault. It's not watching where you're going."

She didn't screech or growl or pound her fists into his chest like she wanted to. No, she took a deep breath in and then out.

She had a job to do, and Grady Carson could break her nose, threaten her sanity, but he could not stand in her way.

Grady didn't like the uncomfortable hitch in his chest at the sight of Laurel's face all bloody. It was her own damn fault she'd crashed into him. He'd heard her coming, of course, but he hadn't known she'd turn the corner at the same exact time he had.

At full speed.

She was entirely to blame, but somehow he felt guilty as he walked her back to the main house. "We'll clean you up, then you can be on your way."

"I'm just going to come back with a search warrant. Clint is the only potential witness in a *murder*, Grady. I can't stop going after him until he answers some questions."

He hated that she was using that reasonable, even-keeled cop tone with him when there was a trickle of blood slowly dripping down her chin.

"Ain't none of my business what you got to do, Deputy," he said as lazily as he could manage, even though he didn't feel lazy at all.

His teenage half brother was a dope, plain and simple. Grady didn't think Clint had actually killed anyone, but he had a bad feeling based on Clint's running away that Clint knew *something*. Considering Clint's mom had kicked Clint out of the house just last week and had lectured Grady on getting him sorted out, Grady could only feel pissed and more of that unwelcome guilt.

He hated feeling guilty. So, when Ty pulled up on his bike, alone, Grady cursed. "Where the hell is he?"

"I don't know, man. Disappeared."

"That's impossible."

Ty shrugged. "Noah took one of the horses to go search the trees. What the hell happened to her?" Ty asked, gesturing toward Laurel.

"Your cousin broke my nose," the infuriating woman stated.

Ty's eyebrows winged up.

"I did not break her nose. She ran into me at full speed and broke her own damn nose."

"Want me to go open the saloon for you?" Ty asked.

Grady nodded and fished his keys out of his pocket. He tossed them at Ty. "I'll be there soon."

"You don't have to do this," Laurel said as Ty rode off. "My nose isn't really broken. It's just bleeding. I can clean myself up in my car."

"How do you know it's not broken?"

She shrugged. She was a tall woman, but narrow. Narrow shoulders, narrow hips. Her hair always pulled back in a bouncy brown ponytail. Her face always devoid of makeup. Her body always covered up. The complete opposite of his type.

Which was why he'd never quite understood why his gaze tended to linger on her when they happened to be in the same vicinity, or why he got such a kick out of pissing her the hell off, and always had, since she'd been a girl hanging around his sister back before Vanessa had decided Delaneys were evil incarnate.

But one thing he did know and always had known—no matter how fragile Laurel Delaney could look on the outside, she was as tough as nails when it came down to it.

"I've had my nose broken before," she retorted. "I know what it feels like."

"You?"

"Yes, me." She glared at him, all piss and vinegar and a special brand of spitfire unique to her. "Meth-head head-butted me once."

"A meth-head head-butted you and your father let you stay in police work?"

"You don't know what I did to the meth-head in return."

Hell. Bloodthirsty was such a turn-on, even on a Delaney. Maybe especially on one. "Come inside so we can wash you up before you slink back to wherever you hid your car."

"I did not hide my car."

Grady raised an eyebrow at her and she returned his look with an arch one of her own.

"I parked it down the hill so I could have a nice, head-clearing walk." She smiled sweetly.

"Sure." Grady pushed the front door open and led

her into the kitchen. "Sit." He pointed to a barstool situated under the kitchen counter.

He grabbed a washcloth and ran it under some warm water before walking around to her.

"I can clean it myself," she said, holding her hand out for the cloth.

Instead he did what he knew would piss her off. He gripped her chin and held her head still as he used the washcloth to wipe away the blood.

She sat there regally, not sniping at him or pushing him away, and he had to fight back a smile over the fact she had changed tactics with him.

He wiped the blood from her nose and where it had dripped down her chin. She was fair-skinned and her nose was faintly freckled. While most Delaneys reveled in the finer things, the more genteel side of life, and her elegant face sure fit all that, Laurel had never been one for elegance and pretty things.

"You sure it's not broken?" he asked, and he was close enough that the hair hanging around her face stirred.

"I'm sure." She stared at him with those golden-brown eyes and there wasn't an ounce of animosity hiding there. He couldn't help that his gaze dropped to her unpainted mouth.

Laurel had always been easy to resist, not because he'd never found her attractive, but because it only ever took him opening his mouth to rile her up enough to have her walk away. But she wasn't bristling like she usually did, and he figured that was all kinds of dangerous.

"I'm not out to get you," she said as sincerely as she'd ever said anything to him.

Her sincerity was good enough to break this particular spell. "You'll have to pardon my lack of belief, considering how many times your father has tried to get Rightful Claim shut down." He stepped away and tossed the cloth in the sink. He crossed his arms across his chest and frowned intimidatingly down at her.

"That doesn't have anything to do with me. Should I blame you for everything your father's ever done? Because I hear it's quite a list."

He wouldn't admit she had a fair point.

"Work with me, Grady," she implored, speaking to him for once like he was a person instead of a Carson. "For your brother's sake. For Bent's sake. Put everything that came before behind us for the sake of *this* case and this case alone. If Clint is innocent, I don't want to be the one who puts him away for murder. I don't want a real murderer to get away with something because of feud crap."

"Haven't you ever heard the old saying that those who fail to learn from history are doomed to repeat it?"

"Well, I don't think there's any chance of me falling in love with you and dying in some army-led Native American massacre, or you and all the Carsons going off to war and eradicating an entire generation. So we might just make it. Did I cover all the idiotic Delaney-Carson fairy tales?"

His mouth curved. "I don't know, the illegitimate Carson who married a Delaney as payback always struck my fancy."

"That poor woman died in childbirth."

"And thus the waters between Carson and Delaney never commingled."

"You're terrible."

"Don't you forget it, princess."

The door squeaked open and Noah entered, slapping his cowboy hat against his thigh so that dust puffed up. "Must have had some help. That boy isn't anywhere out there."

"I need a list of friends, places he might have gone, that sort of thing," Laurel said in her demanding cop way that got Grady's back up like few other things.

But she'd implored him to help, and while helping a Delaney was the first and biggest thing on his *Don't Ever Do* list, this was about Clint. It was about Bent. Much as he might enjoy the feud tales and riling up the Delaneys, he didn't actually want any trouble in town. Trouble wasn't good for business, and as much as he would never admit to anyone, a little too hard on his heart.

He loved the town like he loved his brother. He loved his saloon like he loved the graves of every Carson before him. He might not have sworn to protect this place like Laurel had, but he had the sneaking suspicion they both wanted the same thing.

Damn it all.

"Your best bets are Pauline Hugh or Fred Gaskill," Grady offered.

Laurel hopped off the barstool. "Hugh, Gaskill. Got it. And if he comes back here, call me. Or bring him to me. I only need to question him. The longer he runs, the worse this looks. Please let him know that."

Grady nodded and Noah did, too, and then Laurel was striding out of the house.

"So, we're working with a Delaney," Noah said as if he didn't quite believe it.

"That Delaney and *that* Delaney only. And only until

we get a handle on what Clint's involvement is and how much we need to protect him."

Noah made one of his many noncommittal sounds that Grady usually found funny, but he wasn't much in a mood to find anything funny today. "What's that grunt supposed to mean?"

"Oh, nothing. You just seemed awfully cozy with Deputy Delaney there."

"At least I wasn't blushing in front of her."

Noah bristled. "I was not blushing."

"Just don't get any hooking up ideas of your own." Which was the wrong thing to say. It was beyond irritating, since he always knew the right thing to say, or when to keep his mouth shut. Grady never gave too much away.

Noah's rare smile spread across his face. "You staking a claim, cousin?"

"No, I am not. We just have to be careful how we play this. I'm going to work now. Go shovel some manure or something."

"Oh, there's plenty right here to shovel up," Noah replied.

Grady flipped him off and headed out of the house. He took a second to stand on the porch and look at the blazing sun in the distance, the rolling red hills, the rocky outcroppings of this beautiful Wyoming world.

He definitely wasn't watching Laurel Delaney stride down the long gravel driveway, a woman on a mission.

A mission he was more than a little irritated to find he shared.

Chapter 3

Laurel fumbled with her phone to turn off the beeping alarm. She wanted desperately to hit Snooze, but there was too much to do.

She hadn't gotten home until well after midnight, after tracking down all the names the Carsons had given her yesterday. She'd questioned both teens, but neither one had been able to give her the faintest hint on Clint's whereabouts.

She yawned and stretched out in bed. Oh, she didn't believe any of the shifty teenagers, but she couldn't force them to tell her anything. Which meant today would be another long day of investigating. Even if she got ahold of Clint to question him, she wasn't hopeful she'd get anything out of him.

She didn't have time to find Clint *and* investigate a murder that would be common knowledge in Bent and the surrounding areas by now.

Murder. Who had *murdered* Jason Delaney?

She forced herself out of bed and walked from her small room to the tiny kitchen. It was a cold morning, but it would have to be a quick one. Coffee, shower, get on the road. No time to build a fire and enjoy the cozy fall silence.

She frowned at the odd sound interrupting said silence as she clicked her coffee maker on. Something like a rumble.

Or a motorcycle.

"Hell," she muttered. She could not argue with Grady before she had coffee. Before she even had time to get dressed. She looked down at the flannel pajamas. It could be worse—she could be wearing the ones with bacon and eggs on them, or more revealing ones.

But she wasn't wearing a bra and she very nearly blushed at the idea of being bra-less in the same room as Grady.

She jumped at the pounding on her door, which was silly when she knew it had been coming. But she hadn't expected it to all but shake her little cabin.

Well, no time to fix the pajama situation. Worse, no time to fix the no-coffee situation. So she put her best frown in place and opened the door. "What do you—" But she stopped talking because it wasn't just Grady.

Grady shoved Clint through the door before following, and for a few seconds Laurel could only stand there and stare. Grady had brought her the only potential witness and the main suspect all rolled up into one. He'd brought a Carson into Delaney territory.

Grady scowled at—she assumed—the naked shock on her face. "The sooner you question him, the sooner you can clear him. You said you know he didn't do it, after all."

"I didn't say that," Laurel returned, shaking herself out of her shock and going for a notebook and a pen.

"What do you mean you didn't say that? Never mind, Clint. Let's go."

Laurel stepped in front of him, holding out a hand to stop him. Somehow that hand landed on his chest. Because even though it was something like thirty degrees outside considering the sun was just beginning to rise, he only had a leather jacket on, unzipped, so that her hand came into contact with the soft material of his T-shirt, covering the very not-soft expanse of his very broad chest.

She jerked her hand away and focused on her notebook. "Calm down," she said, hoping *she* sounded calm. "I said I don't *think* he did it. I'm only out for the truth, and if the truth is Clint's nose is clean, I'll make sure my investigation reflects that." She lifted her chin and met his blazing blue gaze.

She'd never seen Grady this riled up before. He was more of the "annoy the crap out of people till they took a swing at him, then gleefully beat them to a pulp" type.

Which was why it didn't surprise her in the least when he relaxed his shoulders and his gaze swept down her chest. "Nice jammies."

She sidestepped him and gestured Clint to a seat at her small kitchen table. "Sit, Clint. I have a few simple questions for you. Now, right now, we don't know what happened, so I need you to be honest and forthcoming, because the more we know, the quicker we can get to the bottom of this."

Clint sat in the chair, slumping in it, looking everywhere but at her or Grady. "Sure. Whatever," he muttered.

Laurel opened up to a clean page in her notebook and quickly jotted down Clint's name, the date and time. She left out Grady's presence, and she didn't have time to wonder about why. "Now, Mr. Jennings said you came to his door around ten asking to make a phone call. Is that true?"

Clint shrugged again, fidgeting and sighing heavily. "Guess so."

"And why did you go to Mr. Jennings's door?"

"Crap car broke down not far from that rancher's house. I walked up, asked to use his phone since mine was dead, and then my girl came and picked me up." He pulled at a thread on the cuff of his jacket. "I wasn't anywhere near that field."

"How did you know the dead body was in the field?" Grady growled before Laurel could voice the same question.

Clint opened his mouth, but no sound came out. Laurel had to close her eyes. The idiot kid couldn't even lie? Hell, she'd come up with one if Grady's furious blue gaze was on her like that.

"You promised me you were telling the truth," Grady said, leaning over the table and getting in Clint's face. "So help me God, Clint, you do not lie to me and get away with it."

"Gentlemen," Laurel said in her best peacemaking tone, smiling encouragingly at Clint and then Grady. "Let's take a calming breath."

She was pretty sure Grady's calming breath included picturing breaking her neck, but he stood stock-still, fury and frustration radiating off him.

If she hadn't grown up in this town, if she hadn't fascinatedly watched against her will, her whole life, how the Carson clan worked, she might have been concerned.

But where the Delaneys were all cold silences and sharp words, the Carsons exploded. They acted, and it was oftentimes too much and foolish, but Laurel had never doubted it came from the same place her family's way of dealing came from.

Love. Family.

Grady was pissed and frustrated—not just because Clint was lying to him, but at the fact Clint was clearly in trouble and Grady couldn't fix it.

"Let's start from the beginning, Clint," Laurel said evenly and calmly. "With the truth this time."

"Why are you making me talk to a Delaney?" Clint demanded of Grady. "She's going to railroad me no matter what I say."

Grady's entire face looked hard as marble, and the way he had his impressive arms crossed over his chest, well, Laurel didn't think she'd mess with him the way Clint seemed to be doing.

Clint sighed heavily, slouching even further in the chair. "Okay, yeah, I saw the body."

"You…" Grady was clearly working very, very hard not to come unglued.

Laurel held up a hand, hoping it kept him quiet rather than riling him further. "And you didn't call the police because?"

"Because me plus a dead body was only going to make me a suspect. I'm not stupid. I know how you cops work. Maybe you got something on Grady or are getting naked with him, but you got nothing on me."

Laurel hated that a blush infused her cheeks. Naked with Grady? Ha. Ha ha ha. What a laugh. But somehow she couldn't stop thinking about how she didn't have a bra on under her pajamas.

Laurel managed to clear her throat and look condescendingly at Clint. "Would you like me to arrest you? Because I can."

Clint began to bluster, but Laurel continued on in her even tone, because she would not be upset by a couple Carsons in her cabin. "Or you can truthfully answer my questions and allow me to investigate this. And, if you had nothing to do with it, this questioning will be all there is to it."

"I stood up for you with your mom, kid. You screw that up, you're out of chances, and you know it."

Clint stared at the table, but clearly, whatever Grady was talking about got through to him. "The story's all true. I just broke down on the other side of the ranch. I was walking up to the door to see if I could make a call when I heard a shot. I thought it was…" He shook his head. "Well, anyway, it was dark. I didn't see anything. But I heard the shot, a thump like a guy fell over, and footsteps running away."

Laurel scribbled it all down, her heartbeat kicking up. This was something. A lead, no matter how tiny, and that was important. "That's all you heard?"

"Think so."

"Thinking isn't good enough," Grady sneered.

"All right. That's enough out of you." Laurel stood and began pushing Grady into her bedroom. "You are officially uninvited to this questioning. You just stay in here until I'm done."

She pushed him and pushed him until he was far

enough in her room she could close the door. Which she did. On his mutinous face.

Grady stared at the rough-hewn wood of the door and tried very hard to resist the urge to punch it.

What did Clint think he was doing? Noah had found Clint holed up in the stables early this morning and they'd all surrounded him and demanded to hear what he knew. To make a plan. To protect their kin.

In *that* moment Clint had said he hadn't seen anything, that he was the innocentest of bystanders. That was the only reason Grady had decided to throw Clint on his motorcycle and drive him to Laurel's place.

If Grady had known the kid had *seen* it? Witnessed the murder go down and walked away? He would have called any lawyer he could afford.

Instead… Grady swore angrily, pacing Laurel's tiny bedroom. His idiot brother had just made everything ten times worse and *in* the house of a Delaney. How the hell was Grady going to get Clint out of this one?

He took a deep breath. He had to curb his temper, because getting angry wouldn't help Clint. He needed a cool head and a plan.

He took stock of the room around him. Neat. Tidy. The bed was unmade, but considering Laurel was still in her pajamas, maybe she hadn't had a chance. Deputy Delaney did not seem like the type to leave a mess lying around.

She had a tiny bed, all in all. Bigger than a twin, he supposed, but not by much. Which was when he knew the best way to find a sense of inner calm in order to formulate a plan. It was not to go out there and bang his head against a hardheaded moron teenager, but to irritate the hell out of Laurel Delaney while she beat *her* head against Clint's teenage woe-is-me.

Grady settled himself in the middle of Laurel's bed. Comfortable, he'd give her that. The sheets were nice, and the pillows firm and plump and a lot better than the ones he had back at his apartment above the saloon or his bedroom at the ranch.

He grinned to himself, imagining asking her about where she got her pillows. Her eyes would do the fire thing, and she'd probably fist her hands on those slim hips.

Hips that had been settled in this bed this morning. In those ridiculous flannel pajamas. Except, he didn't think she was wearing a bra under said pajamas, and he wouldn't mind seeing what Laurel looked like a little unwrapped.

As it was, he could smell her. Something floral and feminine and so unlike her usual asexual appearance he was a little tempted to get his nose in there and take a good sniff.

Which was insane and more than a little perplexing. He didn't care what a woman smelled like. Vanilla. Citrus. Nothing at all. It was all the same to him as long as they were warm, willing and up for anything.

Laurel Delaney would not be up for anything.

Yeah, couldn't let himself go down *that* particular road. At least, not unless he was making her blush while he did it.

The door opened. Laurel stood with her notebook and pen in hand, her mouth opening to say something that was no doubt important.

Then she saw him and fury flickered across her features like a thunderstorm sweeping through the valley. "Get out of my bed, Grady."

"You know, a woman has never ordered me *out* of her bed before," he returned conversationally, crossing his ankles.

"There's a first time for everything. Your brother's answers are sufficient for now, but he needs to stay in town in case I have more questions, and it's very possible he'll still be considered a suspect if I can't find something more concrete. But I don't have enough on him to apply for warrants, so I suggest you do your darnedest to get through to him."

"Will do, Deputy."

"Now, if you aren't out of my bed and my room in ten seconds, so I can get dressed, I will get my weapon and shoot."

Grady folded his arms behind his head and flashed a grin at her. "Go ahead and get dressed. I don't mind."

She made a squeal of outrage, or maybe she was actually having an aneurysm. "You have got to be the most infuriating man alive."

"Part of my charm."

"I'll claim immunity."

"Oh, don't tempt me to test that when I'm in your bed, princess."

"Ten, nine, eight…" She began to count, looking at the ceiling, which he'd count as a bit of a victory, because if she wasn't glaring at him maybe she was at least having a few inappropriate thoughts about him in her bed.

He would have been more than happy to let that countdown run out, see what she did. Would she really pull her gun on him? He doubted it. But whatever fun he was about to have was completely ruined when he heard his motorcycle engine start.

Without him anywhere near it.

Grady swore and hopped off the bed so fast the bed screeched against the hard floorboards. He ran past Laurel and out the door of her pretty little cabin and yelled after Clint's retreating form.

"That little punk will rue the day he touched my bike."

"Rue the day, huh?"

Grady whipped around to glare at Laurel, who was leaning against her open doorway, looking more than a little smug.

"No one, and I mean no one, touches *my* bike."

"It appears he already did."

Clint had indeed, and he would soon find out what it meant to cross Grady Carson, half brother or no half brother.

"I'll get dressed and drive you into town. Just wait for a few minutes," Laurel said, pushing off the doorway and stepping inside. Grady took a few steps toward the doorway, but Laurel lifted an eyebrow.

"Out here," she added. And for the second time this morning, she slammed a door in his face.

Chapter 4

Laurel hummed to herself as she poured her coffee into her thermos. Turned out watching Grady get the crap end of the annoyance stick was quite the morning pick-me-up.

Plus, now she had a lead. It wasn't much of one, all in all, but Clint hadn't heard any yelling. Just murmured voices, which Laurel could safely assume meant Jason knew his murderer. Knew him and agreed to meet him in a field in the middle of nowhere.

Which meant Jason had been more than likely into something shady. So, her investigation needed to start focusing on her deceased distant relative.

It was a relief, in some ways, that it might be personal or even professional rather than random. Random was harder to solve. Random was more dangerous.

But Jason had known who killed him, there was a trail to follow, and she'd do her job to follow it.

With renewed purpose, and the image of Grady nearly losing his crap firmly in mind, Laurel slipped on her coat, hefted her bag and grabbed her thermos before heading outside.

She frowned a little when Grady was nowhere to be seen. Had he decided to walk back into town? No skin off her nose and all that, but quite the long walk in the cold when he didn't have to.

She walked to her car parked on the side of the cabin, and that was when she saw him.

He stood with his back to her, clearly surveying the sprawl of Delaney buildings—houses, barns, stables. Shiny, glossy testaments to the wealth and success of the Delaney clan.

It shouldn't make her uncomfortable. Her family had worked long and hard for their success, *and* they'd always upheld the law while they did it. She was born of sheriffs and bankers and good, upstanding people. She *knew* that.

But no matter how traitorous the thought, she'd always been a little jealous of the Carsons. Not their wildness by any means, but the way they treated their history. They didn't just know the dates and the people, they lived it. Embodied it. A Carson today was not much different than a Carson one hundred years ago, she was sure.

Laurel had always felt a little disconnect at her father's edicts of bigger, better and more when they had so much to be proud of just in who they were.

"Tell me something, princess," Grady said, his voice something like soft. Which might have bothered her, or affected her, if she thought it was sincere. As it was, she figured he was just trying to lower her guard.

"What's that?"

He turned slowly, those blue eyes of his direct. Sometimes she wondered if she couldn't just see the past through them.

Get a hold of yourself, idiot.

"You don't believe in the feud," he said in that rusty scrape of a voice that might have made women weaker than her shiver. "So, what do you believe in?"

She didn't need to think about it, or even look away. "Bent."

He sighed heavily, his gaze traveling to the mountains in the distance. "I was afraid that's what you'd say," he muttered. "I suppose we don't agree about the way people go about it, but I feel the same. As long as Clint's a suspect, Bent's at risk."

"I agree."

"So, I'm going to help you."

Laurel frowned. "I don't need your help, Grady. This is my job."

"And if everything Clint says is true, that relative of yours was in some shady business that got him killed."

Laurel's frown deepened. She hated that he'd put that together, even if it was easy enough. Grady had good instincts, and she didn't want to have to compliment him on them. Or anything.

"And, baby, you don't know a thing about shady. But I do."

"What are you going to do? Eavesdrop at the bar? Beat a few answers out of people? This is a police investigation."

"I can be subtle."

She barked out a laugh. "You're as subtle as a Mack truck. One that nearly broke my nose."

Grady quirked one of those smiles that, if she wasn't careful, could make her believe there was some softness in this man. But that was utter insanity. Grady was and always had been the opposite of subtle or soft.

"I can listen. I can put out a few feelers. I can do it all without anyone raising an eyebrow. It's the beauty of owning a saloon."

"Bar," Laurel muttered. But she didn't get the rise out of Grady she expected.

"This is my brother we're talking about, Laurel."

Her first name. Not *princess*, not Delaney. Just her first name.

"Okay," she said carefully, because even though she knew she shouldn't let it get to her, it did. If the positions were reversed, if one of her siblings were in trouble… Well, she'd probably break a few laws. Who was she to think Grady couldn't uphold a few to save his brother? And Bent. "But you'd have to promise me, really, honestly promise, that we do this *my* way. If there's a murderer out there, I have to be able to build a case on him. One with evidence, and no questions as to the validity of that evidence. Or a *murderer* gets away." She refused to entertain that thought, but Grady had to.

His jaw tightened, but he didn't smile or joke or do anything except nod. Then hold out his hand.

"You have my word."

Laurel could not have predicted this turn of events in a million years. Working with a Carson… It was insane, and risky, but maybe if the town saw a Carson and a Delaney working together for the truth, they'd be able to find something of the same.

She took his outstretched hand and shook, firmly.

"So. We're in this together," she said, because she couldn't quite believe it.

"Only until my brother is cleared and to save Bent from another wave of feud crap."

"I thought you believed in the feud wholeheartedly."

"I believe in enemies. I believe in history. I believe in Delaneys mostly being so high on their horses they don't see anything."

Laurel tried to tug her hand away, but Grady held it in his, his large hand grasping hers tightly.

"I believe violence is *sometimes* the answer. Just like I can believe in the feud, the importance of that history, and think not *all* Delaneys are scum of the earth." His mouth curved into that dangerous thing. Dangerous and feral and so completely the opposite of arousing.

She wished.

"But mostly, Deputy Delaney," he said, holding firm on her hand and even tugging her closer. Close enough she could feel his breath mingle with hers, close enough she could see that the vibrant blue of his eyes matched the blue of the fall sky above them.

"I believe in Bent. And I believe you do, too. So, we'll do this your way until we have the murderer behind bars."

"And after that?"

"After that, I'll go back to doing things my way, princess." The curve of his mouth morphed into a full-blown grin. "So try not to fall in love with me."

"Such a hardship," she muttered, and when she gave one last tug of her hand and he didn't let go, she let her temper take over a little bit. She moved quick and clean and managed to land an elbow to his stomach that had his grasp loosening enough for her to free herself.

"Next time you hold on to me like that, you'll let me go the first time I pull away, or that elbow to the gut will be a knee to the balls."

Grady made a considering noise. "I like that you plan on there being a next time I hold on to you like that. Desperate for another touch?"

"I don't know how you'll hear anything shady going on in that bar of yours over the infernal buzz of your outrageous ego."

"I think I'll manage."

And the irritating part was, she was quite positive he would.

Grady had considered, for a moment or two, hauling her over his shoulder as payment for the elbow to the gut. Maybe he'd even slap that pretty ass of hers for good measure. It was a fantasy with some merit, but it would have to stay a fantasy.

He'd heard enough bedtime stories about a one-hundred-dred-and-fifty-year-old feud to know that Carsons and Delaneys getting mixed up in each other's asses was never, ever a good thing.

Besides, he needed to focus on Clint, which meant figuring out this case. A lot faster than the police would. He got that Laurel had some of the same concerns he did, and he got and respected the fact she knew what she was doing.

But he didn't have time for bureaucratic red tape, or following all leads. *His* goal wasn't so much the truth as it was making sure his brother didn't get wrapped up in this. Laurel could do her police work, focus on her job, and Grady could focus on Clint.

It made them something like the perfect team. Which

made it something like amusing to follow her to her car and get in as a passenger. She tossed her bag in the back, and got into the driver's seat as he stretched out in the passenger's.

"Can't say I've ever sat in the front seat of a cop car before."

"And I've never been pushed into the back of one. Such different lives we've led," she returned dryly, turning the keys in the ignition.

She drove away from the Delaney spread, a monstrosity of glitter and shine, the antithesis of what it should be in Grady's estimation. You built a name for yourself, you ought to give some nod to the past platforms you built yourself on. But the Delaneys liked it slick and *new*. And if he was being honest, at least part of the appeal for the Carsons was finding joy in the old and patched-together.

"You guys really hire *all* your ranch work out?" Grady asked, more because he knew it would make her stiffen than because he didn't know.

"Dylan helps some. Cam might when he comes home. Being a navy SEAL keeps him busy."

Grady made a humming noise he knew would irritate her. "Seems a bit of a misnomer to call it the Delaney ranch, then."

"If you insist," she replied, and though she clearly tried to use cop tone on him, some of her snap crackled through.

Grady grinned. Laurel always gave a hell of a snap. "Where exactly are you planning on letting me out?"

"Rightful Claim," she replied matter-of-factly as she maneuvered her neat, sparkling car down the winding road back toward the town's heart.

"So, you're going to drive through town, for all and sundry to see, and then drop me off at my bar to do the walk of shame?"

Her head whipped to his for a brief second before she returned her concentration to the road. "No one will think that."

"Baby, *everyone* will think that. What better story is there in Bent? Number one: a Carson murdered a Delaney. Number two: a Carson defiled a Delaney. Hell, we could create our very own Civil War."

"That isn't funny."

"It wasn't a joke." Though he couldn't blame her exactly for thinking he took this lightly. He wasn't a man prone to giving away his deeper emotions. Especially to the Delaneys, but he was also no idiot. Once the whisper of murder made it through town and who the suspect was, added to any whisper of him and Laurel spending time together—no matter how ludicrous—things would really get going.

Any romance rumors now would only fan the fire, and make him and Laurel's life harder while they were trying to clear Clint.

Laurel sighed heavily. "So, where do you want me to drop you off?"

"Go out of town to the north, circle around back, and there's a small, gravel access road back of Carson property we can sneak through."

"I should not have to sneak. Or waste half my morning sneaking."

"Lotta things we shouldn't have to do in this life, princess, but we do them anyway."

Her lips firmed, but she posed no other arguments. Her dark hair was pulled back in a ponytail, as it usually was, her jaw clenched tight, also usual. But something about seeing her in her pajamas, lying in her bed—it was like seeing a slightly different, softer side to Laurel Delaney.

He clearly needed more coffee. He didn't needle her the rest of the way. Well, he fiddled with the buttons on her fancy police car dash, even in this unmarked car, before she slapped at him, but other than that he was on his best behavior.

He couldn't imagine Clint had ridden Grady's motorcycle anywhere else but the Carson ranch, because if the kid had, well… Grady wouldn't consider it on account of a bad temper and an insane dislike to people touching his few prized possessions. His bike chief among them.

Morning broke like a glorious blast, rays of sunshine reflecting the gold of everything. Fall in Bent could make the snobbiest of city folk smile. As for Grady, it was always a reminder his soul belonged here. Those roots that bound him to this land and that sky weren't shackles but gifts.

He glanced at Laurel. She did everything efficiently. The turn of the wheel, the checking both ways before making a turn. Always so serious and conscientious. He supposed that was the fascination. He'd never known anyone quite like her, even in the passel of uppity, glossy Delaneys that ran Bent, or tried to.

"Turn here," Grady instructed, gesturing toward a barely visible turn off the highway. Laurel nodded and drove her car through a canopy of green and gold, leaves and pine, until they reached the gate.

"You can walk from here," she said primly.

Something about her prim always made him grin. "A polite woman drops her man off at the door."

"Consider me impolite and you very much not my man."

Grady pushed the car door open and stepped out. "I'll put a few feelers out tonight at Rightful Claim, let you know what I come up with."

She nodded, all business. "I'm going over to the mining company to talk to Jason's boss and any coworkers he might have been friendly with. I'll let you know if I've got a specific lead I want you to listen for."

"Look at that, Deputy, we're acting like partners already."

She rolled her eyes. "We'll be lucky if we don't kill each other."

The grin that had never fully evaporated spread across his face. "Funny, killing each other isn't what I'm worried about."

Her eyebrows drew together, all adorable, innocent confusion. Oh, to be as sweet and rule-abiding as his deputy princess.

"You just think on that, and we'll be in touch." He closed the door and started walking toward the old homestead. The wind was cold, but he didn't mind. It was a good kind of cold. A thinking cold. And he needed to get his head in the thinking game. The keeping-Clint-out-of-trouble game.

When Laurel's car didn't immediately turn around and drive away, he chuckled. He kept walking, but he waited for what he knew would come. Because deputy princess didn't know when to quit.

He supposed that was fair. Neither did he.

"I will never sleep with you, Grady Carson," she shouted through her open driver's side window.

He just raised a hand in salute. He didn't think of "never" so much as a challenge as he considered it a curse. And there were already plenty of Carson and Delaney curses in the air.

Chapter 5

Evergreen Mining existed about thirty miles outside of Bent, and straddled Bent and Freemont counties with its sprawling compound in the middle of just about no-where. Little boxlike things dotted the landscape as Laurel explained who she was and showed her badge to the security entrance.

Laurel didn't know much about the company. No one in her immediate family or group of friends worked this far outside of Bent. She did remember the mine here getting in trouble a few years back for some safety reg-ulations, but she hardly expected her accountant victim to have been involved in any of that.

At best, she'd find a link to someone who might have wanted Jason dead. At worst, it was a dead end and she'd have to start prodding Jason's family. She sighed. She almost wished she knew that line of the family better, but as the son of her father's second cousins, they were so far removed she barely even heard gossip about Jason.

Laurel was led to the office of Jason's boss by a secretary. The secretary knocked on a door and then pushed it open, stepping inside and gesturing Laurel to follow. "Mr. Adams, the police are here to ask you a few questions."

"Yes. Of course." A well-dressed middle-aged man stood from behind a desk and held out his hand. "I'd be happy to assist you in whatever way I can, miss."

"Deputy Delaney," Laurel said, shaking his hand in return.

The man shook her hand, looking at her quizzically. "You're related to Jason?"

Laurel forced herself to smile. "Yes, though distantly."

"Ah. Well, have a seat. I'd be happy to answer any questions you may have. I do have an appointment with my foreman in twenty minutes that I can't miss." He smiled apologetically. "Regulations and all that."

"Of course. I mainly just need a list of anyone Jason had routine contact with, and if you know of anyone he might have had a disagreement with or dislike of."

"Well, our administrative staff is somewhat isolated out here, Miss Delaney."

Laurel bit back the need to correct him. *Deputy, not Miss, jerk.* "Did he have a secretary or an assistant?"

"No. Jason was a satellite accountant, meaning he kept track of our accounting at this plant alone. He would have answered to the head accountant in our main office in Nebraska."

Laurel continued to ask him questions, and Mr. Adams continued to give vague, unhelpful answers for twenty full minutes. Finally, Mr. Adams stood. "I have my meeting. Is there anything else—"

"I'd like access to Jason's things. Did he have an office?"

Mr. Adams frowned but quickly smoothed it out. "Follow me, miss."

Laurel scowled at Mr. Adams's back, but followed him back out into the hallway and down a few doors. Mr. Adams pulled out a key ring and unlocked the door.

"Feel free to look around as much as you'd like. If you need to take anything, I'm afraid I'll have to approve it. Jason did have access to some sensitive documents."

"I'm sure copies can be made of anything that might aid me in my investigation." Laurel smiled brightly at him.

Mr. Adams smiled thinly. "Of course. If you can't find me, my secretary should be at her desk. She can also summon anyone else you may need to talk to. If you'll excuse me."

Laurel nodded and stepped into the office. It was small and cramped, and messy. She sighed. It was hard to find clues when you didn't know what you were looking for. Long, frustrating hours of sifting through crap. Her least favorite part of the job.

But it was part of her job, so she got to work. She didn't know how long she filtered through the papers on Jason's desk before she finally found something of potential interest. A scrap of paper in a file with the name Jennings scribbled on it.

Considering Jason had been found by a Mr. Jennings, that seemed incredibly pertinent. A quick scan of all the papers in the file gave Laurel no clue as to why, but with some closer reading, she might be able to find something.

The door swung open and a man entered, stopping short. He was youngish. Maybe midtwenties, dressed like he didn't belong in the administrative building. Jeans, a heavy-duty jacket and heavy work boots.

"Who are you?" he demanded. "Where's Jason?"

Interesting. She supposed the appropriate thing would be to tell this man what had happened to Jason, but she wanted a little information first. Especially since Mr. Adams considered Jason so isolated.

"Hello. I'm sorry, who are you?"

The man frowned. "Jason get fired or something?"

"Actually..."

"You know what, never mind," the man mumbled and rushed out the door.

Very, very curious. Laurel clutched the file and hurried after him, trying to make her strides look relaxed.

He passed the secretary, busting out the door with a hard push.

Laurel stepped up to the secretary's desk. "Who was that man?"

The secretary didn't even look up. "Hank Gaskill."

Gaskill. Why did that sound familiar? Laurel pushed the file toward the woman, getting out her notebook and writing down the name. "Can I get copies of everything in this file?"

The secretary took the file and frowned. "This was in Jason's office?"

Laurel raised an eyebrow as she placed the notebook back in her pocket. "Yes."

"It shouldn't have been. This is Mr. Adams's file,

and it doesn't have anything to do with accounting or finances."

A lead. A *real* lead, then. "Then I definitely need copies."

The secretary nodded and turned to a copy machine behind her.

"Does Hank Gaskill come to visit Mr. Delaney often?" Laurel asked.

The secretary shrugged. "Lately they've gone to lunch together. Childhood friends, from what I could tell."

Yet, Hank hadn't heard that Jason had been murdered. Interesting. "Thank you." Laurel got her card out of her pocket and handed it to the secretary. "If you or Mr. Adams or anyone thinks of anything else, please be sure to call me."

The secretary handed over the copies and took Laurel's card. "I will. Jason was so young. Such a tragedy."

Laurel nodded and slipped the papers under her arm, heading back out to her car. *Gaskill. Gaskill.* Why was that familiar?

She walked to her car, turning over the events of yesterday in her mind, and that's when it dawned on her.

Fred Gaskill. Clint's friend she'd questioned yesterday.

Oh, damn that kid and his lies.

Grady was in a piss-poor mood as he opened Rightful Claim. He'd spent too much of his morning searching for Clint. The teen had, sensibly, left Grady's bike at the ranch, but had disappeared after that.

Grady had a saloon to run and things to do, and his half brother was putting a dent in both.

"I take it you don't have any ideas on how to bring him to heel," Ty asked, pulling chairs down off the tables. Since Ty had basically just gotten back to Bent after a stint as an army ranger, he was going to be working at the bar until he decided what he wanted to do next.

"I'm washing my hands of that kid," Grady muttered, putting cash in the register for the evening.

"Yeah, you're so good at washing your hands of people."

Grady only grunted. So, maybe giving up on people wasn't exactly his strong suit. But that was because he always did some good. If Clint didn't want some of that good, well, fine. Grady would let him off the proverbial hook.

Soon as he got Clint cleared of murder.

The saloon doors swung open and Laurel stepped into the dim light of the bar. She was dressed exactly as she had been this morning, except her weapon was strapped to her hip.

The fact his spirits lightened enough he could feel a weight lift in his chest was kind of worrying, but he'd wrap that up in sarcasm and irritating the crap out of her.

"She deigns to walk through our doors, Grady. To what do we owe the unwanted nonpleasure?"

Something about Ty giving her a hard time bothered him in a way he did not care for at all. "Watch the bar," Grady ordered gruffly.

He ignored the shock on Ty's face and jerked his head toward the back. "Follow me," he said to Laurel.

She pressed her lips together, but didn't argue. So, instead of leading her to one of the back rooms or the kitchen or anything that might have been easy and safe, he led her upstairs to his apartment.

Her pressed-lips look had morphed into a full-blown scowl as he opened the door and gestured her inside.

"Do we really need to talk up here?"

"Private," Grady returned cheerfully. He entered the apartment and turned to give her an impatient look.

She huffed out a breath but stepped inside. She wrinkled her nose. "Your bedroom isn't even separate from your kitchen?"

"But the bathroom is separate, which is probably far more important." He nodded toward the bed that took up a considerable amount of space in his kitchen/living/bedroom area. "You want to lie down on my bed? Tit for tat and all that?"

"Gaskill," she said firmly, though he didn't miss the way her eyes drifted to his messy, unmade bed. "Fred Gaskill is friends with Clint, and claimed he didn't know anything about Clint's whereabouts."

"Yeah."

"Do you know anything about Hank Gaskill?"

"Fred's older brother. Works at the…mine." Which was where Laurel had been headed today.

"Friends with Jason. He popped into his office today while I was looking through Jason's things. Skittered off like he was afraid." Laurel frowned, a line digging into her forehead. "But he didn't seem to know Jason was dead."

"What does it mean?" What did it mean that one of Clint's friends had a brother who was friendly with a dead man? It could mean nothing in a small, rural county. A coincidence. But Grady wasn't sure he believed in those with a murder having gone down.

"I don't know. I've got some more digging to do, but—"

"What kind of digging?"

"Police digging. Does Hank ever come in here?"

Grady didn't care for the brush-off, but he didn't press it. Yet. "A handful of the mining guys do occasionally. Not much else in the way of a place to hang out and get a drink for those who live on this side of things."

"I need you to call me if they ever come in. Day or night. On duty or off. You call me."

"What? So you can oh so subtly eavesdrop?"

"Maybe."

Grady snorted. "Princess, everyone knows you don't come into Rightful Claim, and this is time number two in a week. Make it a third, especially during working hours, the whole town might implode with the implications of a Delaney in a Carson establishment."

"Carsons bank at Delaney Bank and shop at Delaney General all the time."

"It ain't the same, and you know that."

Laurel blew out an irritated breath. "Regardless. You call me. Something is off with everything I witnessed today. Hank coming into Jason's office, then files on his desk that shouldn't have been. I can't tell if the boss is just a patronizing, sexist douche or an actual criminal."

"Maybe even both."

She frowned. "He called me *miss*."

"So, if I really want to piss you off I should call you Miss Deputy Princess."

She rolled her eyes and made a move for the door, but Grady blocked it.

"Out of my way."

"What's the plan, Delaney?"

"The plan is for me to continue investigating per my job. If you see Hank *or* Fred Gaskill in your bar, or doing anything fishy, you call me."

"And that's it? My kid brother might be on the hook for murder and I'm just supposed to play lookout?"

Some of that pissed-off hard edge softened. "What else is there to do, Grady? I have due process to follow. You can't go with me to search Jason's place, and I can't hand over evidence. Both of our hands are tied."

"I really prefer to do the tying," he joked even though he didn't feel like joking in the least.

Laurel's gaze slid to the bed again before she seemed to shake herself out of it. "Regardless. I need you to sit tight and watch. I need you to have some patience."

Grady ran his palms over his beard. Hands-tied patience. When had he ever not balked at that? But no matter how many times he'd acted against all he'd been told to do, when he *acted* he did so knowing he was right.

The worst part of all this was knowing Laurel was right. He was no cop. He had no authority to arrest or try a murderer, and an eye for an eye wasn't going to work.

"You get really quiet when you know I'm right," she offered with a smirk.

The hands-tied frustration bubbling through him and that self-satisfied smirk of hers right next to his bed was the kind of terrible concoction that led to bad decisions.

Still, holding himself back in one arena meant holding himself back in another wasn't a possibility. So, he stepped forward, and when she lifted her chin to meet his gaze rather than step back, he grinned.

"Do I, now?" he asked quietly, reaching out and taking one of those flyaway strands of her hair between his fingers.

She kept that haughty expression on her face, but he watched her elegant throat move as she swallowed.

"You don't believe in the feud, but do you believe in the curse?"

"What curse?" she asked, clearly attempting nonchalance. But she didn't meet his gaze when she asked.

"The one that says if a Carson and a Delaney even look at each other with so much of an ounce of kindness, or *other* nice things, the whole world goes to hell. Just like my favorite illegitimate Carson and his Delaney bride who died, and the Delaney girl who would've married the Carson boy if not for World War II, and then there's your sis—"

That dark, irritated look returned. "There's no curse. I'm being nice to you, aren't I?"

He twisted her soft strand of hair in his fingers. "Could be nicer."

Her eyebrows furrowed, but she didn't pull away and he'd be damned if her gaze didn't drop to his mouth. But when she looked back into his eyes, there was something he didn't want to notice, even if he did.

A note of vulnerability to invulnerable Laurel Delaney. "What game are you playing, Grady? Because I'm not playing one."

"No games. Just…" He leaned a little closer. "Chemistry. Admit it. Does it hurt so very much to admit it?"

Laurel stared at him for a few humming seconds. Seconds he thought she might have actually considered *chemistry.*

But then she shook her head. "You're not funny." She stepped around him, her hair sliding out of his fingers.

There were ways to stop her, sarcastic things to drawl her way, but he couldn't get over the fact she didn't seem so much irritated by him as something else. Something a lot softer.

Grady didn't poke at soft. He might be his father in a lot of ways, but not that one. "Listen." He turned to face her, frowning at the fact she already had the door open and was striding out of it. "I'll give you a call if anyone from the mine shows up."

She paused in his doorway and straightened her shoulders, but she didn't turn around. "Great. Thanks."

Then she was gone, and he was left in the same piss-poor mood he'd been in before she'd arrived.

Chapter 6

"This isn't going to work."

"Not with that attitude," Jen said to Laurel, all too cheerfully. "This was your idea. Don't start pooh-poohing it after all the work I've put in."

Laurel sat in her sister's tiny bathroom, second-guessing her plan. And then third-guessing it. Until the number got too high to count.

"I watched too many detective shows as a kid. It's infected my brain and this is a terrible idea," Laurel said dejectedly.

"No, the terrible idea is trusting Grady Carson."

"Don't start."

Jen handed Laurel a small mirror and Laurel studied her reflection. The wig didn't look ridiculous, and though she *felt* silly, Laurel knew that on the surface she looked like any normal twentysomething.

The problem was she'd *never* been a normal twentysomething. Her life since she could remember revolved around becoming and then being a cop. No parties, little dating. She didn't go to bars or flirt with guys. Ever.

Plus, she didn't think she'd be able to recreate any of the things Jen had done to make her look different. She was terrible with makeup, felt uncomfortable in decent-fitting clothes and didn't know if she could jab the wig pins into her scalp with as much glee as Jen had done.

"People are starting to talk, Laurel. Murder is murder even without the feud. Add the Delaneys and Carsons, and my store is a veritable gossip station."

"People have too much time on their hands, then. The murder has nothing to do with the feud."

"Then why are you suddenly being seen all over the place with the Carsons?"

It was stupid to be caught off guard by that. Laurel knew how this town worked. The Delaneys didn't go into Rightful Claim, ever, let alone twice in one week. And loud, disruptive Carson motorcycles did not make their way up to the Delaney Ranch. She'd been so focused on the case and clearing Clint, she'd been sloppy with anticipating how the town would react.

Or maybe that's Grady's influence. Just the thought of Grady filled her with… Well, it was irritation, but something in addition to that annoyance Grady normally evoked. And she was all too afraid it was familiar. A tingle. A shutting down of her rational brain. That same stupid thing that used to sizzle through her when she'd been a teenager hanging out with his sister and would catch a glimpse of him.

"Laurel. What's going on? Really. I know you can't share all the police stuff, but you can share the *you* stuff."

Her stuff? There was no *her* stuff. There was her job and her duty to this town and that was her entire life. She was proud of that. She *was*.

But something about Grady's obnoxious comment about chemistry had dug inside of her and stirred up all the lonely she so often ignored.

Like some sort of horrible cosmic sign, her phone vibrated with an incoming text message. Jen snuck a quick glance at the sender's name, which read *GC*, and frowned.

"Yes, I'm going to ask who GC is, and yes, it better not be Grady Carson."

"Jen."

"I thought you grew out of this."

"Grew out of what?"

"Oh, like it wasn't obvious when we were in high school that you mooned over the guy?"

"Pot. Kettle," Laurel said, pointing to Jen and then to herself. "Ty Carson is back in town, by the way."

Jen's entire body stiffened. Yeah, Laurel might be stupid and a little bit weak in the head when it came to Grady, but her sister had no moral high ground to stand on. Laurel had only ever *looked*. She was pretty sure her sister had done more than that with Grady's cousin back in the day.

Ignoring her sister's waves of disapproval, Laurel brought the message up on her screen.

Gaskill here. On alert. Do. Not. Come. Here. Will report back.

"Well. Time to put my plan into motion," she said, taking one last glimpse at herself in the mirror. Anyone who knew her and looked right at her might figure out who she was, but if she stayed in the shadows, kept a low profile, she could sit next to Hank Gaskill and listen to everything he had to say.

Maybe it would be pointless, but maybe it wouldn't. She had to try. She'd sent Hart over to search Jason's place while she'd been at the mine, but he hadn't come up with anything. She'd take another look herself tomorrow, but for now she had to work on the people involved. The leads she *did* have.

"I should go with you."

"I believe the point of the disguise is, you know, Delaneys not going into Rightful Claim."

"Someone should go with you. I don't like you going there by yourself."

"It's police business, Jen. It's hardly dangerous. I'm just going to listen for some information that I may or may not even find. If someone is with me, it ruins the whole point."

"You're going to Grady's bar. That's not *all* police business."

"I don't know why you suddenly think I can't control myself, but I can. Besides, looking at Grady and Grady looking back are two very separate things." Which was probably not the way to convince her sister she didn't have a thing for Grady.

"You don't honestly think Grady Carson has never looked back at you."

Laurel turned her attention from her reflection in the mirror to her sister. After all, she and Jen looked a lot alike. Jen's hair was a shade lighter, and her eyes had hints of hazel. They were only about ten months apart, and they'd always been close.

But Jen had always been into the whole girlie thing. Understanding how to put on makeup and dressing to attract attention. Laurel had never been comfortable with that. She was more interested in police procedure and appearing tough and untouchable. She'd always wanted to be a cop, and a female cop *had* to be a little untouchable.

So, it didn't matter if her mind on occasion wandered to Grady, and touching him. It was all…fantasy. And irrelevant to her current situation at hand. "This conversation is ridiculous. I'm going to go do my job. Beginning and end of story."

"Fine. But I want regular text updates and I want to know when you're home. In fact, I'd feel even better if you come back here when you're done and assure me it was all police work and nothing dangerous."

Laurel stood and stepped out of the bathroom, adjusting the bra holster that wasn't comfortable, but the only way to conceal her gun effectively. At least in the jeans Jen had loaned her, because all of Jen's dresses were far, far, far too short for Laurel's taste.

"I'll text you when I get home."

"I don't like that you're wearing that gun. That means you think something bad is going to happen."

Laurel took a deep breath. "No, it means I'm on duty. You know who you sound like right now."

Jen wrinkled her nose. "Much as I hate sounding like Dad, it *is* a terrible feeling to know you're going off into danger."

"You're not usually this silly about my work stuff. What's going on?"

Jen crossed her arms over her chest. "Nothing is going on except you're not usually walking the line between Delaney and Carson while investigating a murder. A murder of someone we're related to, I might add."

"It's my job, Jen. I do it well." She picked up the purse Jen had laid out for her to match the outfit. A little clutch that made no sense to Laurel. "What do you do with this thing? There's no strap. How am I supposed to attach it to myself?"

Jen rolled her eyes. "You carry it. It's cute. Not everything has to be functional."

"In my world it does." But she was playing a part. A part her sister had helped her get ready for. She turned to Jen and pulled her into a hug. "Thank you for helping me. You know I appreciate it."

"You owe me. Stay away from Grady Carson. Please just listen to me on that. Even if you take out all the feud nonsense, the Carsons are not meant for us. Period. I don't want you getting hurt by that moron."

"You ever going to tell me what happened between you and Ty?"

"Nothing happened between me and Ty. Ty Carson does not exist as far as I'm concerned. You should go. Policewoman business awaits."

Laurel rolled her eyes. She'd always been close with her siblings, but none of them had ever poked much at each other's romantic lives. It was considered a separate, no-go zone. Laurel wasn't sure why things were that way, but she supposed it was small-town complications. Everyone else poked into everyone else's business enough, why add to it?

Besides, Jen's worry was irrational, and Laurel shouldn't keep defending herself. It was pointless. She was not going to get *involved* with Grady Carson. No matter how much chemistry they had or how much he wanted her to admit it.

She had bigger things to worry about than chemistry. Carsons. Delaneys. Bent and feuds. She had a murder to solve.

And solve it she would.

Grady was loath to admit that running a bar and trying to eavesdrop on someone was at cross-purposes. Any time he got remotely close to Hank's table and was able to overhear something of the conversation, someone called his name or clapped him on the back and asked him a question. Men made loud, raucous jokes in his direction and women offered smiles and innuendo and whatever.

It was something he usually enjoyed, the banter and flirting. The noise, the conversations. But today it only served to piss him off.

If he couldn't get any of the information Laurel needed, he'd have to admit he failed. That galled for too many reasons to count.

He was not a guy who had to prove himself to people. He was what he was, and anyone who didn't like it could go to hell. The only person who had ever challenged that had been his dear old deadbeat dad.

And Laurel Delaney.

If he didn't get the information she needed, *she* would, and it seemed like adding insult to injury to fail at this, as well as know that she inevitably wouldn't.

The saloon doors swung open and Grady glanced up at the latest patron as he always did. There were a few people who tried to stir up fights in his bar, and he liked to cut them off at the pass.

But this customer was a woman. She looked vaguely familiar, but he couldn't quite place her. Dark eyes scanned the bar, moving past him rather quickly.

He frowned. She wasn't a regular or a known troublemaker, or he would have been able to place her. She didn't look like any Bent resident he knew. Something prickled through him, though, some kind of omen, as if he *should* be paying attention.

He shook his head. He was being some kind of paranoid, hyperalert idiot because he'd let Laurel's crap get into his head, and that just wasn't acceptable.

He focused back in on his target. If he could go clean off the table next to Hank, he might be able to hear *something* before someone bothered him again.

But just as he pulled the rag out of his back pocket, the woman who'd just entered slid into a chair at the table he'd been about to pretend to clean.

"It's not clean," he said gruffly.

"I don't mind," she replied airily.

Something about that voice… Grady glanced over at her but she studiously ignored his gaze. What was going on here? He thought about asking her if he knew her, but he was a little afraid she was some unhappy ex-lover. He didn't have time for that, and she didn't seem interested in rehashing anything.

"Get you something to drink?"

"A Coke, please," she said, her head turned so far away from him he could only see curly blond waves of hair and the peekaboo of an ear.

"Be right back."

She nodded, tucking her hair behind her ear. Which was when he saw it. The little wink of a silver star earring. Which Grady supposed could be a coincidence.

Maybe tiny silver star earrings were all the rage and young women everywhere were wearing them.

But the woman's behavior, her voice, those familiar eyes darting all over his bar... He reached out and grabbed her wrist. When she jerked her gaze toward him, all flashes of gold fury, he very nearly dropped his jaw.

"What do you think you're doing?" he demanded. He was more than a little angry she'd fooled him for as long as she had with that ridiculous blond wig and clothes that actually fit her all-too-enticing body.

"Nothing," she hissed. "Now, if you would get me my Coke."

He gave her hand a tug. "Come over to the bar so I can get a tab started for you."

She held firm in her seat, staring him down with those dark, expressive eyes. "That won't be necessary," she said, over-enunciating each word.

She nodded her head toward Hank's table as if to tell Grady to stop in case someone in the group might overhear. Maybe he should. But he'd told her not to come in here. He'd told her he could handle it.

But he *wasn't* handling it. Even if her disguise didn't do much, if she sat here and sipped a Coke she had a far better chance of hearing something than he did. No one would recognize her if she calmly sat there. No one would believe Laurel Delaney was in Rightful Claim in a blond wig with an actual hint of cleavage showing.

Damn it.

He released her wrist. "One Coke coming right up," he muttered. Because he was *not* his father, and could back off even when he was irrationally pissed.

"Who's that chick?" Ty asked as Grady moved behind the bar and grabbed a glass.

Grady was an excellent liar in most situations, but he always hesitated at lying to family—especially Ty, Noah and Vanessa.

But this was important and bigger than him. "Some out-of-towner. She said she came in looking for a little Wild West charm."

"Is that a euphemism?" Ty asked with a grin.

Grady filled the glass with Coke and tried not to scowl. "Guess we'll find out," he muttered and headed back for Laurel and her stupid disguise.

Everything about the situation grated. The fact his hands were tied. The fact she was the one sitting there in a blond wig. So, he did what he always did when she irritated him.

"You make a hot blonde."

She glared at him. "Did you know that at a restaurant or bar, you don't have to tip the proprietor?"

"Says who?"

"The law," she returned, giving him a haughty look before glancing over at Hank's table.

He should let her be. Let her eavesdrop. Let her do her *job*, but he slid into the seat opposite her instead. When she didn't object or even send him a nasty glare, he decided he'd do her a favor in return by not asking her how she came upon a wig and clothes that actually fit.

She grabbed the sparkly purse that looked about as much like Laurel as the curly blond hair. Everything about her right now was the opposite of Laurel, and it was a little annoying to find he rather preferred her to be *her*.

She scribbled something on a piece of paper and casually slid it over the surface of the table toward him.

He flipped over the paper and read the question in

her neatly printed letters. *Who are the others at the table?*

He wanted to make a quip about her needing his help, and he doubted the table of three men next to them would notice, but he could be subtle. He wrote down the names of the men Hank was sitting with and returned the paper to her.

She read the names quickly, then slipped the paper into her sparkly handbag. She daintily sipped her Coke and studiously ignored him.

"Most female strangers who come into my bar flirt with me." He flashed a grin.

She rolled her eyes so far back in her head it must've hurt.

"Of course, you don't strike me as the type of person who knows how to flirt."

She curled her lip at him, as he'd hoped, but she didn't snipe back. Merely straightened in her chair.

Grady couldn't help the fact his gaze drifted to the hint of cleavage, and the whole outfit, really. Laurel Delaney actually had a body under there, and he couldn't even be surprised because the baggy clothes and fierce appearance no doubt served her in her job. And, unfortunately for her, in a small town you didn't get to be someone else once you clocked out of your job. Laurel Delaney *always* had to be Deputy Delaney, or risk a lot of things.

Why did he have to *understand* this infernal woman?

The table next to them laughed uproariously, but as Grady glanced over just like Laurel did, he imagined she saw the same thing.

The two men at the table with Hank were laughing, but Hank wasn't. He was staring down the bottom of his drink. Abruptly, he pushed out of his chair. "Going to grab a smoke," he grumbled to his jovial companions.

Hank wasn't even three steps toward the door before Laurel was picking up her purse. Luckily Grady was paying enough attention he could grab her hand before she got up. "Don't you think about it."

She glared at his hand on hers. "Don't *you* even think about telling me what to do."

"What do you think you're going to do after you follow him?" He leaned forward so that no one could hear them, though no one was paying any attention. "Ask for a cigarette? Smoke one? You?"

She jerked her hand out of his grasp. "If that's what it takes. Don't follow me or I will be forced to arrest you for getting in the way of a criminal investigation."

"I don't think that's legal, princess."

"I don't think I care. Stay here."

He could've grabbed her again. He could do a lot of things. But the fact he needed to get through his thick skull was that Laurel was a *cop*. She was investigating an actual murder case, and he didn't have any claim to sit here and tell her what to do.

If she wanted to be stupid and go have a smoke with Hank, as if that would get her any information, well, that was her prerogative.

She stood and walked out the same way Hank had. Grady scowled as he watched her go, her hips swaying mesmerizingly in the tight denim.

Which was *really* unfair, all things considered.

He'd give her ten minutes. Tops. And then he was going after her.

Chapter 7

Laurel pushed through the swinging door and walked out of Rightful Claim with her heart beating a little too hard in her chest.

It had rattled her that Grady had seen through her disguise so quickly. But she'd grown up with Grady. She'd only met Hank Gaskill once in passing. Granted, it had been this morning, but why would he expect the blonde in a bar to be the brunette in Jason's office he'd talked to for five seconds?

She inhaled and exhaled, slowly walking toward where he leaned against the corner of the building, lighting a cigarette. He took a long drag and Laurel steeled herself to approach him.

"I don't suppose I could borrow a cigarette?" she asked, making her voice a little breathless and then berating herself for it. Over-the-top was suspicious.

"How can you borrow a cigarette? Plan on giving it back once you smoked it?"

Laurel couldn't tell if his response was snarky or flirty. That was always the trouble. While she could read murderous intentions or abusive husbands or drug addicts, she really wasn't very good at reading the opposite sex's reaction to her. There were always too many mixed messages and ulterior motives and it just didn't make any sense.

But she was on a job, playing a part. She wasn't Laurel Delaney. She was someone else entirely. So, she smiled as sweetly as she knew how. "Truth be told, I'd just like a puff of one. I quit a few years ago and I have just had the worst day."

"Well, this is the bad day corner," Hank replied and held his lit cigarette toward her.

Luckily, Laurel had seen enough bad movies to know you didn't take a deep inhale of a cigarette when she'd never smoked a day in her life. She put her mouth to the cigarette for a second and then pulled it away, pretending to sigh heavily as if it was a great relief.

"Thanks," she offered, offering the cigarette back to Hank.

He shook his head, tapping another cigarette out of the package he held. "Keep it. Had a rough day myself."

Laurel smiled understandingly. "They must really be going around, huh?"

"Yeah." His gaze moved down her body and back up, a kind of subtle checkout she probably wouldn't have caught if she wasn't looking for clues for a murder case.

"What's your sob story?" he asked.

"Just your average 'lost my job, boyfriend kicked me

out' type thing. You?" she asked, sounding awfully casual if she did say so herself.

He shrugged and stared off into the dark, taking a deep drag of his cigarette before he replied. "Friend died."

"That's awful. Was he sick?"

Hank shook his head, and no matter how badly Laurel wanted to press, she knew that would only look weird coming from a stranger.

He looked her up and down again. "Why'd your boyfriend kick you out?"

"Oh." Laurel worked up her best sheepish smile. She was playing a very strange game here, but if it got her *any* information, did it matter? The important thing was if Hank thought she was available and interested he might tell her more about what he knew of his dead friend.

She had no other leads and a town whispering about murder and Delaneys and Carsons, so, sometimes the end justified the means.

"I may have kissed another guy," she said quietly, conspiratorially. "We'd been together a few years, and it just got boring, you know?"

Hank's mouth curved a little bit. "Wouldn't know. I must get bored before a few weeks is up."

Laurel laughed right along with him.

"You want to go back inside? I'll buy you a drink."

"Your friend died. I feel like *I* should buy *you* a drink."

Hank smiled. "Okay. I'll let you."

Grady wouldn't like that, Laurel knew. He'd think she was being stupid or something. But she couldn't care what Grady would like. She couldn't care what kind of lines she was tiptoeing on either side of right now.

If she had a drink with Hank, he might say *something* that could be a lead. Sometimes strangers were the best people to confide in. It wasn't as though he was the murderer. This morning he clearly hadn't known Jason was dead. But that didn't mean he might not know how or why.

Hank finished off his cigarette and flicked it into the street. Trying to hide how little she'd smoked, Laurel slipped hers into the ashtray canister on top of a trash can.

"Hank," he offered, holding out his hand to shake.

Laurel smiled and ordered herself not to panic at how many lies she was weaving. "Sarah," she offered, shaking his hand in return.

"You're not from Bent."

"No. Fremont. Well, that's where I lived with my boyfriend, but now I need a place to crash. So, I came to Bent to stay with my cousin for a bit."

"Oh, yeah? Maybe I know her. What's her name?"

Laurel fiddled with her clutch, trying to look like she was doing something purposeful while she tried to come up with the best lie. "Dylan Delaney." She figured using her brother's name was better than using that of any of her female relatives. And she couldn't use a Carson name. God knew they'd never back her up.

"Don't you know the Delaneys aren't supposed to be in Carson bars?" Hank asked with a grin.

Laurel smiled as flirtatiously as she could possibly manage. "I've never been very good at doing what I'm supposed to do." What a laugh.

"Well, then let's head inside and let you buy me a drink."

Laurel nodded and tucked a strand of hair behind her ear and turned toward the door.

Which burst open—and hit her square in the face.

Grady slammed his palms against the outward-swinging door, but instead of a satisfying, loud swing there was only a thump followed by a squeak.

It was not possible that he'd...

Gingerly, he pushed the out door again, this time meeting with no resistance, but when he stepped onto the well-lit boardwalk in front of his saloon, blonde Laurel was standing there holding her nose.

Again. For the second time in as many days.

Dark eyes met his, flashing all-too-enticing gold fury. "What is wrong with you?" she demanded.

"Me? I wasn't the one standing on the other side of the *out* door, sweetheart. That's why we have big signs that say *Out* and *In*, so people don't get knocked into unless they're drunk or stupid." No matter how acidic his voice was, his chest pinched painfully. Which was beyond stupid. She'd been the idiot standing on the wrong side of the wrong door.

Hank handed Laurel a bandanna from his back pocket, which she put to her bleeding nose.

"I think you owe her a drink on the house, man," Hank said, a little too cheerfully.

Grady raised one eyebrow at Hank and didn't move another inch of his body. Just stared down the little prick. "You think so?"

Hank wilted and looked away. Coward.

"Come with me and we'll get you cleaned up," Grady ordered Laurel.

"No, thank you," she replied, biting off each word.

"You should let him clean you up, Sarah. Get some ice and we'll get our free drinks. Okay?" Hank patted Laurel on the shoulder, seeming a little too jovial for the situation.

"Shall we… *Sarah*?" Grady offered, gesturing at the door. Specifically the *In* side of the door.

She tried to smile. He could tell she really, really tried. And if she didn't have a handkerchief pressed to her nose, he might have found it all funny. As it was, he took her arm far too gently for his own liking and pulled her inside and through the loud, crowded bar.

He motioned Hank toward Ty. "Ty, get this man two drinks on the house." Ty nodded and Hank walked up to the bar while Grady propelled Laurel toward the back. When he started leading her toward the stairs up to his apartment, she jerked out of his grasp.

"I'm not going to that stupid apartment of yours and you are not ruining this for me." She pulled the handkerchief away from her nose. He didn't think it was quite as bad as the last one, but there was a slight smudge of blood underneath.

She looked at the bandanna and shook her head. "How. How is it possible? Twice in one week you smash me in the nose."

"Might I remind you that in the first instance, *you* ran into me. And in the second instance, I was going out the *out* side of the swinging doors. That's why they have the signs on them. You don't stand next to the out one, because people push *out* of them."

She closed her eyes, standing still as she breathed in, and then out. In and then out. Clearly trying to calm herself. When she reopened her eyes, all of that fury had been smoothed out of her features. "Grady, why were you coming out at all?"

"Guess I just wanted to witness how far you were willing to go for a little information. Call it curiosity."

"You are..." She shook her head. "I cannot work with you. I don't know why I ever thought that would actually be beneficial. Stay out of my way. Stay out of this case."

"You can't be serious."

"I can't include you in this if this is how you're going to act. I need you to listen to me. I need to trust that I can do something without you swaggering in and breaking my nose."

"It isn't broken." And he was behaving like a...like a contentious, surly teenager. "Stay here," he grumbled before stalking back to the kitchen. He grabbed one of the ice packs they kept in the freezer for bar fight injuries.

When he returned, he held it out to her. She took it, and placed it on the bridge of her nose with a wince.

He hated what he knew had to come next. Hated it beyond measure, but he hadn't gotten through life without having to do a few things he hated. He had a strict moral code for himself, no matter how a Delaney might sneer her nose at it. It didn't allow acting like a punk.

"I'm sorry."

She blinked at him, and he wanted to rip that idiotic wig off her. "What did you say?"

"I said, I'm sorry," he repeated, shoving his hands into his pockets. He wasn't going to *explain* that he'd charged out of the saloon and pushed that door far harder than he'd needed to, but he would apologize for causing some harm.

"For what part?"

"The nose part."

"Is that all you're apologizing for?" she asked coolly.

"You're right that's all. We're in this together, and I wasn't about to let you get dragged off in the dark by some—"

"We aren't in this together. This is not an equal partners thing. I am the detective. You're an informant at best. I need you to act like one instead of the over-the-top, makes-trouble Starsky to my Hutch."

"I'm sorry… Did you just make a Starsky and Hutch reference? What thirty-year-old makes a Starsky and Hutch reference?"

She all but growled in frustration. "I'm going back to Hank. You are not going to interrupt me. You are not… Is it me?" she demanded.

"Is what you?"

"That people think I can't hack it at my job. All of a sudden I have a *real* case and people are worried about me and think I can't handle myself. That I need help or protection or whatever. So, based on you and my sister's actions today I'm wondering, is it me? What kind of vibe am I putting off that makes you think I am incapable of handling myself?"

She flung her arms up in the air, clearly exasperated and pissed and maybe even a little hurt, and why could he *see* all that in the set of her mouth and the lines in her forehead? As if he knew what she was feeling just by looking at her. As if he'd spent a lifetime memorizing every emotion that flitted across her face.

Bull.

"Speaking from your sister's standpoint, she cares about you. I think if she were in some sort of dangerous situation, no matter how well-equipped she might be, you would worry about her, too. And express that worry. I believe that's called family love and devotion."

"Okay. Fine. Maybe you're even right. What's your excuse? Don't you think a woman can hack it?"

"Vanessa is my sister. Believe me, I know what women can hack."

"Then what? Why is it that you can't stand down and let me do my job? I'm a Delaney? You think I'm soft? You—"

"Maybe I don't like watching you smile and flirt with a stranger." Which shut her up. And was the only reason he said it. Not because it was true.

Her eyebrows drew together and he didn't know how a woman who was clearly intelligent and yes, fantastic at her job, could be so completely dense.

"Why would that bother you?" she asked as if there was no reasonable answer.

"Maybe, on occasion, I'd like it if you smiled at me." Which in fairness to Laurel wasn't a *reasonable* answer.

"That doesn't make any sense," she persisted.

"Why not?" he demanded, leaning closer. Closer and closer, making her eyes widen and the air between them crackle with electricity. It was an electricity he'd avoided his entire adult life out of duty, out of a healthy belief in the history of Carsons and Delaneys and Bent and destruction.

But Laurel stood there staring at him, her eyes a shade of dark, unfathomable brown, and no matter that she had that wig on, and makeup making her lips redder and her eyes smokier, she was so wholly *Laurel*.

"You're a Carson," she said on a whisper.

He stared at her for something like a full minute, and

then he laughed. Because Ms. Doesn't Believe In The Feud thought he couldn't want her to smile at him. All because of his last name and hers.

He supposed he had two choices here in this little back room, empty since everyone working was up front at the bar. He could let her go back to Hank, find out whatever information she'd hoped to find, and wash his hands of messing with her or her investigation.

Or, he could do what he should have done fifteen years ago when he'd caught Laurel Delaney snooping around his room after a sleepover with his sister.

She dropped the ice pack from her nose, clearly still confused, and clearly ready to get back to cop mode.

"Grady, I—"

But he couldn't stand it. He cupped his hand around her neck and pulled her mouth to his.

Chapter 8

Grady Carson was kissing her.

On the mouth.

She was sure there was something she was supposed to do about that, but her brain was all crackling static while her body…took it. She absorbed the feel of those full lips on hers, the warmth of his rough hand on the back of her neck, holding her still and there as his mouth took hers like they'd been doing this for centuries. Like everything about this kiss was right exactly as it should be.

She knew, somewhere, that was all wrong, and yet sensation seemed to mute that knowledge. Sweep it away into some strange, distant part of her. So distant it didn't seem weird to lean against him, to open her mouth to him, to press her palm against the hard, hot wall of his chest.

When he broke the kiss, slowly, so slowly, easing her

body away from his, she had to tell herself to breathe, to open her eyes, to *think*. But all she saw was the vibrant blue of Grady's gaze, and the only thoughts she could manage were in gibberish.

She tried to inhale but it was shaky, the exhale unsteady. Everything felt jittery and unstable, and somehow she was still leaning toward Grady, only his arms keeping her upright.

She shook her head, trying to find sense or reason or some grasp of what was happening. She managed to rock back on her heels, holding herself upright so Grady's arms fell away.

He didn't say anything. He didn't move. If it weren't for that intense, heady gaze of his, she might have thought he was wholly unaffected. She wasn't sure he was *affected*, but he wasn't exactly…

Well, she didn't know. *He'd* kissed *her*. She didn't know why. She didn't know why she'd kissed him back. She didn't *know*, and that was her least favorite feeling in the world.

"I… I don't know what that was." She wasn't even sure she knew her name.

Laurel Delaney. Delaney. Deputy Laurel Delaney, and if you recall, you have a murder to solve, not a Carson to kiss.

Kiss. Grady had kissed her. Kissed her with his mouth. His tongue. She could only stare at him because surely, surely no matter how…*wow*…that kiss was, he'd lost his mind.

His mouth curved in that infuriating way, except now she knew what that felt like against *her* mouth and she couldn't muster irritation because she was just…jelly. Boneless, spineless, thoughtless jelly.

"In my world they call it a kiss."

In her world it was something far more primitive than a kiss. Kisses were nice. Affectionate. Not a wild, all-encompassing thing.

"Go on back to your informant, smile some information out of him, and then…" He tilted his head, studying her with something in his expression she couldn't read. It was like humor, but not mean. He wasn't making fun of her, like she might have expected, but she certainly didn't know what he felt, or what he saw when he looked at her.

"Then what?" she asked, feeling entranced no matter how much she told herself to come back to reality.

"We can finish this discussion."

"I thought it was a kiss."

"Oh, princess. It was both."

Before she could make any sense out of *that*, he turned and walked away, disappearing into the main room of the bar while she stood in this little back area by herself.

By herself. Which was good. She could jam her brain back into gear by herself. She could think and plan and somehow compartmentalize, because she was here not to get even more confused about Grady. She was here to get information from Hank.

Hank, who was out there drinking a free drink and waiting for her. Hank, who certainly hadn't killed Jason, but might know *something*. Or have some clue whether he knew it or not.

Her job was her life. Had been since she'd joined the police academy. When she'd made time for any kind of…man-woman thing, it had been a relationship. Not a surprise kiss in the back of a bar from a man she wasn't even sure she *liked*.

It was all so complicated and confusing, and the point of being a cop was that it wasn't those things. There was right and wrong, legal and illegal, and the blurring of lines was only ever to find justice or the truth.

Which was what she needed to focus on. Grady had left, was clearly just messing with her or something. Which might make sense if he'd laughed or teased her for kissing him back, but he'd only told her to do her job and come back later to talk.

Talk.

Did he really mean talk?

She could not be worried about that. She placed the ice pack to the bridge of her nose, willing the icy jolt to get her to focus. On Hank, murder and her job. With a stern nod to herself, she walked back into the noisy, crowded bar, repeating four very important words over and over in her head.

Don't look at Grady. Don't look at Grady.

She focused on Hank, who was now sitting on a bar-stool, two empty glasses in front of him as he watched the TV above the bar intently.

Laurel approached, keeping her gaze steady on Hank and Hank alone. There was a phone placed on the seat next to him.

Laurel swallowed and picked it up. "Saving this seat for me?" she asked in her best throaty tone.

Hank glanced over at her and smiled. "'Course. You're my free drink ticket." He winked as if it was a joke, but Laurel had to admit she wasn't so sure it was.

Which was fine. Drinking a little too much might

convince Hank to tell her what he might know. Something Jason was into. Someone who was bothering him.

She placed his phone on the bar and slid into the seat. Hank waved at Ty down at the other end of the bar, and Ty made no bones about ignoring him.

Hank spared her a glance. "Don't worry. He owes you a drink. I'll get you one."

"No, it's—"

But Hank was already off his chair, striding down the bar to where Ty was serving.

Hank's phone vibrated and Laurel glanced at the screen. A text window popped up, and since Hank was occupied trying to scam himself into another free drink, Laurel nudged the phone so she could read the text.

There was no sender's name, only a number. The message read, Eagle Creek Park. 7. Bring folder.

Laurel frowned. Eagle Creek Park was an isolated state park that barely functioned as a park anymore. She didn't even think they had full-time staff. It was an odd place to meet anyone, unless you were teenagers hoping to get drunk or high. Which certainly didn't require any folders.

Hank returned, grumbling. "Said I had to wait my turn." He slid back into the seat, his hand going over his phone. "Maybe you should try…" He trailed off as he read his text.

"Everything okay?" Laurel asked.

Hank scratched a hand through his hair, then took one of the empty glasses and brought it to his mouth, trying to shake the last drops onto his tongue. His hand shook.

"What's wrong?" she asked, hoping it sounded like worry and compassion and not a cop demand.

"Nothing. Just gotta run. Hey, give me your number so I can hit you up sometime."

"Oh, sure, you want me to type it in?" she asked innocently, holding out her hand.

"Nah, just tell it to me." He sat, fingers poised on his phone screen, but Laurel didn't miss the way his eyes darted around the room.

It was almost ten o'clock, so he couldn't be rushing to meet the guy. Unless seven meant something else besides time. But what else could it mean? Eagle Creek Park was the location, and its address wasn't seven.

She rattled off a fake number. Much as she'd like to use this particular fake flirting to her advantage, she didn't want to push it too far. Especially when she might have to interrogate him as herself.

"Hope I see you around."

"Hope so," she offered cheerfully even though she wanted to stomp her feet and demand he tell her the answers. Instead she let him walk away.

But she had *something* to go on. Eagle Creek Park. Either seven tomorrow morning or seven tomorrow night. She'd be there both times and get to the bottom of this one way or another.

Grady watched Hank slink out of the bar. Based on the frustrated expression on Laurel's face, she hadn't gotten what she'd wanted out of him.

Grady shouldn't be happy about that. But, regardless, he had a few questions of his own. He slipped out the back, grabbing a half-full bag of trash as a prop, and pushed out into the parking lot. The Dumpster was right there, and he made a big show out of tossing the bag into the bin.

Hank approached a beat-up old truck and Grady cleared his throat. "Hey, Gaskill, right?"

Hank looked over at him suspiciously, so Grady did his best not to look intimidating. He probably failed in the dim light of a bar parking lot, a big man with a gruff voice.

"Fred Gaskill your kid brother?" Grady asked when Hank didn't respond.

"Yeah. What of it?"

"Clint Danvers. *My* kid brother. Who didn't get mixed up in trouble until good old Freddy came along." Which was a bald-faced lie, but might lead him somewhere at least. There were too many connections going on here, connections that led to his dumb brother.

Hank scoffed. "First of all, bull. Second of all, it ain't Freddy, and it ain't Clint, it's that chick that's got 'em wrapped around her pinky finger."

Which was certainly news to Grady. "Which one?"

"Lizzie Adams. She's got four kids in Fred's class following her around town, doing her bidding like she's some kind of TV mob boss. Those idiots are hard up enough to think she's going to put out if they do what she wants. Whatever trouble Clint's got, I guarantee you it started with her."

Lizzie Adams. Grady committed that name to memory. "Well, thanks for the tip, man."

Hank shrugged. "I've been telling Fred to stay out of her orbit for weeks, but he's seventeen. Imagine Clint is the same."

"More than," Grady grumbled.

Hank got in his truck and Grady offered a wave before heading back inside. Lizzie Adams. He didn't think a bunch of teenagers were really involved with murder, but something wasn't right.

He walked back into the bar, stopping at the sounds of crashing coming from the little kitchen. He peeked in to find Vanessa slamming things around with seemingly no purpose.

"Everything okay?"

She glared at him over her shoulder. "Fan-freaking-tastic. What's a Delaney doing in our bar? In a wig?"

"Don't worry about it."

Vanessa fisted her hands on her hips and glared at him, but he wasn't about to be intimidated by his little sister. "Hey, you used to invite her into our house. Consider this payback."

"I was a kid."

"And today I happen to be a grown man." He flashed her a grin that had her reaching for something to throw at him, so Grady picked up the pace and hightailed it into the main area of the bar.

Scanning the people sitting at the barstools, he was gratified to find Laurel still sitting there, typing things into her phone. Notes, no doubt. But she hadn't scurried off to do that. Her target had left, and she was still here. In his bar.

He wondered how long she'd stay. If she would share her information with him. If he should share his information with her. Or if all she wanted was to finish their discussion from earlier.

He grinned to himself, and as if that was some kind of beacon, Laurel glanced up and looked over at him.

She didn't grin back. She scowled. But when he nodded to the back room she slid off her stool and headed toward him. He didn't mind Laurel Delaney walking toward him at all, even in a blond wig.

"I need to talk to you. About the case."

His grin didn't falter. "That all?"

"Yes."

He made a considering noise to rile her up. "Upstairs is the only private place around here."

She rolled her eyes. "Fine."

He stepped through the opening into the back and headed for the stairs, but Vanessa stormed out of the kitchen.

"What are you doing?" Vanessa demanded. When Grady opened his mouth to tell her to mind her own business, she wagged a finger. "Not you." She moved the finger to point at Laurel. "You."

Laurel leveled her with a cool look, and didn't even pretend to be blonde Sarah. "Police business. That's all I care about, remember?" And with that she sailed past Grady and up the stairs.

Grady glanced at his sister with an eyebrows-raised questioning look, but Vanessa only huffed and stalked into the bar to start her shift.

Women.

He took the stairs, slowly, because he kind of liked the idea of Laurel waiting for him. She was tapping her foot when he reached the top.

"Can we move this along? I have things to do."

"At your command, princess," he said, pulling his keys out of his pocket and unlocking the door to his apartment. He dramatically gestured her inside.

Once he closed the door, she didn't hesitate to start in on cop mode.

"I need some information out of Clint, and I don't think he's going to give it to me."

"I don't think he's going to give it to me, either."

"What about another family member? Vanessa, maybe?"

"Because she's known for her reason and charm? Pretty sure you were just on the brunt edge of that. What happened between you two?"

"A question only your sister can answer. I have no idea."

"Dad was pretty hard on her about being friends with you."

"Yeah, so was mine."

"He ever hit you?"

Laurel stilled, but she didn't wilt. "No. He didn't." She blew out a breath. "I am not here to drudge up ancient history. Or Delaney-Carson nonsense. I saw a text Hank got that I can only assume is important or linked, and I need to know what Clint knows about Eagle Creek Park."

"You mean the place all the high school kids go to get high?"

"Yes. Exactly."

"I could probably get someone to ask him that without him bristling. Why do you need to know?"

"Because."

Grady crossed his arms over his chest and frowned down at her. "Try again."

"It's confidential."

"Fine, then I won't tell you what Hank told me out there in the parking lot."

"Hank didn't tell you anything."

Grady raised an eyebrow. "You calling me a liar? I

believe back in the day that ended up with shoot-outs in the streets and a lot of Delaneys on the wrong side of a standoff."

"Tell me, and *then* I'll show you the text."

"Promise?"

She wrinkled her nose, clearly balking, but eventually she pushed out a breath. "Fine, I promise."

"Hank said his brother and Clint and a couple of the other idiot boys they hang out with are all gone over this girl, and she's the cause of any trouble they get into. Girl named Lizzie Adams."

"Adams? The man in charge of the mine is named Adams. These kids are connected somehow."

"I agree."

Laurel started moving toward the door, but Grady grabbed her arm. "Hey, you have to show me the text."

"I have to go, Grady. I have to look into this. Make sure Lizzie Adams is—"

"You promised, princess," he said, not letting her arm go no matter how she jerked it. "Now, spill."

She grunted in frustration, but she pulled her phone out of her pocket with her free hand. "Let me go now."

He did so, but stayed alert, because he wouldn't put it past her to make a dash for it. And if she did, he'd have no compunction about throwing her over his shoulder. He'd enjoy it.

She held the phone out to him and he read the notes she'd typed.

"This is what his text said, verbatim. And this is the number."

"Eagle Creek Park. 7. Bring folder."

"So, I need to be at Eagle Creek Park at seven, and

if he's not there in the morning, I'll go at night. But if Clint can get me some information—"

"What if it's not a time?"

"Huh?"

"What if seven isn't a time? It could be a…hike marker, a cabin—it could be a campsite. Hank wasn't just meandering out of here after a few drinks. If he didn't have somewhere to be, he'd be trying to get into your pants." Because it was damn weird Hank had high-tailed it out of here.

"I have to go."

"Like hell."

"Grady, this is police bus—"

"Then call backup because I'll be damned if I'm let-ting you go to an isolated park all by yourself. I don't care if it's me or some cop crony of yours, but there's gonna be somebody."

"I don't have time for this. He's got a good ten-min-ute head start on me, and Hank could be going into danger. Another isolated place like we found Jason? I'll call for backup on my way." She jerked the door open, but he followed.

"Fine, but I'm at your side until that backup shows up."

"Grady," she growled, already jogging down the stairs.

But he jogged right after her. "Sorry, princess, you don't have time to argue."

Chapter 9

Laurel didn't have time to argue, and while she had half a mind to pull out her gun and use it on Grady to keep him put, she knew where night shift zones were, and she knew she could get to Eagle Creek Park long before any of the deputies on duty.

It *wasn't* smart to go alone, but it was hardly smart to go with a civilian. Especially this one.

But what choice did she have? She couldn't help thinking Hank was in danger, and she couldn't ignore that and wait for backup.

So, she got into her car, and let Grady get into the passenger seat no matter how much she shouldn't.

"Don't say or do *anything*," she instructed. She pulled her radio out from the glove compartment and switched it on. She relayed the information, what there was of it. A mysterious location in a big park, no idea of who was involved or if it was even criminal. It could be some romantic assignation. With folders.

She focused on the road, ignoring Grady's large presence in her passenger seat.

"You gonna take off the wig?"

She cursed under her breath and started digging for the pins keeping the wig in place. Every time she found one she plucked it out and tossed it over her shoulder. When Grady's fingertips skimmed her ear, she nearly jerked off the road.

"Easy," he murmured, far too close as she sped down the highway out of Bent. "Just going to help."

Somehow she focused on the road as Grady finished pulling all the pins out of her hair. Admittedly, her heart was beating too hard against her chest, but she could chalk that up to adrenaline and worry about Hank over the feel of Grady's fingers in her hair.

That man kissed you!

She could not even begin to think about that right now. Once it felt loose enough, she tugged off the wig and threw it in the back.

"Stick with brunette, princess."

"I'll keep it under advisement," she muttered, flipping on her brights as they approached the park.

She squinted, surveying the side of the road. She knew the sign for the park had long ago been knocked over and not put back up, so the entrance was hard to find in the dark if you weren't looking for it. When she reached the entrance, she switched the lights back to normal. It would be hard to sneak up on anyone in a car, with the lights, the sound of an engine and the tires on the road, but she and Grady couldn't exactly hike the whole park, either.

"Do you know your way around?"

"I know the campsites are in the back. You take that left there," he said, tapping the windshield in the direction of a small gravel one-way street. "Campsites are numbered one through however many there are, if I'm remembering right. Road goes up, then around a cul-de-sac, so seven should be on our right as we drive up there."

Laurel nodded and navigated the turn onto the narrow road. She scanned the dark for the sign of a vehicle, a person, or anything that might lead them to believe someone was out here.

"How much space between campsites?" Laurel asked as her headlights flashed against a crooked sign that read *Campgrounds closed.*

"Not much, so if we're only going to seven, we could stop here and walk. Can't imagine it taking more than ten minutes. We could surprise them. Well, assuming they haven't already heard the car."

Laurel nodded. It would be at least another twenty before backup could get to the park. She radioed out the plan to the officer en route, then brought the car to a stop in campsite one. She backed in, in case they needed to get out of here quick, before grabbing her flashlight and utility belt, and fishing the gun out of the bra holster.

She ignored Grady's raised eyebrows as he watched her, and got out of the car. She snapped everything into place except the flashlight, clicking it on as Grady quietly closed the passenger door and met her at the hood of the car.

"You should stay in the car," she said, knowing she was wasting her breath.

He huffed out a laugh. "Lead the way, Deputy."

She sighed heavily. "Stay behind me. Don't make any noise. If you try to be a hero, I'll shoot you myself."

"Sure you will."

It was so incredibly annoying he knew her threats didn't hold any weight. But they didn't have time for bickering. She started walking up the gravel drive, training her flashlight on the ground and the signs alternatively, keeping her ears tuned to the sounds around them.

Wind whistled through the trees and against the grasses. Animals scurried through both. The dark took on a life of its own, a moving, unpredictable thing. Laurel kept her hand on her gun, and her flashlight at the ready.

As they reached the sign for campsite number five, she flicked off the light. Grady didn't say anything, and she gave them a few moments to adjust to the dark. It was a clear, cold night, but even the vibrant glow of the stars and moon above didn't make the dark any less daunting.

Laurel began to inch forward, keeping one foot on the gravel and one foot on the grass to make sure she was following the path of the road. When a hand grabbed her shoulder, she nearly screamed, but she bit it back in time, reminding herself *Grady* was behind her.

"Listen," he whispered into her ear. He was suddenly close enough she could feel his body heat, the slight movement of his breath against her hair, but she had more important things to focus on.

Listening.

It took a few moments, but finally she heard it. It sounded like the wind at first, but the more she listened, the more she picked up the cadence of speech in whispers.

She reached up and moved Grady's hand from her right shoulder to her left, then placed her own left hand over it. She patted it, trying to make a nonverbal sign for him to keep it there as they inched forward.

She needed to be close enough to hear what the whispers were, and she needed to know where Grady was. So, she stepped forward, and Grady followed, his tight, warm grip on her shoulder.

She pulled out her gun, wanting it at the ready in case whoever they came upon was armed as well. She hated that she wasn't wearing her vest, but she also hated Grady unprotected behind her and the fact Hank was in danger, no matter if he'd gotten himself in it.

The whispers got louder, but still Laurel couldn't make out the words, and couldn't tell how close they were getting. With the open spaces and sparse clusters of trees, sound bounced everywhere.

Still she inched forward, forcing herself to breathe evenly, to focus on her mission. Keep Hank safe. Keep Grady safe. Then, find out what was going on.

There was a quick shout, and then the unmistakable sound of a gunshot.

Grady's hand clamped on her shoulder, but Laurel jerked out of his grasp and ran toward the shot.

Was she crazy? Grady understood Laurel was a cop and all, but what woman went running toward a gunshot?

Then again, what unarmed, civilian man ran after a woman running after a gunshot? Apparently him. So maybe he had to question his own sanity.

When he caught up with her, she was crouching over a body. The flashlight was on a bloody spot on the guy's shirt.

Hank.

"Hank, can you hear me? Can you focus?"

Hank just groaned as Laurel pulled her cop radio to her mouth, relaying the need for an ambulance ASAP, while her flashlight moved back and forth across the ground, clearly looking for clues as to where the shooter had gone.

She shoved the radio into its slot on her utility belt as she stood, then tossed Grady the flashlight and her phone. "Call 911 and have them walk you through keeping pressure on the wound."

"What are you going to do?" he demanded, and maybe he should have cared more about the fact Hank was moaning on the ground below him with a gunshot wound, but he was a little more concerned about Laurel ending up this way.

"I'm going to find the man who did this." He opened his mouth to tell her something to the effect of *over his dead body* when sirens sounded in the distance.

"It won't be the ambulance, but it will be the cops. Call 911. Look after Hank. Let the police handle this."

And she meant *her*, which was against every impulse inside of him. Unfortunately, so was leaving a man bleeding profusely from a gunshot.

Laurel had taken off, already murmuring into the radio that she needed the park secured. She'd left him the flashlight and it was all he could do not to grab it and rush after her. But Hank moaned, clearly trying to say something and unable to do so.

Grady cursed and used Laurel's phone to dial 911.

How she had service out here he'd never begin to know, but as the 911 dispatcher answered, he explained his emergency and was given instructions on how to deal with the wound.

Hank groaned and thrashed as Grady applied pressure to the wad of fabric that had once been Hank's jacket. He placed the flashlight on the ground, beam pointed toward the wound, so he'd have both hands to work with.

"Didn't get it," Hank rasped, squinting at Grady as if he didn't see him. But he was talking, so he saw something.

"Didn't get what?"

Hank's hand thrashed around, his breathing becoming more labored even as Grady pressed on the wound. The ambulance needed to hurry.

"Pocket," Hank rasped, pointing to his left side.

Keeping the pressure as even as he could manage while also reaching across Hank's body, Grady grimaced and shoved his hand into the other man's pocket.

And pulled out a crumpled piece of paper.

"He didn't get it," Hank managed, his breathing getting shallower, his movements less erratic.

Grady frowned, trying to uncrumple the paper with one hand and read it in the beam of the flashlight. It was handwritten notes on a piece of graph paper. A list of dates, and next to each one a note. Most of it was nonsense to Grady. Names he didn't know, words he'd never seen before. But there was one line, dated two weeks ago, that was written in all caps.

CLEANUP WILL NOT MEET EPA STANDARDS.

Which meant nothing to Grady, and he doubted it would make sense to Laurel, either. But he figured out that whatever Hank, Jason and the man going around shooting people were involved in, it was centered at the mine.

It also meant whatever was going down at the mine was a big enough deal to kill, or try to kill, two men over. Blatantly. Without too much worry about being caught or repercussions if someone did put it all together.

And Laurel was out there in the dark.

If he hadn't been thinking about Laurel, about how many men she had out there with her now that the sirens had stopped and clearly the other cops were searching as well, he might have missed it.

A slight shuffle of leaves, the unmistakable sound of someone stepping on a twig or a branch or something. Then the eerie silence that followed.

Grady didn't move. No doubt if it were Laurel or any of the officers, they would announce themselves. Especially knowing they had a shooting victim.

It could be an animal, but animals typically didn't pause after they'd made a loud noise.

Grady didn't make any sudden movements. Whoever was out there had too good a vantage point, and hadn't shot yet. Which didn't mean he wouldn't, but it certainly meant he was considering not shooting him, too.

So, slowly, almost imperceptibly, Grady began to turn his head to look over his shoulder.

"Don't move," a faraway-sounding voice rasped.

"All right," Grady replied, keeping his head exactly where it was, inflicting his tone with as much ease as he could manage.

"Who are you?" the man growled in an undistinguishable voice that didn't stay still. Grady couldn't tell if the man was pacing or just moving around.

"You think I'm going to tell a strange man in the woods who I am?" Laurel wouldn't approve of this particular method of dealing with a man and, presumably, a gun, but Grady had known his fair share of desperate men. He could handle this one.

He hoped.

The ambulance had to get here soon, and if it didn't, the officers would have to circle back. So, maybe at worst he ended up with a bullet to the gut like Hank and lived to tell the tale.

Worst-case scenario is probably bullet to the head, genius.

Grady pushed that thought away and focused on the task at hand. "Just trying to help a guy out here. I don't want any trouble."

The man made some scoffing sound and Grady tried to focus on his surroundings. Was there anything he could use as a weapon? Did Hank have anything on him that could be grabbed and used as a weapon before the guy shot him?

He just needed the thug to come closer so Grady could knock him down. He had no doubts he could win in a fair fight, no matter how big the guy was, but this man had a gun, and Grady had nothing.

"Step away from Hank."

Grady looked down at Hank's form illuminated by the flashlight beam. He'd gone still, but his breathing continued, labored as it was. Grady wasn't sure the man could survive if he lost any more blood.

And you're not going to survive with a bullet to the brain.

But he'd never been very good at backing down to bullies. "Why don't you just let my friend here—"

"What's in your hand?" the man demanded, and he'd either forgotten to use his raspy voice or just didn't care.

Grady looked at the paper. The last thing he wanted to do was give the evidence up, but if he could remember the date, and the exact verbiage of the all caps message, plus some of the names...

Suddenly the paper was torn from his grasp, which gave Grady the chance he needed. He immediately kicked out, making contact with the man's shin. The man howled in pain, but unfortunately he didn't go down.

Which meant Grady had to take the pressure off Hank's wound. It would be precious time and probably precious amounts of blood, but they were both going to end up dead if Grady didn't fight.

So in a stealth move, Grady got his feet underneath him in a crouching position. As the attacker raised his arm, moonlight glinting off the gun in his hand, Grady lunged.

He rammed into the attacker, which sent them both sprawling, and Grady hoped the clattering sound mixed with crunching leaves was the gun falling out of his attacker's grasp.

Suddenly, over the sound of their grunts, Grady heard sirens, loud and clear. He looked up to see the flashing red, which was stupid, because it gave his attacker just enough time to land a blow that had his world going black.

Chapter 10

Laurel swore and then swore again. She'd scoured the back of the park as much as she could manage with no artificial light, but there was no sign of the shooter. The only men she'd run into were the two officers she'd called in for backup.

"He could be anywhere. We just don't have the manpower for this kind of search," Deputy Clarion said disgustedly.

He was right, but that didn't ease Laurel's irritation or anger. Having someone *else* shot while you were investigating a murder wasn't exactly the thing stellar detective careers were made of. Especially when she had no suspects, no clues. Only forest and darkness and questions.

This was all her fault. She did everything in her power to push away the crushing sense of failure, but it rooted deep. She'd missed clues and hadn't thought things through, and another man was hurt because of her and could very well end up dying.

"We need to head back and make sure he hasn't doubled back," Laurel ordered, a little sharper than necessary, but she felt sharp and pissed.

She'd left Grady behind unarmed, and it was more than possible a man with a gun had outsmarted them, circled back, and was going to do his best to finish off the job of killing Hank. Because they were dealing with someone who was desperate enough to murder one man, and attempt to murder another. She didn't think he'd stop to consider the moral implications of murdering Grady as well.

She swore and increased her pace. "Keep your eyes peeled, but our focus right now is getting back to the victim," Laurel called over her shoulder, breaking into a jog. "If our suspect gets away, we're just going to have to chalk it up to a loss, but if our victim is finished off, or a civilian is, that's on us."

Her, really. She'd been the idiot to let Grady strongarm her into bringing him here, and then she'd been the fool who'd left him to fend off anything that came his way with a dying man and no weapon. She'd left him defenseless.

The idea of Grady being defenseless was *almost* laughable. Grady was big and strong and inherently capable of handling himself, but he wasn't Superman. He couldn't fight off a bullet.

She heard the two other deputies huffing behind her so she walked faster. Through the trees and dangerous open areas, back to the campsites where she'd left Hank and Grady. Moonlight lit her way, and as she got closer, the flashing lights of the ambulance helped lead her exactly where she needed to be.

The fact the ambulance was there eased some of the worry clogging her chest. It had made it to the correct location, which meant Hank had a chance and Grady hadn't been hurt. Surely they'd gotten to Hank and Grady before anything had happened.

The suspect had probably made a run for it without a second thought to look back. He probably figured Hank was as good as dead and had gotten what he was after.

And yet somehow Laurel didn't feel any better. She got close enough to see Hank's body strapped to a stretcher and being lifted into the ambulance, but no Grady.

She swallowed down the panic. He was around here somewhere. Had to be. "Where's the other man?" she demanded of the paramedic as he closed the doors.

"What other man?"

"There was a man here guarding Hank, the victim."

The paramedic raised his eyebrows. "I didn't see anyone, and I've got to transport this man. He's lost far too much blood and is unresponsive."

"Wait. There was another man. There was another—"

"I have to go, Deputy, if you want this man to—"

They both stopped arguing when a loud groan came from somewhere nearby, along with the rustling of leaves.

Laurel immediately moved toward the sound and she was gratified the paramedic didn't take off.

"Grady?"

The response was a string of truly filthy curses.

"Give me your light," Laurel demanded of the paramedic. He handed her a flashlight and she flicked it on, moving the beam of light up toward the groaning and cursing.

"Grady." He was sprawled out in a shallow gully. As she moved closer, he rolled onto his side, clearly tried to sit up and failed. "Don't move," she ordered, scurrying down the little swell of earth and kneeling at his side. "Oh, my God. Are you shot?"

"I don't know," he grumbled. "Am I?"

"Grady." She tried to run her fingers over his chest, but the paramedic was pushing her out of the way.

"Where does it hurt, sir?"

"Probably the bleeding wound in my head," Grady snapped back, and though he had some fire to his responses, even in the weird illumination provided by the ambulance lights and flashlights, Laurel knew he looked pale.

"Simon, we have to go," the other paramedic yelled from the ambulance. "This guy isn't going to hold on much longer."

"Got another one, Pete. Blunt force trauma to the head. Lost consciousness. Bring out the other stretcher."

Pete swore, but moved quickly and efficiently.

"I don't need a stretcher." Grady pushed at the paramedic, and nothing made Laurel's blood run colder than the fact he didn't even budge the paramedic. Big, strong Grady Carson's push was ineffective at best.

She swallowed at the fear trying to lump itself in her throat. "Let them put you on the stretcher, Carson." She turned to the other officers she'd almost forgotten about. "You two, canvas the area. Anything you can find, you bag up. Got it?"

"Piece of paper," Grady mumbled as the two paramedics worked to move him.

"What?"

"Hank had a piece of paper. Something important. It's all a little fuzzy." He lifted a hand, but dropped it.

"A piece of paper. Okay, I'll look for one."

"What did that guy hit me with? I knocked his gun away."

He'd knocked the shooter's gun away, dear God. The paramedics started hefting him to the ambulance, and Laurel had to order herself to focus. Not on Grady, not on how badly he might be hurt, but on figuring out who did this.

"We're looking for a gun, something that could have been used as a blunt force trauma weapon and a piece of paper," she announced to the two deputies searching the area.

The ambulance revved its way out of the campsite parking space and Laurel had to force herself not to look at it. Grady was in good hands.

And hurt. Because of you.

She wasn't sure she'd ever been so close to crying on the job, but she ruthlessly blinked back the tears. "Anything you even question for a second, bag it. We need a clue."

She moved her beam to the gully Grady had been lying in. She didn't see anything outright, but it was covered in leaves. She reached into the part of her utility belt she kept rubber gloves in and pulled one on.

She began to sift through the leaves, looking for anything at all that wasn't natural debris. Anything that could have been used to hit Grady over the head.

She found the tiniest scrap of paper, white and dry, which meant it couldn't have been here long. She squinted at the words, but there weren't enough to make any sense out of it. Still, she placed it in her evidence bag.

Then her hand ran into something hard. She pulled it out of the pile of leaves and studied it. A shoe. A nice shoe at that. Men's. Big enough. With a sole hard and sharp enough to do some damage.

Laurel slipped that into the bag. She probably couldn't get an identity with a shoe, but it was certainly *something*.

"I found a gun," one of the deputies said a few yards south of her.

Laurel nodded. A scrap of paper, a shoe and a gun. It wasn't much.

But it was something.

Grady hated hospitals. They were so white and every noise was so mechanical. He'd watched a few too many people die in hospital rooms. He'd been with all of his grandparents, holding hands or murmuring prayers, because his grandparents had raised him right in the shadow of everything else.

Then there was the time Dad had died. Grady trying to shield Vanessa, being pushed away as monitors went crazy and nurses jumped into action. And somehow feeling sad when all was said and done, even though his father had never been anything more than a mean SOB.

Grady blew out a breath and glared at the door. They'd stitched him up and talked over his head about concussions and being watched overnight, and he was about ready to lose his usually impenetrable cool.

They were going to release him soon, or he was going to fight his way out. One way or the other. He just had to figure out whom to call. Noah or Vanessa or

Ty. Hell, he should call Clint and demand some payment for what a mess he was in because of the kid.

But the only person he wanted to call was Laurel, and that was messed up.

When the door opened, Grady was ready to go after whatever poor soul dared darken his door without discharge papers.

"Mr. Carson," a young, timid thing asked, hovering there as though she were afraid of him. "There's a police officer here who wants to speak with you, and I couldn't find—"

"Is it a woman?"

"Um, well, yes."

"Send her in, then."

"Oh. Right. Well."

"Now," Grady growled, sending the girl scurrying out the door. A few seconds later, Laurel appeared. She was still wearing what she'd been wearing in his bar earlier, sans wig. She'd tamed her hair back, though, in one of those serviceable braids she tended to favor. And she looked serviceable and a little bit formidable on top of it.

Hell, he wanted to get her into bed.

"Why are you torturing that poor candy striper or whatever it is she is?" Laurel asked, and he noted she hovered close to that door opening even as her gaze scanned his bandage.

"Because no one will let me out of this hellhole."

Her mouth flattened and she jammed her hands into her pockets. "Well, I need to take your statement."

"You came all this way to take my statement, princess?"

"Yes. Is your head a little clearer now, or should I wait until morning?"

"My head is just fine," Grady said, willing the snap out of his tone and failing. "Everything about me is just fine." To prove it, he slid off the hospital bed and into a standing position.

"Sit back down right this instant," Laurel demanded, crossing the room as if she was going to push him into bed herself.

"You ain't in charge of me, Deputy," Grady returned, folding his arms across his chest and fighting back the dizziness that had taken over him. "The doctor is working on my discharge papers, so I can stand just fine." He glared down at her, but that scowl she'd been using seemed to fall away as she took in the bandage on his temple.

She looked…defeated. Sad. Guilty.

Hell.

"I just need to get your statement," she said quietly. "We don't need to argue."

"But arguing is what we do best."

Laurel shook her head faintly, and that weird cloak of sadness didn't leave her. "Did you get a look at the attacker?" she asked, pulling her ever-present notebook out of her pocket, along with a pen. "Any identifying marks or facial features that might distinguish them from other people? A height, weight or build."

It galled that he didn't have any answers, but he couldn't exactly make any up, so he had to be honest. "No. It was dark and I couldn't see anything except for the fact he had a gun. Did you guys find it?"

She swallowed and gave a sharp nod, her dark eyes soft and something else. Something he couldn't recognize no matter how many other emotions on her he could.

"Yes," she said, her voice rough. "We found it. Ideally it's traceable and this is over, but…"

"The murderers of the world don't usually use traceable guns."

"No, they do not. We also recovered a shoe, which was the weapon that…" Her eyes darted to his bandage again. "Did you have to get stitches?"

"Yeah. Ten. Must've been some shoe."

"It was sharp. Hard-soled." She inhaled shakily and he didn't understand what this was. Just guilt over someone hurting him? He wasn't sure he understood why she should feel that way. Which made it hard to know if he wanted to comfort her or tease her.

"I'm so sorry," she said, all earnestness and Laurel. Just Laurel, this bastion of right and fighting wrong.

Which answered that question for him. He didn't want to tease her when she was all soft. "For what?" he demanded a little bit too brusquely.

"I shouldn't have left you there. I shouldn't have taken you there at all, but I really shouldn't have left you with a hurt man completely unarmed. I should have known or predicted he'd double back and… He could've killed you, Grady. So easily. He could have killed you both, and I wouldn't have been able to do anything about it. And that… It was shoddy police work and I'm sorry that you got caught in the middle."

"See, I just thought it was one of those instances where you did your best but bad things happen because life is unpredictable," Grady returned gruffly, because he didn't want her guilt or her apologies. Not when he'd forced her hand, and not when… Well, she had done her best. He was no idiot.

"I should've known better," Laurel said firmly.

"How?"

"Because as a police officer you're trained to deal with these things. You are trained—"

"You're trained to know exactly where a murder suspect might go in the dark? In an isolated, enormous park that no one has been to in years and therefore has no brush cleaned up, no identifying markers, no nothing?"

"I am trying to give you an apology," she said through gritted teeth.

"I don't want your apology. I was the one who made it impossible for you to go without me, and I'm sure glad I did. Because the fact I could stay with Hank made it certain *you* didn't both end up dead."

"It would've been in the line of duty. It would have been my job. It's not your job. You shouldn't have been there, and you shouldn't have gotten hurt, and it's my fault that you did."

"How long you going to self-flagellate, because I'm out until you're done."

Laurel threw her arms up in the air. "You are insufferable. And ridiculous. I'm trying to be nice and… and…be a good person, and you're throwing it back in my face!"

Even though his head was starting to throb, Grady couldn't help smiling. Maybe it was sick, but he sure liked seeing her irritated more than he liked seeing her…contrite or upset or whatever that was.

"I need your statement," she snapped, hitting her pen against the notebook, eyes flashing angry gold. "Tell me everything that happened once I left."

To placate her, he did just that. He went through calling 911, and trying to stop Hank's bleeding. He remembered the paper, but then things started to get a little gray. Not quite linear. There was something about a paper. Hank had a paper?

"You can't remember?" Laurel asked gently and he scowled at her.

"I remember. Some things. Bits and pieces, but I can't seem to put it all back together in the right order."

"I think that's a fairly common concussion symptom."

"It's not a serious concussion."

"But it is *a* concussion. And ten stitches."

"And not your fault. I probably would have gotten knocked around a lot worse if I hadn't been thinking about you." Which was not an admission he needed to make, except he was tired. Exhausted. His head hurt, and he didn't… He didn't want her guilt or her cop crap. He just wanted her.

"What do you mean you were thinking about me?"

"I was worried about where you had gone, and what might be happening to *you*, and I was listening for you. I heard a twig break and shuffling of leaves and then I knew someone was there. Which gave me time to prepare and fight back." But he couldn't remember much of the fight.

"You don't have to worry about me," she said, shoving her notebook and pen into her pocket. "I'm the cop."

"You're not invincible because of a badge," he snapped, wanting to shake some sense into her.

"No, but—"

"Just shut up," he bit out, because if she spent any more time talking about her line of duty, he was going to end up kissing her until they both forgot their last names.

Which was the number one thing he wanted, and not just because of this night. He couldn't remember a time he hadn't wanted a piece of Laurel Delaney, and the events of this night made him tired of pretending.

"I found a scrap of the paper you mentioned," Laurel said, using that cool cop tone that seriously tested his self-control. "It doesn't make any sense to me. But I took a picture of it." She took her phone out of her back pocket and handed it to him.

He looked down at the screen. It really was just a scrap. Two dates listed, then not even two full words after. He knew he'd looked at this. He'd looked at this paper and...

"It's okay if you don't remember," Laurel said gently. "It'll come to you. In the meantime, we have a shoe, a gun and the first real evidence-related lead we've had this whole investigation. And, unless either comes back as being Clint's, which I find very hard to believe, your brother is off the hook. Which means so are you."

Off the hook. Because Clint would be proven innocent. It didn't make him feel any better. In fact, it pissed him right off. "Like hell I am."

Chapter 11

Laurel didn't think Grady would ever make any sense to her. He should be relieved. He should be skipping out of the hospital room. Free.

But he was fuming. *Fuming.*

"Clint isn't a part of it," she repeated. Maybe the concussion was making it hard for him to think straight or understand everything properly. "Which means I don't need your help anymore. At least, there's no reason for you to help me. Your brother is in the clear. Probably."

"You really don't think I have a reason to still be involved in this?" Grady asked incredulously.

"Well—"

"Someone hit me over the head with a shoe and gave me a concussion. It could have been a lot worse, too. So, I am going to be a part of bringing him down."

"Grady," she began, doing her best to find a reasonable tone.

"Do not argue with me, princess. I am in this now. No one knocks me out and gets away with it. I've got a little revenge to enact."

"My job isn't about revenge. It's about justice, so you wanting revenge can't—"

"Consider my revenge justice. Now—"

A knock sounded at the door and an older woman in nurse's scrubs stepped in. "I have your discharge papers, Mr. Carson." She smiled pleasantly at Laurel. "And good, you have someone who can drive you home."

Laurel opened her mouth to argue. She should not be driving him home. He needed to call one of his cousins, or his sister or even Clint. Anyone who was not her.

She needed some distance from Grady. No matter if he had revenge *or* justice on the brain. She had let herself be compromised by all his irritating goading and charming smiles and that kiss, and she had done things she knew went against protocol.

Laurel *never* went against protocol.

But Grady flashed the nurse a charming smile. "Yes, I got myself a ride home. Now let's get me out of here."

"We just have to go over some paperwork, I'll need a signature, then you'll be free." Again the nurse turned to Laurel. "Will you be staying with Mr. Carson overnight?" she asked innocently.

Grady grinned. "Yeah, I think she owes me that."

Again Laurel opened her mouth to protest, but there was no point in arguing in front of the nurse. There was no point in arguing, period. Grady would get her to do what he wanted. He always seemed to.

So, she would get him home to the Carson Ranch. The other Carsons would kick her out so fast her head would spin, and the fact that idea disappointed her was reason enough to go through it. She needed a Grady-ectomy and stat.

"Here is a list of symptoms you may have for the next few weeks," the nurse said, handing Grady one of the sheets of papers she'd brought in. "You should avoid driving for at least twenty-four hours and tonight, if you're sleeping, you should be woken up every two hours to make sure you're responsive. All of these papers have information on how to deal with a concussion and when to call us, but mostly the main concern is if you're unresponsive or your symptoms get significantly worse." She went through the medications Grady could take and rattled off more instructions before letting him sign his release form.

"You are free to leave whenever you're ready," the nurse said cheerfully. "Take care of Mr. Carson," she added to Laurel before striding out of the room.

"Come on, driver. I'm ready to go home."

"I'm going to take you to the ranch and drop you off with your family," Laurel said firmly. No matter that looking at the bandage on his head made her want to touch his face. Press her cheek to his chest and listen to his heartbeat.

Maybe *she* had been hit over the head.

"You'll drive me to Rightful Claim and take good care of me all through the night," Grady returned, that sharp, wolfish smile on his face as he gathered his belongings.

What was wrong with her that she *wanted* that, and so much more? And, worst of all, she always kind of had, but she'd learned to keep her distance, to force her focus elsewhere. But Grady Carson had always been that thing she couldn't want or have, and so she'd turned it off.

But it was impossible to turn off when he was *here* all the time, when he'd kissed her, when he was saying 'take good care of me all through the night' with that glint in his eye.

She wanted to be him for a second. To say outrageous things and not give a crap. She wanted to be *free* of all the rules and protocols she'd placed on herself. "I'm pretty sure she said no vigorous activity," she retorted.

Grady barked out a laugh and she hated the part of herself that was warmed by that. Encouraged. The part of her that wanted to fuss over him and, yes, have a little vigorous activity. It was a lot more than a concussion standing in her way of all that.

"That makes me wonder all kind of things about you, Laurel."

"I'll drive you to Rightful Claim, but I'm not your nurse. Someone from your family should come stay with you." Because she did not trust herself. A sad, pathetic fact.

"Someone from my family isn't the reason I have a concussion."

She knew he was trying to use her guilt against her. She knew she absolutely shouldn't let him. A good cop knew they weren't at fault for something that went wrong. It was the fault of the bad guys. Murderers and rapists and burglars—they were at fault when bad things happened.

But knowing something and feeling something were two very different things—hence her current predicament. She walked down the squeaky hospital corridor and toward the exit, warring with herself. With knowing and feeling.

She knew better than this and yet some part of her wanted to take care of Grady. She wanted to talk over the details of the case with him, and she wanted to be there when he remembered what he would inevitably remember. Something about that paper.

Grady slung his arm across her shoulder, casual as you please. "Don't think so hard, princess. You're giving me a headache."

"I think the concussion gave you a headache."

"Nah, it's you."

They stepped into the cold chill of late-night autumn. Or, more accurately, way-too-early morning. She led him to her car and felt a sudden wave of exhaustion roll over her. This had been the longest night and it felt as though nothing concrete or impactful had been accomplished.

You have evidence. You are making progress.

She was, but it was the knowing versus feeling thing again. She didn't *feel* progress. She couldn't seem to feel anything that wasn't futility, despair or frustration.

She glanced at Grady sitting in the passenger seat of her car. He had his eyes closed, and the white bandage stuck out against the tan skin and dark beard of his face.

It really wasn't fair he was so handsome, and that he was here, the living incarnation of her current life crisis. He was so many things she couldn't want, and yet did. Why couldn't her emotions ever follow the reason she was so desperate to live by?

"We going to sit here all night?" he asked, eyes still closed, voice a rumble in the quiet of the car.

"I'm not going to sleep with you," she said firmly,

because if she put it out there, in real, spoken words maybe she could be sure.

"You've said that a few times now. I can only assume that means you think about sleeping with me an awful lot." He turned his head to face her, eyes open and far too blue, and he grinned.

But Laurel didn't have it in her to grin back. There was this out-of-control thing inside of her she didn't know how to rein back in, and she didn't know what to *do*—when knowing what to do was all she'd ever done.

"For the record," Grady drawled. "I don't think I have it in me tonight. But I never say never."

Laurel turned on the car and pulled out of the parking spot. "I didn't say never," she grumbled.

Grady felt nauseous and his head was pounding and if he had any energy at all, he would be tracking down the person who'd done this to him and bashing his head in.

He pulled his keys out of his pocket and unlocked the back doors of Rightful Claim, Laurel hovering behind him. Her presence was the only thing that kept him from actually punching something. Because somehow just her being there felt comforting.

He'd never thought to look for *comforting* in a person he spent time with before, but Laurel gave him all sorts of interest in the feeling. Especially considering his body felt like hell and working up any other interest probably wasn't happening.

Grady stepped inside and Laurel followed. He locked the door behind her and walked toward the stairs to his apartment. He paused at the bottom of them. Stairs he undoubtedly ran up and down a thousand times a day suddenly seemed daunting. Too much.

"They should've kept you overnight," Laurel observed in a brisk tone.

He scowled in her direction. "I'm fine."

"You're struggling," she said firmly.

"Then why don't you help me up the stairs and take good care of me?" he asked, trying to flash a cocky grin her way and failing mostly. All he could seem to do right now was grimace.

She rolled her eyes, but she stepped closer to him so that they were side by side. With a huff of irritated breath she cinched her arm around his waist.

"Come on. Let's go."

He looked down at her incredulously. She really thought she was going to help him up the stairs? "You're a slip of a thing."

She made a scoffing noise. "I only seem like a slip to you because you're ginormous."

"Ginormous, huh?"

He noted the faint blush that crept across her cheeks and wished he had the wherewithal to lean down and capture her mouth with his.

"I'm sturdy enough," she continued, gauging the stairs in front of them. "Probably kick your ass in the PT test."

"No. Definitely not."

She began to take steps with him, and he didn't lean on her so much as let her presence be a guide in keeping his dizziness at bay.

"We can test that theory sometime, but not today."

Grady grumbled irritably and let her help him up the rest of the stairs. It was just that all of his limbs felt heavy. His body, his head, everything felt stone-like and sluggish.

"I cannot fully express the unfairness of being rendered this weak by a shoe."

She patted his back sympathetically. "It was a very hard shoe."

"Don't placate me." They reached his apartment door and he unlocked it before pushing it open and stepping inside. It was good to be back in his own place. In his own air.

"Go lie down."

"Yes, ma'am. I find your bossy so hot."

She muttered something under her breath and went over to his little kitchenette. She started looking through his cabinets, muttering all the while. Grady toed off his boots and sprawled out on the bed. The covers were all tangled at the end of the mattress and it seemed like far too much work to pull them up.

"Don't you have any tea?" Laurel asked, rummaging through his stuff.

"Yes, Laurel, I keep *tea* on hand. Do I seem like a *tea* guy to you?"

"Don't you have anything warm and comforting?"

He patted the bed next to him. "I have you."

He thought he saw her mouth curve a fraction and he'd mark that down as a success.

"You know you're impossible, right?" she asked, fisting her hands on her hips and doing her best to glare at him.

"You would not be the first person to tell me that. I believe that was the lullaby my mother used to sing me to sleep with."

"You should call Vanessa. She'd be in a much better position to take care of you."

"Vanessa? My sister Vanessa? She couldn't take care of a pet rock."

"Fine. Noah? Ty? They're your family." She had that soft, earnest look about her and he much preferred the almost smile he'd earned a few seconds ago.

"Right. Which means I don't get nearly as much enjoyment out of pissing them off."

"I'm not pissed off."

"No, you're guilty. Which pisses *me* off. Come sit next to me."

"I am not sitting on the bed with you."

"Can't control yourself around me, princess?"

"Grady."

"I want you to show me the picture again. I want you to go through everything that happened, and if you go through it, maybe it'll jog my fuzzy memory and I can put these pieces back together."

"I think you should sleep. I have to wake you up in two hours and see if you're responsive. Then we can go through all that."

"Then you're staying?" he asked.

"If you're not going to call anyone else, what choice do I have? I don't have any of their numbers. I could wrestle your phone from you, but I have a feeling that wouldn't end up the way I'd like it to."

Grady chuckled. "No, baby, wrestling would not end the way you want it to."

"Get some sleep."

"I need to work through this or I'm never going to fall asleep." And he wasn't even just trying to get her into his bed. It was eating at him, all those murky pieces he couldn't remember.

She sighed heavily and shook her head as though she couldn't believe what she was about to do. Then she walked over to the bed. Gingerly and hesitantly she rested her butt on the very edge opposite him. She handed over her phone. "Here's the picture of the scrap we found."

"If I start scrolling through your pictures am I going to find something interesting?"

"In your dreams."

"Yes, interesting images of you have appeared in many of my dreams."

"Grady," she scolded exasperatedly.

"Okay. So we got there, and we heard the gunshot. We found Hank, and then you took off."

"First you argued with me, and then I took off," Laurel corrected, sliding just a little bit more into the bed so she could stretch out her legs and rest her back against the headboard.

"Semantics," Grady replied. "I called 911. They told me to put pressure on the bullet wound. He was losing a lot of blood. I remember all that clearly." Grady looked down at his hands. For a moment he could almost see Hank's blood on them, but they'd washed that off at the hospital.

"How is Hank?" he asked, surprised at how rusty he sounded.

"He lost a lot of blood. He's still alive, but it's fairly critical. Out of surgery. They'll call me if anything changes or when he wakes up," Laurel said gently.

He'd never much appreciated gentle. Gentle tended to get trampled in this life, but Laurel's gentle was some-

how steel, too, and it washed over him like a soothing balm.

"He said something to me. He said 'he didn't get it.'
Then he gestured to his pocket and I pulled out a piece
of paper. I read it over and tried to remember what it
said. Something important."

Grady stared at the picture of the scrap of paper on
Laurel's phone. He knew there was something he was
supposed to remember, and it was just somewhere in
the gray, frayed edges of his mind.

"You can't beat yourself up about it. I think the more
you focus on trying to remember, the harder it's going
to be *to* remember."

"I have an excellent memory and never forget anything. I could probably name every person who's ever
walked through the doors of my bar."

"Saloon," she corrected for him, and when he
glanced at her there was a hint of a smile.

He didn't have words for how badly he wanted to
kiss that smile. "I'd probably remember more if you
scooted a little closer."

"Grady, you have to understand that I have already
put my investigation in danger because of you."

"Excuse me?"

"I don't mean that as a blame on you. It's a blame
on me. For whatever reason, I have a hard time..." She
looked away, clearly embarrassed and irritated with
herself. "I have a hard time saying no to you. I should
have put my foot down and not brought you with me."

"So you could have been shot?"

"If I'd waited with the deputies..."

"Hank could be dead. The what-ifs work both ways.
Good and bad. What if-ing it is pointless, and I think

you know that. You haven't compromised your investigation. Not because of me, and not because of you. Your investigation is fine. Things just aren't going easily."

"Maybe I'm used to things going easily."

"Thankfully for you, I'm not. I'll teach you."

"The thing is, Grady… Maybe there is this weird pull between us. Attraction or chemistry or, I don't know, DNA. Carsons and Delaneys forever attracted to each other like magnets only to ruin everything. But we are night and day. Opposites in every way except the one that has us working together. I am serious and permanent and all the things you avoid like the plague."

"Maybe I'm not serious about everything, but I'm serious about plenty. My family. This town. And that's permanent. I'm not all one-night stands and parties or whatever it is you think of me."

"Then what are you?" she asked, looking at him with earnest brown eyes. So earnest and pretty and, yeah, everything that wasn't usually *him*.

She was right. They should be oil and water but their Carson and Delaney roots somehow acted like soap, mixing them all together.

"Probably no good for you, princess deputy."

"It's not about being good or bad for—"

He reached over and curled his fingers around her upper arm. He was tempted to give her a good jerk, till she was sprawled out on top of him, but his body wasn't up for it. "Come over here."

"Grady—"

"Now, Laurel."

No one was more shocked than him when she obeyed.

Chapter 12

Laurel knew she was losing her mind, but it felt so good. Because letting Grady pull her toward him, until she was practically sprawled across half of him, felt like a relief. It cleared all the arguments in her head and released nearly all of the tension in her body.

"How often do you think you've called me by my actual name?" she asked.

"Haven't exactly kept track." He curled his finger into a strand of her hair, wrapping it around and around. "Still not going to sleep with me?"

She sighed, glancing up at the bandage on his head. "Nope."

He grinned. "Because of doctor's orders?"

She could lie. She could go back to her usual circuitous denials, but he was warm and comfortable to lean against. She didn't feel much like lying or denying or focusing. So, she told the truth. "Yes, that is why."

He pulled on the finger he'd wrapped some of her hair around, drawing her face closer to his. "Doctor's orders don't last forever."

"Maybe I don't want them to."

His eyebrows went up and she couldn't ignore the fact she got a thrill out of shocking him. Except, the thrill was immediately followed by exhaustion. "I am so tired, Grady, and I have so many things to do." So many things and all she wanted to do was rest her cheek on Grady's chest and sleep.

For a second, just one little second, she gave in to the impulse.

"Set the alarm on your phone, princess, and we'll take ourselves a little rest."

"Like this?" she asked incredulously.

Before she could explain to him that she wasn't about to take a nap curled up on top of him when he was suffering from a concussion and they weren't even…whatever it was they weren't, he'd shifted lower on the bed and they were both prone.

She was on her side, all but curled against him, her head resting on his shoulder. His arm was around her, strong and protective. She should get up. Roll away. She wasn't going to sleep with—actual sleep—with Grady. It was wholly incongruous to him and what they were or weren't and yet her eyelids were already drooping. Where it usually took her a good hour to shut up her brain and fall asleep, she already felt relaxed. Safe.

The next thing she knew her phone was jerking her out of sleep. At first she thought it was her alarm, but as she pawed on the mattress to find it, she saw the name of the hospital flashing on her screen.

She hit Accept as fast as she could, somehow all

tangled up with Grady in the dark. "H-hello?" she answered breathlessly, trying to roll away from him and being caught in a hard, uncompromising grasp.

"Deputy Delaney?"

"This is her."

"Hank Gaskill is awake and doing well enough to receive very brief visits, if your questioning is absolutely necessary."

"It is. It is. I'll be there soon." She clicked End, already scooting toward the empty side of the bed so she could slide off without any physical contact with Grady. "Hank's awake. I have to go."

"We were asleep for an hour," Grady said. "You can't keep going at this pace."

She pulled on her jacket, patting herself down to make sure she had everything. "I have to. Now, can you please, *please*, call someone?"

He sighed heavily but he held up his phone. "Ty should be around."

"Promise me you'll call him, and make sure he follows the doctor's instructions. A promise, Grady. Your word."

"You think my word means anything?"

She studied his face, all sharp edges and challenge, and yet she knew what she'd always known about Grady Carson. He might be wild, he might be antagonistic and frustrating and not necessarily law-abiding, but he was not a man who went back on his word. "Yeah, I think a promise from you means something."

Something on his face altered into an expression she couldn't read and wasn't sure she'd ever seen on him, at least not directed at her. "This case won't stand in our way forever, Laurel."

She met his gaze, and she knew he was right in the same way she knew Carsons and Delaneys would never get along, and never leave Bent. Even with an hour's sleep under her belt, she didn't have the energy to argue. "I know it won't. But I still have a job to do. Call Ty. I'll…check on you later."

He smiled, back to slick charm and self-satisfied humor. "I'll be waiting."

She couldn't let that mean anything. She had a job to do and a case to focus on, and Grady… Well, everything all jumbled up with him would have to wait. No matter how nice it had been to simply lie next to someone and feel safe and comfortable.

She drove back to the hospital, pushing away the exhaustion that dogged her. She'd grab a cup of coffee, then question Hank, then… She'd have to grab a few hours. The sun was just hinting at the horizon, ready to start a new day.

And you're still no closer to an answer.

So far. So far. That wasn't final.

She parked at the hospital lot and made her way up to Hank's floor. After a lot of asking around, she found his doctor.

"I don't know how lucid he'll be, and he shouldn't be agitated. So this needs to be quick and low-key. In a few days, he should be recovered enough to handle more."

Laurel nodded at the doctor before following her into the room. Hank was connected to all sorts of machines and monitors. His eyes fluttered open.

"Mr. Gaskill, this is Deputy Delaney. Do you feel well enough to answer some questions?"

"Yeah," Hank rasped. "Yeah. Did you find who did this?"

"I'm afraid not," Laurel said. "Is there anything you can tell me that would help me identify and apprehend the man who shot you?"

"I don't know who it was. It could have been someone I know. It could have been a stranger. It could have been a hit man for all I know. It was dark. Everything so dark."

Laurel eyed all the beeping machines nervously. "It's okay, Hank. You've been seriously shot. I'm going to do everything in my power to find out by who. You don't have to have all the answers."

He stilled a little. "I don't have any proof, but Adams has something to do with it. Jason was sure of it."

"Do you know why Jason met with whoever killed him?"

Hank closed his eyes, and Laurel knew she was running out of time. This was too much for a man who'd been shot a handful of hours ago.

"He was going to blackmail the higher-up. There's someone higher up who knows, and Jason wanted to get paid to be quiet. He was going to pay me, too."

"What higher-up?"

Something beeped shrilly and the doctor moved, nudging Laurel out of the way. "Deputy, you'll need to leave. I'll alert you when he's up to a more thorough questioning."

Higher-ups and blackmail, and none of it made any sense. But she had her next step. Not sleep like she'd hoped, but Mr. Adams.

"A shoe?"

Grady glared at Ty, who was sprawled out on a recliner in the corner. "It was hard, everything was dark, and I was a little busy knocking a gun out of his hand."

"Would have been more badass to have gotten a concussion from a gun over a shoe."

Grady scowled. "I'll keep that in mind next time I'm accosted while trying to save a man's life."

"See that you do," his cousin replied good-naturedly. "Hurt?"

"Fading," Grady lied. His head was still pounding, and every once in a while he felt sick to his stomach, but it was getting better. Maybe.

He glanced at his phone again. No updates from Laurel. It had been a little less than an hour. Plenty of time to get there and question Hank.

"A watched phone never rings from an inappropriate wannabe hookup."

Grady looked up from his phone with a doleful expression. "I'm not allowed to have an interest in this case?"

"Well, considering you said it looks like Clint is in the clear, yeah, you shouldn't. The dead Delaney wasn't anybody to you."

"That how you felt in the army? Dead guy. Not my problem."

Ty's expression went blank, and Grady regretted bringing it up. His cousin was an army ranger, had done some dangerous, amazing things in his time serving this country, and no matter how pissy Grady was, he didn't have a right to poke at that.

"Listen—"

But Ty held up his hand as his eyebrows drew together. An odd swishing sound went through the apartment, then the squeak of one of his stairs. He didn't hear footsteps, but the stairs outside didn't squeak without someone standing on them.

Grady flung the covers off his legs, but again Ty's hand stopped him. Ty moved out of the chair, cat-like and silent. When he reached the door, he picked something up off the ground. A piece of paper. His quizzical frown went furious.

He tossed it on the bed. "Be right back," he whispered.

"What the—" But Ty was already gone. Grady picked up the paper and felt as though he'd been transported into some kind of movie. Little magazine letters had been cut out and pasted onto the paper.

Watch your step and your back.

He was out of bed before he'd made it to the last word, but by the time he pulled on his boots, Ty was back.

"Gone," Ty muttered in disgust. "Someone must have been waiting. Though I didn't hear a car, which I would have." Ty shook his head. "I imagine this is about Delaney's case and not some wronged ex-lover."

"I imagine," Grady returned.

Ty sighed heavily. "Call your little deputy, Grady. If this is about the case, she needs to know."

Part of him wanted to leave her out of it. He could handle whatever coward thought he could intimidate a Carson, but it *did* have to do with the case, undoubtedly, which meant there might be a clue.

He grabbed his phone and pulled up Laurel's number. When she answered, she sounded exhausted and pissed.

"Grady—"

"I received a little message under my door about ten minutes ago."

"A message?"

"I'm afraid you're going to need to come check it out."

"Is this a joke? Because—"

Grady held out the phone to Ty. "Would you tell her?"

Ty rolled his eyes but took the outstretched phone. "Delaney? Ty. Stop being difficult and come do your job, huh?"

It was Grady's turn to roll *his* eyes. "Charming as ever," he noted, grabbing the phone back. "Laur—" But the call had ended.

"Does it always have to be antagonism?" Grady demanded of Ty.

"To a Delaney? Yeah, I'm pretty sure that's how it works."

"It doesn't have to work that way. Did it ever occur to you that the people who fed us all that feud garbage weren't exactly good people?"

Ty's eyes widened. "You slept with her."

"No, I haven't," Grady returned, irritable and edgy. "But I am thirty-three years old and playing cops and robbers is getting old. My dad was a miserable SOB. My mom wasn't much better. Blaming the Delaneys for everything wrong in their lives never got them anywhere but more miserable."

"Sometimes the Delaneys *are* the source of a person's misery, and before you start reading into *that*, let me just say that if you're letting some woman convince you everything our entire family, and lives, and town are built on is crap, then maybe you need to get a hold of yourself."

"Maybe I don't want my life to be built on a feud that's older than my saloon."

"Then you aren't the Grady Carson I know, and I'm not sure one I want to."

Grady clenched and unclenched his jaw, enough unspent fury pumping through him he wouldn't mind a little bit of a fight. Except he had a concussion and he *was* tired. Tired of fighting and feuds and things that only existed because they always had.

He still believed in Bent and history, but he wasn't a boy playing at a man anymore, and he wasn't going to let history or this town dictate how he lived his life.

"Guess you can go, then."

"Guess I will," Ty replied, grabbing his coat and striding out the door.

Grady gave in to the impulse to slam his hand against the wall, and immediately regretted the way it jarred his head.

When Laurel finally made it back, she didn't knock or even pause. She barged right into his apartment. She looked around, frowning.

"Where's Ty?"

"Left."

She fisted her hands on her hips. "He was supposed to take care of you."

"Yeah, well, he was being an ass. So I booted him. Now, are you here to do police work or what?" He handed her the paper.

She read, her expression going flat and hard, and Grady wasn't surprised to see some mean-edged cop on her, or the fact it turned him on. But she also had dark circles under her eyes and her usually creamy complexion was near gray.

"You're going to crash, princess."

"Sooner or later," she agreed, frowning at the paper. "I don't like this."

"Can't say I care for it, either."

"You can't be alone. Not until we figure this out."

He offered her a smile. "You going to play bodyguard?"

"I have an investigation to run."

"I can help."

"I'm going to take you to the Carson Ranch. There's enough of you to keep an eye on things."

"On a big spread like ours? I'm not taking this to the ranch and potentially endangering my family. You want me not alone, you're up. Since you're already involved."

He could tell she wanted to argue, but in the end, she nodded. "Unfortunately, you're right."

"Well, now, those are words I never thought I'd hear from you. 'Unfortunately' notwithstanding."

"But there are conditions."

"Of course there are."

"You go where I go, not the other way around. You listen to me. You *obey* me. Because this isn't a joke, and it isn't a game. I have a ticking time bomb of an investigation, more and more people in danger by the second. You're going to have to swallow your Wyoming-sized pride and do what I tell you to do."

Grady gave her a grand mock salute, but she didn't even crack a smile.

"I don't want anything to happen to you," she said in that earnest way that made him feel something close to *vulnerable*. Which was crap.

"Get it through your head that the same goes, okay?"

She sighed. "Well, let's get going, then."

"Where are we off to?"

"We have to question a possible suspect."

"Please tell me it's not my brother. Or any Carson."

Laurel quirked a tiny smile at that. "It's your lucky day. This suspect is as Carson-free as you can get."

"So, he's a Delaney?"

"Worse. An outsider."

Chapter 13

It wasn't easy to pretend the warning letter to Grady didn't rattle her, but she knew she needed to present the tough cop facade right now. Not just because Grady was now under her protection, no matter how laughable that seemed, but also because she had to face Mr. Adams in a professional, smart way that hopefully led to a confession or more of a lead.

It was hard to believe the pudgy, middle-aged manager of an unassuming mine could be a cold-blooded killer, strong enough to hit Grady so hard with a *shoe* it gave him a concussion, and agile enough to slip through darkened woods and out again without getting caught.

But she couldn't rule it out, either.

The town of Clearwater was quite a bit larger than Bent. Many of the nonlocal mine workers lived here, so there was a sprawling residential area. Since the town had sprung out of meeting the needs of those workers, everything was more modern than Bent. Fast food, a Walmart, even stoplights.

"How much you want to bet this guy lives in the nicest house in town?" Grady asked, clearly not impressed.

"Well, he is the mine manager."

Grady made a rude noise. "You think this guy is the one who knocked me out?"

"No," Laurel said firmly, turning onto the street Mr. Adams lived on. "But he's involved. Now, we need to go over a few procedure ground rules."

"Of course we do."

Laurel ignored the sarcasm. "You can't go in with me."

"I thought I was under your protection, Deputy," Grady returned, all mock innocence.

"It's tricky and it's complicated, but I can't have you shooting off at the mouth. It will call into question my investigation and if there is a trial, and Mr. Adams is accused of some wrongdoing, your presence and interference will be noted and used to undermine everything. I can't risk it."

Grady was silent as she pulled to a stop in front of the Adams residence. She turned to him, surprised when he hadn't mounted an argument, but also not convinced he would listen to her. When did he ever listen to her?

"Stay put. For the sake of making a murderer, and possibly his accomplice, *pay*."

"What about a little creative use of the truth?"

Laurel frowned, but he had said truth, and Grady might be all manner of wild, rule-breaking things, but he tended to dwell in the truth of it all. "I'm listening."

"We'll say I'm looking for Clint, since we know he's

been hanging out with Lizzie. He's not here, I say fine. Then you can question Mr. Adams in a separate room and I can quietly and patiently wait."

"You can't snoop."

Grady grinned. "I can't snoop and tell you about it, but I can snoop for my own peace of mind." He put a hand to his heart. "My brother could be missing."

"And is more likely at the Carson Ranch sleeping off teenage idiocy."

"More than likely, but you never know. Might as well give it a shot."

Laurel blew out a breath. She didn't know if it was genius or stupid and that was always the problem with Grady. He obscured both with those sinful smiles and mischievous glances.

"It's like having a partnership with mayhem," Laurel muttered, pushing out of the car.

"I'll take that as a compliment *and* agreement."

They walked up the well-kept path to the door side by side. Laurel reached out and pushed the doorbell as Grady surveyed the yard and house.

"I was right about the nicest house in town," Grady mumbled as Mr. Adams slowly pulled the door open.

His eyebrows were furrowed and he was clearly surprised and concerned to see her. "Uh, Deputy. I'm sorry, I don't recall your name…"

"Deputy Delaney. Mr. Adams, do you have a few moments to answer some questions for me?"

Mr. Adams looked nervously from Laurel to Grady's bandage and back to Laurel. "Erm, I suppose. Is…is something the matter?"

"We hope not. I have a few more questions about the Jason Delaney murder case, and Mr. Carson here is looking for his missing brother, who was last seen with your daughter."

Mr. Adams blinked at that. "I don't know anyone named Carson."

"His last name is Danvers. Clint Danvers," Grady supplied, and Laurel was quite impressed with how concerned brother he sounded.

"Oh, Clint. Yes, he and Lizzie have been working on a school project together."

Laurel did her best not to snort. She'd have almost felt bad for the guy for being so clueless if it wasn't for the fact he might be linked to murder.

"I haven't seen him in a while, and I have to say I'm starting to get awfully worried. I don't suppose Lizzie is around so I could ask her if she knows where he is."

Mr. Adams blinked in surprise and clearly balked at the request, so Laurel fixed her kindest smile on her face.

"If you'd feel more comfortable with a woman asking her, I can do it."

"Why don't I go get her and we'll… We'll all discuss it together." Mr. Adams smiled thinly. "She's in her room."

"Do you mind if I come with? I have some—" she glanced at Grady, then back at Mr. Adams "—confidential questions I'd like to ask you."

"Oh. Oh. Well, I suppose."

Laurel followed Mr. Adams from the entryway toward a staircase. She glanced back at Grady, who was whistling as he wandered the large entryway. She wanted to roll her eyes, but instead she focused on Mr. Adams.

She had to consider her words carefully. Hank's not-quite-clear answers didn't give her specifics to go on, so she had to fill in some blanks and hope she was right. "Were you aware Jason Delaney had evidence something criminal was going on at the mine, and was threatening to blackmail a higher-level official within the company?"

Mr. Adams stopped in his tracks. He looked genuinely surprised, but his next question left Laurel more than a little suspicious.

"How do you know that?"

She smiled apologetically. "I'm not at liberty to say."

"I… I had no idea." Mr. Adams resumed his pace up the stairs, but Laurel noted he'd gone pale.

"There's some concern you could be involved, Mr. Adams."

Again he paused, this time at the top of the stairs. He licked his lips, looking around nervously. "Involved… I… I didn't know… I…" He cleared his throat. "You've caught me quite by surprise."

"Clearly." Though Laurel didn't know if it was the right kind of surprise. "Please understand, I have to do my due diligence, and I hope if you know anything at all, you'll pass it along to the police. It's always so much worse on someone when they try to hide the truth."

He was all but sweating now, swallowing nearly convulsively as he reached out for a doorknob.

"This is Lizzie's room," he said, his hand shaking, his voice weak. When he tried to turn the knob, he frowned. "Locked. How odd." He knocked on the door. "Lizzie. Are you awake? I'm afraid I need you to come talk to some people for me." He chuckled weakly and looked at Laurel. "Teenagers do love their sleeping in."

"Mr. Adams. If you don't answer my questions in a

forthright manner, I will be forced to investigate you further. Not just for whatever criminal activity is happening at the mine, but the murder of Jason Delaney, as well as attempted murder of an unnamed victim and the attack on another man. Do you understand?"

Mr. Adams nodded, jiggling the doorknob desperately. "Of course, Deputy. I don't know a thing about any of those things. I swear."

That Laurel didn't believe for a second, but the door swung open and a young, blonde teen answered, flushed and nervous-looking. "Hi, Daddy." She gulped. "Who's this?"

"The police, sweetheart. They're looking for your school friend Clint."

Lizzie's eyes widened at Laurel. "Clint?" she squeaked. "Uh, why?"

Laurel noted a boy's boot was partly visible, as though someone had attempted to shove it under the bed, along with a pair of men's jeans crumpled on one side of the room. Laurel decided to go for a little creative truth herself.

"His brother's been injured and—"

A rustling sounded and Clint tumbled out of the closet. "Grady's been hurt?" he demanded.

Mr. Adams made an outraged, choking sound.

"Grab your pants and head downstairs," Laurel said, stepping between the fuming Mr. Adams and the half-dressed teen. "I suggest you hurry."

Clint scrambled to gather his clothes and darted out the door while Laurel stood in front of Mr. Adams. When he made a move for the boy, Laurel put her hand out.

"Let's all calm down now."

"You little slut!" Mr. Adams shouted.

The poor girl began to cry and Laurel wasn't exactly gentle pulling Mr. Adams out of the room. "I suggest you calm yourself."

But he pushed her away, heading for the stairs Clint had just run down. "I want him arrested! This instant!"

"Your daughter is eighteen. There's nothing arrest-worthy happening here. Now, if you would stop—"

Clint skidded to a stop in front of Grady.

"What are you doing here?" they asked each other in unison.

"You're not that hurt," Clint said, frowning at Grady's bandage.

"But apparently you're that dumb," Grady muttered in return, glancing up at the furious Mr. Adams.

Clint quickly shoved his legs into his jeans, then his feet into the boots he'd been carrying. "I gotta go."

Laurel took the moment of surprise and confusion to move past Mr. Adams on the staircase. "Let him go," she mouthed to Grady, nodding at Clint.

Grady moved out of the way of Clint's escape, but he stepped side by side with Laurel to block Mr. Adams from him as Clint slipped out the door.

"He… He defiled my daughter!" Mr. Adams shouted, pointing at Clint's retreating form, his face growing redder and redder.

Grady raised an eyebrow. "Seriously?"

"Mr. Adams," Laurel said as calmly as she could manage. "Your daughter is eighteen. And upset by your behavior. You should calm yourself and have a civil conversation with her."

Mr. Adams poked his finger wildly at her "I don't need *you* telling me how to handle my daughter."

"Clearly," Laurel replied sarcastically before she could bite back the response. She forced herself to retrieve a card from her pocket. "If you have any further information you'd like to divulge on the mine, Jason Delaney, et cetera, please give me a call."

Mr. Adams stared at the card, but seemed to regather his wits and took it. "I assure you, I know nothing about any of that."

Laurel nodded. "I hope my investigation reflects that, for your sake." Laurel turned for the door, ushering Grady out.

"That asshole is lying," Grady said flatly.

"Through his teeth," Laurel agreed, pulling her phone out of her pocket. "I need search warrants ASAP."

"How long is that going to take?"

A question she didn't want to answer. "Long enough for him to tip off whoever's got a hold on him."

"What about the girl? You think she might know something?"

"Maybe. Maybe." Laurel slid into her car and waited for Grady to get in the passenger side. "We'll go to the station so I can apply for the search warrant. Then… Why don't you call Clint? See if he can get Lizzie to come over for dinner at the Carson Ranch."

"Dinner?" Grady asked.

"Get her there under the guise of meeting Clint's family. Get her away from her father and in a neutral, safe space, and she might feel comfortable enough to talk. Maybe she doesn't know anything, but if she does I doubt she's going to tell me under her father's roof, and I don't want to drag a young girl into the police station if I don't have to."

"And that's legal?"

Laurel shrugged. "Depends on what she says. If I have to go the straight and narrow route with the search warrant, I can get a little creative in the questioning department."

"My, my, my, Deputy Delaney, you are full of surprises."

"Don't you forget it."

Grady had spent more than his fair share of minutes trying to rile Laurel up, but watching her reaction to the judge denying her search warrant application was like nothing he'd ever seen.

She swore admirably. She fumed. She ranted as she drove from the sheriff's department all the way to the Carson Ranch.

"I don't think I've ever been more turned on," he offered once she took a breath.

"Oh, shut up," she returned, wholly unamused. Which, admittedly, served to amuse *him* more.

"Still no word from Clint?" she asked irritably.

"Not since he picked Lizzie up. They should beat us here, though."

She shook her head. "Something doesn't feel right. Something is off. I'm *missing* something."

"Then we'll find it."

She took a deep breath and let it out, straightening her shoulders as she drove up the bumpy, curving drive to the main house.

He liked that he'd calmed her some, and wished he could feel it inside of himself, but mostly he felt the same way she did. Something didn't feel right, and he didn't know what.

"You have to deal with this every case?"

"Deal with what?"

"That dogged not knowing what is going on?"

"Not every case, but some. A lot of not knowing is part of the job."

"Your job blows."

Her mouth curved. "It's not such a bad thing, putting it all together, knowing you can."

"Well, if you know you can, you can. So, you should stop ranting."

"I thought it turned you on."

Grady chuckled, but it died when they reached the house. "He's not here."

"He could have parked in one of the outbuildings, couldn't he?"

"Could have, but wouldn't." Clint wasn't that thorough. Grady shaded his eyes against the setting sun and looked around the property before turning his attention back to Laurel. "We should head back into town. Retrace what would have been his steps. They might have stopped somewhere to make out or something, but..."

"But maybe not. Is Ty in town?" she asked, already reversing the car and heading back the way they'd come. "We could split up our search and meet in the middle."

"Good thinking." Grady sent a quick message off to Ty as Laurel sped down the drive they'd just ambled up. Her gaze was shrewd on the road, hands grasped tight on the steering wheel, and it was an odd thing to not be in charge and not have it grate.

But his little brother might be in trouble and there wasn't a lot of room for any other emotions above fear.

"Keep your eyes peeled and tell me if you see anything," Laurel said. But as they drove, all he saw was road and the expanse of a Wyoming landscape.

"He's dead to me," Grady muttered, pissed off beyond belief the way fear gripped him. But he'd been attacked and threatened, a man had been killed, and now his brother was nowhere.

"Keep trying his cell," Laurel instructed calmly.

Anyone else's calmness in this situation would have only served to stoke his irritation higher, but something about Laurel's no-nonsense approach and the clear seriousness she took this with soothed rather than rattled.

"Let's stop at the gas station, see if anyone noticed anything. Ty should be catching up with us soon."

"Okay."

Laurel pulled into the gas station's parking lot and pushed her door open, but she glanced at him before she stepped out. She reached over, squeezed his forearm. "We'll find him. We will."

He took in those serious brown eyes and the determined set of her jaw and he nodded, some of that panic settling into something a lot more peaceful.

He stepped out with her and heard his name shouted. Clint burst from the front door of the station, blood dripping down his face. "Grady!"

Grady grabbed his brother, trying to figure out why he had blood all over him. He opened his mouth to demand answers, but Clint was already talking.

"Someone grabbed her. Just…grabbed her." He turned to Laurel, all heavy breathing and fear and desperation. "You gotta find her."

"Did you call the police?" Laurel asked composedly, though her whole body had tensed next to his.

"You are the police!"

Laurel didn't respond to that, but immediately began speaking in low tones into her radio.

"What was she wearing?" Laurel asked.

"Uh. Jeans. A T-shirt. Pink, I think. Pinkish. She had my jacket on. Leather jacket."

"What can you tell me about the car?" Laurel asked gently.

Clint swallowed, tears clearly swimming in his eyes. "Black. Slick." Clint rattled off a few possible makes and models. "The plate wasn't Wyoming. It was yellow, I think. Yellowish or something close."

Laurel relayed the information into her radio as Ty roared into the gas station, screeching to a halt on his motorcycle in front of them. "What's going on?"

"We need to get him to a hospital," Grady said roughly.

"No way, man. I have to find her."

"That gash is nasty. You need stitches. Did you lose consciousness?"

"No, I'm fine. They just knocked me down and I hit my head. He was gone by the time I got back up."

"Did Lizzie know the man who took her?" Laurel interjected.

"No! He had a ski mask thing on. I was gassing up and he just got out of his car and pushed me down and grabbed her. It took me a minute to get up and he shoved her in the car and left."

"He knocked you out."

"Whatever, man," Clint replied, pushing Grady's concerned hand away. "We have to find her. We have to."

"We've got a lot to go on. Write anything else you can think of down, okay? Ty, you take him to the hospital. I'll send an officer to watch and take Clint's statement."

"And what are we doing?" Grady asked.

"This time, we're getting consent to search Adams's house without having to wait around for a search warrant." She stopped midstep toward the car and then turned to him. "I mean, you don't have to come with me. I've given Lizzie's name and description to county, and I've sent the closest officer to the hospital to question Clint. You'd be safe there, if you want to be with Clint. I'd under—"

"I'll be safe with you, too. Let's go."

Chapter 14

Laurel knocked on Mr. Adams's door for the second time in two days. When Mr. Adams opened the door, his face was red, his thinning hair wild. "Did you find her? Is she—"

"Mr. Adams, I need consent to search your house. We're looking for any clues that might help us find Lizzie."

"My…consent." The man choked on something like a sob, but Laurel couldn't let that sway her. "My daughter is missing."

"Yes, and the Bent County Sheriff's Department is doing everything in their power to find her. Including this. If you give us consent, Deputy Hart and I will search the entire house." Laurel nodded at Hart, who was standing behind her. "We'll take anything that might aid us in finding her whereabouts."

"I…" Mr. Adams raked his shaking hands through his hair. "All right. You can search the house."

"Sign this, please." Laurel nodded to Hart, who held out the consent form. With shaking hands, Mr. Adams signed it.

"If you'd leave the door open while we search, and find somewhere out of the way to be." She glanced back at Grady, whom she'd instructed to stay in the car.

He, of course, wasn't *in* the car, but leaning against it, looking somehow lazy and lethal at the same time, the stitches on his head adding to the dangerous vibe. She sighed heavily. She didn't like leaving him out there, but there weren't a lot of choices right now.

"I… You…" Mr. Adams made another choking sound, but he finally got out of the way of the door.

"Upstairs. First door on your left," Laurel directed Hart.

Laurel herself headed through the lower level of the house while Mr. Adams trailed after her, sputtering in-effectively. What she wanted to find was some kind of home office or place where he'd have things related to work. "I don't suppose you have any information as to who might have taken your daughter, or why."

"Miss Delaney, I don't know who's responsible," Mr. Adams rasped.

"If you say so," she returned evenly, ignoring the Miss instead of Deputy.

"No, I mean, I don't know their name or anything to identify them by. The man I've been working for is a nameless, faceless entity. I get messages, and I act on them. I don't keep my job if I don't act on them."

Laurel whirled on the admission. "So this has some-thing to do with the mine?"

Mr. Adams sank into a chair, rubbing his hands over his face. "Yes. I guess. I was just told to get rid of some papers. To cover some things up. When Jason started poking around…" He looked up at her plaintively. "I didn't kill him. I don't have anything to do with this except paperwork."

"I need to know everything about the paperwork. I need a list of anyone who is above you and would be affected if the information you destroyed got out. I need everything you know, Mr. Adams. For Lizzie's sake."

He swallowed audibly and nodded. "My office is upstairs. I don't have anything specific, but I can write down some things. They took Lizzie because she's been…" His voice broke and he cleared his throat. "I don't know why, but she's been poking around my work. Asking me questions about the mine, about Jason, and I didn't know what was going on. I figured she'd get bored of it, but—"

"Delaney," Hart called from above. "I found a license plate number written on a scrap of paper."

Laurel met Hart at the bottom of the stairs, glancing at the looping scrawl of what had to be a license plate number.

"Call it in. Have someone check it out," she said.

Hart nodded and started talking into his radio.

Laurel turned her attention to the man behind her. A man who'd clearly done some illegal things, but was scared sick by his daughter's disappearance and his worry for her.

"Show me your office."

He started walking and she followed him up the stairs while Hart stood in the entryway, relaying his information to dispatch.

Mr. Adams led her to a small room at the end of the hall. It was nicely decorated, dominated by a huge desk. There was a recliner in the corner and everything was neat as a pin.

"I don't bring anything home, and everything I was told to destroy, I destroyed, but I... Lately I've been getting nervous, what with the murder and all, so I started keeping a list." With shaking hands, Mr. Adams opened up a drawer, then reached toward the back, popping something that turned out to be a false bottom.

But instead of a piece of paper or anything innocent, there was a gun. Clear as day. Mr. Adams gasped.

"It isn't mine," he whispered, his voice sounding strained. "I don't own a gun. I don't."

Laurel pulled rubber gloves out of her utility belt and put them on. She picked up the weapon. It was exactly the kind of gun that could have killed Jason Delaney. She closed her eyes for a minute because she wasn't stupid.

Mr. Adams wasn't the murderer, but someone sure wanted her to think he was.

"My notes. They're gone," Mr. Adams gasped, pawing around the false bottom. But it was empty save for the gun. "Oh, God. Oh, God."

"Hart," Laurel barked.

After a few seconds, the deputy appeared. His eyes widened when he saw what Laurel was holding.

"I need you to run the serial number on this gun." She rattled it off to him and Hart relayed the number to dispatch. She racked her brain for a reason to take in Mr. Adams so they could have him in custody while they ran ballistics on the weapon, because as long as his daughter wasn't safe, neither was he. Neither were Clint and Hank, for that matter.

The radio squawked and everyone in the room heard the results clear as day. "That gun has been reported as stolen."

Laurel glanced at Mr. Adams, who looked panic-stricken. "Stolen? I don't own a gun. I haven't stolen a gun. That isn't mine! My notes are gone!"

"Hart. Arrest him."

"No. No! I didn't do anything. Please, understand. I didn't… They're making this…"

"Mr. Adams," Laurel began firmly so he'd stop blubbering and listen. "You have a stolen weapon in your home. I have to arrest you. We'll need to run ballistics on it, and if it comes back as the murder weapon in the Jason Delaney case—"

"What have I done? Oh, God." Mr. Adams began to cry, and Laurel almost felt sympathy for the man, but he'd gotten himself mixed up in some ugly business.

"Consider this the best thing for you right now, Mr. Adams. You'll be safe, and this might be leverage we can use to get Lizzie released. If whoever has her is worried about being linked to the murder, having someone arrested for it might lower their guard. If it's the murder weapon."

He calmed a little bit at that.

"Hart, I want you to arrest him and take him to the station, and get a recording of everything he can remember about the documents he destroyed. Along with anyone he might want to implicate."

Hart stepped forward and went through the steps to arrest Mr. Adams while Laurel continued to look through all the drawers. She sat down at the desk as

Hart led Mr. Adams away. She didn't know what she was looking for, but she could confiscate the computer along with the murder weapon.

She wasn't sure she believed Mr. Adams was completely ignorant of who was behind all of this, but a trip to the station and videotaped questioning might help jog his memory. If nothing else, she truly believed it would convince the real killer they weren't still looking for him.

"I thought we decided he wasn't the murderer."

Laurel glanced over her shoulder to find Grady taking up the entire doorway. "You shouldn't be in here," she said, though the words were a waste and she knew it. "I don't think he's the murderer, but someone wants us to think he is. I don't have any proof he's *not* the murderer. A stolen weapon in the house is enough to bring him in."

She turned back to the desk. "I have to search everything. Once I'm done, and I've compiled all the evidence I've found, we'll drop it off at the station, then head over to the hospital and see if Clint remembers anything."

"You have to sleep at some point, princess."

Her shoulders slumped and the wave of exhaustion she'd been fighting off with sheer adrenaline threatened to topple her. "Yeah, at some point. But not yet." A few more steps and then she could think about sleep.

Grady's large hand covered her shoulder, squeezed. She looked up at him with a million snippy responses she knew she needed to give him. But all she wanted to do was lean into him. Rest against him.

Which wasn't something she could allow herself. "Wait downstairs. Don't touch anything. I'll be down as soon as I'm done."

He didn't remove his hand. Instead, the other came up and cradled her cheek, gentle as could be. Something like a lump lodged itself in her throat at the sheer *wanting*. Wanting him. Wanting sleep. Wanting to just *rest*.

"I'll go downstairs. You've got half an hour to finish up. Then you'll drop off anything you need to at the station. After that, you're heading straight for bed."

"Is that an order?"

He grinned that horrible, lust-inducing grin. "Yeah, I think it is."

It was the simply *kind*, almost caring way he said it that made the lump in her throat impossible to swallow. "Decided you're my caretaker now?" she asked through a tight throat.

"I think we mutually decided that for each other. Get to work, Deputy. I'm tired, too."

On a deep breath, Laurel pulled out of the grasp of Grady's rough hands and did just that.

Grady'd had his fill of waiting for people. He'd also had his fill of Laurel looking like she was about to keel over, and then pressing forward as if her sheer force of will could keep her awake for years.

Hell, maybe it could. She walked out of the sheriff's department looking with-it and strong no matter that legions of shadows existed under her eyes. So much so he could see them even in the parking lot lights.

"How's Clint?" she asked.

"Hospital released him. Ty's taking him back to the ranch and him, Noah and Vanessa will keep him out of trouble. I gave him your number in case he remembers something important."

She nodded. "Good."

He hopped off the hood of her car, where he'd been sitting and waiting. "I'm driving."

She rolled her eyes. "You can't drive my county-issued vehicle, Carson."

"Why not?"

"It's against the law. Plus, you've had a concussion."

"I believe that was something like twenty-four hours ago. Which means I'm okay to drive now."

"God, has it been twenty-four hours?" She raked her hands through her hair, which had come out of its band at some point between finding Clint and now.

"Heck of a twenty-four hours."

She huffed out something close to a laugh. "I suppose." She pulled her keys out of her pocket. "If anyone asks, you put a gun to my head before I let you drive my car."

"Got it." He took her keys, trying to tone down his self-satisfied smirk a *little* bit.

She slid into the passenger seat, her eyes already drooping, and he turned the keys in the ignition.

He didn't bother to talk. He let her lean against the window by her side as he drove them away from the sheriff's department and toward Bent. The long way. Because he had a bad feeling that wherever he stopped, she'd pop back up into Deputy Delaney mode and never get any real rest.

So he drove through the glittering late night, enjoying the peace and the stars, and only finally heading to Laurel's place when he started to come perilously close to dozing off himself.

As he drove Laurel's car up the smooth, curving drive that led to her cabin on the fancy Delaney spread, he couldn't help wondering at this *thing* inside of him.

He'd been bred to hate Delaneys. Told stories of their wrongdoings over the centuries. He'd reveled in that. Being the underdogs, the dangerous ones. He'd used it to excuse the things he'd wanted to excuse in his life.

But Laurel had never fit with all that fiction he'd allowed himself. Something vibrant and good with this odd tug between them he'd always known was there, but had sought to avoid.

But there was no more avoiding. It was here, stronger with every passing hour as they tried to solve this mystery together. The fact of the matter was, a fact he wouldn't likely admit to anyone possibly ever, he cared about Laurel Delaney.

Not just attraction, or that teenaged desire of something that was off-limits and too good for him besides. Not just this lifetime of a wait, the anticipation, the holding himself back since he was a kid and believing he could control that tug.

This was more, and that was what had made the wait endure all those years. That he knew her and understood her. That he *liked* her. That her work ethic made *his* pale in comparison and he'd never met anyone who'd come close.

He parked on the little square of gravel and looked over at her sleeping form in the dim glow of moon and starlight filtered through the car windows.

Even as his body hardened, because she was gorgeous, his heart did some painful twisting thing. That care lodged far too deep to ignore anymore, to avoid, and he was very afraid burrowed too deep to ever be mined out.

"Wake up, princess, or I'm going to have to heft you over my shoulder," he said, far too gruffly. Because truth be told, he didn't know how to do care without a lot of gruff to cover it up. To hide the softness. Ward off the inevitable attack. Wasn't that what dear old Dad had taught him?

Laurel blinked her eyes open, staring out the windshield and then at him. "Oh. You brought me home." She frowned at the clock. "That was a heck of a drive."

"I figured it ensured you at least got an hour."

She pushed out of the car into the frigid night air and took a deep breath. "Feel like a new woman." She grinned over the hood of the car at him. "Now I don't need to sleep at all." But that confidence was underscored when she yawned.

"Uh-huh," he replied, rifling through her keys until he found one that looked like a house key. He tried it in the lock and it worked.

She stepped inside, yawning again as she flipped on a light. When she turned to face him, she frowned.

"Where are you going?"

"To the saloon."

"You can't be alone. You really can't be alone in my car."

"What do you suggest, then?" It was something of a challenge, one he probably shouldn't have laid down when they were both exhausted and no real breaks in the case had been made.

Her gaze held his, unwavering and potent, that thing always between them crackling with a new kind of electricity. Because they'd both acknowledged it now, because they were both operating on less than full capacity. Or just because it was *time*.

"I guess I suggest the inevitable," she said quietly, yet in that self-possessed, certain way she said everything. She stepped forward, as if she had no doubts or concerns, and slid her arms around his neck.

"Is that what it is?" he asked, his voice a rough rasp as she stared up at him, her mouth parted and *right there*. "Inevitable?"

"It feels that way," she replied, her tall, lithe body pressing to his, those brown eyes never leaving his gaze. As if one hour of sleep had given her all the power she needed. "But maybe I just want to." Then her mouth slid against his, soft and hot.

It felt like centuries of waiting even though he'd just kissed her the other day. Her mouth insistent, determined, so *her*, and he wanted to taste every contour of it until it was etched in his very bones.

He didn't seem to be alone in that desire. Her tongue moved against his, her arms clamped around his neck as if she could keep him there, devouring her mouth.

More, his mind chanted. *More, more, more.*

"Grady, I *want* you," she murmured against his mouth. "Now."

He kicked the door behind them closed before moving her toward her bedroom, their arms still wrapped around each other.

"Consider it me taking advantage of your exhaustion," he gritted out, backing her toward the bed. "Then you can pretend you regret it in the morning."

"I won't." She met his gaze then, her brown eyes dark and serious. "I won't." She pulled his mouth back to hers as they tumbled onto the bed together.

Chapter 15

Laurel had never been all that concerned with sex before. When she was in a relationship, it was nice to have, certainly. A kind of physical comfort, two bodies coming together.

There was nothing easy or particularly comfortable about Grady on top of her, pushing her into her mattress, his mouth unrelenting and perfect against hers, his hands molding to every curve of her body as if he couldn't stop himself. Not because it hurt or she was in an awkward position, but because there was this desperate ache inside of her, growing and growing without getting any closer to being fulfilled.

This was not the precursor to sex she knew. This was wild and desperate and she felt like if she didn't feel Grady's naked skin against hers and soon, she might simply combust and turn to ash. Or, worse, beg.

She could feel his erection against the apex of her

thighs and it made her wonder if all the minimal sex she'd been having in her life had just been bad. Or if not bad, adequate. Decent and all, but not…this all-encompassing, reason-killing thing.

She pawed at his shirt, wanting to see the grand expanse of his chest, wanting to feel it under her fingertips or pressed against her body.

She'd had a lifetime of occasionally catching glimpses of Grady without a shirt on, but here in her bedroom, in her *bed*, it was, well, it was something else as he sat up and pulled off his T-shirt.

She could see every fine line of his tattoo that took up most of his shoulder and weaved its way down to his elbow. She could reach out and touch the delineation of each impressive muscle, and she could truly absorb and enjoy just how *big* he was. She didn't have to fight that or prove she was just as strong or could take him down. She didn't have to be Deputy Delaney here. For a little while she could just be Laurel.

He reached out and jerked her shirt off her in one quick pull. There was a jolt of self-consciousness that lasted all of five seconds, because his gaze was hot and blazing on her as if he could eat her alive.

She could recognize it in him, because she felt the same way, and that was the thing about whatever it was that existed between them. Maybe it had never made sense, and they'd certainly both ignored and avoided it, but they had always both *felt* it.

He reached forward and palmed her breasts, still clad in her bra, but then he jerked the bra down, not even bothering with the clasp. His hands rasping against the sensitive skin there as his mouth descended onto her mouth, kissing down her neck to her breasts. His beard scraped against her skin everywhere he kissed. It was abrasive and harsh and somehow that made every feeling deep inside of her sparkle brighter and higher.

Abruptly, Grady's mouth left her and he got off the bed. She tried to formulate a question, but she was breathing too hard as he yanked his phone out of his pocket and tossed it as if he didn't care if it landed on a hard surface and broke apart. His keys were next, but when he got his wallet, he flipped it open and pulled out a condom.

She exhaled harshly and maybe she should have been put off by the fact he had a condom, but she didn't care. She flat-out didn't care how or why or how long, as long as he used it with her.

"Take off your pants," he ordered.

Laurel gladly scrambled to comply as he undid the button and zipper on his own pants. As she kicked off her khakis and her underwear, she watched all of Grady come into view. Everything about him strong and broad and beautiful.

There was some dim part of her mind reminding her this was Grady Carson and she wasn't supposed to be getting involved with him. Certainly not like this.

But every other part of her didn't care. Because Grady, for all his swagger and outward appearance and sarcastic jokes, was good and kind and he might not want to ever admit it, but he cared about her. The same way she cared about him. An indelible fact they'd both spent too long trying to falsify.

He was standing there at the foot of her bed, completely naked and impressive. She sat on her bed, naked save for the bra he'd pushed down to her waist.

He flicked a glance at it. "Get it off."

She didn't even hesitate to do as he demanded. To do anything he demanded. Because she had always been in charge in life. She'd never cared for following anyone else's moral compass or rules. She had her own strident ones. She knew how she wanted to live her life, and she did it. Always.

But she'd never felt wild. She'd never been consumed by need or desire, and so why not follow his every order? He was the expert after all.

Grady put one knee on the bed, looming like an incredibly sexy conqueror. She would gladly be conquered. Exhaustion and feuds be damned. All she wanted in this moment was Grady.

He opened the condom wrapper, rolling on the latex before covering her body with his. And she was completely covered. Being flattened into her mattress was a delicious feeling. To live in this world that was only Grady, hard and hot and demanding on top of her.

His hands explored her body, and she smoothed her hands down his expansive, smooth back. His mouth nuzzled against the curve of her neck until she was sighing with pleasure, arching herself against him, desperate for him to enter. Her body somehow both relaxed and coiled at the same moment.

When he finally slid inside of her, there was a moment where they both paused. Holding on to each other, watching each other. Connected. As though she could see over a century in his eyes and vice versa.

Inevitable. That word kept repeating itself in her mind. Because this felt nothing short of inevitable. This was where she belonged. He was everything she needed. She didn't believe in feuds. She didn't believe in curses of Carsons and Delaneys commingling. But she understood in this moment it was not for the faint of heart. This joining, this meeting. It was only for those strong enough to handle it.

It was a very lucky thing she was strong enough. And so was he.

Grady surged inside of her in a long, slow, inexorable glide as if he felt it, too. The inevitability. The strength it would take and how much they were made for it.

His mouth claimed hers as he moved against her, over and over again, bringing her to a blinding kind of climax she'd never experienced before, shattering around him and chanting his name as he brought her to that peak again.

Her name from his lips against her mouth as together they tumbled off the edge of something that felt nothing short of perfect and meant to be.

Grady figured he must be dreaming when a repeatedly shrill noise sounded and he was all wrapped up in a very naked Laurel. Surely this was an alternate universe he found himself in. Because there was no way the things he remembered from the night before could be real. Just no possible way.

In this dream, she was as perfect as he might have imagined. And in this dream, it felt as though no possible outcome of his life could be anything other than Laurel in it. In his bed. Always.

Yes, it had to be a dream.

But Laurel's sleepy voice was very real as it murmured a hello next to him. Her warm and very naked body next to him making him instantly hard again absolutely happening in the present.

He opened his eyes, noting the room was still dark.

Which meant at best they'd scored one or two hours of sleep. They both definitely needed more.

Laurel's hand slapped against his bare chest and he winced.

"Where?" she demanded into her phone receiver. "She's all right?" Laurel covered the receiver with one hand. "They found Lizzie," she whispered. "A little beat-up but mostly okay."

"Does Clint know?"

She shook her head, so Grady got out of bed to find his phone. It was somewhere on Laurel's side of the room so he walked around. Her floor was neat as a pin except where their discarded clothes and his tossed phone, keys and wallet dotted the hardwood.

Laurel was barking demanding questions into her phone and clearly getting at least some of the responses she wanted. Grady picked up his phone and typed a text to Clint that Lizzie had been found and was okay.

He watched Laurel as she picked up a pen and note-pad from her nightstand and balanced it on her lap. The sheet covered her legs, but her upper body was completely bare, and Grady wanted nothing more than to crawl back into bed and toss her phone and notes away.

But this was her job, and he was an intuitive enough man to know she would not compromise her priorities. He wished he didn't admire that so much about her.

There was something like panic beating in his chest because he wanted… Well, for the first time in his adult life he wanted something that was out of his control. He could fight for his name, for Rightful Claim, for Bent, but what lay before him with this woman wasn't a fight.

It would be something like a give-and-take, and

sometimes he wondered if deep down inside he was just his parents—all take.

But he wasn't a coward. Wouldn't allow himself to be. Panic didn't rule him, and neither did fear. If he wanted to give and take, he damn well would.

Laurel finished writing something down, then clicked off her phone and set it neatly on the nightstand.

"They haven't found who took her. Apparently she was dumped back at the same gas station she was taken from. She doesn't have a description, but they did find that the license plate Lizzie had written down in her room was a Nebraska plate, and Nebraska plates are yellow, which means the plate we have and the car that took her are probably one and the same."

"You think this is all the work of one man?"

"I'm not sure. But one man has the answers and I need to find them. Apparently Lizzie knew her father was in trouble and had been doing her own poking around—mostly with the help of Clint. She's been pretty tight-lipped about what happened while she was kidnapped, so I'm going to go question her. Maybe she'll feel more comfortable with a woman." Laurel was already out of bed, pulling on a T-shirt.

Belatedly she noticed it was his. She shook her head and moved to take it off again, but he stopped her, putting a hand to her abdomen.

"And if she gives you a tip-off to who did this? What are you going to do?"

She looked up at him, then blinked as if to focus herself. Her gaze slid down his naked body, which he had to say he didn't mind.

She shook her head as if to clear it. "I'll follow procedure to bring whoever it is in for questioning. We both need to get dressed and I'll drop you off at the Carson Ranch."

Grady bit back all the jumbled worry inside of him. It had only been a few days of working side by side with her, and she'd been a cop for a long time, but he didn't like... Well, the idea of not being there when she went up against a man capable of murder.

"I need to check on things at the bar," he forced himself to say. "When Vanessa runs things, I tend to find myself a mess. Drop me off there."

She chewed on her bottom lip for a second before reaching out and touching his bare chest. "Just because we have a lead doesn't mean you're not still in danger. You should be somewhere protected, and with people."

"You're in danger all the time. Just by being a cop, right?" he said quietly, because he knew it was true. He *knew* that. He understood that. He just wanted her to understand... Something.

She absorbed those words, seeming to take in their weight. She didn't brush that statement off, she considered it. Which meant something, maybe something more than it should.

It was another layer. They didn't necessarily have to talk every step through for them to understand each other.

"There is a slight difference," she said carefully.

"Rationally, I get that."

"And irrationally?"

"Irrationally, I want you by my side always so I can know you're safe. *I* want to keep *you* safe."

She stared up at him, her fingertips on his chest, and it was like a moor to this world. She was his anchor to this world. This Delaney cop. Somehow it made all the sense. Because she was the last thing he should ever want, of course she was the only one who fit.

She got up on her tiptoes and brushed her mouth across his. "I don't…" She took a deep breath and squared her shoulders, all the while looking him in the eye. "I don't want last night to be a one-time thing."

"Good, because it's not," he returned gruffly.

"And I don't just mean the sex."

"I know what you mean."

"You feel the same way?" she asked him directly, so brave and certain and good.

It grated somehow, because he wasn't all that good, and she probably deserved someone better, but he'd be damned if he let her have another man. He took her mouth with his, the opposite of her sweet little peck. He kissed her long and hard and hot. "You are mine, Laurel Delaney. End of story."

Her mouth curved, almost as if she was indulging him. "And you are mine, Grady Carson." She patted his chest. "I'm surprised you're not being a baby about it."

"Maybe once I've had a good night's sleep I'll work up a good tantrum."

She smiled at him, but it didn't ease this feeling inside of him. Separate from all the being each other's.

"I don't think we should separate right now," he said, even knowing it was a losing battle to go against what she needed to do.

"I need to question Lizzie alone, and I need a few hours to concentrate. Besides, they let Lizzie go of their own volition. Things are de-escalating. There might still be danger out there, but I think it's weakened. Besides, you have work to do as much as me. You know it."

Grady grunted, irritated she was right. "Something

doesn't feel right. Just like the other night when Clint didn't show up. Something doesn't… Something isn't adding up."

"I agree. That's why I need a few hours at the station. Talk to Lizzie. Look at some documents Hart found. I need my concentration on this case for a good two hours. And I can't do that with you around."

"You flatter me, princess."

"Get dressed. I'll drop you off at Rightful Claim, as long as someone can be there with you. I don't want you being alone. I'll put in my few hours at the station, and then…" She chewed on her bottom lip again.

"And then what?"

She trailed the fingertips over his beard. "I'll come and find you."

"You had better." He kissed her, meaning for it to be soft, subtle, just to prove he could. But it evolved somehow, as it always did with her. Wildfire and need. "We both need showers before we go, don't you think?"

"We are not both going to fit in my shower," she said with a breathless laugh.

"But we could give it the old college try," he returned, tugging her toward a door that had to lead to the bathroom. And when she went with him willingly, laughing and naked, he figured things might just be all right after all.

Chapter 16

Laurel drove toward the Bent County Sheriff's Department after dropping Grady off at Rightful Claim, not exactly feeling rested. She was still tired, because she'd grabbed maybe just three hours of sleep. But it had been good, heavy sleep. And something like giddiness was keeping her going.

She was a little embarrassed at that. How much excitement and drive this whole Grady thing had given her. She should calm down. She should be rational.

She and Grady were in some very odd circumstances and it was likely causing heightened feelings…or something. The reality of themselves was possibly a little different outside of the bedroom.

Which was all her fear talking, actually. Because last night and this morning had been good. The kind of good that was overwhelming. The kind of good you had to work for and sacrifice things for. In equal-ish measure.

She blew out a breath. She didn't have time to really work through all that. She had to question Lizzie, and see if the ballistics report had come back yet. Her focus had to be the job, and then she could figure out her personal life.

Because that was the priority list of her life. Always had been.

Why did it suddenly feel like a weight?

She shook her head, focusing on the sun rising behind her. Which was when she realized the same car had been following her for a while now. The same kind of car Clint had mentioned when describing the man who'd taken Lizzie.

The car was far back enough she couldn't make out the letters and numbers on the plate, but she could tell it was yellowish. Just as Clint had described.

She inhaled, then slowly breathed out through her mouth, focusing on being calm and following procedure.

What if they've been following you since before you left Rightful Claim? What if someone is following Grady?

She couldn't focus on *that*. She had to focus on what to do in her here and now. Because she'd left Bent city limits, and the sun was only just beginning to rise. The highway out of town was deserted, and the current stretch she was on was at a high enough elevation that the shoulder was mostly guardrail to prevent cars from going off the slight rocky cliff.

Taking a glance in her rearview mirror as often as she could, she grabbed for her radio without looking at it.

"Dispatch. 549. Rush traffic," she said as calmly as she could manage.

"Go ahead 549."

Before she could get the next words out of her mouth, an engine roared close—too close. She flicked a glance in the rearview mirror just in time to see the black car plow into the back of hers.

She jerked forward, her face smashing into the airbag as she felt her car skid forward and then sideways, metal screeching against the guardrail. That noise reminded her of how precarious her situation was. Because if this car succeeded in pushing her over it, she'd be tumbling down a pretty steep, rocky drop.

She ignored the pain in her head and focused on her grip on the wheel. She jerked it as far to the right as the airbag would allow, braking as hard as she could while she did so.

She had to get out of the car. While it offered some protection, she could be more agile on foot. And possibly run down the steep ravine without plunging to her death.

She couldn't see anything with the airbag in her vision, but the screeching of the guardrail had stopped and so had her movement. She imagined the attacker was reversing to plow into her again, so she had to act fast.

She pushed hard, opening the door open and scrambling out of the car as she disentangled herself from the airbag and seat belt. She grabbed her gun out of her belt as she looked around, trying to find the other car.

It had indeed reversed and was now speeding toward her. Laurel didn't have time to think twice—she ran and jumped over the guardrail, half running, half stumbling down the rocky hillside.

If she drew him into a chase, she could shoot him. Of course, he likely had a gun himself, but at least she'd have a chance to fight back. She glanced behind her—nothing but rocks and bent guardrail.

She surveyed the landscape in front of her. It was mostly open, though there were a few swells of land she might be able to hide behind with enough of a head start.

The biggest problem was she didn't have her radio or her cell. All she had was her gun. So, she kept running, checking over her shoulder every few minutes for signs of someone following her.

She was maybe halfway to a decent cover of rocks and swell of land when a figure appeared, stepping over the guardrail. He was wearing all black, including a ski mask, just as Clint had described the man who'd taken Lizzie.

Well, he was not going to take her. She raised her gun, tried to aim, only to realize her vision wasn't clear. Blood was dripping down into her eyes. Blood? Where had that come from?

She tried to blink it away, finally becoming cognizant of the fact her head was throbbing and burning. In the adrenaline of the moment, she hadn't realized she'd been hurt, but some of that reality was getting through to her now. The world tilted, but she breathed through it and fired off a shot in the direction of the man in black.

She didn't even try to see if she'd hit her target. She started running again, trying to figure out where she was. If there was somewhere she could go. She was injured and isolated, but she wasn't outnumbered, probably, and just because she was hurt didn't mean she was witless.

After another scan of the area, and remembering where she'd been on the road, she realized she was close to the back entrance to the Carson Ranch she'd dropped Grady off at the other day.

She didn't want to lead this man to the Carsons, but she didn't have a choice. She needed a phone. She needed help. If she at least got to the property, she might get hurt, but maybe someone would find her before she was killed. Maybe.

A shot rang out and she winced at how close it sounded, but nothing touched her. Still, it was too close for comfort, and proof the man was armed with a deadly weapon.

Lungs burning, everything in her body a painful, aching throb, Laurel tried to pull up her shirt and wipe away the blood that was impeding her vision as she ran.

But even without blood in her eyes, her vision was getting blurrier. She felt dizzy and sick but she knew she had to keep running. Someone was after her. The man who'd killed Jason, who'd kidnapped Lizzie. It had to be him.

She got to the back entrance of the Carson Ranch without the man catching up to her or firing off another short. She just had to get to the house, or maybe Noah would be out somewhere close working. Someone who would hear something, do something. She had to hope and pray for that, because she knew her time was running out.

Her legs buckled and the world around her was suddenly dark instead of the picturesque fall morning. She didn't quite realize she'd fallen until her shoulder hit the hard ground.

She tried to get up, but her body wasn't listening to her mind. She could hear approaching footsteps closing in on her.

Dimly she hoped Grady was okay and at Rightful Claim, working and giving Vanessa a hard time. She swallowed at the nausea threatening, praying she'd left enough clues and wreckage for whoever found her to figure out who this man was and where he'd come from.

Somewhat belatedly, she realized she still had her hand on her gun. The gun. She placed her finger on the trigger and when it sounded like the man was right on top of her, she managed to roll onto her back and shoot.

Grady frowned at his phone with growing irritation. He'd been patient all morning and not called Laurel to see what was going on. But it was nearly two o'clock and there'd been no word from her. Not to him. Not to Clint.

Grady tried to convince himself she'd found a lead and was following it. He tried to convince himself she was doing her job. If something had happened, wouldn't he have heard something? If not from Laurel herself, from *someone*.

Then again, why would anyone think to tell him about the goings-on of Laurel Delaney?

When Dylan Delaney stormed into the bar before they'd officially opened for the day, everything in Grady went cold and still.

The Delaneys did not come into his bar.

"Where is she? What have you gotten her messed up with?"

Grady stood behind the bar, willing his temper to behave. He'd never cared for Laurel's brother the slick, arrogant banker who only'd ever looked down at any Carson in his bank. But Dylan *was* her brother, and maybe he knew something that Grady didn't. It'd grate more if he wasn't so worried.

"What do *I* have your *cop* sister mixed up in?"

"She might be a cop, and this might have more to do with the case she's working on, but when Carson property is involved, so are you. I know it."

"What are you talking about?" Grady demanded, keeping himself unnaturally still. He couldn't *react* yet. First he needed facts.

"My sister disappeared. They've traced footsteps and blood to *your* property, and there's a lot of talk about how you left the station with her last night. So I want to know what you did to her."

Grady pushed out from behind the bar, ignoring Dylan's demands. He pulled his phone out and dialed the ranch. No answer. He dialed Noah's cell, which went straight to voice mail. Ty was in the back, and if he'd heard anything, he would've told Grady by now.

"Ty," Grady called, already to the door. "Lock up. Meet me at the ranch." He didn't wait to see if his cousin would listen. He called Vanessa. Nothing.

He took his keys out of his pocket as he swung out the front doors.

"You don't walk away from me, Carson," Dylan threatened, hot on his heels.

"I'll fight you after your sister's been found, if that's what you're gunning for. But I've got more important things to do right now than deal with you." He got on his motorcycle.

"I'm following you," Dylan shouted over the roar of the motorcycle's engine, as if that was some kind of deterrent. Grady didn't even respond.

He took off, breaking every possible traffic law to get to the ranch. There was a cop car parked at the front of the house, but he didn't see anyone in it. He scanned the land, heartbeat thumping painfully in his chest.

Blood. Blood. She was bleeding somewhere, and he couldn't do a thing about it.

Except she'd gotten here. His property. There had to be something he could do. Had to be.

Dylan's car pulled up next to him, windows down. "I don't know what you think you're going to do."

"I'm going to find her," Grady replied. Some way. Somehow. There was nothing else *to* do.

"Why are *you* going to do anything? The police are searching for her, and if you had anything to do with—"

"I don't have anything to do with it. I love her." Which was not exactly a *surprise* admission, just an uncomfortable one.

"That's… You're a *Carson*."

"Yeah, I'll worry about that some other time." He scanned the area again, trying to figure out where to start. He had to stop jabbering with Dylan and actually think. Formulate a plan.

"They're at the back entrance," Dylan offered. "What's the quickest way?"

Grady frowned at the sleek sports vehicle Laurel's brother drove. "That car isn't going to make it over this hard terrain."

"It will," Dylan said, everything about him severe and determined. "Now, what's the quickest way?"

"Follow me." Grady took off, narrowly missing wrecking out when he went over a swell of land too fast, but it didn't matter. Nothing mattered aside from finding Laurel.

When they reached the back entrance, there was a whole area taped off with caution tape. The deputy who'd searched the Adams's house with Laurel the other day frowned in his direction as Grady swung off the motorcycle and stormed toward the tape.

"You're going to have to stay back," Hart said firmly.

Grady only did so because he knew the guy was trying to do his job. He glanced at the crowd. Three deputies. And Noah.

He went to stand next to his cousin. "Tell me what you know."

"No signs of a vehicle," Noah said. "But Laurel's car was found crashed into a guardrail on the highway. Someone rear-ended her, but the car that caused the accident is nowhere to be found. The cops found a trail of blood that led here."

"That's a mile at least."

Noah nodded grimly. "Vanessa's with Clint and another officer at the house. I've offered to search the higher elevations on my horse, but they're still making a decision."

"Screw that." Grady looked at Noah's horse tied to a tree, placidly standing a few yards off. "I'm going."

"There's the old stone church up on the ridge. It's the only kind of place to hide anywhere near here," Noah said quietly, angling them away from the deputies gathering evidence and talking earnestly. "Unless someone picked her up on the road, but the cops don't think so. I told them about the church, but—"

Grady shook his head. "They've got their procedure, but we don't. I'm not waiting around. I'm going to take your horse up there. You and Delaney go back and get more horses, rifles, whatever you can. We search for her ourselves."

Noah looked suspiciously at Dylan. "You really want to take him?"

"I'm her brother," Dylan interjected. "Finding Laurel is all that matters."

Noah nodded at that. "All right."

"Wait until I'm gone, then take my bike. It'll be quickest to get back to the barn." Grady handed Noah the keys. "I'm going to ride Star right up the property line to the stone church. You cut up from the barn the opposite direction. Got your cell?"

Noah nodded.

"You see anything, anything comes up, call. I'll do the same. Something big happens, 911, cops, whatever. The only important thing is finding her safe, and keeping yourself out of harm's way. Got it?"

"What about keeping *your*self safe?"

Grady didn't bother to lie. "I'll do what I have to do. Whatever it takes."

"Grady—"

But he was done arguing and standing around. He strode over to Noah's horse and untied the reins from the tree. He mounted Star and gave her neck a quick pat before leading her away from the group and tape.

Once he had a little space, he urged her into a trot. Straight toward the ridge that would lead him up to the old stone church that had been abandoned probably a century ago, and sat just off Carson property, owned and tended by no one.

"Hey, where are you going?" one of the deputies shouted.

Grady didn't bother to answer. He was going to find Laurel. One way or another.

Chapter 17

Laurel heard voices. Unfamiliar voices. She knew she had to open her eyes, but she couldn't seem to manage it. Her head hurt, with so much pain she could barely think past it.

But there were voices, and even though everything hurt and jumbled together, something inside of her knew she had to listen to those voices.

"What kind of idiot are you? There's no way out of this. You've screwed everything up," a man's voice hissed, all restrained fury.

"We could kill her," the other voice suggested, as if he were suggesting getting dessert at a restaurant.

"*You* could kill her," the man retorted. "She did shoot you, after all. We could call it self-defense, perhaps."

"I've done all your dirty work," the second man returned, clearly not happy about it. "All of it."

"That's what I pay you for, and this... You've made

this an irreparable mess. You should do all the dirty work when you were the one to muddy it all up. A simple job."

"Simple? Kill two guys and kidnap a girl?"

"You failed at one of those, and the girl was safely returned. You're in the clear there."

The second man laughed bitterly. "I'm not doing another thing for you until I get my full compensation."

"No full compensation until we take care of this problem."

Nausea rolled through Laurel, but she tried to breathe through it. Some of the confusion in her mind cleared, even with the constant ache in her head. The fact they hadn't killed her yet meant *something*.

She had a chance. A chance to live. A chance to escape. If she could only act.

Breathe in. Breathe out. Focus.

She thought she could maybe open her eyes now, but figured it would be best if she gathered her wits before she gave any indication she was conscious. Formulate a plan. Obviously they had weapons. There were two of them, and only one of her.

She blew out a breath, willing herself not to throw up. She was sitting on the cold floor, and her arms were behind her back. Which meant they were tied together. She catalogued the rest of her body as much as she could with her eyes closed and her brain still scrambled.

There was something around her ankles as well. Something hard and cold behind her back. She was cold. So cold.

Focus.

Except she must have said that out loud, or moved, or something.

"She's conscious," the angrier man muttered.

Laurel blinked her eyes open. The man all in black was pulling his mask back down, and she missed any identifying markers. The other man wasn't anywhere she could see, but she was afraid to turn her head to fully search the room.

"Where am I?"

The man in black laughed. "Jupiter, sweetheart."

Dark eyes glittered behind the ski mask and Laurel knew without a shadow of a doubt she had to escape quickly. Even if the other man didn't want to kill her, this one did.

"I'm going to throw up."

He rolled his eyes, turning to somewhere just outside Laurel's vision. She tried to turn her head but pain pierced her skull.

"Just kill her," Angry Man was saying. "*You* this time. So we're both in this and I know you're not going to try and pawn this all off on me."

"Take her outside until she's done. Then bring her back. If we decide to kill her, we need to make sure we have everything we need first."

Angry Man grumbled, but he walked over to her. Laurel was shaking, and no amount of breathing helped that. When two rough hands grabbed her and pulled her to her feet, she swayed and closed her eyes.

He pushed her back roughly against the wall, and she leaned against it, trying to make the world stop spinning. She realized somewhat belatedly he'd untied her legs.

"Walk," he ordered gruffly.

Weaving and swaying, Laurel began to walk. She didn't make an effort to change her weakened gait.

The weaker he thought she was, the better. But moving helped. Stepping outside helped.

Except for the fact nothing around her gave her any clue as to where she was. There were trees and sky and rocky ground.

"Well? You gonna throw up or not?"

Laurel bent forward. "I need my hands. I have to use the bathroom."

The man laughed harshly. "Like hell. Stop talking and start retching or we're going back in there right this second." He waved his gun in her face. "If I wasn't trying to prove a point, I would've blown your brains out hours ago."

Hours. Had it been hours? She didn't recognize this place, though it still looked like Wyoming. But maybe it wasn't. Maybe she was far away from home and help.

She bent over, pretending to gag, trying not to cry. Slowly she raised her gaze, trying to find…something. Anything. A place to run and hide. A clue as to where she was.

"You run, I'll only shoot you. Somewhere that'll take a long time to bleed out so you can die a long and terrible death."

She turned her head to look at this man. "Why?"

He shrugged. "Why not?"

Something rustled behind them and the man pushed her down. Since her hands were tied behind her, she couldn't stop the fall. She could only turn her head and brace her body for impact. The sound that came out of her when she hit the hard, cold ground was loud and involuntary.

"Shut up," Angry Man said, giving her a swift, painful kick to the leg. "And don't move."

Laurel sucked in a breath and tried not to sob as she blew it back out. She tilted her head to see where Angry Man had gone. He was slinking around the side of the building, gun held at the ready.

Laurel couldn't help but think it was a squirrel or raccoon or something. Who would stumble upon this…

She looked around her as best she could in her prone position. It was a clearing, the building behind her stone and clearly abandoned for a long time. Windows gone, any clue to what it could have been completely gone.

Except the cross at the very top of the roof.

Oh, God, she knew where she was. She and Vanessa had snuck up here once as kids and spent the night telling each other ghost stories. One of the few times she'd been convinced breaking the rules wasn't the worst thing in the world.

That time was long past, but that church was Wyoming. It was home. She was so close to the Carson Ranch she still had a chance, a real chance, to escape. As long as Angry Man didn't shoot her first.

But he'd disappeared around the corner of the building. And yes, he could likely outrun her in her current injured and tied-up state, but maybe…

A shot rang out, jolting her. She rolled herself onto her side and managed to leverage herself up to her knees. Her vision blurred, but she pushed through it and up onto her feet. She had to… She had to…

When a figure rushed around the corner of the building, Laurel thought for sure she was hallucinating. She had to be. Maybe she'd died. Or was unconscious and dreaming.

Grady stopped short, then swore roughly. Before she could blink, he was in front of her, gingerly touching her shoulder.

"Are you all right?"

"There's another one, Grady," Laurel said, surveying the stone church. They were like sitting ducks out here, and the man inside had to have heard the gunshot.

Except in the next moment, a man was stepping out of the church. He didn't wear a mask or all black and she didn't even see a weapon on him.

"Thank God. Thank God. I was so scared," he said, moving toward her and Grady.

Grady pushed her behind him, holding his pistol up. "Don't come any closer," he ordered the man. "Hold on to me," he whispered to her.

"Please, you've got to help me," the man implored.

Laurel frowned, holding on to Grady's shirt. From everything she'd heard, this man was the leader of the whole debacle. But maybe in her jumbled head she'd been confused.

"That man you shot was holding me captive, much like you." The middle-aged man looked imploringly at her. "Thank God we're both all right."

"Laurel?" Grady asked.

It didn't feel right, but everything was so topsy-turvy and she couldn't trust what she'd heard and what she hadn't.

"The police are on their way. They can sort out whether or not that's true," Grady said firmly, his aim of the gun not wavering from the man's chest.

"Something isn't right," Laurel whispered, more to herself than to Grady.

"What isn't right?" he returned, as quietly and under-his-breath as she'd spoken.

"I don't know." She just didn't know.

Grady wasn't about to lower his weapon on this guy, no matter what he said. Or Laurel said, for that matter. While he wasn't dressed like the man he'd shot on the other side of the church—no mask, no weapon—he was still here. Unharmed, while Laurel's entire face was streaked with blood.

He couldn't think about that, though. If he did he might sink to his knees at the sheer pain of it. That she'd been this hurt, and was somehow still alive. Still here. He had to get her safe.

"I'd feel so much better if you put the gun down," the guy said with a nervous chuckle.

Grady didn't move. "I wouldn't."

"Then maybe I should just go back inside until the police—"

"Don't move."

Something about the guy's expression didn't sit right with Grady. Something about this whole thing didn't sit right, and if the cops didn't get here soon, he'd be forced to act. Because he wasn't going to make Laurel stand through much more of this.

"Why don't you sit down," Grady said. When the man started to bend his knees, Grady rolled his eyes. "Not you. Her."

"Oh," Laurel breathed behind him. "I better stay standing."

"Laurel!"

If Grady wasn't mistaken, it was Dylan's voice,

which meant Dylan and Noah had arrived. The cops couldn't be too far back.

"Someone call an ambulance," Grady barked. "Noah, can you ride Laurel out of here without banging her up any more?"

Noah dismounted, about five seconds after Dylan. Both men charged up the hill, taking in the scene around them.

"I'll take her myself," Dylan said hotly.

"I don't know if a horse ride would be the best thing for her in this condition," Noah said calmly. "Head injury—"

"She'll be fine. She needs a doctor fast."

"If all the men could stop posturing and listen to what *I* have to say," Laurel interjected, but she was leaning against Grady and shaking.

"I'm sorry, are any of you a police officer? Or someone who could convince this man to stop pointing his gun at me?" the man Grady hadn't taken his eyes off said.

Grady exchanged a look with Noah, but Noah didn't seem too keen on the idea, either. "How'd you get up here?" Noah asked.

The man tugged at the collar of his shirt. "I... I don't know. I was brought here against my will."

"How?" Laurel asked from behind Grady.

"W-what?" the man said.

"How did one man bring you and me here against our will?" Laurel asked, her voice sounding stronger and clearer than it had.

"I'm not sure how you arrived, but I was brought here yesterday. Now—"

"Why weren't you tied up?"

The man stood stock-still, everything about him frozen. "I…was."

"No you weren't," Laurel returned, and she moved from where she'd been leaning against Grady's back, to stand next to him. She leaned on him for support, which was certainly a concern, but she stood there, determined. "I saw you. I heard you."

The man's eyes darted around where they all stood in the clearing.

"There isn't anywhere to go," Grady said fiercely, noting that Noah and Dylan had raised their rifles to aim at the man as well.

"And even if you got out of here, I'd find you," Noah said calmly. "I can find anything in these mountains."

The man licked his lips nervously. "I… I don't know what you're all talking about. I don't… I'm a victim. And I haven't done anything wrong. If you do anything to me, I will sue you."

"And who will I sue for paying that man to run me off the road?"

"I did no such thing—" he smirked a little "—that you'll be able to prove."

"Do you own a black sedan, Nebraska license plate 85A GHX?"

The man visibly paled, and it was Grady's turn to smirk. "I think you might be on to something, Deputy," he offered cheerfully.

"I'm going to go out on a limb and say you're employed by the company that runs Evergreen Mining."

"I don't see what that has to do with anything."

"But I do," Laurel said. "I heard your conversation with the other man, and I've got so much evidence built up. All I needed was the man behind it, and here you are."

"You can't…" He shook his head, looking around more desperately. "You're lying."

"I guess we'll find out how much when the police arrive. Noah or Dylan, will you walk around and see if you can find the car?"

"Gladly," Dylan said, sounding about as lethal as Grady felt.

The only thing that kept Grady in place was Laurel leaning against him. Otherwise he'd be more than a little tempted to beat this guy to a bloody pulp.

"You can't do this. My lawyers will have a field day with this. None of you know what you're talking about and…and… This is ludicrous. I'll take you for everything you're worth."

"That supposed to be scary?"

"You have nothing to hold me on. Nothing."

"Cops are here," Dylan called from the other side of the stone church. "And I found the car. Just as Laurel described."

The man darted for the woods, but Grady fired his weapon, hitting him in the upper thigh. The man fell to the ground with a howl. And again, Grady would have gladly gone over and gotten a few kicks in, but Laurel was leaning, saying his name.

"Grady."

He glanced down at her. Her eyes were drooping, and underneath the awful blood all over her, her complexion was gray.

"Open your eyes, baby."

She shook her head almost imperceptibly. "Can't."

"Come on, princess. Stay with me here." He moved the arm not holding a gun around her waist, holding her up. She clutched his shirt, but it was as though her legs didn't hold her up. Her legs buckled.

"I really don't feel well."

"Laurel." But her eyes had rolled back, her body going limp. Grady looked up wildly, heart beating with panic against his chest. "Hart," he barked when the deputy came into view. "Get your car up here now."

Grady had to hand it to the young deputy—he didn't balk at taking orders from a civilian. Hart turned and ran back down the hill, shouting orders to the other deputies with him.

Chapter 18

Laurel wasn't a fan of waking up from unconsciousness not knowing where she was or what had happened. She vaguely remembered the stone church, something about the man who'd been responsible for all this.

She definitely remembered Grady. He'd held her up and kept her safe.

"Grady?" Whatever sound that came out of her mouth certainly didn't sound like his name. She cleared her raw throat and tried again. "Grady?" She tried to open her eyes but it was all too bright.

"Shh. We're right here." Jen's voice. Her sister.

"Jen. Where's Grady?"

"I can't believe she's saying that Carson's name. She must be delirious."

"Hello to you, too, Dad." She felt a large hand on her arm. She imagined it was her father's, and despite all his blustering she was sure he was worried sick. "Can someone dim the lights."

"That should be better," another male voice said.

Laurel's eyes flew open. "Cam." Her brother closest in age to her had been deployed for a while and she hadn't seen him in over a year. But here he was, in her hospital room.

Hospital. Why was everyone here?

"Oh, God, am I dying?"

Jen took her hand. "No, but you certainly gave us all a scare. You lost a lot of blood and needed a lot of stitches. Collapsed lung, bruised ribs and a broken nose." Jen let out a shaky breath. "And Dylan said it could have been so much worse."

Laurel looked around at her family in the hospital room, and she knew she should want this and this alone. She was healing and her family was here because they loved her.

"I need to see Grady." She turned to Jen, imploringly, figuring Jen would be her best, softest-hearted bet. "Please. He saved me, you know." She looked around at her stone-faced father and an even stonier-faced Cam. "He saved me. I need to speak with him."

"I'll get him," Dylan surprised her by saying.

Dad sputtered, Jen soothed him, and Cam ushered all of them out of the room, pausing at the door to look back at her. "I didn't expect to come home and find you looking like hell, sis."

"Are you home to stay?"

"Yeah."

"I'm very glad," she said, feeling overly emotional. She'd blame that on whatever machines she was hooked up to or whatever was in the IV.

"Me, too." And then he disappeared, and only seconds later, Grady stepped in. He was big and strong and she wanted to *weep*. Because he was here, and he'd saved her. "You're here," she managed to rasp.

"Where else would I be, princess?" he asked gruffly.

"What happened?"

"You were hurt—"

"With the guy. The head guy. It's all a blur after I told him I had evidence and—"

"He made a break for it."

She squeaked in outrage.

Grady's mouth curved grimly. "I shot him."

"Oh. I don't remember that. Is he dead?"

"No. Fared better than you. Other guy's in critical. The leader of this whole thing has a million lawyers crawling all over the place, but you built a pretty tight case against the guy. Evidence all over his car that he had Lizzie. And while the other guy may have been driving the car, it's registered to the main guy. Not quite the criminal mastermind he fancied himself."

"So who was the not-head guy?"

"Hired muscle. Basically a hit man he was using however necessary to try and cover all this up."

"Was he really doing all this for EPA violations?"

Grady shrugged, still standing near the door. "We don't know. He's got enough lawyers to block every cop in America, I think."

"Why are you standing all the way over there?" she demanded.

"Because I want to touch you so bad it hurts," he said, hands jammed in his pockets, something like but not quite fury vibrating off him.

"You can touch me."

"You look terrible, princess."

"I'll heal. Come here."

Slowly, he took a step forward, and then another, until he was standing over her, looking at her face as though she'd jabbed a knife in his chest.

He put a fingertip to her collarbone, she assumed since it wasn't bruised or scraped.

"You gave me quite the scare," he murmured, his fingertip warm and gentle on her skin.

"It wasn't exactly roses and unicorns from where I stood, either."

"Laurel." He looked so grim, so serious. Like he was about to deliver the most terrible news on the face of the planet. With her actual name to boot. "I love you."

She blinked. "What?"

"You heard me," he returned grumpily, shoving his hands back in his pockets.

"But…"

"And I'm not prone to saying that, so don't expect me to repeat it."

"Grady," she reached out for him, but he stepped away from the bed.

"Oh, fine," he grumbled. "If you're going to be that way about it."

"What wa—"

"I love you," he blurted as if she'd somehow *forced* the admission out of him, and she was to blame for all of it. "I love you. Grady Carson loves Laurel Delaney. Are you happy?" He raked his fingers through his hair.

She wanted to laugh. He'd lost his mind, and he loved her. Really. "Grady."

"And don't think you're getting out of this," he said,

pointing at her. "You started it. You're stuck with me now."

"Come here," she said as forcefully as she could manage. "And calm down."

He looked at her with that same desolate expression he'd used to say he loved her. "You could have died."

A lump clogged her throat, but she spoke through it. "So could you. You came in guns blazing, all by yourself."

"Hours," he said, his voice breaking just there at the end. "You were gone hours before we found you."

"Grady."

"What?" he snapped.

She cupped his face with her hands, reveling in the sharp spikes of his beard. "I love you," she said, looking directly into those beautiful blue eyes, knowing without a doubt that whatever crazy Bent feud nonsense was thrown their way, no matter how many murder investigations went awry, they would make it through together.

He kissed the spot on her collarbone he'd touched earlier. "You're darn right you do, princess."

Two weeks later

When Laurel Delaney sauntered into Rightful Claim on a snowy day, dressed in a drab Bent County PD polo and baggy khaki pants, with her badge attached to her hip, Grady Carson wondered how he'd ever thought he could fight the feeling in his gut he got every time she walked into his bar.

A century-old feud hadn't stood a chance against this wave of possession. Love. She was his. He was hers. Beginning and end of story.

"So, the doctors clear you?" he asked casually.

She slid onto a barstool. "Desk duty," she said disgustedly, some of the cuts on her face still red and a terrible reminder of that day not so long ago. "I can work in-house and lose my marbles."

"I'm guessing that's wise."

She made a rude noise. "I'm fine."

"That's not what you said last night."

She wrinkled her nose. "You just hit my ribs the wrong way. I don't plan on getting naked and sweaty with anyone I'm investigating."

"Good to hear."

"I did get some good news today," she said leaning forward on the bar, then wincing.

He winced right along with her. He thought it had been bad enough seeing her bloody and passed out, or in that horrible white hospital bed, but watching her *heal* and push herself too hard was a new pain he'd never known.

"What's that?" he asked, sliding her a Coke.

"The muscle woke up yesterday. Lawyered up, but he made a plea bargain. Looks like he's going to turn on Mr. Head Guy."

Head Guy. Aaron Zifle. The head of the mining corporations safety department, drowning in safety violations and trying to keep his pretty young wife sparkling in diamonds. Apparently he'd been about to lose his job and so desperate to keep the well-paying position he'd decided the only way to deal with Jason Delaney's accusation had been to kill.

At least that was Laurel's theory after her nonstop investigating while she'd still been forced to spend most of her days in bed. Grady was inclined to believe her since he spent most of his days at her bedside, listening to her chatter.

Vanessa had nearly run his bar into the ground, at least in his estimation, but it still stood, and he was back to work, and Laurel was trying to be.

"That is good news. Make his trial airtight, won't it?"

"Yes. They'll likely up his bond with that information, too. The chances of him getting out of what he's done, even with his team of lawyers, is pretty slim."

"We should celebrate."

"How?" She rubbed at her rib. "I'm not sure I'm up for any serious celebrating."

"How about this. After I close up, I pack all my things up and move them to your cabin."

Her eyebrows furrowed together. "Move. Into my cabin. You?"

"Yes, I believe that's what I meant."

"But… We… We've barely dated," she said, her eyebrows furrowing deeper.

"True."

"My family… A Carson living on Delaney land? The town might have us tarred and feathered."

"Could be."

"And the bar." She gestured around to encompass all of Rightful Claim. "Don't you have to be here at all hours?"

"Not *all* hours. I was thinking about giving Vanessa more control, and the apartment—she's been angling for it for months."

Laurel blinked at him, beautiful and strong and absolutely everything he wanted to wake up to. Go to bed with. Build a life with.

"This is crazy," she said, shaking her head.

But she hadn't said no, and he knew her well enough. "Absolutely insane. So, what do you say?"

Her face broke out into a grin. "How soon can you close up?"

When he leaned across the bar and gave her a nice, hard kiss, a few cheers went up around them. A few mutters. One boo he was pretty sure came from Ty.

But Grady Carson didn't care much, because Laurel Delaney was his. Like it was always meant to be.

* * * * *